THE
MIRAGE

THE
MIRAGE

MATT RUFF

HARPER

An Imprint of HarperCollins*Publishers*
www.harpercollins.com

HarperCollins books may be purchased for educational,
business, or sales promotional use. For information, please write:
Special Markets Department, HarperCollins Publishers,
10 East 53rd Street, New York, NY 10022.

FIRST EDITION

Designed by Jo Anne Metsch

Library of Congress Cataloging-in-Publication Data
Ruff, Matt.
The mirage / Matt Ruff.—1st ed.
p. cm.
ISBN 978-0-06-197622-3 (hardcover)—ISBN 978-0-06-197623-0 (pbk.)
I. Title.
PS3568.U3615M57 2011
813'.54—dc22
2011012895

12 13 14 15 16   OV/RRD   10 9 8 7 6 5 4 3 2 1

FOR

MY PARENTS

When God wants to punish you,
He grants your wish.

—AMERICAN PROVERB

Contents

Prologue

11/9

This is the day the world changes.

It's 21 Shaban, year 1422 after the Hijra. Or as the international trade calendar would have it: November 9, 2001. Sunrise in Baghdad is at 6:25, and as the first rays strike the Tigris and Euphrates twin towers, an old man stands in the main dining room of the Windows on the World restaurant, gazing out at the city.

The morning commute is well under way, cars streaming in along the expressways from Fallujah, Samarra, Baqubah, and Karbala. Across the Tigris, the 6:30 Basra Limited loops around the old World's Fair grounds and runs briefly parallel to the Sadr City El before both trains plunge underground into the central station. There's traffic on the river, too: passenger and cargo barges, water taxis, the racing shells of the Baghdad U rowing team, the hydrofoil ferry from Kut.

Looking down at it all, the old man feels a sense of vertigo that has nothing to do with fear of heights. He tells himself it's the motion, the city's ceaseless motion, which the rush hour only amplifies.

The old man grew up in Yemen. His family owned a bakery, and he and his brothers all worked there. It was hard work, long hours, but every day, five times a day, everything stopped, employees and customers alike stepping out to go to mosque, leaving only a Christian behind to mind the ovens. It wasn't just the town's businesses that shut down: A witness viewing that landscape from above would have seen the roads empty too, even long-distance travelers pulling over to pray.

Baghdad, city of the future, doesn't pull over for anything. Here when the old man steps out of the kitchen for dawn prayer, it's not just Christians who stay behind working. Here attendance at mosque varies, as if it were the world's schedule, not God's, that needed to be accommodated. Here the traffic flows round the clock, pausing only for accidents and gridlock. Little wonder that the sight of it disorients him, producing the flutter in his chest and inner ear that says *This is not the place you were made for.*

Or so he tells himself. But really, what else could it be?

Someone calls his name from the kitchen. It's time to get back to work. There's another round of pastries to get out before breakfast service starts at seven, and then he needs to begin prepping for lunch.

A helicopter buzzes past the windows, and the sun continues to rise, revealing a sky streaked by contrails. The heavens are in motion, too.

7:15 a.m. In a broadcast studio just blocks from the towers, Baghdad's mayor, Anmar al Maysani, is appearing on the *Jazeera & Friends* morning talk show. Today's topic is the skyrocketing murder rate: 463 people have been killed in Baghdad since January, and the year's final tally is expected to top five hundred. It's the worst violence the city has seen since the mob wars of the early '90s.

The mayor has some explaining to do. After being introduced as a "noted feminist," she's braced to spend the allotted time discussing whether some jobs aren't better left to men after all, and is surprised when the host's first question is about another subject entirely.

"Madam Mayor, there are many who believe that the increase in lawlessness we are seeing is an inevitable consequence of the secularization of society, and that what's needed is a new Awakening, a rejection of modernity and a return to traditional religious values. What do you say to this?"

"Well," the mayor replies, "the first thing I would say is that God is great, and nothing is more important than the struggle to live righteously. If citizens are inspired to rededicate themselves to that struggle, that's the best news that could come out of this unfortunate situation. But I don't agree with the connection you're trying to draw between so-called secularization and lawlessness. If you look closely at the statistics, you'll find that the increase in murders is being driven by a rise in organized crime activity. When men turn to violence in their pursuit of illegal profits, the problem isn't that they've failed to submit to God; the problem is that they're gangsters."

A dry cough from the show's other guest, the publisher of the *Baghdad Post*, gets the host's attention. "Mr. Aziz? You have a comment?"

"I'm just a poor Christian," Tariq Aziz says, "and I wouldn't dream of lecturing my Muslim brothers and sisters on the struggle to be righteous, but if men are choosing to become gangsters, that would seem to me a clear sign that they are *not* submitting to God . . ."

"Madam Mayor? Your response?"

"If Tariq Aziz feels he's a *poor* Christian, I won't argue with him," the mayor says. "Perhaps it would benefit Mr. Aziz to contemplate a line from the Psalms of David: 'I will not have an evildoer for a friend.' There are several verses from chapter 63 of Holy Quran that I might also recommend to him . . ."

"I'd recommend the mayor review the laws against slander," Aziz shoots back.

"I'm only too happy to focus on the law," the mayor says. "It's through law and order that we'll solve this problem, God willing."

"But that raises another issue, doesn't it?" says the host. "For several years now, you've been the public face of the law in this city. And yet things have gotten worse."

"Recently they have, but—"

"Yes, recently, even as you've been given greater authority by the city council. Some people might say that's a sign you've been given too much authority, that you're not up to the responsibilities of your office. Some might go farther, and say that God has placed a natural limit on how much responsibility any woman can handle, and that you've tried to exceed that limit, with predictable results. *Madam Mayor . . . Your thoughts?*"

7:59. Down by the river, it's time for another round in the War on Drugs: A young boat pilot, having just tied up to a pier under the July 14th Bridge, finds himself surrounded, not by the smugglers he was expecting, but by uniformed agents of Halal Enforcement.

The lead agent is a big man named Samir with a bodybuilder's physique. "Before you lie to me," he says, wagging a warning finger in the youth's face, "I want you to think about something. We know your name is Khalil Noufan. We knew you were coming here, and we know what your cargo is. We know you have an uncle Ziad who's up to his ears in gambling debts. We know all that, so ask yourself: What else do we know?"

The boy blinks slowly, his expression suggesting he'll never win any science prizes. When he speaks, it's as if he's reading off a cue card: "I'm transporting fruit."

"Right." Another agent has boarded the boat and is prodding a pile of boxes whose labeling indicates they contain bananas. Hearing a telltale clink, he jokes: "It must have been very cold out on the water this morning." He tears open a box at the top of the pile and extracts a glass container. "Look at that, frozen in the shape of a wine bottle. What are the odds?"

The boat pilot blinks a bit faster and switches to his fallback story: "It's for the Jews. To use in the main synagogue."

Samir laughs. "You hear that, Isaac?" he says to the agent in the boat. "Your grand rabbi's smuggling Sabbath wine again."

"Ah, I hate it when he does that."

Samir turns his attention back to the boy: "Why would Jews smuggle wine when they can import it legally?"

"To, to save on the taxes . . ."

"What, they're going to risk jail for a few riyals?"

"They're Jews!"

All of the agents laugh at this. On the boat, Isaac breaks the seal on the "wine" bottle and extracts the cork. He sniffs, then sips, the contents.

"Well?" Samir says.

"A fine Scottish vintage." Isaac takes a more substantial swallow from the bottle. "Around eighty proof, I'd say."

"'Proof?'" The boat pilot is beyond his prepared script now. "What's 'proof'?"

"Hard liquor, asshole," Samir tells him. "That's a class-A felony charge. Multiple felony charges, if we decide to count each box as a separate shipment. How many boxes, Isaac?"

"At least forty. And it looks like there are two dozen bottles per box, so if you really want to be a hard-ass you could count them double."

Samir whistles. "Eighty felony charges . . . And that's with a mandatory five-year sentence per charge. I know you're probably no good at math, but do you understand how fucked that makes you?"

"No! It's wine! They told me—"

"'They' who? Hey!" Samir grabs him by the chin. "Look at me. Who hired you?"

"No one . . . The Jews."

"The Jews!" Samir snorts in disgust. Still gripping the boy's chin, he leans in close: "Eighty felony charges. That's as good as a life sentence, you get that?"

"I . . . I . . ."

"Oh, that's good, start crying. That'll really help, where you're going . . ." Leaning in even closer, as if for a kiss, his voice dropping to a seductive whisper: "You have beautiful eyes, you know that? The other prisoners at Abu Ghraib—I bet they'll *love* those eyes . . ."

8:23. At Baghdad International Airport, a pair of ABI agents have set up a surveillance post on the roof of the air traffic control tower. The object of their interest is a palatial estate to the east, located on an island in the middle of an artificial lake. A causeway lined with other, lesser mansions links the island to the lakeshore, and the control tower offers an excellent vantage for recording the license plates of vehicles on the causeway.

While the male agent, Rafi, peers through a camera-equipped telescope at the estate, the woman, Amal, chats with an airport manager who's followed them up here. Ostensibly the conversation is about a baggage-theft ring the manager claims to have knowledge of, but Amal suspects what he's really after is her phone number.

". . . Persians with forged work visas," the manager is saying. "They sneak across the border through the marshlands and pay the local riffraff to provide them with fake papers."

"Persians." Amal grasps the subtext readily enough. The manager's southern accent and dialect mark him as a native of the Gulf peninsula, and because Amal and Rafi are federal agents, he has apparently concluded that they are at least honorary Riyadhis—and Sunnis. As opposed to the no-good Persians and Iraqi marshlanders, who are Shia. "You know, we're pretty familiar with the local riffraff," she says, gesturing towards the lake estate, "and I have to tell you, he's not so fond of Persians. Or the people of the marshes."

"Ah, that's not the riffraff I'm talking about. He's a wicked man, it's true, but the criminals you should be investigating are the ones in city hall."

Amal feigns astonishment. "You're saying the Baghdad mayor's office is corrupt?"

"Are you kidding? That incompetent woman comes from the same swamp that the Persians are always sneaking through, so what does that tell you?" The manager pauses, momentarily entranced as the breeze stirs a loose strand of Amal's hair. "You know," he continues, "you look a bit like her."

"Well, that's flattering!"

The manager smiles. "I said she was corrupt and incompetent, not ugly! And of course you're much younger than she is."

"Yes," Amal says. "Young enough to be her daughter, in fact." Behind her she hears a sound that she at first takes to be Rafi snickering, but it's actually the camera shutter. "Something happening?"

"One of the sons is on the move," Rafi says. "Uday, I think."

Amal takes a look. A yellow sports car has just exited the front gate of the estate and is racing down the causeway. "That's Uday all right. Qusay drives the red one." She turns back to the manager, who's still smiling in a way that makes her wish she'd worn a bigger headscarf. "Anyway . . ."

"Please." The manager stops her. "I can see you're busy. Perhaps . . . we could talk more later?"

Amal has to make an effort not to roll her eyes. "I'll tell you what. Why don't you give me your card, and I'll see if—"

He's already reaching for his wallet. But before he can fumble out a business card, his cell phone rings. "Yes . . . ?" As he listens to the caller, his smile fades.

"What is it?" Amal asks, after he hangs up. His face gone grave, he ignores the question, reaching past Amal to tug at Rafi's sleeve. "Excuse me . . ."

"What?" says Rafi, annoyed.

"I'm afraid there's a problem."

"Yes, we know. Give Amal your card, like she said, and we'll—"

"No," the manager says. "This is something else. Something serious. An Arabian Airlines flight out of Kuwait City has been—"

His phone rings again. More bad news.

"What's going on?" says Amal. "Has the plane been hijacked?"

No response. It's like she's suddenly invisible. The manager stares at Rafi, but Rafi stares right back, waiting for the guy to answer Amal's question.

"Two," he finally says. "Two planes . . . At *least* two."

8:41. Another Halal agent, a thin, wiry man with a mustache, arrives at the riverbank. The agents already on scene have opened up additional bottles of "evidence," and the gathering now seems less like an arrest and more like a party, with everyone except the handcuffed guest of honor in a festive mood.

"Hey, Mustafa!" Samir calls to the new arrival. "About time you got here!"

"What do we have?"

"Another Jewish wine-smuggling conspiracy." Samir laughs and offers him an open bottle, but Mustafa waves it away.

"What is it really? More Scotch whiskey?"

"A mixed assortment. Whiskey mostly, looks like, but also some vodka, and some horrible cherry concoction."

"This one tastes like coffee!" Isaac calls from the boat.

"I'm hoping for a nice arak, myself," Samir says.

"Just the thing, with Ramadan coming up," says Mustafa, his tone more than his words causing Samir to raise an eyebrow. Mustafa nods at the weeping boat pilot. "This is our smuggler?"

"Yes," Samir says, still reacting to the Ramadan comment. "A real hard case, as you can see."

"I suppose you didn't wait to see if anyone would show up to meet him."

"Why bother? If we know about this shipment, you can bet Saddam knows we know. The real shipment's probably being unloaded upriver somewhere while we're busy with this decoy."

"Busy." Mustafa shakes his head. "You'd better hope no one with a camera catches you being 'busy' with that bottle."

"What's gotten into you this morning, Mustafa? Why are you late?"

"My car wouldn't start."

"And for that you're being an asshole? You've been fighting with the wives again, haven't you? Which one, Noor?"

Mustafa points to the dusty hatchback he drove to the pier. "Does that look like something I'd borrow from Noor?"

"Ah," Samir says. "Fadwa then. That's a shame. Still, no need to take it out on me."

"Let's just knock this off before the *Post* does an exposé on corruption at Halal."

"Fine, fine," Samir says. "All right everybody, let's start wrapping things up—"

The other agents, clustered by the boat, are all staring at something in the sky to the south. Even the boat pilot has stopped crying and raised his head to look.

"What . . . ," Samir says, turning. "Huh. He's awfully low . . ."

Mustafa is the last to look around. He catches only the briefest glimpse of the jet before it passes overhead, engines screaming. The impact is hidden from view by the structure of the bridge; they'll watch it later, of course, replayed endlessly on television, but in the moment it's only a loud *boom,* followed by the screams of people who can see it.

Then for just a second there is silence, a pocket of stillness during which some instinct makes Mustafa look not towards the hidden tower but at the car that brought him here. "Fadwa," he says, and a shockwave passes beneath his feet, leaving a different world in its wake.

Book One

The Mirage

THE LIBRARY OF ALEXANDRIA
A USER-EDITED REFERENCE SOURCE

United Arab States

> This page is currently **protected** from editing to deal with **repeated acts of vandalism.** To suggest changes, please **contact an administrator.**

The **United Arab States** is a federal constitutional republic made up of 22 states, one federal district, two religious districts, and several territories. Situated largely in the Eastern Hemisphere, it occupies the entirety of the Arabian Peninsula and the Levant, most of Mesopotamia, North Africa, and Northeast Africa, and numerous islands in the surrounding waters. It shares land borders with Turkey, Kurdistan, Persia, and various African nations.

At over 14 million square kilometers and with more than 360 million people, the United Arab States is the world's second largest country by total area and third largest by population . . .

HISTORY

Birth of a nation

The UAS was born from the ashes of the Arab League, a loose federation of Middle Eastern states that broke away from the Ottoman Empire near the end of the 19th century. Having successfully—if tentatively—declared independence from the Empire, the members of the League fell almost immediately to fighting amongst themselves along clan and sectarian lines. The bloody civil war continued until an attempt at reconquest by the Ottomans caused the League to once again unite against a common foe. Supported by a newly independent Egypt and the armies of the House of Saud, the League routed the Ottoman invasion force.

Following the armistice, the victors gathered in Egypt to discuss their future. In what became known as the miracle of Alexandria, the various parties managed to set aside their differences and agree on a plan to form a new and more lasting union, "One nation under God."

At its founding the UAS consisted of thirteen states—Arabia, Bahrain, Egypt, the Emirates, Iraq, Jordan, Kuwait, Lebanon, Oman, Palestine, Qatar, Syria, and Yemen—and the religious district of Mecca-Medina. The nation's capital was initially at Cairo, but within a few years, during the presidency of Abd al Aziz ibn Saud, it was moved to Riyadh.

Early growth

The new nation's geographic location made it a nexus of international trade, and despite an ongoing feud between Egypt and the federal government over control of the Suez Canal, the economy grew rapidly. The discovery of major petroleum reserves in the 1910s added further to the economic boom. While Christian Europe tore itself apart in war, the UAS embarked on an ambitious project of industrialization . . .

The world at war

Towards the end of the 1930s, war broke out again in Europe and Asia. The UAS attempted to remain neutral, but German and Italian threats against the Muslims of North Africa, and Japanese aggression in Malaya and Indonesia, made this impossible . . . In 1941 the UAS unleashed its military might against the Axis . . . By 1943, Libya, Tunisia, Algeria, Morocco, and Mauritania had all been liberated, and joined the union . . . In July 1944 a newly armed and trained Maghrebi invasion force stormed the beaches of southern France while allied Arab, Persian, Turkish, and Kurdish forces captured Rome and the Russian Orthodox Army launched its own series of offensives against the German eastern front . . . In the Southeast Asian Theater, Arab and Indian marines liberated the last of the Indonesian archipelago and struck north into the Philippines . . . In August 1945, after a third atomic bomb was dropped on Tokyo, Japan surrendered, ending the war . . . In December 1946, Adolf Hitler was beheaded at Nuremberg . . .

1948: Israel, the Orthodox Union, and the beginning of the Cold Crusade . . . President Nasser and the Arab Unity Party . . . "One small step for a Muslim . . ." The Islamic Awakening and the war in Afghanistan . . . "Black Arabs": Somalia and Sudan join the Union . . . The Mexican Gulf War . . .

11/9 and the War on Terror

On November 9, 2001, Christian fundamentalists hijacked four commercial passenger jetliners. They crashed two of them into the Tigris and Euphrates World Trade Towers in downtown Baghdad, Iraq, and a third into the Arab Defense Ministry headquarters in the federal district of Riyadh. The fourth plane, which is believed to have been bound for either the Presidential Palace in Riyadh or, possibly, Mecca (see Controversies and Myths of 11/9), crashed in Arabia's Empty Quarter after its passengers attempted to retake control from the hijackers.

Responsibility for the attacks was claimed by the World Christian Alliance, a North American white supremacist group based in the Rocky Mountain Independent Territories. In retaliation, UAS airborne troops captured the city of Denver, and UAS Special Forces backed by strike aircraft launched raids against Alliance strongholds in the surrounding countryside. Thousands of Alliance troops were captured or killed, but the Alliance leadership remained at large.

Even as the fighting in the Rockies continued, President Bandar used his 2002 State of the Union address to announce a broader War on Terror that would include preemptive attacks against "regimes that aid, harbor, or sponsor terrorists." The president made special mention of America, the United Kingdom, and North Korea, branding them "an Axis of Evil" whose attempts to develop weapons of mass destruction would no longer be tolerated . . .

In March of 2003, Coalition forces launched a successful invasion of America . . . A provisional government was established in the so-called "Green Zone" in Washington, D.C. . . . Hopes for a quick transition to a stable democracy were dashed by outbreaks of violence between

rival American factions and by the rise of an anti-Arab insurgency . . .
In 2006, with Coalition casualties mounting and no end to the war in
sight, the <u>National Party of God</u> suffered heavy losses during the mid-
term Congressional elections. Candidates closely affiliated with the
House of Saud fared especially poorly . . .

Now, with the <u>Arab Unity Party</u> once again in control of both Congress and the executive branch, there is hope that the <u>War in America</u>
will soon be over. But even as the first troops return home, there are
rumors of new terror threats against the Arab homeland, and fears that
Arabia's most challenging days still lie ahead . . .

The crusader was staying on the eleventh floor of the Rasheed Hotel. He'd arrived in Baghdad in the early afternoon and registered under the name John Huss. Among his possessions was a five-kilogram box of plastic explosives stolen from the army base at Kufah.

Arab Homeland Security knew all about him, or thought they did. His real name was James Travis. A citizen of Texas, he was in the UAS on a student visa that had expired nine months ago. During his last year of medical school, he had fallen in with a band of Protestant fanatics and was now working as their courier. Tomorrow he would meet with the leader of a sleeper cell to deliver the explosives.

AHS headquarters in Riyadh wanted to capture the whole cell, so rather than arrest Travis immediately, a plan had been hatched to disarm him. An agent dressed as a hotel maid waited down the hall from Travis's room with a dummy munitions box filled with harmless clay. When Travis went to get dinner, the agent would swap out the real plastique and plant tracking devices in Travis's other luggage.

It was a decent plan, but it did require Travis to leave the room, something that, as of 7 p.m., he showed no sign of doing. As the clock crept towards eight, one of the men staking out the lobby grew bored and began making prank radio calls to the eleventh-floor maid station.

"Amal, room 1169 needs fresh towels."

"Very funny, Samir."

"Amal, the gentleman in 1124 would like his pillows fluffed."

"Very funny, Samir."

"Amal—"

"Very funny, Samir."

Silence for a bit. At quarter to eight, Mustafa asked: "Do we know if he's awake?"

A member of the surveillance team watching the hotel room from across the street clicked in: "He's still got the window shades drawn, but it looks like the lights are on."

"His television's on, too," added Amal. "I can hear it from here."

"You know what would be great?" Samir said. "If we had a working camera and microphone *inside* the room."

"Very funny, Samir"—this time from the surveillance man. "I told you twice already, the equipment worked fine when we were testing it."

"Do you want me to knock on the door?" Amal asked. "I could tell him the other guests are complaining about the TV noise."

"No," said Mustafa, "I just want him to get hungry. Abdullah? Anything?"

Abdullah was monitoring the hotel switchboard. "He hasn't tried to call room service. No other landline calls in or out either, and e-comm unit *says* he hasn't used a cell phone . . . What if he's too nervous to eat?"

"A nervous terrorist, that's just what we need."

"Maybe his conscience is bothering him," Samir suggested. "What kind of Christian did you say he was, Mustafa?"

"Methodist."

"Are those the ones who handle snakes?"

"Hey," Amal said. "The TV just switched off . . . He's coming out."

"All right, everyone check in," said Mustafa. They were supposed to respond in sequence, but excited by the prospect of something finally happening, everyone spoke at once, and a confusion of voices filled the radio channel.

"He just stepped on the elevator," Amal announced as the babble subsided. "I'm inside the room . . . Oh, damn it."

"Amal?"

"Damn it, damn it, damn it . . ." Breathless now, as if she were running: "He's not a courier."

On the ground floor, Samir and three other agents made a dash for the elevator bank, arriving just in time to see the descending car pass the lobby without stopping. All the other cars were engaged on upper floors; Samir pounded the down button uselessly, then barked a warning into his radio as he and his companions scrambled to find the stairs.

The crusader, unaware of the flurry of activity above him, stepped out into the quiet of the hotel's underground parking garage. Although it was a hot summer night, he wore a heavy, oversized sport jacket and kept his left hand tucked inside it.

As he walked across the garage, he recited under his breath: "I believe in one God, the Father Almighty, maker of heaven and earth and of all things visible and invisible . . . And in one Lord Jesus Christ, the only-begotten Son of God, begotten of His Father before all worlds, God of God, Light of Light, very God of very God . . ."

A spark from the shadows to his right brought him up short. A thin man with a mustache, cigarette dangling from his lips, stood beside a black van, trying to coax a flame from an ancient brass lighter. The man looked up at the crusader staring at him. "My friend," he said, "can you help me?"

The crusader didn't answer. The man took a step towards him, gesturing with the cigarette: "Please, sir. Can I have a light?" He repeated this entreaty in Hebrew and French, and then, when the crusader still didn't respond, in fractured English. At last the crusader's left hand came out from inside his jacket. As the crusader reached into his front pants pocket, the man with the mustache took another step forward and punched him in the throat.

The crusader ended up belly-down on the ground, his left hand still trapped in his pocket, his right arm flung up and out, fingers splayed against the concrete. His assailant straddled him, pointing a gun at his sideways-turned head as he gasped for air.

"Easy, Mr. Travis," Mustafa said, his English dramatically improved. "The only person you can kill now is yourself, and Jesus won't reward you for that."

The crusader finally caught his breath, but instead of relaxing he tensed, his face turning an even darker shade of red.

"Don't . . . " Mustafa warned, then hesitated, smelling something. Smoke? With a cry the crusader reared up underneath him. Mustafa pulled the trigger but the gun misfired, and then he was bucked off. He scrambled up into a crouch, but the crusader was up too, something shiny and bright appearing in his hand; as Mustafa wielded the gun like a brick, the crusader leaned in and drew a line along the side of Mustafa's neck. The pain was sharp, simultaneously searing and cold, and Mustafa's collarbone was suddenly wet. He dropped his gun and clapped both hands to the wound.

He swooned, falling onto his back. The crusader stood over him, arms raised, a wire trailing from his left hand into his jacket. Nearby voices were shouting orders—"Stop! Drop it!"—but the crusader began his recitation again, his own voice rising to drown them out: "And I believe in the Holy Spirit, the Lord and giver of life, who proceeds from the Father and the Son, who with the Father and the Son together is worshiped and glorified, who spoke by the prophets. And I believe in one holy Christian and apostolic Church, I acknowledge one Baptism for the remission of sins, and I look for the resurrection of the—"

Two shots rang out, and something ugly happened to the back of the crusader's head. Mustafa, his field of vision starting to narrow, watched fascinated as the dead man swayed a moment more on his feet, left thumb twitching spasmodically.

"God willing," Mustafa whispered. Travis's knees buckled and his corpse fell forward. The world grew dim but did not disappear, and then a woman in a maid's uniform was leaning over Mustafa with a still-smoking pistol in her hand. She called his name.

The next Mustafa knew he was in a hospital bed, shading his eyes against the light from a window whose curtains had just been thrust open. A dark figure stood at the bed's foot, and in the moment before his vision adjusted Mustafa had the fleeting thought that it might be Satan. Of course that was foolish. Satan doesn't stand in the light; Satan comes from behind and whispers in your ear.

The figure spoke: "Have you been watching Al Jazeera?"

Not Satan, no. Just Mustafa's boss. "Hello, Farouk," he said, his voice a dry whisper. He raised a hand to his neck and felt a thick bandage covering the place where he'd been cut.

"The reason I ask," Farouk continued, "is that Jazeera's newscasters have picked up this habit, lately, of referring to our crusader friends as 'homicide bombers.'" He shook his head. "*Homicide* bombers . . . What does that even mean? A man builds a bomb, of course he wants to kill someone. It's the *suicide* part that makes them special."

A water pitcher and two glasses sat on the bedside table. Mustafa took his time pouring himself a drink. "I thought I could take him alive," he said finally.

"You say that as if it were a sane idea."

"I had him on the ground with a gun to his head, Farouk. He should have surrendered."

"Yes, that's what a rational criminal would have done." Farouk fished a small object from his suit jacket. "Here," he said, offering it to Mustafa. "A souvenir."

Mustafa turned the slender bit of polished steel over in his hands several times before recognizing it as a lighter.

"Taken from his pocket," Farouk said.

"How did you know—"

"That you'd asked him for a light? I know all things. I gather the idea was to get his hand away from the bomb trigger. That would have been genuinely smart, if you'd followed up by shooting him in the face."

Mustafa found the igniter button, and a focused jet of blue flame hissed from the side of the lighter. "He tried to set the explosive on fire?"

"No, himself. The autopsy found burns on his inner thigh and genitals." Mustafa glanced up sharply at this, and Farouk shrugged. "Maybe he was fighting the temptation to surrender. Maybe he just wanted a burst of adrenaline. The point is, you were trying to reason with a man who'd sooner burn off his dick than be taken alive . . . Tell me this isn't about Fadwa."

"Farouk . . ."

"Because I know all things, I know the official declaration finally came through last month. In light of that, I could overlook a certain amount of idiocy. But a death wish is out of bounds."

"I'm not trying to get myself killed because of Fadwa, Farouk."

"No? What is it about then, the other wife?"

"You called Noor."

"Of course I called Noor. Do you know what she said when I told her you were in the hospital?"

"She asked if I was dying. When you said no, she told you to call her back if that changed."

"That's it almost word for word. What kind of woman talks that way about her husband?"

"You said it yourself: the *other* wife."

Farouk shook his head again. "The more I learn about plural marriage, the more I thank God for making me a Christian."

Mustafa smiled gamely at the jest, but the reminder that Farouk belonged to the suspect class concerned him: "Is Riyadh giving you a hard time about the mission?"

"They'd like to," Farouk said. "Unfortunately it was their bad information that screwed things up. The outcome was as good as could be expected, considering. Of course my report glossed over a few details."

"If you need someone to blame—"

"What I need is the rest of that terror cell. And no more non-sense." He sighed. "It appears you were right about Amal, at least."

Amal, a recent transfer to Homeland Security, was the newest member of their team. As a politician's daughter, she came with two strikes against her, and Farouk had only accepted her under protest. He'd wanted to keep her out of the field, but Mustafa, after reviewing her personnel file, had argued that she deserved a chance.

"How is she?" Mustafa asked. Because he'd seen her records, he knew she'd never killed a man before.

"Quite pleased with herself," Farouk said. "As she should be. Two head shots from fifteen meters is impressive." He studied Mustafa's expression as he said this and didn't like what he saw. "You'd rather she'd just wounded him? Shot the detonator out of his hand, maybe, like on TV?"

"I'm happy to be alive."

"You're lucky to be alive. For that matter so is Amal. Fifteen meters is still well within the lethal radius of a suicide vest. And in case you were too busy bleeding to notice, there were four other agents within blast range as well."

"You've made your point, Farouk. Next time I'll shoot him in the face."

The comment only seemed to irritate Farouk more. He brought out another souvenir: Mustafa's pistol. "Next time," he said, tossing the gun on the bed, "try loading the fucking thing."

THE LIBRARY OF ALEXANDRIA
A USER-EDITED REFERENCE SOURCE

Baghdad

The city of Baghdad, population 6.5 million, is the largest city in Iraq and the second-largest city (after Cairo) in the United Arab States. Founded in the year 762 by Abu Jafar al Mansour, it was the capital of the Abbasid Caliphate until its sack by the Mongol Hulagu Khan in 1258. Under the Ottoman Turks, who ruled the city from the 16th through the 19th centuries, Baghdad went into decline, but its role in the founding of the UAS helped restore its fortunes. Today it is once again an important commercial and cultural center.

Baghdad has many nicknames, among them "The City of Peace," "The City of the Future," and "The City That Never Sleeps." Less flattering nicknames include "The Crime Capital of Mesopotamia" and "The Modern Babylon."

Since the 11/9 attacks, Baghdad and its residents have become symbols of Arab resistance to Western terrorism . . .

BAGHDAD IN POPULAR CULTURE

The diversity of its population has made Baghdad a popular setting for films and TV series—like the children's program *Open Sesame!*—that seek to promote greater religious and ethnic tolerance. One of the high-water marks of televised ecumenism was surely *Baghdad Police Story*, which debuted on the Arabian Broadcast Company in 1971 with the tagline "Shafiq: he's Sunni. Hassan: he's Shia. They fight crime." Part cop drama, part soap opera, part morality play, the series concerned the lives of two undercover detectives on Baghdad's east side. The recurring cast included characters who were Sufis, Christians, and Jews; there was even a Zoroastrian, a Persian counterfeiter named Qaisar. Episodes typically offered one or more moral lessons, the most common of which was "Respect the other People of the Book—even if you don't like them very much."

A very different Baghdad—one sadly more representative of the post–November 9 ethos—is seen in the contemporary hit series *24/7 Jihad*, each season of which chronicles a single day in the life of anti-terrorist Jafar Bashir. Bashir is a Unitarian Sunni, a portrayal that has drawn criticism from religious authorities who feel that his casual use of violence and torture is un-Islamic. Still greater controversy surrounds *Jihad*'s depiction of Shia. Although the series' main villains are Christian fundamentalists, Bashir must also cope with double agents within his own organization. Of the six identifiably Shia characters who have appeared on *Jihad* to date, *all* have been traitors (and all have died horrific deaths). In a 2007 interview on Al Manar, *Jihad* executive producer Jamal Sur insisted that this was a coincidence, and that the show in no way intended to suggest that Shia Muslims as a group were disloyal to the state. He added, "I think certain people are a little too in love with the idea of being martyrs." This prompted Omar Karim of the anti-defamation group Shia in Media to respond, "Chapter 25, verse 63 of Holy Quran instructs us to meet the taunts of the ignorant with the blessing of peace. Mr. Sur: Peace be unto you."

Mustafa lived with his father, Abu Mustafa, in a two-bedroom apartment in Baghdad's Rusafa district, east of the Tigris.

Abu Mustafa was a retired BU history professor. For a long while after the death of Mustafa's mother, he had chosen to live alone, the better, he said, to entertain the rich Baghdad widows who find elderly bachelors irresistible. The line about the widows wasn't entirely a joke—Abu Mustafa had always appreciated the company of women—but Mustafa knew he also enjoyed being on his own, free to socialize when he wanted to, to visit with family and friends, and then relax, at the end of the day, with his books and his own thoughts.

Mustafa had helped find and pay for the apartment, which was in an older building convenient to the riverside promenade and the shops and cafes along Sadoun Street. The neighborhood was religiously mixed, which, at the time they'd first got the place, hadn't been a problem. Since 11/9, though, hate crimes were up all over the city, and you didn't have to be Christian to find yourself in trouble. Mustafa's father was Sunni; his mother had been Shia. Asked what that made him, Mustafa had always replied, "A Muslim, of course." But to some Baghdadis, who'd seen God's judgment in the fall of the towers, that was no longer a good enough answer. Almost every day now the news carried a report of some Muslim getting roughed up, or worse, for belonging to the "wrong" sect.

Mustafa worried about his father becoming the target of some idiot who thought "God the All-Merciful" was code for "God the Head-Basher." He worried, as well, about his father's declining faculties. Sometimes when Abu Mustafa went out these days, he had trouble finding his way home. He blamed his confusion on mysterious changes to the city—once-familiar landmarks that had been altered, or that weren't where they were supposed to be. No doubt some of this was due to new construction, but when Abu Mustafa began talking about the streets being laid out differently, Mustafa knew something more was going on.

Abu Mustafa dismissed any suggestion that he move to a quieter, "less confusing" neighborhood, so the family had come up with an alternate plan. Mustafa's uncle Tamir and aunt Rana took an apartment in the same building. They had eight children, so there was always a spare niece or nephew available to keep an eye on Abu Mustafa. Mustafa himself, after protracted negotiations, moved into his father's spare bedroom. The face-saving cover story was that this was for Mustafa's convenience, to shorten his commute to work.

Mustafa and his father got on OK, as long as Mustafa was careful not to be overly protective. It wasn't always easy. Recently, Abu Mustafa had developed an animus towards air-conditioning. At first Mustafa thought it was the sound that bothered him, and he offered to pay to have the apartment refitted with a quieter system. But Abu Mustafa said it wasn't the noise; the problem was that the air-conditioning was *wrong*.

"What do you mean, wrong? You think it's a sin to be comfortable?"

"I didn't say sin!" Abu Mustafa grew flustered. "It's not immoral, it's just . . . wrong."

Two or three times a week now—invariably on the hottest nights—Mustafa would wake up sweating because his father had shut off the AC. Then, last week, there'd been a new development: Mustafa had awakened to find the air-conditioning still running, but his father's bedroom empty. After a frantic search, he discovered that Abu Mustafa had taken a mattress pad and gone up to the apartment building roof to sleep in the open air—the way Baghdadis had used to do, long ago, before the city was electrified.

"What's the matter?" Abu Mustafa asked, puzzled by Mustafa's concern. "You think I'm going to fall off?"

"In your sleep, anything is possible," Mustafa said. "It's not safe up here."

"God willing, it's as safe as anywhere in the city. And I like it up here. Even with the city lights, you can still see the stars. The stars are as they should be."

Talking to Farouk from his hospital bed, Mustafa had been embarrassed, but he didn't feel true shame until he saw his father in the hospital waiting room. As Abu Mustafa embraced him and kissed him on both cheeks, Mustafa felt his eyes welling up, and he apologized through tears for his carelessness in nearly getting himself killed. Of course, Abu Mustafa forgave him; but he knew he'd be reminded of it the next time he told Abu Mustafa to be careful. So for that, as much as for his own sake, Mustafa resolved to be less foolish in the future.

It was not the first time in his life he had made that particular pledge.

Mustafa spent the next day resting at home, but he asked Samir and Amal to come by and update him on the investigation.

It was Amal's first time at the apartment, and like many first-time visitors, she was drawn to the bookshelves that covered every free centimeter of wall space. While Samir went into the kitchen to help Abu Mustafa make tea, and Mustafa relaxed on a couch by the window, Amal stayed on her feet, moving from shelf to shelf.

"How many languages does your father know?" Amal asked.

"Half a dozen well, and another half dozen well enough to muddle through. Which sounds impressive, unless you'd met my mother."

"What was she, a translator?"

"Restless," Mustafa said. "She always wanted to travel around the world, but North Africa on holiday was as far as she ever got. So she took foreign language courses, scores of them. As a boy I was her study partner."

Amal had come to a shelf filled with photographs instead of books. "Is this her?"

Looking where she pointed, he said: "Yes. That's from the honeymoon—she and my father took a boat trip on the Nile."

"She's beautiful," Amal said.

"She was," Mustafa agreed. "That next picture, in the silver frame, that's my uncle Fayyad and my sisters, Nawrah, Qamar, and Latifa."

"Do your sisters live in Baghdad?"

"Nawrah and Qamar live in Fallujah. Latifa lives in Palestine; her husband manages a beach resort in Haifa."

Next in line were Mustafa's own wedding pictures. Amal glanced at them but didn't say anything.

"Yes," Mustafa said, broaching the subject for her. "My two wives. That's Fadwa on the left, Noor on the right. I'm sure the office gossips have told you all about them by now."

"It's not my place to gossip about my colleagues."

"You're kind, but it's OK. I'm used to it . . . You know, I heard the speech your mother gave in the Senate last month, about the Marriage Reform Act. I thought she was very courageous to challenge the House of Saud the way she did."

"'Courageous' is not the word her own colleagues would use," Amal said. She continued, choosing her own words with care: "My mother feels strongly that polygamy, however much tradition defends it, is fundamentally unfair to the women involved."

"Your mother is right," said Mustafa.

The most famous photograph of Amal's mother had been taken just after sunrise on the morning of November 10, 2001. Mayor Al Maysani had been up all night directing the emergency response, shuttling about the city from trouble spot to trouble spot; she'd been to Ground Zero twice already, but as dawn broke she set out again, intending to get her first clear look at the site in daylight.

She left her command post at City Hall and stepped out onto Haifa Street. Eschewing her official car, she headed north on foot, trailed at first only by a handful of aides and security people. Within a block, others began to fall in behind her: exhausted cops and firefighters, paramedics and EMTs, as well as scores of ordinary Baghdadis who, out of stubbornness or shock, had ignored the evacuation order.

By the time a bend in the road brought the shattered ruin of the towers into view, the procession numbered in the hundreds. When the mayor raised a defiant fist into the air, the multitudes behind her did the same, and the cry went up: "God is great!" That moment, captured on camera and published in newspapers across the country, became known as The Moment: The Moment we got to our feet; The Moment we began to fight back; The Moment we said, we will never be broken.

The Moment, as well, that Anmar al Maysani was transformed from a failed one-term mayor into a politician of national standing.

Amal had seen the picture many times, of course. People liked to show it to her, and to describe, often through tears, what it meant to them. These outpourings of emotion could be difficult to listen to, and while Amal did her best to be courteous, she was always a bit on guard around new acquaintances, never knowing when they might spring The Moment on her.

Today she was spared that. The tea conversation focused on Amal's own heroism—a novel topic, but not an unpleasant one—and when Abu Mustafa inquired about her family, he showed more interest in her father than her famous mother. Amal's father had been a police union official, murdered in the line of duty, so the subject was not without pain, but Amal was grateful to anyone who remembered that her dad, too, had once been a hero.

"I'm sure he would be very proud of you," Abu Mustafa said.

"I would like to think so," Amal said. "Did you ever meet him, Abu Mustafa?"

"Once," Abu Mustafa said. "At a Baath function, a union fund-raiser held on the university grounds. It was not a great evening—there were some unsavory characters there, I'm afraid—but your father impressed me. A good and decent man . . . We're fortunate you follow in his footsteps."

Amal blushed.

"Well," said Abu Mustafa. "I will thank you once more for saving my son's life and remind you that you are always welcome in my home, and then I will leave you to your official business."

"You're going out?" Mustafa said, as Abu Mustafa stood up.

"Just downstairs, to see your uncle Tamir. Don't worry."

"I'm not worried," Mustafa lied.

With a smile and a nod to Amal, Abu Mustafa turned and left. After the apartment door clicked shut behind him, Mustafa sat quietly for a moment. Amal did too, thinking of her own father. Samir poured more tea.

"All right," Mustafa said. "Tell me where we're at."

Amal went first. The search of James Travis's hotel room, she said, had turned up nothing of interest, other than the tools he'd used to assemble the suicide vest. "The bomb-disposal guys say it was a decent job. He'd been well trained by somebody."

"So it definitely would have gone off?"

"Oh yes."

"Do we have any idea what his target was?"

"The Abu Nuwas Street Mall," Samir said. "Travis had a tourist map of the waterfront. The mall complex was circled."

"And what's Riyadh saying? Do they have any new intel for us? Preferably something more in line with reality?"

"They're 'reevaluating their sources, in light of recent events,'" Amal said. "The good news is, we may have caught a break in Kufah . . ."

For the past few weeks, Travis had rented a room at a guest workers' hostel not far from the Kufah army base. "My old Bureau partner Rafi has been working down there on a different investigation, so I asked him to tag along when ABI swept the hostel yesterday. The room was clean—Travis threw out everything he didn't take with him—and according to the manager, garbage pickup was yesterday morning. So at first it seemed like a dead end . . ."

"What did they do, search the garbage dump?"

"There was some discussion of doing that. But then Rafi got suspicious and made a phone call."

"Turns out the manager was lying," Samir said. "Garbage pickup in that part of Kufah is actually on Mondays—*if* you've paid your garbage bill. But the manager discontinued the service over a year ago, without telling his boss. He was pocketing the money for himself and having whichever tenants were behind on their rent help him haul the trash to bins on other people's property. So, long story short, ABI had the guy out dumpster-diving all night."

"They found Travis's garbage around three o'clock this morning," Amal said. "They're still sifting it for clues, but one of the first things they found was a camera—"

"A *broken* camera," said Samir. "Smashed, like Travis took a hammer to it. Only he must have been asleep the day they taught destroying evidence in terror school, because he screwed up and left the memory card intact . . ."

Amal switched on her cell phone. "Rafi emailed me the pictures. Take a look at this."

The scene was of four men seated at a long wooden table, indoors, in a close and poorly lit space. Travis, the picture-taker, was in the foreground, holding the camera at arm's length, the flash highlighting the pinkness of his cheeks. He'd evidently consumed a large quantity of alcohol—Mustafa could make out the tops of several foam-flecked glasses on the table in front of him. Behind Travis, holding glasses of their own, were two blond men; their features were hard to discern on the small screen, but an enlargement might provide enough detail for computer identification. The fourth man, a surly red-haired fellow, had been caught in profile jabbing a finger at Travis, his mouth open to deliver a rebuke.

"What do you think?" Amal said.

"I think this redhead may be the one who smashed the camera. And if I'm counting empty glasses correctly, I think I know why he overlooked the memory card."

"But do you think these are our guys? The rest of the cell?"

"It's possible," Mustafa said. "Though I'm frankly stunned that even drunk crusaders would be this stupid. This room that they're in . . ."

"A rat cellar," Amal said. "Rafi's checking with Halal to see if they can identify it."

A rat cellar: an illegal bar catering to foreign guest workers, primarily Europeans. There'd be home-brewed beer, misappropriated Sabbath and communion wine, and probably hard liquor as well, though not the good stuff. As for the location, it might be a literal cellar or an aboveground structure like a warehouse—any place the local cops could be bribed to turn a blind eye to.

"Those blond guys in the back," said Samir. "They look like Germans, don't they?"

Mustafa smiled. "I suppose they might be German, or Austrian. But I don't know, Samir—they could be Scandinavian."

"Scandinavian terrorists? Mustafa, please!"

"As long as their faces are clear enough for a computer match, what difference does it make whether they're German or Scandinavian?" Amal asked. "Shouldn't ICE have them in the system either way?"

"ICE should, which doesn't mean ICE will," said Mustafa. "But if they're German, Samir has an excuse to call in our friend Sinbad."

"And who is Sinbad? Naval intelligence?"

"Mossad," Samir told her.

"There's an Israeli named Sinbad?"

"It'll make sense once you've met him," said Mustafa.

The Library of Alexandria
A USER-EDITED REFERENCE SOURCE

Israel

This page is currently **protected** from editing to deal with **repeated acts of vandalism**. To suggest changes, please **contact an administrator**.

The modern **State of Israel** is a country in Central Europe. It is bordered on the north by the North Sea, Denmark, and the Baltic Sea, to the east by Poland and the Czech Republic, and to the west, in part, by the Netherlands. The rest of its western and southern borders are officially defined by the courses of the Rhine and Main rivers, but since the 1967 Six-Day War Israel has occupied most of Bavaria, Swabia, and the West Bank of the Middle Rhine. Israel's capital is Berlin . . .

HISTORY

Following the defeat of the Third Reich, the UAS spearheaded a plan to partition Germany into two states, one Jewish and one Christian . . . The same 1948 act of Congress that officially recognized Israel's sovereignty also established a new religious district in Jerusalem, Palestine and guaranteed Israeli citizens access to the holy city through special visitor visas. (In the aftermath of the 11/9 attacks, new security restrictions were placed on these visas; see the 2002 Arafat-Abbas Amendment to the Law of Return . . .)

Both Israel's existence and its geographical location remain controversial . . . British Prime Minister David Irving is only the most recent of Europe's leaders to call for the Jewish state's destruction . . . Meanwhile, many North American evangelical Christians would like to see the Jews permanently relocated to the site of the historical Land of

Israel, believing this to be one of the necessary preconditions for the End of Days . . .

Despite recent tensions, the UAS continues to be Israel's closest political and military ally, with the two countries operating as partners in the War on Terror . . .

Sinbad's real name was David Cohen. He was a twenty-nine-year-old Mossad agent who'd done two tours as a commando in the Israel Defense Forces—a good man to have around, Samir joked, if you needed to kill a roomful of bad guys using only a rolled-up newspaper. Or if you needed to seduce a roomful of women—for in addition to his combat skills, David Cohen had been blessed with the good looks and charisma God usually reserves for pop stars.

Mustafa and Samir had met him several years ago at an international security conference in Cairo. Samir, who was in the midst of a divorce, had gone clubbing with Cohen every night in hopes of being a secondhand beneficiary of his attractiveness; Mustafa had skipped the discotheques but listened dutifully to Samir's tales of their adventures.

On the last day of the conference, Mustafa and Samir were called away to a terrorist incident unfolding just blocks from the conference site. Cohen tagged along.

The "terrorist incident" turned out to be a robbery gone bad. Five masked men had held up a bank, only to be caught in traffic as they tried to make their getaway. When police surrounded their stalled car, the men had opened fire, and in the ensuing gun battle one cop and two of the robbers were killed. The three surviving bandits had retreated on foot into a small movie theater, taking the patrons hostage. Homeland Security had been alerted after the bandits, claiming to have explosives as well as guns, threatened to blow up the building unless their demand for safe passage was met.

When Mustafa, Samir, and Cohen arrived on the scene, they found the local AHS chief, Hamid Darwish, poring over a set of blueprints. Darwish, a political appointee who'd gotten his job through party loyalty rather than strategic acumen, had decided to end the standoff by pumping gas into the theater's ventilation system.

"Tear gas?" Mustafa asked.

"No, something much better," Darwish replied. "Something I've been wanting to try . . ." He pointed to a pair of his subordinates who were unloading several large canisters from the back of a van. Each canister was stamped with a lengthy chemical name and bore numerous warning labels.

Mustafa wasn't familiar with the chemical, but David Cohen was. "It's a sleep agent," he said. Looking at Darwish, he added: "You're an idiot."

"Who is this person?" Darwish demanded.

Cohen introduced himself, then explained why the plan was madness: Even if the bandits and their hostages all weighed the same amount and shared identical metabolisms, there was no way to ensure that they'd inhale the gas at the same rate. "Some will pass out while others are only numb—and if you pump in enough gas to make sure they all lose consciousness, you'll kill some of them."

"We know what we're doing," Darwish said. "Besides, we have no choice—these men are desperate, and they say they've wired the building with dynamite."

"They're lying. Why would they have dynamite?"

"You ask that, and yet you call *me* an idiot?"

"The whole point of robbing a bank in the daytime is that the vault is already open. These men don't have explosives . . . and gassing them is stupid."

"Get this fucking *Israeli* out of my face," Darwish snapped.

"That was diplomatic," Mustafa said to Cohen, after he had, with difficulty, convinced him to back off.

"That man's as dangerous as those bank robbers," Cohen said. "You have morons running things here."

"Yes, welcome to Egypt," Samir said smiling.

"The thing about morons," said Mustafa, "is that they don't respond well to being *called* morons."

"Ah, he wouldn't have listened even if I'd been polite. He wants to use his stupid gas."

"And what would you suggest we use? Is there something better, something we can control the dosage of, maybe?"

"Yes," Cohen said. "Bullets." He looked up the block, to where the Cairo SWAT team were cooling their heels around their own van. "Give me a minute . . ."

The crowd of local and federal cops around the theater was growing, as more men from the security conference wandered by to see what was happening. Mustafa searched the crowd, trying to find someone reasonable who outranked Darwish.

Samir tapped Mustafa on the shoulder. "Look up."

David Cohen, wearing a SWAT jacket and with a rifle slung across his back, was standing on the roof of the department store next to the theater. A broad alleyway separated the two buildings. Cohen took a running start and leaped across the gap. It was then, seeing how gracefully he sailed through the air, that Samir gave Cohen his nickname: "Hah! Sinbad the Jew!"

Having landed safely on the theater's roof, Cohen vanished from view. Moments later, gunfire erupted inside. The real SWAT team members came alive at the sound, but before they could do anything, Cohen called out on a walkie-talkie to announce it was all over.

Two of the bank robbers were dead and the third had surrendered. None of the hostages were harmed. Darwish was furious. He had Cohen arrested as soon as he came out of the theater, and would have shot him if he could have gotten away with it.

But within hours the situation changed, as the news spread that one of the freed hostages was Diala Mahfouz, the grandmother of Cairo's mayor. The old woman had a weak heart, and while the excitement of Cohen's impromptu commando raid hadn't been great for it, gas would have been far worse.

By nightfall Cohen had been sprung from the holding cell Darwish had put him in and was up on a stage with the mayor and other officials, being hailed as a hero in front of dozens of news cameras. Mustafa and Samir stood near the back of the auditorium where the press conference was held, Samir beaming as if he were the one onstage.

"What did I tell you, Mustafa?" he said. "Is this guy cool, or what?"

As they waited for Sinbad outside the Israeli embassy, Mustafa suffered an attack of vertigo. He couldn't remember when these spells of dizziness had first started, but he'd had them off and on for at least the past few years. They came most often during moments of idleness: He'd be staring at the city skyline, or contemplating some perfectly ordinary street scene, and suddenly be struck by a powerful sense of dislocation. The last time, he'd been in Riyadh, about to step into a crosswalk, when he happened to notice that all the cars lined up at the red light were driven by women.

This time it was the embassy flag that set him off. He heard it snapping in the breeze overhead and glanced up. The Star of David, fluttering proudly above Al Kindi Street, somehow made him aware of the earth's rotation beneath his feet. He staggered backwards and might have fallen, if not for the support of a concrete barricade.

"Are you all right?" Amal asked.

Mustafa fingered the bandage on his neck. "I still need a bit of rest, I guess."

"Here he comes!" Samir said.

Amal turned to look, and Mustafa, imagining he saw something in her expression, said, "Ah, you've been talking to Umm Dabir." Umm Dabir was Farouk's secretary. She'd met Sinbad during one of his visits and developed a not-so-secret crush.

"I'm sure I don't know what you mean," Amal said.

"I understand many of the women in the office are in love with him."

"Not just the women, apparently." Amal nodded towards Samir, who'd already run up to embrace Sinbad and was now walking alongside him with an arm slung over his shoulders.

"Hey, man, good to see you!" Samir was saying. "But what's this about you already being in town and not calling us?"

"No time to party this trip," Sinbad said. "I'm due on a redeye to Berlin tonight . . . Hello, Mustafa." He flashed a smile at Amal. "And you must be Mustafa's new bodyguard."

"Yes, she protects me from Christians, and the lions of my own foolishness," Mustafa said. "Amal bint Shamal, meet David Cohen. Sinbad to his many admirers." As they shook hands, Mustafa took note of the attaché tucked under Sinbad's arm. "You have something for us?"

"I do," Sinbad said.

"Let's find a place to sit, then. I'm feeling a little lightheaded today."

They went to a tea shop around the corner from the embassy. The proprietor greeted Sinbad as warmly as Samir had, and Mustafa felt his vertigo flaring again. But he felt better once he was seated with a steaming glass of tea in front of him, listening to Sinbad explain that Samir had been right—the two blond men in the photograph were German.

"Peter and Martin Hoffman, of the Lutheran National Socialist Brotherhood," Sinbad said, producing two Interpol files from his attaché. "Both alumni of the Munich Polytechnic. Peter is a chemist, Martin an engineer—but their main occupation, since graduating, has been organizing attacks on Jewish settlements in the Rhineland. Last year Peter was captured at a car-bomb assembly site in Koblenz. He killed a soldier and escaped. We think he and his brother fled to Turkey on forged guest-worker visas. From there . . ."

From there, sneaking into the UAS would have been a relatively trivial exercise. Despite millions of riyals spent to secure the Turkish-

Syrian border, it remained a popular route for undocumented European immigrants.

"This is helpful," Mustafa said. "But if they are in the country illegally, finding them won't be easy."

"Ah, but there's more," Sinbad said. "I also ran a check on your dead suicide bomber, James Travis . . ."

"Interpol has nothing on him."

"No, but Mossad does. Two summers ago, Travis was part of a humanitarian mission in the Rhineland that was detained, briefly, on suspicion of providing aid and comfort to terrorists."

"What sort of humanitarian mission?" Amal said.

"Medical," Mustafa guessed. "He was a student doctor, remember?"

"Yes," Sinbad said. "And one of the other doctors detained with Travis was an American named Gabriel Costello." He opened up his attaché again. "I think you'll recognize him."

The photo attached to the new file he handed them was full-face rather than profile, and the subject looked somber rather than angry, but there was no mistaking the red hair.

"This is an ICE file," Mustafa noted. "How did you get—"

"It's not important," Sinbad said. "What matters is, Dr. Costello has a green card . . . and a Baghdad address. I looked it up, it's an apartment in the western suburbs, near the airport."

Directly beneath Costello's home address, the file listed his current occupation and place of employment. "I don't believe this," Mustafa said. "He's a trauma surgeon at Karkh General Hospital." He explained to Sinbad: "That's where I got patched up the other night. It's just minutes from here. We should go over, see if Costello is working now . . ."

"He's not," Sinbad said. "I checked that too. The receptionist I spoke with said Dr. Costello's next shift starts at two p.m. So you have time to finish your tea."

Samir was beaming again.

"You know, David," Mustafa said, "if you wanted to skip that flight to Berlin tonight, I'm sure we have some other cases you could solve."

"Let's see how this goes, first. I'm not interested in Costello, but if we can find the Hoffman brothers, maybe I'll stick around."

By quarter to two they had plainclothes agents in place inside and outside the hospital. Half a dozen Baghdad police units, a bomb-disposal team, and a Hazmat crew were all on standby.

Mustafa, Samir, and Sinbad were parked across the street from the hospital's ambulance bay. Sinbad had offered the use of his embassy car as a mobile command post and Mustafa had accepted, thinking it would be more comfortable than the black van. Also—and this was somewhat embarrassing—the Israeli diplomatic corps, at least that part of it that was actually Mossad, had better communications gear than Arab Homeland Security did. Instead of juggling two sets of radios, Mustafa could use Sinbad's dash-mounted system to monitor and transmit on both the AHS and local police frequencies.

Amal was in the parking structure adjacent to the hospital, posing as a booth attendant. Mustafa had hoped that an unfamiliar woman in the booth would be less likely to raise suspicion, but this part of the plan was working too well: The doctors and male nurses arriving for the 2 p.m. shift were stopping to chat Amal up, creating a small traffic jam at the garage entrance. Some of the other agents began teasing Amal about her "new boyfriends"; then Abd al Rasheed, an older agent who'd re-embraced Islam in a big way after 11/9, came on air to berate them for the crudeness of their comments.

"Enough!" Mustafa said, breaking into the transmission. "Peace be unto all of you, and knock it off! It's almost two. Does anyone see our target?"

"Mustafa?" a voice answered almost immediately. "This is Hamdan. I think we may have him. You said Costello drives a white motorcycle?"

Mustafa glanced at Sinbad. "That's our information, yes." He recited a license plate number.

"That's the one. He's here."

"Is he headed for the parking garage?"

"He was. He just pulled over to the curb and checked his pager. Now he's making a cell phone call . . ."

Mustafa looked at Sinbad again and nodded hopefully towards the radio scanner. Sinbad shook his head.

"Mustafa?" Hamdan said. "Do you want us to grab him?"

Before Mustafa could answer, Abdullah clicked in from the hospital switchboard: "Mustafa, Costello's on the line right now . . . He says he's going to be late to work."

"Does he say why?"

"Family emergency."

Mustafa took his finger off the transmit button. "Did I miss something in Costello's file about relatives in Baghdad?"

"No," Sinbad said. "He's got no family here. Nearest thing is a fiancée who got killed in Gaza City a few years back."

"So who paged him?"

"Two guesses," Samir said from the back seat.

Hamdan: "Mustafa? The guy is on the move again. What do you want us to do?"

"Follow him," Mustafa said, making a decision. "Keep him in sight but don't take him yet. He may be on his way to meet with the Hoffmans . . . Hamdan, do you copy?"

An oath accompanied by the blare of a car horn erupted from the radio.

"Hamdan?"

"Ah, we're stuck behind some idiot who won't move . . . Costello was able to squeeze around. He's turning south onto Union Boulevard."

Sinbad already had the car in motion. Thirty seconds later they too were on the boulevard, the white motorcycle visible a block ahead of them.

"Everyone please pay attention," Mustafa said into the radio. "Costello is southbound, approaching the July 14th Bridge. We want to see where he's going, so I'd ask my friends in the Baghdad PD to please stay back with your sirens off. Anyone *not* driving a marked car, we could use your help with the pursuit. And can I get a helicopter overhead in case we lose him?"

Costello didn't appear to be aware that he was being followed, but he was a naturally impatient driver willing to take chances, and Sinbad, whose car could not slip through the same gaps as the motorcycle, had to work hard to keep up with him. The bridge, where six lanes became four, proved a special challenge, but Sinbad managed to keep Costello in sight by means of several death-defying swerves into oncoming traffic.

They crossed the river, coming onto the narrow peninsula formed by the sharp bend the Tigris made as it flowed south out of midtown. Baghdad University's main campus occupied the peninsula's western tip, and Costello headed that way. "Abdullah," Mustafa said into the radio, "can you get BU campus security on the phone and have them stand by?"

"Wait," Samir said. "He's pulling over."

They were on a commercial strip near the eastern edge of the campus. In the middle of the block was an Ali Baba supermarket with a Forty Thieves coffee shop tucked in beside it. Costello parked his motorcycle in front of the coffee shop. Two blond men sitting at a table on the sidewalk stood up to greet him.

"Look at that, the whole gang." Samir pounded Sinbad on the shoulder. "Dude, you bring good luck." But Sinbad was less enthused. As Costello sat down with the Hoffman brothers, Sinbad pointed to a green knapsack under the table beside Peter Hoffman's chair. "What do you suppose is in that backpack?"

Mustafa said: "We recovered all the stolen explosives."

"All the stolen explosives from the army base," Sinbad said. "But you can find explosives in a university engineering department, too. Or make them in a chemistry lab."

"So what do you suggest we do? Call in SWAT and have them loan you a rifle?"

"I've got a rifle in the trunk. But if I use it we've got no one to interrogate." He thought a moment, then reached forward to toggle a switch on the dashboard. A warning panel lit, reading AIR BAGS DISABLED.

"David?" Mustafa said.

"Unbuckle your seat belts and brace yourselves. Be ready to jump out as soon as the car stops moving."

He drove forward before Mustafa could argue with him. When the car was almost at the coffee shop, Sinbad gave the steering wheel a hard jerk to the right and leaned on the horn. As the car swerved onto the sidewalk, Costello and Martin Hoffman jumped up and dove out of the way. But Peter Hoffman bent down and reached for the backpack. Sinbad hit the gas and plowed into the table moving faster than he'd intended; the car clipped the front corner of the coffee shop and slewed around to a stop.

Mustafa, despite bracing for impact, was thrown forward into the dashboard. By the time he stumbled from the car, Costello had hopped back onto his motorcycle and Martin Hoffman was fleeing on foot. Peter Hoffman had disappeared—or so Mustafa thought, until he looked down and saw a hand sticking out from under Sinbad's car.

Costello kicked the cycle into life. Samir grabbed his wrist and tried to haul him off the bike, but Costello swung his helmet with his other hand, catching Samir in the face. Samir tumbled backwards and Costello twisted the throttle and raced away in the direction of the campus.

"Go after Hoffman!" Sinbad shouted. "I'll get the American!" He reversed into the street and roared off after the motorcycle.

Martin Hoffman had run to a car parked across the street at the east end of the block. He stood beside it, slapping his pockets for keys, then looked back helplessly towards the coffee shop. He saw Mustafa coming for him and ran into the Ghost Music superstore on the corner.

Mustafa entered a moment later with his gun drawn. A few dark-haired students circulated among the racks of magazines and comics at the front of the store, but there was no sign of Hoffman. Searching for the German, Mustafa's gaze was drawn to a display of bright yellow books offering easy education in divers subjects: *Algebra for the Ignorant; Desktop Publishing for the Ignorant; Yazidi Culture for the Ignorant;* and in a special pile, the post-November 9th bestseller, now heavily discounted, *Christianity for the Ignorant.*

Samir came into the store, followed closely by Amal, Hamdan, and several other agents. They spread out into a line and began a systematic sweep. In the video-game aisles, an exchange student stood up suddenly from behind a shelf of cheat manuals; he looked nothing like Hoffman save that he had blue eyes and pale skin, but it was only the grace of God that kept him from becoming a news story.

Mustafa found himself in an open aisle between two entertainment mediums and two warring sociopolitical viewpoints. To his left, in the DVD section, a bank of flat-screens showed the governor of Lebanon, in his previous career as an action-movie superstar, maneuvering a jump jet between the skyscrapers of Beirut and using the plane's nose-cannon to annihilate an army of terrorists, all of whom looked like relatives of the man Mustafa was chasing. To his right, in pop music, a wall of speakers and subwoofers blasted out the punk band Green Desert's anti-war, anti-Saud anthem, "Arabian Idiot."

And straight ahead, taking no political stances but offering both DVDs and CD soundtracks for sale: a cardboard cutout of the Bollywood Aladdin. Mustafa looked away, then looked back again. A fringe of blond hair was visible above the curve of Aladdin's turban. Mustafa turned and made eye contact with Samir, who nodded; he'd seen it too.

A woman in an abaya and veil came out of the DVD section, dragging a small boy behind her. Martin Hoffman darted from his hiding place. He knocked the boy aside and grabbed the woman to use as a shield, raising a knife to her throat. The woman struggled. Her veil tore loose, and Mustafa blinked in surprise. "Fadwa?" he said.

Shrieking, the little boy launched himself at the man who'd grabbed his mother. He sank his teeth into Hoffman's leg. Hoffman's grip on the woman loosened, and for an instant, Mustafa had a clear shot. His gun snapped up, seemingly of its own accord; this time it was loaded. Hoffman cocked his head to the side and opened his mouth as if he'd heard something shocking. He dropped his knife and fell backwards into the Aladdin display.

As the woman scooped up her son and fled for safety, more gunfire erupted. Mustafa thought at first that one of the other agents had opened up with an assault rifle. But it was movie gunfire—the Governator, slaughtering Christians in Beirut. Green Desert retorted with a lyric about Arab imperialism. Martin Hoffman didn't react, just bled silently onto the pile of mixed media that had become his final resting place.

"You had to do it, man."

Mustafa and Samir were on the sidewalk in front of the store. Inside, a team of paramedics, having made a pointless attempt to revive Hoffman, now stood milling around the body with the cops and federal agents. Mustafa had stepped away once the wisecracks started. Samir mistook his attitude for regret: "You had to do it. He'd have cut that woman's throat."

"I know, Samir," Mustafa said.

The woman sat in the back of an ambulance, hugging her son to her breast. Her veil was still askew. Mustafa studied her face and wondered what had come over him. She wasn't Fadwa; she didn't even look like her.

"Hey," Samir said. "That little boy had some fire in him, didn't he?"

"Yes." With an effort, Mustafa turned away from the ambulance. He waved to Amal, who'd been conferring with the head of the bomb-disposal team about the contents of Peter Hoffman's back-pack. "So?"

"Two kilos of commercial blasting gel," she said, joining them. "Maybe from the mining-engineering school, maybe stolen from a demolition site—they're tracing the lot number now. There was hardware in the bag, too, and tools. Everything you'd need to put a time-bomb together."

Mustafa frowned. "It wasn't wired up yet?"

"No," Amal said. "Also, I was asked to tell you, blasting gel's pretty stable, but all the same it's not a great idea to drive over it."

"Thanks, we'll pass that along," Mustafa said. Sinbad's car had just pulled up to the police cordon at the end of the block. The car had suffered severe front-end damage—two broken headlights, a crumpled grill and hood—but through the cracked windshield they could see that Sinbad had a passenger. A live passenger.

"Hear me, O Israel!" Samir called out, as Sinbad pulled Costello from the vehicle. "You are the *man!*"

"He led me quite a chase," Sinbad said. "Did you catch my German?"

"We got him," Mustafa said, not wanting Costello to know that Martin Hoffman was dead. "He's inside."

Sinbad read the truth in Mustafa's eyes. "Ah . . . That's good, then."

The right front tire of Sinbad's car had been punctured and was beginning to deflate. "So, David," Mustafa said. "Can we get you a ride to the airport?"

Miranda warning

A **Miranda warning** is a statement of legal rights that must be read to any criminal suspect taken into police custody within the United Arab States, before the commencement of questioning that seeks to elicit potentially incriminating information. Incriminating statements made by a suspect who has not been properly "Mirandized" are not admissible as evidence.

The exact text of the Miranda warning varies from jurisdiction to jurisdiction, but the following script, used by police in the state of Iraq, is typical: "By the grace of God the All-Merciful and Compassionate, you have the right to remain silent. If you give up the right to remain silent, anything you say may be used against you in a court of law, where, God willing, justice will be done. By the grace of God the All-Merciful and Compassionate, you have the right to an attorney. If you cannot afford an attorney, one will be appointed for you by the court. Do you understand these rights as I have described them to you?"

The warning gets its name from the 1966 Supreme Court case *Miranda v. Morocco*. The case concerned Arturo Miranda, a Catholic of Spain arrested in Marrakesh for the kidnapping and rape of a young Berber woman. Miranda admitted his guilt to the police and was subsequently tried and convicted. His lawyer argued on appeal that as a non-citizen who did not speak Arabic, Miranda had been unaware of his right to silence under the UAS Constitution, and that therefore his confession should have been excluded. The Supreme Court agreed, in a landmark 5–4 decision.

The Court's majority opinion was written by Chief Justice Alim al Warith. Among other authorities, Al Warith cited a traditional saying of the Prophet Mohammed (peace be unto him) which states, "None of you truly believes, until you desire for your brother what you desire for yourself." Wrote Al Warith: "Surely any man, when confronted by the overwhelming power of the state, would want, at a minimum, to be made aware of his inalienable rights."

Law enforcement reaction to the ruling was initially negative, with some police and prosecutors predicting a total collapse of the justice system. Al Warith had anticipated this in his opinion: "There are those who will say that by advising suspects of their right against self-incrimination, we eliminate any chance of obtaining a confession. In the case of *innocent* suspects, of course, this is a desirable outcome. As for the guilty, by treating them with honor and dignity, we hope to reawaken their consciences and lead them back to the righteous path; but those who persist in wickedness will, we believe, be undone by their own moral weakness. Though they be warned ten thousand times not to speak, still Satan will loosen their tongues and bring them to doom."

Although the wisdom of the ruling continues to be debated, a 1976 study by the Arab Civil Liberties Union, *Ten Years of Miranda,* found no significant decline in the number of confessions obtained by police. The report did note a drop in the percentage of convictions overturned on appeal, which it attributed in part to the use of signed Miranda waivers to document suspects' consent to be questioned.

As for Arturo Miranda, he received a new trial. Even without his confession, prosecutors had enough evidence to convict him for a second time. Miranda served 7 years in Rabat State Prison; upon his release, he was deported to Spain. The judge who signed the deportation order urged Miranda to consider the fate of his soul on Judgment Day and mend his ways.

This particular "Miranda warning" went unheeded. In 1974 Miranda was implicated in the hijacking of a bank truck carrying Spanish government funds, including a rumored 6 million pesetas from the personal account of General Francisco Franco. The Madrid police, in an effort to get Miranda to divulge the whereabouts of the truck, subjected him to a brutal interrogation. He died in custody. The stolen money was not recovered.

Arab Homeland Security's regional Baghdad headquarters was located in an eight-story building within shouting distance of Ground Zero. The building, formerly owned by the underwriter who'd insured the twin towers, had undergone extensive renovation since 2001. Part of the remodel had been the addition of a state-of-the-art "interview suite": three interrogation rooms surrounding a single, central observation room.

The basic setup would have been familiar to anyone who'd ever watched a television police procedural. But unlike the interrogation rooms on *Law & Order: Halal* or *CSI: Damascus,* these came with million-riyal price tags. The bulk of the money had gone towards special sensors that turned each room into a walk-in polygraph machine. In addition to the lie-detecting equipment, there were multiple cameras and microphones; these were supposedly on a closed circuit, but Mustafa had long suspected the existence of an undocumented line out that allowed the higher-ups in Riyadh to monitor the questioning.

Other aspects of the interrogation rooms would have given a civil libertarian pause. The climate controls could be set for temperatures outside the normal human comfort range. Shutters in the air vents allowed the rooms to be hermetically sealed; this was billed as a safety feature for preventing the release of smuggled-in biological or chemical weapons, but a cynical mind could not help asking whether there might not be some other reason for restricting a detainee's air supply.

And then there was the matter of the wall outlets. The ceiling lights provided more than adequate illumination, and there were, as noted, plenty of built-in recording devices. So why had the designers opted to include so many electrical sockets?

"Well, you know how it is," Samir had said, when Mustafa pointed this out to him. "Some power drills have really short cords."

Now, as he looked through the one-way glass into interrogation room A, Mustafa tried to map out an interrogation strategy that did not involve the use of power tools.

"Abdullah," he said. "Did you remember to offer Dr. Costello a Bible?"

"I did, Mustafa," Abdullah said. "But you see how he's sulking in there. He wouldn't even look at the cart."

Whatever other rights might be stripped from them in the name of state security, every prisoner was entitled to a holy book. This could be a thorny proposition where Christians were concerned, for while there is only one Quran, there are many Bibles. Woe unto the Muslim who gave an angry crusader the wrong translation or selection of apocrypha.

Sensing an opportunity, Mustafa had filled a library cart with as many different Bibles as he could lay his hands on: the Latin Vulgate; various incarnations of the King James; the Luther Bible; the Revised Standard; the Ignatius Bible; the Scofield Reference; the Reina-Valera; the Louis Segond. Mustafa's goal was not so much to have something for everyone, but rather, by demonstrating an awareness of Christian sensibilities, to show respect, and thereby establish trust and good will. It was a surprisingly effective tactic, even with prisoners who refused all hospitality.

The observation room door opened and Amal and Samir came in. "Well?" Mustafa said.

"Gaza City PD came through," Amal told him. "It was a convenience-store robbery. They faxed over the report and a photo of the crime scene."

Mustafa studied the photograph Amal handed to him. It showed a woman sitting with her back against the door of a cold-beverage case, her head lolling to one side. Her close-eyed expression was peaceful, as if she'd just nodded off to sleep, but below the neck she was a bloody mess.

"So what's the plan?" Samir asked. "You going to play the sympathy angle with this guy?"

"Something like that," Mustafa said.

"Hello, Dr. Costello," he began. "My name is Mustafa al Baghdadi. I'm here to speak with you about your recent activities."

Costello sat with his elbows propped on the interrogation room table, his gaze fixed on the short length of chain that ran between the cuffs on his wrists. "I have nothing to say to you."

"Perhaps you'll just listen, then," Mustafa said. "If you don't mind, I'm going to speak Arabic. I understand you're fluent in the language, and while I do have English, those who are observing us"—he gestured at the cameras, the mirrored glass—"are not so fortunate."

Costello made no direct answer to this, but sat back in his chair with a sigh. Mustafa held up the folder containing Costello's ICE file; he'd padded it with a couple hundred pages of unrelated office correspondence, so it made a weighty thump as he set it on the tabletop. "This is everything we know about you." He sat opposite the doctor, and rather than open the folder, looked straight across the table and began to recite from memory.

"Your full name is Gabriel Brennan Costello. You were born in Boston in 1973. In 1988, following the death of your parents, you went to live in London with your maternal grandmother. In 1991 you received a visa to pursue undergraduate studies at Baghdad University. From 1995 to 1998 you attended the Ain Shams School of Medicine in Cairo. You completed your surgical residency at Jaffa Medical Center in Palestine. Four years ago you returned to Baghdad to work in the trauma unit at Karkh General Hospital. Since then, you've taken several leaves of absence to go on foreign missions with the humanitarian group Médecins Sans Frontières.

"I must say, it doesn't sound like the résumé of a terrorist. Of course you're an American, and a Christian, and those Doctors Without Borders missions have all been to help other Christians wounded in the German *Volksaufstand*. In the eyes of some of my colleagues, any one of these facts would be enough to brand you a threat, with no further explanation necessary. But I try to be more open-minded than that, and as a resident of this city, I'm naturally curious. You know, right after 11/9, all of Arabia asked itself Why? Why do they hate us? The rest of the country has tried to move on since then, but here in Baghdad, still living with the aftereffects of that day, we find it much harder to put the past behind us. We still want to know: Why do you hate us, Dr. Costello?

"Is it because you're American? The War on Terror hasn't been kind to your native country, it's true, but you were young when you left home, and there's nothing in your record to suggest a nationalist streak.

"Is it because you're Christian? It's tempting to believe that, but even if I didn't know better, I can still count. There are nearly two billion Christians in the world, and if you were all wicked by nature, things would be very bad indeed.

"So what is it, Dr. Costello? What turned your heart against us? Arabia welcomed you in, gave you an education and a profession, a stake in a civilized society. Was there something else, some basic courtesy we failed to extend? Did we offend you somehow? Why do you hate us?"

Mustafa paused to give Costello an opportunity to respond—perhaps to take issue with Mustafa's description of Arabia's generosity. But Costello wasn't interested in complaining about his immigrant experience. He slouched in his chair and stared at the table in silence, projecting weary resignation.

"Maybe instead of asking *why* I should ask *when*," Mustafa continued. "On your residency application, you listed your own and your parents' religion as Episcopalian. I confess, I had to look that up on the Library of Alexandria. LoA describes it as an American offshoot of the Anglican Church. Is that the answer to the riddle, Dr. Costello? Did the Church of England get its hooks in you during your time in London? Did the Archbishop of Canterbury brainwash you in one of his parish schools? You know the British prime minister has threatened to unleash a wave of destruction against the Muslim world if we or our allies interfere with England's nuclear-bomb program. He claims to have sleeper agents in place all across Arabia and Persia. Is that you, Dr. Costello?"

A thin smile of derision appeared on Costello's lips and he snorted softly. "What, you think it's a funny idea?" Mustafa said. "I assure you, my superiors would have no problem believing such a thing . . . I'd be inclined to believe it myself, if this were 1981 and the Israelis had just blown up the nuclear reactor in Suffolk. But there's been no new provocation, and for all his bluster, I don't think either the prime minister or the men who pull his strings are really that eager to go to war with us.

"So no, I don't suppose England is the answer. I have a different theory. I think the poisoning of your soul took place much more recently. I think it had less to do with faith, or politics, than with a woman.

"Tell me I'm wrong, Dr. Costello. Tell me this isn't about your fiancée."

Costello's smile went away. But he was looking at Mustafa now.

"Jessica Lamar, of Texas," Mustafa said, acknowledging the eye contact. "She was working as a physical rehabilitation specialist in Jaffa when you did your residency. Is that how you met, through work? Did you share a patient? Or did you meet at a chapel service? She was a member of the United Methodist sect, which I understand is another branch of Anglicanism, so that would mean you could worship together, yes?" Costello didn't answer and after a moment Mustafa went on: "You applied for a marriage license in spring of 2005. By then you'd already been accepted onto the staff at Karkh General, so I guess the plan was you'd get married over the summer and move to Baghdad to start work in the fall. But in early June, you got a call from the police.

"She was visiting outpatients in Gaza City. Gaza . . . not the nicest part of Palestine. But because it's so poor, plenty of residents join the military in hopes of escaping to a better life—and now, thanks to the war, there are plenty of injured veterans needing care. So your fiancée was on a mission of mercy to help soldiers wounded in the invasion of *your* native country . . . and her reward for this was to be shot down senselessly by a couple of petty thieves."

A muscle started jumping in Costello's cheek.

"According to the Gaza PD," Mustafa continued, "the gunmen were members of a street gang that calls itself the Islamic Resistance Movement. You know the joke the Gaza City cops tell about the IRM, Dr. Costello? They say the Movement is very successful—it's been resisting Islam's message of peace for over thirty years now."

Mustafa placed a hand on the case folder. "The police report of your fiancée's murder is in here," he said. "There's a picture. Would you like to see it?" Costello blinked and his head jerked back. "No, I don't suppose you would . . . But there's another photo I would like you to take a look at." As Costello eyed him warily, Mustafa got out his wallet and removed a worn snapshot that had been laminated in plastic. He placed it on the table and slid it forward, watching the doctor as he did so and seeing, in his mind's eye, the mother from the Ghost Music store.

"I don't know this woman," Costello said.

"No, you wouldn't," said Mustafa. "Her name was Fadwa bint Harith. She was my wife. On the morning the towers fell, we had an argument. I was at fault, and knew it, and so naturally I was very angry. When I had to leave for work and my car wouldn't start, I took hers. She had an appointment downtown as well that morning, not far from where I was going, but rather than drive her I left her to take the subway. She would have been riding on the number two line, one of the trains that passed beneath the Tigris and Euphrates Plaza.

"You can guess how the story ends, Dr. Costello. And perhaps you wouldn't think it presumptuous if I said that I thought I understood something of how you felt, losing your Jessica. But really, that's too simple. We have this thing in common, you and I, but there are also differences.

"One difference," Mustafa said, placing his hand on the folder again, "is that there is no photo of my wife's body for me to be afraid of. Fadwa is one of the 11/9 missing. I know she is dead—indeed, I would say I knew it even before it happened—but there is no actual proof of that.

"Now, I don't know how much you know about Islamic legal tradition, Dr. Costello. In the matter of missing persons, the authorities vary widely in how long you must wait before declaring them dead. The strictest standard, from the Hanafi school of jurisprudence, holds that in the absence of positive proof you must assume the person is alive until such time as they would die of old age. In the case of a young person vanishing, that can mean a wait of as much as sixty or seventy years. It's a very strict standard, especially for women, who can only have one husband at a time.

"Here in the state of Iraq, we follow the much more liberal standard of the Maliki school, which specifies a waiting period of only four years. But there's a catch: The four-year clock doesn't start until you go before a judge to report the person missing.

"In Fadwa's case, I resisted going to the judge. I knew she was dead, I didn't doubt it, but still, out of some selfish impulse, I delayed. Fadwa's father was very angry with me when he found out—he accused me of being cowardly. Eventually, my own father convinced me to do the right thing. But because I delayed so long, it's only very recently that the official declaration of death came through. That was hard; I was surprised by how hard it was, after so much time. My behavior since then has been . . . erratic. My boss, he's actually worried about my sanity.

"What about you, Dr. Costello? Did having your fiancée's body make it easier or harder for you, do you think? I can't imagine it was much easier. Did you go mad? I think perhaps you did. And I am tempted, again, to say that I understand.

"But that brings us to the other difference between us."

Mustafa flipped open the folder and pulled out not just one death-scene photograph, but several. He began dealing these onto the table, and Costello, who had been listening attentively, now recoiled in his seat as if Mustafa were chucking hot coals at him.

"Take a good look, doctor," Mustafa said. Costello tried not to, but before he could avert his eyes one of the images caught at him, and he looked; and then his expression changed, as he realized that the people in these pictures, though unquestionably murder victims, were not, any of them, his fiancée. They were Arabs, Iraqis: two men, dead in the front seat of a bullet-riddled car; another man, tied to a post with his hands behind his back and shot in the head; a woman, garroted in her bedroom; and saddest of all, three small children, lying like dolls in the wreckage of a blown-up storefront.

"Yes, take a good look," Mustafa repeated. "This is what you signed on for, when you joined the Hoffmans." This wasn't, strictly speaking, true. Mustafa had taken these photos from an open case file forwarded to AHS from Halal Enforcement. Although the use of explosives automatically made it a terrorism case under post-11/9 rules, these were almost certainly organized crime slayings. The killers would be Arabs as well, their boss—Mustafa could guess who he was—a Muslim. Still, the goal of these murders was the same as those planned by the Hoffmans: to spread terror. *Morally,* there was no difference.

"Let me tell you something about myself, Dr. Costello," Mustafa said. "I'm no pacifist. I'm not above thoughts of vengeance. If the men who flew the planes on 11/9 were brought alive before me, I'd show them no mercy. Likewise, with the men who sent them on their way. But this"—he waved a hand at the pictures—"this slaughter of innocents, it's beyond me. Not even in my darkest dreams am I tempted to such savagery. I look at this woman, here, and all I can think of is Fadwa in her last moments. God willing she didn't suffer long, but to imagine even an instant of her pain and fear, and then to imagine choosing to inflict that same pain and fear on some other blameless woman . . . No. No, that is beyond me. And these children, little children who can have done nothing, *nothing* to deserve this . . . I don't understand it. Can you explain it to me, Dr. Costello?

"Is this Christianity? I'm no expert on your New Testament, but I have read parts of it. The prophet Jesus, peace be unto him, said that there were two great commandments: to love God with all your heart and soul, and to love your neighbor as yourself. True words, Dr. Costello, words that any Muslim would be bound to agree with, for we believe the same thing. But even a very poor Muslim such as I am would have a hard time seeing how you get from those words, to this. Can you explain it to me? Think of your Jessica, in her last moments. If she were here now, and knew what sort of acts you'd been contemplating, what would she say?"

Costello's lips moved in a soft murmur.

"What was that, Dr. Costello? I didn't quite hear you."

"I said, I'm sorry."

"I would like to believe that," Mustafa said. "It would help me to believe that, if you'd talk to me about your dealings with the Hoffmans: What you were planning. Who else was involved. Anything you can tell me that might prevent the deaths of more innocents."

But Costello shook his head. "It doesn't matter."

"To the contrary, Dr. Costello, it matters very much. Certainly it matters to those who may die. It matters to their families. It matters to me. And as a human being and a child of God, it should matter to you. I won't lie to you: Even if you choose to cooperate fully, you're facing a long stretch in prison. For security reasons you'll be kept in solitary confinement, which means years in a small room with only your own conscience for company. You may not think it now, but over time, over *long* time, guilt and regret can eat you alive. And if that doesn't happen? You still have to answer to God on Judgment Day. So I would urge you, for your own sake, to care. Care *now,* while you can still do some good."

Not a bad speech, Mustafa thought, but even before he finished, he could tell that it was wasted. Whatever brief connection he'd established with Costello had already evaporated. The doctor had mentally withdrawn, or maybe *sidestepped* was a better word—when he spoke again, it was from a different, and very strange, place.

"It doesn't matter," Costello said, "because none of this is real."

"What's not real, Dr. Costello?"

"This world."

"The world isn't real?"

"*This* world." Costello tried to spread his arms in an all-encompassing gesture, but, restrained by the cuffs, had to settle for flapping his hands. "This country."

"I'm not following you, Dr. Costello."

"The 'United Arab States.' It's not real."

"You're saying you don't recognize the authority of the UAS government?"

"No, I'm saying it doesn't exist. It's a mirage. There is no Arab superpower, no union of Arab states. In the *real* world, you're just a bunch of backward third-world countries that no one would even care about except for oil . . ."

"Dr. Costello, what are you—"

"It's a *mirage*! All of it: This country. This world. Everything you think you know, about what is, is just an illusion. A dream." He paused, stymied momentarily by Mustafa's incredulous expression, but then pushed on. "America. America is the true superpower."

"America," Mustafa said. "Really."

"I don't expect you to believe me—"

"That's good, Dr. Costello, because I don't. I don't know what sort of game you think you're playing at here, but if you want to talk about what's real, then I'll tell you, my superiors—the men in charge of deciding your fate—they *really* don't have a sense of humor when it comes to terrorism. So if you've got some half-baked notion of pleading insanity—"

"I'm not crazy," Costello said. "I'm not pleading anything. I accept my fate. I'm trapped in the mirage, as long as God sees fit to maintain it."

"This mirage you speak of, it's God's doing?"

Costello nodded. " 'The last shall be first, and the first last . . .' God's turned the world upside down."

"And why would He do that?"

"To punish us."

"The Americans?"

"Yes."

"For what sin?"

"Pride," Costello said. "Failure to submit to His will. We turned away from Him, so He turned away from us. He sent the mirage, and put you people in charge."

"The Arabs are instruments of God's wrath?"

"Something like that."

"And those Gaza City thugs who killed your fiancée. They work for God too?"

Costello was silent.

"And if you believe that," Mustafa pressed him, "why fight against us? How does that make sense, to terrorize God's own agents?"

"It's not *about* you," Costello said. "It's about us. About demonstrating our faith."

"Through murder?"

"I told you I was sorry."

"Dr. Costello—"

"I'm sorry about your wife. I'm sorry you're in pain. I mean that . . . But it doesn't matter. You'd be in pain anyway. Your suffering isn't part of the mirage. It's just your lot."

"My lot."

"All of you," Costello said. "You're the losers. It's not fair, but it's how it is: God's plan has winners and losers, and you're the losers. *You're* the losers. That's reality . . . And we'll kill as many of you as we have to, to get back there."

Listening to this, Mustafa was once again aware of the motion of the earth beneath his feet. He felt a tingle in his hands as his nails dug into his palms, and imagined a reality, quite close, in which he leaned across the table and began battering Costello with his fists.

Just as well that Abdullah chose that moment to knock on the glass.

"He's not lying," Abdullah said.

"You mean this life really is just a dream?" said Samir. "Can I be rich when I wake up?"

"Obviously the story is nonsense. But according to the machine, he believes what he's saying."

"You pulled me out to tell me the man's insane?" Mustafa said, still flushed with anger. "I knew that already, thanks."

"It wasn't me," Abdullah said. He jerked a thumb at Amal.

"Umm Dabir just called down from Farouk's office," Amal explained. "She said Farouk's on the phone with Riyadh. She said you told her to let you know the next time that happened during an interview."

"Riyadh's calling now? About *this* guy?"

"Umm Dabir didn't say what the call was about. But if that's what you were waiting for, I guess so."

Seven times over the past two years, Mustafa's interrogation of a terror suspect had been interrupted by an official call from Riyadh ordering that the questioning cease immediately; in each case, senior AHS agents had arrived soon after to transfer the prisoner to a "special location." For a long time, he'd thought little of it.

Then about a month ago, he'd tried to do some follow-up on one of these special prisoners—a French smuggler named René Arceneau—and discovered that the files pertaining to his arrest had vanished. His name had been scrubbed from the computer databases, not just the AHS databases but all of them. ICE, the Bureau, Halal Enforcement's Maghreb division, even the Algerian Department of Motor Vehicles, all parties to Arceneau's capture, now claimed to have no record of him.

This was unprecedented. Even in cases of extraordinary rendition, where prisoners were shipped overseas to be questioned in a human-rights vacuum like Texas, the Arab government didn't deny that the prisoners were in custody, it merely lied about what was done to them. Mustafa wondered what would be bad enough to make the state destroy evidence of a person's very existence.

He also wondered why he cared so much. It wasn't as if he hadn't already known that "special location" was a euphemism for a torture facility. And once you assent to a person being drugged, starved, beaten, hung by the wrists, burned, frozen, choked, drowned, electrocuted, and kept in sensory deprivation until his mind breaks, why should it bother you to think that he might also be murdered, and once murdered, erased?

Maybe it was the timing. The day Mustafa learned that René Arceneau had become an unperson was the same day he'd gotten Fadwa's death certificate.

We close our eyes to sin, but God sees all.

Mustafa's subsequent attempt to learn more about Arceneau's fate had uncovered only one additional piece of information: The order to have him removed to special custody had come not from AHS headquarters but from Congress, from the office of the head of the Senate Intelligence Committee. Mustafa learned this from Farouk, who'd warned him to stop rattling the knobs of doors he had no business opening.

That the warning hadn't taken proved beyond all doubt that Farouk was right to be worried about his sanity. Who's more dangerous to wrestle with, a suicide bomber or a senator? Clearly the latter: A suicide bomber only has one way to destroy you.

"Mustafa?" Amal said. "What's going on?"

"That's a very good question," Mustafa replied. "Who's handling the search of Costello's apartment?"

"Sayyid and Abu Naji."

"Why don't you and Samir hurry over there and help them?"

"Do you think that's a good idea?" said Samir.

"Please, just do it." Mustafa held out his hand. "Can I borrow your cell phone while you're gone?"

"My cell phone . . ." Samir sighed and reached into his pocket. "And what about Amal's cell phone, eh?"

Amal, who still didn't know what was going on here, but was smart enough to guess at a few details, said: "My battery charge is very low. I may have to leave the phone switched off to conserve power . . . What are you going to do, Mustafa?"

"Keep talking to Dr. Costello. While he's still with us."

Mustafa stared through the glass at the man in the interrogation room. Something about you scares the men in power, he thought. It can't be this crazy story you're telling, so what is it? What secret are you hiding? What does Osama bin Laden not want me to know?

The Library of Alexandria
A USER-EDITED REFERENCE SOURCE

Osama bin Laden

Osama bin Mohammed bin Awad bin Laden (born March 10, 1957), a Sunni Muslim, is a senator from the state of Arabia. He is a member of the National Party of God. Since the year 2001 he has been the chairman of the Senate Intelligence Committee.

EARLY LIFE

Osama bin Laden is one of 25 sons of Mohammed bin Laden, whose Bin Laden Construction Company (now part of the Saud/Bin Laden Group) is responsible for such projects as the expansion of the Grand Mosque in Mecca and the Prophet's Mosque in Medina, and the restoration of the Dome of the Rock in Jerusalem.

Osama was born in a suburb of the federal district of Riyadh and grew up in Jeddah, Arabia. He attended Jeddah's elite Al Thagr School and studied economics and business administration at Jeddah University.

HOLY WARRIOR AND STATESMAN

In 1980, displeased with the Arab government's "tepid" response to the Russian Orthodox invasion of Afghanistan, Osama left school and traveled to Peshawar, Pakistan. There along with Abdullah Azzam he founded the Afghan Services Bureau, an organization that helped deliver money, weapons, and recruits to the Afghan resistance. Desiring a more direct role in the conflict, Osama eventually established a camp within Afghanistan and became the leader of his own mujahideen unit.

Following the defeat of the Russians and the breakup of the Orthodox Union, Osama returned to Arabia a hero. In 1990 he ran for Congress, easily winning election as Jeddah's representative in the House. He

served two and a half terms, then in 1995 won his Senate seat in a
special election held after the untimely death of the incumbent, <u>Wafah
al Saud</u>.

FACTS ABOUT OSAMA BIN LADEN

· At nearly two meters in height, he is the tallest man ever to serve in
Congress.

· He has been married five times and divorced once.

· His personal worth is estimated at 50 million riyals.

· An extremely religious man, he does not listen to music, attend
movies, or watch any television programs other than news.

· His relationships with both the <u>Party of God</u> and the <u>House of Saud</u>
have been described as "complicated." It is rumored that upon his
return from Afghanistan, Osama initially intended to run for office as
an independent candidate; only after numerous meetings with high-
level party officials did he agree to join the <u>POG</u>.

· He was an early, ardent supporter of the <u>War on Terror</u> and the <u>inva-
sion of America</u>. He is one of very few invasion supporters not to have
suffered politically as a result.

· He is often mentioned as a potential presidential candidate; many
pundits were surprised when he decided not to seek the POG nomi-
nation in 2008. When asked whether he would run for president in
2012, he said that he might, "if there still is a presidency." Asked to
explain what he meant by this statement, he replied, "The <u>Day of
Judgment</u> may come at any time."

Costello's apartment was in one of four identical towers surrounding a dusty cul-de-sac. It was after 10 p.m. when Samir and Amal arrived, but a group of boys were still outside playing soccer. A pair of police cars were parked in front of Costello's building, and a cop leaned against one car's back trunk, smoking a cigarette and watching the game.

Samir pulled up beside the police cars, and he and Amal got out and showed their IDs. "Are our colleagues inside?"

"No," the cop told them. "They cleared out twenty minutes ago. They said they were done." His tone was accusatory, as if Samir and Amal were breaking a promise by showing up this way.

"So what are you still doing here?" Samir wanted to know.

"Securing the premises."

Amal, only too familiar with the ways of the Baghdad PD, chuckled at this.

"We need to get into the apartment," Samir said. "You want to take us up, or should we just ring for the super?"

"One moment," the cop said. He stepped away, speaking quickly and softly into his walkie-talkie. A few minutes later, another policeman appeared inside the building lobby and opened the door for them.

Two more cops waited in the hall outside Costello's apartment. A warning notice had been taped to the apartment door, and a red Homeland Security seal placed across the crack between the door and the doorframe. The seal was broken.

"'Securing the premises,'" Samir said.

The first cop, who'd ridden up with them in the elevator, just shrugged. "They said they were done."

"Yes, and now you're done, too. Open this door for us and get the hell out of here."

A whirlwind had been through Costello's living room, yanking cushions from seats, knocking objects from shelves. A plastic date palm had been uprooted from its pot and now lay on the floor, pretending to be dead. A wooden hutch held a few DVD cases—all popped open, the discs tossed aside—but there was no player to go with them. Bolted to the wall above the hutch was a pair of reinforced bracket mounts that had, until quite recently, held a flat-screen TV.

"What do you think?" Amal said, gauging the size and spacing of the brackets. "One-and-a-half-meter widescreen?"

Samir nodded. "One of those nice plasma jobs, probably."

Amal looked past a serve-through counter into the kitchenette. The whirlwind had been in there too, opening cabinets and dumping out cans and boxes. "I guess the microwave wasn't worth stealing . . . So what are we looking for?"

"I don't know," Samir said. "But if we find a second plasma, it's mine."

A wooden cross hung on the wall in the apartment's single bedroom. Samir checked the closet, finding only a few shirts and a threadbare suit. Amal peeked under the bed, then turned to the dresser—its contents had already been pawed through, but she removed each drawer in turn, checking to see if anything was taped to the backs or undersides.

Samir stepped to the window. There was a scatter of paperbacks on the sill and on the floor below it. The books were in English and German, neither of which Samir could read, but he recognized some of the covers. In addition to a Bible and what appeared to be some sort of catechism, there were several volumes of the *Left Behind* series and a new edition of Martin Luther's 16th-century polemic, *On the Jews and Their Lies*.

"Nothing here," Amal said. "What've you got?"

"Typical Christian hate literature. No secret blueprints hidden between the pages."

They checked the bathroom next. While Amal tugged at the mirror above the sink, Samir investigated the toilet tank, known colloquially to Halal Enforcement as a "Bavarian ice chest" because of its popularity as a hiding place for bottled beer. But the tank lid was askew, and any contraband had already been taken by the cops or the federal agents who'd been here before them.

"Hey," said Amal. "I need a tall person here."

Concealed near the top of the mirror frame were a couple of sliding catches; when Samir pressed on them, the mirror tipped forward and came loose, revealing a hole in the wall. Inside the hole was a pistol, a banded stack of riyals, a bottle of whiskey, and a wrinkled newspaper in a plastic pouch. "One of these things is not like the others," Samir said.

They opened up the newspaper. The ornate typeface at the top of the front page was opaque to Samir, but Amal, whose high school French had given her a firmer grasp of the Roman alphabet, was able to deduce that this was, or at least purported to be, an American publication: *"New York . . . Times,"* she read.

The above-the-fold photograph had an eerie familiarity: twin skyscrapers, one partially obscured by the black smoke pouring from its sides, the other wreathed in an expanding billow of flame. But these were not the Tigris and Euphrates towers, nor did the stone-piered suspension bridge in the foreground resemble any of Baghdad's bridges.

"Something from the war?" Amal speculated, sounding doubtful.

"I'm leaning towards Photoshop," Samir said. "I don't think America has buildings that tall. Besides, it looks fake. Can you make out the headline?"

"'U.S. attack . . . destroys towers,' then something about a pentagon. And the last word is 'terror.'"

"Wait." Samir tapped his finger on the dateline. "What month is this?"

"September. September 12, 2001."

Samir laughed. "September 12 . . . So the day before was September 11 . . . 9/11, get it? These towers, they're located in the magical American superpower. And the guys flying the planes into them, they must be those poor loser third-world Arabs . . ."

There was a loud thump from the front of the apartment. They heard footsteps in the living room. "Maybe I spoke too soon about the microwave," Amal said.

Frowning, Samir leaned his head out the bathroom doorway. "Hey!" he called. "Who's out there?"

No answer but abrupt silence. More annoyed than concerned, Samir walked forward through the bedroom, saying: "This is Homeland Security! Whoever you are, if you don't have a federal badge you'd better start running n—"

As Samir entered the living room, he was attacked from the side, punched in the head and spun around to face the wall. He tried to jab behind him with his elbow, but a sharp blow to the kidneys dropped him to his knees, and then he felt a gun muzzle press against the back of his neck.

A second assailant had darted into the bedroom to grapple Amal. Samir heard her cry out, and the clatter of her pistol being knocked to the ground. He watched from the corner of his eye as she was dragged by the hair into the living room and shoved to the floor; her attacker squatted on her and aimed a submachine gun at the base of her skull, commanding her to lie still. About the only good news in all of this was that the gunman was an Arab, which meant he probably wasn't a terrorist.

A voice demanded: "Who are you?"

"I told you, we're Homeland Security," Samir said, then hissed at a jab from the gun muzzle. "Homeland Security, damn it! My ID is in my pocket." A rough hand was already inside his jacket, removing first his pistol and then his identification.

"Homeland Security has been ordered off these premises. What are you still doing here?"

"We received no such order."

"You are lying." A pause, as the speaker examined Samir's ID. "Samir Nadim . . . Where do I know that name from?"

"Oh God," Samir said. That voice . . . "Idris?"

He was dragged to his feet, turned around, and shoved back against the wall. His assailant, like Amal's, was armed with a submachine gun, but Samir barely glanced at the weapon before focusing his attention on a third man, a tall bearded figure who stood behind and slightly to the left of the gunman.

"Idris," Samir said, not at all happy. "It is you."

"Baby-fat Samir," Idris said. "Not so fat anymore I see. But you still insist on trespassing where you don't belong."

Samir bristled. "We have every right to be here. We are conducting an investigation—"

"The investigation has been reassigned, as you well know. You are trespassing." Idris bent to pick up the copy of the *New York Times,* which Samir had dropped during his brief scuffle. "Where did you get this?"

"We found it in the bathroom. Costello had a—"

"Who else has seen it?"

"No one," Samir said. "We just—"

"I will tell you what I think," Idris interrupted him. "I think you are not with Homeland Security. I think you are a common thief, one of the Shia riffraff who infest the slums of this city. I think you heard this apartment was vacant and broke in to see what you could steal."

"Right . . . Fine then. Arrest me."

"No. I don't think so."

"What, then? . . . Wait." His eyes widened. "Idris. You can't be ser—"

"Shoot them both," Idris said.

"Wait a minute!" Samir shouted. "Idris, you can't— . . . Do you know who this woman is? She's Anmar al Maysani's daughter! Do you have any idea what kind of trouble—"

"Anmar al Maysani's daughter. And whose daughter are you, eh?"

"That is a very rude thing to say," a new voice spoke up. "Is this what passes for manners in the capital these days?"

"Farouk!" Samir said. "Mustafa! Thank God!"

"It's all right, Samir," Mustafa said. "Relax."

"Yes, relax," said Farouk. "We'll discuss your disregard for protocol some other time."

"Farouk." Idris took a moment to hide his irritation before facing him. "We seem to have a misunderstanding here."

"Indeed," Farouk said. He nodded to where Amal was pinned to the floor. "Please tell your lackey to get off my agent."

"Of course. Abu Asim, release her." Freed, Amal got up slowly, rubbing the back of her neck. Idris asked: "What are you doing here, Farouk?"

"I've had a call from Riyadh."

"Yes, I—"

"No, sorry," Farouk corrected himself, "I've had *two* calls from Riyadh. It's the second call that brings me out. There's been a change in plan."

"Senator Bin Laden hasn't told *me* anything about a change in plan."

"Senator Bin Laden's wishes are no longer relevant, I'm afraid. The president has asked me to retake control of this investigation."

"The president?"

"The commander in chief," Farouk said. "Surely you've heard of him?"

"Why would the president—"

"That brings us back to the subject of disregard for protocol, and, oddly enough, to Senator Bin Laden." Stepping forward to pluck the *New York Times* from Idris's grasp, he continued: "Let's discuss this back at my office, shall we?"

THE LIBRARY OF ALEXANDRIA
A USER-EDITED REFERENCE SOURCE

Al Qaeda

Al Qaeda is an alleged <u>clandestine agency</u> of the <u>Arabian government</u>, supposedly specializing in <u>anti-terrorist operations</u>. Although Al Qaeda's existence has never been officially confirmed, it is a popular subject of <u>Internet rumor and speculation</u>, particularly among <u>conspiracy theorists</u>.

CLAIMS MADE ABOUT AL QAEDA

- Al Qaeda's purported mission is to hunt down and destroy "the worst enemies of God and the state." It is said to operate outside the bounds of <u>civil law</u> and to be answerable to only a handful of government officials.

- It is claimed that Al Qaeda was founded by combat veterans of the <u>Afghan War</u>, and that service in that or another <u>holy war</u> is a prerequisite for membership. Another common claim is that members must be devout <u>Sunni Muslims</u>.

- Most accounts hold that Al Qaeda was created as a direct response to the <u>11/9 attacks</u>, but there are a few stories that suggest it actually predates the <u>War on Terror</u>.

- Public figures whose names have been linked to Al Qaeda include <u>Senator Osama bin Laden</u> (POG-Arabia), his chief of staff <u>Ayman al Zawahiri</u>, and his former campaign manager <u>Abu Yusuf Idris Abd al Qahhar</u>.

- One popular Al Qaeda rumor holds that the group's existence was first uncovered by a *Baghdad Post* reporter who died under suspicious circumstances after revealing what he had found. The *Post*'s publisher, <u>Tariq Aziz</u>, has denied this rumor, joking that "No one gets killed at my newspaper unless I order it."

AL QAEDA IN POPULAR CULTURE

· In the second season of *24/7 Jihad*, it was revealed that super-agent Jafar Bashir is a former Al Qaeda member expelled for being "too overzealous" in his pursuit of terrorists.

"He's a Wahhabi fanatic," Samir said.

"His family are Unitarians," Mustafa demurred. "Idris always struck me as a member of the cult of Idris."

"But who *is* he?" asked Amal.

They were on the roof of AHS headquarters, watching the moon rise over the Tigris. Inside, Farouk and Idris were in the second hour of a conference call with the powers that be in Riyadh. Mustafa and the others had come up here to get away from the shouting.

"An old schoolmate," Mustafa told her. "Idris was an upperclassman at the boys' academy where Samir and I first met. He was popular, but also a bully. Some of the other students called him 'Iblis' behind his back."

"Satan?" Amal glanced at Samir, who was scowling at some private memory of humiliation.

"He dropped out of school a month before graduation, to go fight in Afghanistan—"

"Where he would have *died*, if there was any justice in the world," Samir interjected.

"—and after that, we didn't hear anything of him for years. Until one day he turned up on Al Jazeera as a spokesman for the Bin Laden campaign. He had a family by then, and went by 'Abu Yusuf,' but it was the same old Idris."

"The Party of God political strategist?" Amal said. "*That* Abu Yusuf?"

"You've heard of him, then. Ah, of course . . ."

"When my mother ran for the Senate, Abu Yusuf Abd al Qahhar was in charge of the POG's smear campaign against her."

"The 'Whore of Baghdad' robocalls." Mustafa nodded. "I remember the uproar over those. Didn't one of your brothers threaten to kill whoever was responsible?"

"Not just one of my brothers . . . So this is the same guy? And what is he now, Bin Laden's personal hatchet man?"

"Abu Yusuf's current job description is a matter of some speculation. Officially he's attached to Homeland Security as 'special liaison' to the Senate Intelligence Committee. Unofficially . . . I assume you've heard the stories about Bin Laden forming his own private anti-terrorism squad?"

"Al Qaeda? I've heard of it. It's an urban legend."

"No doubt," said Mustafa. "But if Al Qaeda did exist, and if Bin Laden needed someone to run the day-to-day operations while he was busy in Congress, Abu Yusuf is the sort of man you'd expect him to pick."

"That's just great!" said Samir. "The acting head of Al Qaeda, and we've gone and gotten him pissed at us. At *me*."

Half an hour later they were summoned back downstairs. As they filed into Farouk's office, Idris regarded them coldly, his gaze lingering on Samir until Samir began to squirm.

"Now that the jurisdictional question is settled," Farouk said, "let's get down to business. Abu Yusuf, I understand you're already acquainted with Mustafa and Samir. And you've met Amal, though I imagine there was no formal introduction—"

"I know who she is," Idris said. "Are you certain the president would want you to involve a woman in this matter?"

"Amal is a fine agent."

"Yes, I'm sure you employ the daughter of Anmar al Maysani for her *fine skills*."

"No doubt Senator Bin Laden has a similar appreciation for the skills of Abu Yusuf," Amal said.

"If I may, sir," Mustafa spoke up, before another round of shouting could erupt. "What is all this about?"

"It's about the mirage," Farouk said. "Earlier tonight, the prisoner Costello told you a rather incredible story. What you don't know is that the story is not unprecedented. Other interrogation subjects have been spouting the same legend: that this world we live in is false; that God loves America, not Arabia."

"How many other interrogation subjects?"

"Many. I can't give you a more precise answer because—as the president was disturbed to learn recently—there has apparently been an effort by certain elements of the intelligence community to conceal the existence of this legend."

"There's no cover-up!" Idris said. "This so-called legend is obviously propaganda dreamed up by Christian fanatics to inspire suicide bombers. If the president wasn't informed about it, it's because it isn't important enough to merit his attention."

"The president does not agree with Abu Yusuf's assessment," Farouk said. "He desires an independent investigation into the question of the mirage."

"So he called you?" Amal said, immediately regretting it. "I'm sorry, sir, I don't mean to imply—"

"No, it's a fair point. I am a Christian, and as we all know, in the current environment Christians—even *Egyptian* Christians who have never had any connection with terrorism—are viewed with suspicion. But as one would expect of the leader of the Arab Unity Party, the president is a true ecumenist."

"And he's from Cairo," Mustafa said, having gotten it at "Egyptian." He turned to Amal and explained: "Farouk and the president come from the same neighborhood."

"Yes," Farouk said, with a small smile. "As it happens, my third cousin is married to the president's half brother."

"Sir," said Samir, still casting nervous glances at Idris, "about this investigation, I don't think I—"

"I know you are only too happy to do whatever your commander in chief asks of you, Samir," Farouk said, "but please restrain your expressions of enthusiasm while I finish. The president has asked me to oversee a reexamination of all existing intelligence pertaining to the mirage legend. He wants to know where this story originated and how it's being spread. He wants to know what it means. And he wants to know where *these* are coming from . . ." Farouk held up the newspaper Amal and Samir had found in Costello's apartment. "Many of the most fervent believers in the legend have in their possession objects, like this one, that they claim are artifacts from the 'real' world. Forged props, obviously, but we need to find out who's making them."

"Does Homeland Security have any more of these artifacts?" Mustafa asked.

"Yes. In fact Abu Yusuf, in what I am sure will be a continuing spirit of cooperation, has just turned over a number of items that he obtained earlier today from the ABI office in Kufah. We have them down the hall, in Conference Room B."

One of Idris's thugs—the same one who had tackled Amal in the apartment—stood guard outside the conference room door. When he saw them coming he moved to bar the way, but Idris waved him aside.

There were four objects laid out on the table inside the room.

The first was a small flag. The red-and-white stripes were familiar, but in the upper left-hand corner, the golden cross and the IESUS NAZARENUS REX IUDAEORUM motto had been replaced by a blue field with a plain array of white stars.

Next were two maps, one of Iraq, the other a regional map of the entire Middle East. Mustafa studied the latter, feeling like a child working one of those puzzles in which the goal is to spot all the mistakes in a picture: The state of Arabia was, at least technically, misnamed. Persia had become Iran, "Land of the Aryans," and Kurdistan had disappeared, its territory divided between the state of Iraq, "Iran," and the sovereign nation of Turkey. Most curious of all—and impossible to ignore, once he'd noticed it—Palestine had also vanished, leaving in its stead a Christian fundamentalist prophecy come true. "I'm beginning to understand why the president is concerned," said Mustafa.

The fourth and final artifact was the top half of a front page torn from another newspaper, the Paris *Le Monde*. It was dated September 13, 2001. The banner headline read *"L'Amérique frappée, le monde saisi d'effroi"*—"America attacked, the world seized by fear." In a column to the right was a smaller headline: *"Nous sommes tous Américains."*

He must have made a sound. Amal looked up from the Iraq state map and said, "What is it?" Mustafa didn't answer, just shook his head, caught in a moment of vertigo.

Nous sommes tous Américains.

We are all Americans.

Book Two

The Republic of
Nebuchadnezzar

A sandstorm had blown through Baghdad overnight, leaving a thick layer of grit on the streets and rooftops. Clerks arriving at the state courthouse found that the filters on the building ventilation system had become clogged. Mindful of the celebrity trial that was scheduled to conclude today, they made an emergency call to maintenance; by 9 a.m. the filters had all been replaced, and the air-conditioning was once more functioning properly.

Nevertheless, when the judge in Part 14 gaveled court back into session shortly before noon, there were a dozen men in the room whose faces were sheened with sweat.

"Members of the jury," the judge said. "Have you reached a verdict?"

"By the grace of God, your honor, we have."

"Are you quite certain?" The judge didn't try to keep the disgust out of his voice. "You've just heard five weeks of testimony, yet you deliberated for less than an hour. Wouldn't you at least like to wait until after lunch?"

The lead defense attorney rose to object: "Your honor—"

"Shut up, you." Glaring at the jury foreman: "Well?"

"We're . . . We're very sure, your honor."

The judge signaled the bailiff, who stepped forward to take the folded verdict sheet from the foreman's trembling hand. The judge examined the paper. "This is your unanimous decision?"

"It is, your honor."

"And . . ." The judge let out a sigh. " . . . you come to this decision freely?"

"We do, your honor."

The judge passed the sheet back to his bailiff, who returned it to the jury box. "The defendant will rise." Smiling confidently, the defendant did so. "Please read the verdict for the record."

"Y-yes, your honor . . . On the charges of conspiracy to commit murder, conspiracy to transport and sell forbidden substances, conspiracy to promote and profit from immoral activities, usury, bribery of a public official, bribery of a police officer, and conspiracy to suborn perjury, we find the defendant, Saddam Hussein, *not* guilty."

The street in front of the courthouse had been closed to regular vehicle traffic, and the police had set barricades along the far curb to keep pedestrians at a distance. A limousine idled near the foot of the courthouse steps, ready to whisk the man of the hour away to his victory celebration.

But Saddam was in no hurry to leave. As he came out of the courthouse—flanked by his sons, his legal team, and his buddy Tariq Aziz—he raised his arms and called to the crowd behind the barricades: "Hel-*lo*, Baghdad!" A cheer went up. Saddam's most fervent supporters—Baath organizers receiving bonus pay for their presence here—raised signs bearing his picture and the phrase LONG LIVE THE KING! A chant began: "Saddam! Saddam! Saddam!"

Saddam kept his right arm in the air, rotating his hand in a regal wave. His eyes grew distant as he soaked in the adulation. After about a minute, Tariq Aziz touched him gently on the shoulder, as if waking a sleepwalker, and guided him down the steps towards a waiting gaggle of reporters and news cameras.

The chief defense lawyer had prepared a statement, but Saddam cut him off almost immediately and began to take questions: Yes, praise be to God, he was pleased with the trial's outcome. No, he wasn't surprised that the jurors—"honest Baghdadis"—had chosen to do the right thing. No, he held no ill will against the prosecutors, though as an honest citizen himself, he did wish the district attorney would focus more on *actual* criminals . . .

While his father held court with the press, Qusay Hussein kept his eyes on the crowd. His older brother was supposed to do the same, but Uday's attention focused instead on a young female journalist who'd been shoved to the back of the gaggle. Uday circled around to her and asked if *he* could answer any questions.

Across the street there was a commotion as someone in the crowd held up a new sign, a homemade placard showing a caricature of Saddam with bloodstained hands, its one-word caption reading BUTCHER! The nearest Baathists reacted furiously, using their own signs as bludgeons. As the police moved in to prevent a riot, a portion of the barricade was left unguarded.

Two men slipped through the gap. They crossed the street undetected and approached along the sidewalk, drawing snub-nosed pistols from their waistbands. Qusay spotted them just as they were taking aim; he cried out a warning and knocked his father to the ground.

The press scattered as the men opened fire. Uday, his face registering glee rather than shock, turned towards the gunshots. He drew his own pistol and shot the closest assassin twice in the chest. The second gunman panicked and tried to flee back into the crowd. Heedless of the other people in the line of fire, Uday squeezed off several more shots, one of which connected. The gunman stumbled and fell to his knees; before he could get up, the police piled onto him.

Qusay helped his father to his feet. Saddam checked himself carefully for bullet wounds; finding none, he looked around at his entourage. "Tariq?"

"I'm OK," Tariq Aziz said, though in truth he looked ill. He was staring at Saddam's lead attorney, who lay gushing blood from a hole in his Adam's apple. One of the other lawyers bent down with a wadded handkerchief, saying, "Put pressure on it, put pressure on it." Aziz turned away and vomited, and Saddam raised a hand to his own throat, feeling a sudden chill. "God is great," he whispered. He said it again, louder: "God is great!"

Uday meanwhile strolled over to where the cops were sitting on the second gunman. As he approached, more police moved in around him, forming a ring that screened him from the view of the cameras. He held out his hand, and an officer passed him a wooden baton.

"Please," the gunman begged. "Mercy! In the name of God, mercy!"

"Hold him tightly," Uday said.

The Library of Alexandria
A USER-EDITED REFERENCE SOURCE

Saddam Hussein

> This page is currently **protected** from editing to deal with **repeated acts of vandalism**. To suggest changes, please **contact an administrator**.

> The **factual accuracy** of this article is **disputed**. Please see the discussion on the **talk page**.

Saddam Hussein Abd al Majid al Tikriti (born April 28, 1937), a Sunni Muslim, is an Iraqi labor organizer, philanthropist, bestselling novelist, and reputed gangster and bootlegger. Though he emphatically denies having anything to do with the manufacture or sale of alcohol, he is more coy on the question of whether he has other ties to organized crime. To date, he has been indicted nine times on various felony and racketeering charges. He has never once been convicted.

EARLY LIFE

Saddam was born in the village of Al Awja, near Tikrit. His father, Hussein Abd al Majid, died while Saddam was still in the womb, so Saddam was raised by his maternal uncle, Khairallah Talfah, in Baghdad.

In 1957 Saddam became an organizer for the Baath Labor Union, which represented construction, garbage collection, and river transport workers in Iraq and Syria. The Arab Bureau of Investigation suspected that the Baathists were also engaged in smuggling and other illegal activities, but did little about it. At the time, the ABI was far more concerned with investigating corruption among two other, much more powerful Iraqi labor unions: the Royal Order of Hashemites, which was controlled by the Hashem family, and the Free Officers Union, led by retired Iraqi state police colonel Abd al Karim Qasim.

THE LABOR DAY MASSACRE AND THE RISE OF THE BAATHISTS

On the morning of July 14, 1958, the Hashem clan leader Faisal II was on his way to a Labor Day celebration when he was approached outside his Baghdad home by a group of men in police uniform. Faisal, his bodyguards, and several other Hashem family members were ordered to stand against a wall with their hands raised; when they did so, they were machine-gunned. By the time the real police arrived on the scene, reports were flooding in from all over Iraq of other Hashemites being murdered or simply disappearing.

It was widely believed that Abd al Karim Qasim had organized the massacre, but local law enforcement would do nothing against him, and federal agents found their own investigation stymied at every turn. Meanwhile, the surviving Hashemites decided to take matters into their own hands. An orgy of violence ensued, with the Hashemites taking the worst of it; by the end of the year, most members of the clan had either died or left Iraq.

In October 1959 masked gunmen ambushed Qasim as he left the Free Officers Union Hall. This was only the most recent of a series of attempts on Qasim's life, and like the previous attempts, it failed. What was different was that this time the attackers were not Hashemites, but Baathists. Five of the six gunmen were killed by Qasim's bodyguards; the sixth escaped. An hour later, Saddam Hussein showed up at a nearby hospital with a bullet wound in his leg. He claimed to have been mugged.

Qasim went into seclusion and Baathists began to die in large numbers. Saddam boarded a plane to Egypt, where he remained for the next four years. In interviews he has said he went to Cairo University to study law, "something I had long planned to do," and that his departure from Iraq on the eve of a major gang war was a coincidence in timing.

The Free Officers and the Baathists traded bullets and bombs until February 1963, when Qasim was caught in another ambush and shot

82 times at close range. Following Qasim's death, ABI agents—having received a mountain of incriminating evidence from an anonymous source—swooped in and arrested over two hundred Free Officers, effectively breaking the union's back. Most of the professions that had been represented by the Free Officers now switched their allegiance to Baath.

In March 1963 Saddam Hussein returned to Baghdad and was appointed secretary treasurer of the Baathists. In 1968 he was promoted to union vice president. Finally, in 1979, after the surprise resignation of union president Ahmed Hassan al Bakr, Saddam was elected leader of the Baathists, a position he holds to this day.

PHILANTHROPIST, NOVELIST . . .
AND PROFESSIONAL DEFENDANT

1979 also marked the first time Saddam was indicted by the federal government. The case, which concerned the bribery and intimidation of workers on an oil pipeline between Kurdistan and Iraq, never went to trial. A furnace malfunction at the hotel where the government's witnesses were sequestered flooded the guest floors with carbon monoxide, asphyxiating four dozen people.

In 1982 the government tried again, accusing Saddam of having rigged the election in which his uncle Khairallah became mayor of Baghdad. On the morning of the second day of jury deliberations, the jury foreman was found hanged in a courthouse restroom. An alternate juror was summoned and deliberations continued; Saddam was acquitted.

By 1986, with two additional acquittals to his name, Saddam had become a national celebrity. He gave regular press interviews and went on television to proclaim, with a wink, his innocence. He suggested that his legal troubles were a result of "high and mighty persons in Riyadh" failing to understand "the rough and tumble nature of life in Iraq."

In 1987 Saddam established the Saddam Hussein Foundation, a char-
itable trust that gave money to schools, mosques, and hospitals, and
the Baath Union Scholarship Program, which helped Iraqis from poor
families attend college. Federal prosecutors, noting that Saddam's
personal charity donations exceeded his declared income by a factor
of ten, charged him with tax evasion. He was found not guilty . . .

In December 1998 Saddam held a press conference to announce he
was publishing a pulp-fiction novel. "For years, government lawyers
have been telling outrageous stories about me," he said. "I thought
it was time to try telling one of my own." The book, *Zabibah and the
King*, concerns a labor organizer from Tikrit who reluctantly turns to a
life of crime after his mistress, Zabibah, is murdered by gangsters; in
due course, having exacted revenge on the killers, he becomes the
(benevolent) king of the underworld.

The *Baghdad Post* called *Zabibah and the King* "sublime," but most
other reviews were lukewarm at best, and initial sales were disappoint-
ing. Then the Baghdad district attorney attempted to use the book as
the basis for a murder conspiracy charge, arguing that the climax of
the story was a thinly fictionalized account of the killing of Abd al Karim
Qasim that included details only someone privy to the murder plot
would know. A grand jury rejected the DA's request for an indictment,
but the resulting publicity pushed *Zabibah* onto the bestseller lists.

Saddam Hussein has since written three sequels to *Zabibah,* also
bestsellers: *The King's Castle* (2001), *The King and the City* (2003),
and *The King Says Devil, Begone* (2006). According to Saddam's literary agent, a fifth "King" novel is nearing completion; state and federal prosecutors are said to be eagerly awaiting their advance review
copies.

FACTS ABOUT SADDAM HUSSEIN

· He married his cousin Sajida Talfah in 1963. They have five children,
  including two sons, Uday (b. 1964) and Qusay (b. 1966).

- In 1986 Saddam married a second wife, <u>Samira Shahbandar</u>. Owing to "friction" between her and Saddam's first wife, Shahbandar lives abroad in an undisclosed location. It is not known whether she and Saddam have any children.

- Saddam's eldest son, Uday, was arrested in 1988 for pistol-whipping a valet outside a Baghdad discotheque. He has had numerous other run-ins with the law since, and unlike his father, he has not always been successful at avoiding jail time. Most recently, he spent three months in <u>Abu Ghraib</u> for assaulting a model he had been dating.

- Saddam's personal net worth is not known, but he and his family have extensive property holdings, including at least seven houses in Baghdad. In addition to the salary he draws as head of Baath and the royalties from his novels, his primary declared source of income is what he describes as a "small" import/export business he "runs on the side . . ."

That night, Mustafa found himself suddenly wide awake for no reason he could determine. The neighborhood was quiet; the air-conditioning in the apartment was still on, and when he stood outside his father's bedroom, he could hear Abu Mustafa snoring steadily within. All seemed well, but a quickening in his blood told Mustafa he wouldn't be getting back to sleep anytime soon. Rather than fight insomnia he decided to make use of it, taking a mat from a closet shelf and heading to the roof to catch up on his prayers.

As a boy he'd rarely missed a prayer time; his mother had seen to it. Whenever he tried to beg off—most commonly in the dawn hour, when a few extra minutes' sleep seemed more compelling than submission to God—his mother told him to think of the millions of other Muslims all around the world, all bowing to Mecca at that very moment. Did Mustafa really want to exclude himself from that community? This was usually enough to get him out of bed.

Then one day in school, Mustafa's class did a unit on the space program. Two questions arose: How do astronauts orient themselves towards the Qibla? And how do they know when to pray? The latter question baffled Mustafa. What, did they not have a clock in the lunar lander?

Mustafa wasn't the only student confused about this, but he was the one who raised his hand, so he was the one who got to stand at the front of the room—while his more knowledgeable classmates snickered at his ignorance—and hold a flashlight above a spinning globe.

That evening Mustafa spoke to his father, who confirmed that, yes, time zones existed. "But then it's not true that all Muslims pray together!" Mustafa said. "If it's morning in Baghdad and midnight in Jerusalem . . ."

"I think you need to study your geography some more," Abu Mustafa said. "As for God, He's not a boy looking down at a globe. He need not perceive time the way you do."

"But if God can see time any way He likes, why do I have to get up early?"

"Because it's what God wants. And if that's not good enough: Because it's what your mother wants. You want to make your mother happy, don't you?"

Well, of course he did. But doing something to please your mother is different from doing it to please God. Your mother isn't always around. As a child in his parents' house, Mustafa remained dutifully observant, but as he got older and more independent, he became more like his uncle Fayyad, who treated his religious obligations the way he treated his financial debts, as something to be honored at his own convenience. In his second year of college, after his mother died, Mustafa had for a long time stopped praying and going to mosque altogether. Since then, he'd been on again, off again. When he married Fadwa, who like his mother was pleased to see him behave like a proper Muslim: on. When he married Noor, and it became clear that pleasing Fadwa was no longer in the realm of possibility: off.

And now, in this strange changed world, with Fadwa dead and Noor estranged from him: on. Sort of. Looking back over the choices that had brought him here, Mustafa had no illusions about what God must think of him. He wasn't sure what he himself wanted from God, or what he really believed. But whatever else was true, he knew he had a lot to make up for.

The sand from the previous night's storm crunched beneath his feet as he stepped onto the roof. Mustafa arranged his prayer mat, then washed his face, hands, and feet at the spigot that jutted from the side of the stairwell enclosure.

He said fifty sets of prayers back to back: ten days' worth, a lot to do all at once but fewer than he owed. When he began, the wound on his neck was smarting, but by the time he finished the pain was gone and his body felt light as air; he seemed to float up off the mat.

He drifted to the roof's edge and looked out over the city. A warm breeze was blowing off the river; the thermometer atop the Trans-Arabia building read 92 degrees Ferran, 33 degrees Khalis. Mustafa engaged in a brief staredown with city councilman Muqtada al Sadr, whose face graced the rooftop billboard at the end of the block. (AL SADR FOR GOVERNOR, WITH GOD'S HELP, the ad slogan ran, and beneath that, in smaller letters: Paid for by the Mahdi Army.)

Footsteps echoed in the street below, and Mustafa looked down to see a bobbing blond head. Another Hoffman brother? He checked for Mossad agents in pursuit, but the blond man wasn't fleeing: He was jogging. He jogged to the corner, his pace slowing, and stopped to catch his breath under a streetlamp.

Metal tags dangled from a chain around the blond man's neck as he bent and clutched his knees. When he straightened up again, Mustafa saw the word ARMY printed, in English, across the front of his T-shirt and along the edge of his running shorts. Not one of the Mahdis, Mustafa thought wryly, and considered calling down to ask if he was lost.

The blond man took a drink from an oddly shaped brass canteen. As he wiped his mouth, he saw Mustafa on the rooftop, and waved. Mustafa waved back, and once again thought to call down, but before he could speak the blond man continued on his way, rounding the corner out of sight. "Peace be unto you, brother," Mustafa said.

"And also unto you, brother."

Mustafa turned towards the voice, half expecting to see his father. But the speaker was a stranger, an Arab of uncertain age who stood on an unbroken stretch of sand to the right of the stairwell enclosure. He was dressed in a long tunic similar to the dishdasha Mustafa himself wore, but of a style more common in the south; a black-and-white keffiyeh was draped around his neck, and his feet were clad in leather sandals.

Mustafa, assuming the man was another of the building's tenants, spent a moment unsuccessfully trying to place him. Before the silence could grow awkward, the stranger said: "I hope I'm not disturbing you."

"Not at all," said Mustafa. "I'm sorry, have we met before?"

The stranger chuckled. "If you have to ask that, I can't have made a very strong impression." He bent to light a cigarette. The jet of blue flame with which he did this reminded Mustafa of the suicide bomber Travis's lighter, but some trick of perception—the way the man held his hands, perhaps—made the fire seem to come directly from his fingertips.

"Did you," Mustafa asked next, "come up here to pray?"

"Here?" The stranger shook his head, exhaling smoke. "I wouldn't pray here." It wasn't clear whether he referred to the rooftop or the city. "My family has a mosque in the Empty Quarter. I prayed there this evening. At the proper hour."

"The Empty Quarter? But that's fifteen hundred kilometers away," Mustafa said. "It's not that late. How could you have gotten to Baghdad so quickly?"

"You're forgetting about the time zones."

"Ah, of course." Then: "No . . . Wait . . ."

The stranger chuckled again. "I'm just teasing you. You're right, it's a long way to travel."

"Then how—"

"I suppose I must have flown. Like this . . ." Raising his hand, he flicked the lit cigarette into the air. It described an arc of sparks through the night sky, growing in size and fury as it did so, until, passing above Mustafa's head, it changed into a screaming missile. The missile continued along its arc, diving towards the TransArabia building, which had itself been transformed from an elegant tower into a squat concrete box bristling with antennae.

The box became a pillar of fire. A visible pressure wave swept outward from the blast, seeming to gain rather than lose force as it expanded. Mustafa backpedaled from the roof's edge but the wave caught him and threw him off his feet; the roof gave way and he tumbled into darkness, sand and debris raining down after him. Then he was back in his bed, fighting free from a tangle of sweat-soaked sheets.

"Mustafa?" His father stood at the bedroom door, looking in concerned, the two of them having swapped roles for once. "Are you all right? You were shouting."

Driving into work, Mustafa heard a news report that shed some light on his dream. Saddam Hussein's not-guilty celebration, held at his riverfront estate in the Adhamiyah district, had included an unlicensed fireworks display. The midnight barrage of star shells had woken up the neighbors and prompted a number of alarmed 911 calls. Saddam had already issued a public apology and promised to pay a fine for disturbing the peace.

At headquarters, Samir had more details about the "disturbance." After the fireworks had run out, Saddam and some of his guests had broken out hunting rifles. "At first it was the usual yahoo shit, firing into the air," Samir said. "But then Uday had one drink too many and decided to take potshots at boats on the river. He put a tug pilot in the hospital with a burst femur."

"Where did you hear about this?" Mustafa asked.

"From Abu Naji. His brother-in-law is the police watch commander for Adhamiyah. He and a bunch of his patrolmen were at the party."

"But Uday's not under arrest." A statement, not a question.

Samir shrugged. "You know how it is. They're treating it as an accident. The tug pilot will get some money to keep quiet—or if the leg turns septic, his family will."

Amal sat nearby, sifting through a box of folders marked TOP SECRET. "So here's a crazy thought," she said. "Is there any way we could pin a terrorism charge on Saddam? Get him and his family declared enemies of the state and ship them off to Chwaka Bay?"

"Believe me, it's been discussed," Mustafa said. "The problem is, Saddam is the wrong kind of terrorist."

"What would it take to make him the right kind of terrorist?"

Samir laughed. "First we need to convert him to Christianity . . ."

"Speaking of Christians," Mustafa said, "are those the mirage files from Riyadh?"

"'Files' may be an overly generous description. You know that old joke about the intelligence service having stock in companies that make toner cartridges?" Amal held up a sample sheet from the folder she was leafing through. Everything except the page number had been blacked out.

"Idris warned us there would be redactions," Mustafa said.

"It looks like they've redacted anything of substance," Amal told him. "For example, I *think* this is an interrogation transcript. It's got the prisoner's name, his nationality, and his religious sect, but the actual Q&A—forty-nine pages' worth—is a solid wall of black."

"And they're all like that?"

"Most of the ones I've looked at. With a few, the pages are missing entirely."

"Very well," said Mustafa. "If Idris and Senator Bin Laden insist on being difficult, we'll just have to go to Riyadh with a presidential order granting us access to the original files."

"And pray we don't end up like Costello," Samir added.

Gabriel Costello had been transferred to the maximum-security wing of Abu Ghraib. Less than a day after his arrival—and before Mustafa could conduct a second interview—he'd been found in his cell with his prison-issue jumpsuit wrapped around his neck and tied to the edge of his bed frame. The official cause of death was suicide by self-strangulation, though the autopsy showed unexplained bruising on his wrists and ankles.

"I don't think we have to worry about Al Qaeda murdering us," Mustafa said. "Not yet."

"And why is that?"

"Because unlike Costello, we're replaceable. If we die, the president will assign other agents to continue our investigation—and he'll know there's something for them to find. I doubt the senator wants that. So he'll use delaying tactics, threats, perhaps bribery and extortion. But unless we uncover something truly devastating, he won't send assassins."

"Such comforting logic," Amal said laughing.

"Don't forget about Idris," Samir said. "What if he decides to make this personal?"

"We'll just have to hope his Al Qaeda training instilled him with a sense of discipline . . . Now come on, let's take a closer look at these files and see if there's anything the censor missed."

Amal shook her head. "I'm telling you, there really isn't much here."

"Nationalities and religious affiliations, you said. Let's make a list."

Prior to 11/9, national security experts had only had to concern themselves with a handful of Christian denominations.

The biggest and the baddest were of course the Russian Orthodox. The Orthodox Union had had a multimillion-man army, a dream of world domination, and from 1952 onward, the ability to split atoms. Moreover, their church was part of the same eastern branch of Christendom that had produced many of Arabia's Christians, a fact that caused no end of paranoia during the Cold Crusade. But those fears had ultimately proved overblown. Capable of ending the world, the Russians chose not to; instead of attacking Arabia directly, they fought a series of proxy wars—in Yugoslavia, in Chechnya, in Tanzania— before making their last, fatal lunge into Afghanistan, after which defeat their Union had simply evaporated. Though the church lived on and the men who ran Moscow still worshipped under an onion dome, their real god, these days, was Mammon.

Farther west, and so far proving more intractable, were the Lutherans and Roman Catholics of Germany and Austria. The creation of the modern state of Israel had displaced many northern German Protestants into the largely Catholic south. In hindsight, it was clear that the Allied architects of postwar Europe should have given more thought to the consequences of this; instead, they'd simply taken it on faith that the defeated Christians would learn to embrace one another, and their Jewish neighbors, in a spirit of true Muslim brotherhood. It hadn't quite worked out that way.

The British Revolution of 1979 had added Anglicans to the list of Christians to watch out for. Their nuclear ambitions were worrisome, but they were really more of an annoyance than anything else, being content for the most part to stay on their rainy island, chanting "Death to Arabia! Death to Israel!" and defiling images of the Prophet in a pathetic bid for attention.

Orthodox, Lutheran, Catholic, Anglican: a simple enough taxonomy to keep straight. And then the events of November 9 had thrown North American Protestantism into the mix, making everything a thousand times more complicated.

The list that they compiled from the mirage files contained Methodists, Pentecostals, Baptists, Disciples of Christ, Adventists, and a few members of more obscure sects that even Mustafa had never heard of, like the Branch Davidians.

"What is 'PMD'?" Amal asked, indicating one of the more cryptic sect designations. "'MD,' that's the English abbreviation for doctor, isn't it? Is there a Christian denomination composed of medical students?"

"I wouldn't rule out the possibility," Mustafa said. "But in this case I think 'PMD' stands for 'premillennial dispensationalist.'"

"Heh." Samir chuckled. "Try saying *that* three times fast."

"Dispensationalism isn't actually a sect," Mustafa explained. "It's an apocalyptic belief system—a prophecy—shared by multiple sects. A lot of these Methodists and Baptists are probably dispensationalists as well."

"This is that rapture thing?" said Samir. "Where the Jews return to Palestine?"

"That's part of it."

"So it's a Zionist belief, then," Amal said.

"Not really," said Mustafa. "According to the prophecy, most of the Jews die in a holocaust shortly after they reclaim Jerusalem."

"I saw some of those rapture novels in Costello's apartment," Samir said. "Maybe this mirage legend is a new twist on the story."

"Maybe." Mustafa thought a moment. "You know who'd probably know, is Waj."

"Is Waj another Israeli friend?" Amal asked.

"No, he's a librarian," said Mustafa. "*The* librarian, as a matter of fact . . ."

The Library of Alexandria
A USER-EDITED REFERENCE SOURCE

Wajid Jamil

Wajid "Waj" bin Jamil (born July 8, 1966), a Sunni Muslim, is an Arabian computer programmer and Internet entrepreneur best known as the founder of The Library of Alexandria open-source encyclopedia.

Jamil was born in Tripoli, Libya. His father, Jamil al Sindi, was an IT specialist serving as a technology advisor to state governor Muammar al Gaddafi. His mother Parmita was a mathematician distantly related to legendary Hindu library scientist S.R. Ranganathan.

After attaining dual master's degrees in computer science and finance from Baghdad University, Jamil became one of the first generation of online day traders, using a software program of his own devising. His profits—which came as much from the sale of his trading software as from his actual investments—served as seed money for his later online ventures . . .

In addition to his work on The Library of Alexandria, Jamil has contributed expertise and investment capital to the eBazaar online auction company, the Hawaladar e-commerce site, and the classified ad site safwanslist. He is also a co-founder of Christian Media Watch, a watchdog group that monitors Western television, radio, and newspapers for anti-Islamic and anti-Semitic propaganda.

Wajid Jamil had originally wanted to name his online encyclopedia the House of Wisdom, after the famous library and translation center established in Baghdad by the Abbasid Caliph Al Mamun. But that URL was already taken, and the cybersquatter who'd grabbed it demanded an absurd sum. So Jamil went with the cheaper library-ofalexandria.org instead, saving the House of Wisdom tag for his corporate headquarters.

The building was located in Al Mansour Square. A mural above the entrance depicted the great scholar Ibn al Haytham lecturing to his students. Auditing the class from the back of the room were two visitors from the future: Wajid Jamil, in his hacker's djellaba and flip-flops, and beside him, in a gold-embroidered caftan, Muammar Abu Minyar al Gaddafi.

People unfamiliar with Jamil's family connections could be forgiven for wondering if this was a joke. Al Gaddafi had struggled for decades to be taken seriously as an Arab leader, but outside Libya—where the crooked state election board, staffed by his old National Guard comrades, ensured his return to the governor's mansion every four years—he was regarded as little more than a comical human interest story: the governor-for-life, who slept in a nomad's tent and was protected by an all-female bodyguard squad.

His big moment in the national spotlight had come in 2000, when he'd run for president as an independent candidate. Asked during a debate which of his accomplishments as governor he was most proud of, Gaddafi gave a rambling answer about infrastructure projects, including a program that had made Tripoli and Benghazi the first two cities in North Africa to provide free wireless web access. When the governor finished speaking, rival candidate Bandar al Saud inquired in a tone of gentle derision, "I'm sorry, are you telling us you invented the Internet?" Though this was not even close to what Gaddafi had said, the line got a huge laugh and was soon being reported as fact. A few days later, during a Congressional debate over a new anti-obscenity bill, the Speaker of the House appeared to have Gaddafi in mind when he described the Internet as "a series of intestines, laid out by a goatherd's son, spewing bile at both ends."

After that it became a full-on Net meme. Someone created a screensaver showing a goat sticking its tongue out above the caption IM IN UR INTESTINES, SPEWIN MAH BILE. Joke posts appeared on technical support boards, crediting the Libyan governor with miracles both positive and negative: "Invoking the name of Al Gaddafi cured my blue screen of death"; "Spoke ill of Tobruk soccer team last night, now I am beset by malware. Halp!" Even as Gaddafi's presidential ambitions went down in flames—he got less than half a percent of the popular vote, stealing just enough support from the Unity Party candidate to clinch the election for Bandar—the denizens of cyberspace anointed him a king, the Mighty Jinn of the Interwebs.

Remarkably little of this made its way into the Gaddafi entry on the Library of Alexandria. The encyclopedia's article on the governor was respectful to the point of obsequiousness—and it stayed that way, no matter how many amateur editors tried to spice it up with irreverent anecdotes and LOLgoat photos. The man Wajid Jamil knew as Uncle Muammar might not have real magical powers, but what he did have was the Tarhuna Data Center, the largest state-subsidized server farm in the country, buried under the mountains south of Tripoli: unlimited data storage and the bandwidth to go with it, available at rock-bottom prices to those the governor counted as his friends. Wajid took pains to remain among that number.

The receptionist at the House of Wisdom told them that Waj would be free shortly and invited them to wait in a private cybercafé lounge.

While Samir helped himself to pastry and Amal checked out the art on the walls—watercolor landscapes of the Libyan Sahara, painted by the governor—Mustafa got tea and sat down at a computer.

The web browser defaulted to the Library of Alexandria, but a few mouse clicks brought him to the homepage of Christian Media Watch, a site devoted to the proposition that however frightened you were of Jesus's Western disciples, you weren't frightened enough. The banner art showed a scene from the *Volksaufstand*: a screaming Teuton with a bloodred cross on his chest winding up to throw a Molotov cocktail at a line of Israeli police in riot gear. Superimposed on this was the quote "Onward, Christian soldiers, marching as to war . . ." which the tagline attributed to POPULAR CHRISTIAN ANTHEM.

Mustafa remembered the first time he'd heard that song. It was his last year at BU, and he was sharing an apartment with Samir, Wajid, and an Ethiopian exchange student named Kidane Sellasie who spent most of his waking hours building cardboard models at the architecture school. Wajid was similarly dedicated to his studies, but on Thursday nights he liked to unwind by smoking hashish and watching funny videos: cartoons, bad movies, old TV shows.

On the night in question, Waj had rented what he'd thought was a collection of computer-animated shorts from the Tunis Film Festival. But there'd been a mix-up at the video store, and the tape inside the case was actually a documentary about American Christian fundamentalists. On the theory that anything could be entertaining with enough smoke, Waj loaded up his hash pipe and popped the tape into the VCR. Samir joined him on the couch, but Mustafa, who had exams the next week, went to his room to study.

Half an hour later, the sound of raucous laughter drew him back out again. "What did I miss?"

Samir was laughing so hard he was gasping for breath: "Rewind! Rewind!"

Waj rewound the tape. When he pressed play, a children's choir was singing the anthem:

> *Onward, Christian soldiers, marching as to war*
> *With the cross of Jesus going on before*
> *Christ, the royal Master, leads against the foe*
> *Forward into battle see His banners go!*

"I don't get the joke," Mustafa said.

Samir made a clumsy grab for the remote: "You went back too far!"

"I know!" said Waj, "I know!" To Mustafa: "Just wait, there's another song after this one . . ."

The next song was a folk number about the different kinds of Jew and how much better it was to be a member of Christ's flock:

> *I wouldn't want to be a Pharisee (No!)*
> *A Sadducee (No!) or a Maccabee (No!)*
> *I'm glad that I'm a Lamb of God*
> *Baa! Baa! Baa!*

"Baa!" bleated Samir. "Ba-a-a-a-a!" Waj went off on an extended riff about Christians and their livestock that Mustafa didn't think was funny but which, to his lasting shame, he laughed at anyway. Then he heard footsteps and turned to see Kidane Sellasie, home for once, standing in the apartment doorway with a sad look on his face.

Mustafa immediately apologized and Samir at least managed to keep his mouth shut. But Waj dug himself in deeper by trying to explain away the insult, insisting that he hadn't been making fun of *all* Christians, just the fanatical, Jew-hating, American variety.

"I'm glad you are so comfortable with your prejudices, Wajid," Kidane Sellasie said.

These days, Mustafa reflected, wincing at the memory, Wajid was even more comfortable with his prejudices—though he no longer found American fundamentalists a laughing matter.

Mustafa typed the word "rapture" into the Christian Media Watch search box and the screen filled with video thumbnails. He clicked one labeled "FOX News, January 2002" and the site began streaming an interview with a man identified as FAIRFAX COUNTY EVANGELICAL PREACHER.

"So you aren't worried by the Arabians' threat to invade?" the interviewer said.

"Worried?" said the preacher. "No sir, why would I be worried?"

"You're very close to Washington, here. And you know the president has promised a massacre if enemy troops try to enter the capital."

"Well sir, God bless the president, but it's not *man's* promises I care about . . . Tell me, have you accepted Jesus into your heart?"

"I attend church regularly, yes."

"That's not what I asked. If you've accepted Jesus as your personal savior, as I have, then your place in heaven is assured and there's nothing you need fear. But if you haven't, there's no place on this earth that's safe . . ."

"You talked earlier about the Great Tribulation," the reporter said. "Do you believe the Arabian invasion could be the start of that?"

"It's too soon to say. We have heard reports that the head of the Israeli Knesset and the grand rabbi of Berlin are meeting in secret with the leaders of the UAS and Persia. There are also rumors that we may soon see a huge influx of Jews into Palestine. If that happens, it would definitely be a sign of the coming Tribulation."

"And what would your reaction be?"

"I'd say, 'Bring it on!'" The preacher smiled. "I'd say bring the Arabs on, too—but they'd better be ready for a surprise when they get here."

"You think God will . . . smite them?"

"No sir, I think they'll arrive to find this land empty. Empti*er*, anyway . . . Come the rapture, I know *I* won't be home . . ."

Amal, done looking at art, now stood at Mustafa's elbow watching the video. She said of the preacher: "Do you suppose he's with God now?"

"He might be, if he stayed in Fairfax. But I doubt he was transported bodily to heaven the way he was expecting."

Though the Coalition assault on Washington had not been without casualties, the massacre promised by the American president had failed to materialize. A year later, however, after insurgents in a village called Langley had murdered a group of civilian contractors, the UAS Marine Corps had gone into Fairfax County to restore order. The resulting engagement had been one of the deadliest of the occupation, with Marines ultimately using white phosphorous shells and napalm bombs to drive the insurgents from the dense urban zones in which they'd entrenched themselves.

Mustafa studied the face of the preacher, frozen now in the final frame of the video clip. Were you still there when the sky started raining fire? he wondered. What went through your mind? Did you think God had abandoned you? That you'd been left behind in your rapture? Or did you immediately start looking for a new prophecy, one that would make sense of the loss you didn't believe you could ever suffer?

Powdered sugar like a swirl of fine ash trickled down in front of the computer screen. "Mustafa," Samir said, through a mouthful of pastry. He indicated a secretary who'd just entered the lounge. "I think Waj is ready for us."

"A lovely name for a lovely woman," said Wajid Jamil. "Is she going to be number three, Mustafa?"

"Excuse me?" Amal said.

"I'm kidding, of course." Waj smiled to indicate no offense was intended. "I'm sure you're already married . . . And a mother, perhaps?"

This was another of Wajid's post-11/9 obsessions, the population race between Islam and Christendom. Muslims on average had larger families, but because there were so many more Christians to start with, it would be many decades yet before they achieved parity. And that was assuming nothing changed: Women like Amal, who put career before family, were a reminder that birth rates aren't fixed.

Mustafa had his own reasons for not wanting to get started on this topic. "With respect, Wajid," he said, "we didn't come here to talk about marriage. If you want to have an in-depth discussion of the subject, you should take it up with Amal's mother, the senator."

"The senator?" Waj's smile underwent a subtle phase-shift as he put it together. "You're Anmar al Maysani's daughter?"

"She is. And you, Waj, aren't you working with the senator on some sort of legislation?"

"Yes. I've been lobbying her on Uncle—on Governor Gaddafi's behalf, about the new telecommunications bill . . ."

"Good luck with that," Amal said.

"Well," said Waj, moving right along. "Let's get down to business, shall we?" He retreated behind his desk, a massive executive cockpit equipped with multiple computer screens. "Please, all of you, sit down. Tell me what the House of Wisdom can do for Homeland Security . . ."

They sat. Mustafa described his interrogation of Costello and the search of Costello's apartment, then gave an edited version of the meeting in Farouk's office. He omitted all mention of Idris and spoke of the president only indirectly, saying that they had been asked "by Riyadh" to look further into the mirage legend. "We thought if anyone would know about a new Christian myth making the rounds, it would be you, Waj," he concluded.

"'The mirage,' hmm . . ." Waj tapped on his desktop keyboard, consulted his screens. "It doesn't look like there's anything in my databases yet . . . You say this is related to rapture theology?"

"It's a theory."

"Yes, well, that would make sense. These rapturists, they're like any Christian End Times cult, always expecting the apocalypse next week, and then when next week comes and the world's still here, they fall all over themselves trying to explain why. With so much theological innovation it's hard to keep up, even with computers . . . Tell me more about these objects you found. Can I see some of them?"

Mustafa opened his attaché and passed the map of the mirage Middle East to Wajid.

Waj spotted it immediately: "Israel is in Palestine?"

Mustafa shrugged. "God willing, anything is possible."

"Heh, and Kirkuk is part of Iraq. The guys who manage the Kurdish edition of the Library would love *that*." Waj laughed. "This is actually kind of cool, in a completely demented way. Is there more?"

Mustafa showed him the newspaper they'd found in Costello's apartment. "*The New York Times*," Wajid read, his English as good as Mustafa's. "'All the news that's fit to print . . .'"

"It's a ghost paper," Mustafa said. "According to our research, there was a *New York Times*, but it was shut down by the American government in 1971 for revealing state secrets. The publishers were executed for treason."

"Well, it looks real enough. Professionally printed."

"That photo is obviously a fake, though," Samir put in. "What do you think, Waj? Photoshop?"

"Could be." He pointed to the bottom right-hand corner of the front page, where a rectangle of newsprint had been neatly excised. "What happened here? Somebody clip out a recipe?"

"We're not sure how that happened," Mustafa said. He'd first noticed the cutout about an hour before he received the call informing him Gabriel Costello was dead. "There are some pages missing from the inside, as well."

"Would it be all right if I made a copy of this?" Waj asked. "I'd like to read it through, maybe show it to a couple of my research guys."

"As long as you keep it in-house."

"Don't worry, I won't post it on the Library . . . Hmm, that's interesting."

"What?"

"According to this, these September 11 attacks took place on a Tuesday."

"Sure, just like 11/9," Mustafa said.

"Yes," said Waj, "that's the problem . . ." He pulled up a calendar on one of his computer screens. "Yeah, see: September 11, 2001, was a Saturday, not a Tuesday."

Samir snorted. "What a surprise, even the date is fictional."

Wajid stared at the calendar. "You think about it, it's too bad September 11 *wasn't* a Tuesday . . ."

"Why?" said Mustafa.

"Because then November 9 would have been a Friday."

Friday: first day of the weekend. Mustafa heard the Fairfax preacher: *Come the rapture, I know I won't be home* . . . "The towers would have been empty."

"Empti*er*, anyway," Waj said. "Janitors, security people, probably some office workers clocking overtime. But the restaurant would have been closed, and the evacuation would have gone a lot faster . . ."

Samir, bemused, said: "What are you talking about?"

"In Christian countries, the weekend starts on Saturday," Mustafa explained. "Or Sunday."

"Yeah, I *know* that," Samir said. "And I know crusaders can be idiots. But do you really think they wouldn't have checked to make sure the towers would be open for business that day?"

"What if they hadn't, though?" Mustafa said. Just imagine it: the planes, themselves emptier because of the holy day, crashing into mostly vacant offices, silent halls and stairwells. Of course it still would have been a great tragedy, and the shock of the towers' destruction would not have been lessened in the slightest. But once the smoke cleared and word began to spread of the even greater tragedy so miraculously averted, might history not have proceeded down a different path? Maybe leveler heads would have prevailed. Maybe the pointless war with America could have been called off. The thought of this alternate reality, in which not only the thousands of lost soldiers but even that silly Fairfax preacher got to live out their natural lives, filled Mustafa with a sudden, irrational joy.

Then he thought, Fadwa, and his joy faded.

"Dude," Wajid said, reading some or all of this in his expression. "Forget about it. Samir's right. They would have checked."

"I know," Mustafa said.

"And even if they hadn't . . . The guy who sold them the plane tickets would have said something."

Waj stepped out of his office to arrange the copying of the newspaper and Samir tagged along with him. Mustafa and Amal remained seated, both looking quietly out the window.

"'Number three,'" Amal said finally, unable to help herself.

"I apologize for that," Mustafa said, embarrassed. "I assure you I've told Waj nothing about you that would imply an inappropriate relationship. But he has a fertile imagination, and he lacks a proper filter between his brain and his mouth."

"So I gather."

"Also, he takes a very personal interest in my marital affairs. He's prouder of my marriage to Noor than I am at this point; he believes he's responsible for it."

"And why is that? Did he introduce you to her?"

"No," Mustafa said. "He made it possible for me to afford to marry her. Stock options," he explained. "Waj sold me some of his shares in eBazaar, a few months before the IPO."

"EBazaar! But you must be rich, then. Why are you still in government service?"

"I *would* be rich, if I'd taken all the shares Waj offered me. But I decided to hedge my bet by investing in some other Internet stocks that didn't perform nearly as well . . . Still, it was quite a windfall. I *thought* I was rich. Rich enough to behave very stupidly, for a while."

"Forgive me," Amal said, "but I still don't understand how you could do such a thing."

"Oh, it's not hard. There's actually an 800 number you can call, to get information on the practicalities of taking multiple wives. A website, too, government-funded, courtesy of Al Saud . . . At least that used to be the case. I suppose your mother's efforts in Congress may have led to some changes."

"That isn't what I—"

"I know what you meant," Mustafa said. "The short answer is, you do it by deliberately confusing what is permitted with what is right. Money makes the confusion easier." He looked at her, then continued in a softer tone: "It's OK, I don't expect you to understand. You kind of had to be there."

The Library of Alexandria
A USER-EDITED REFERENCE SOURCE

Female infertility

(Redirected from **Barren**)

Female infertility is a condition in which a woman either cannot <u>conceive</u> or cannot carry a <u>pregnancy</u> to term. There are many types of infertility and many possible causes, such as <u>genetic defects</u>, <u>physical abnormalities</u>, <u>hormonal disorders</u>, and the effects of various <u>diseases</u>.

Female infertility is one of the most common grounds for <u>divorce</u> . . .

Fadwa was praying to the Virgin Mary on the night Mustafa met Noor.

Mustafa had known Fadwa since childhood. She was the daughter of his mother's oldest friend, and whenever Umm Mustafa went home to visit her family in downstate Iraq, or when Fadwa's parents came up to Baghdad, the two of them ended up playing together. When he was very young, Mustafa's sisters sometimes teased him by saying that he and Fadwa were going to be married one day.

Then, just as the two of them were reaching an age when boys and girls were expected to play separately, Fadwa's father got a job abroad, in America of all places. Umm Mustafa was sad to see her friend leave, but she was also excited, because she thought her own dreams of travel would now be realized. But visiting Fadwa's mother in her new home proved insurmountably difficult: Americans were stingy with tourist visas, and both times that Umm Mustafa successfully navigated the bureaucracy, the trip had to be canceled at the last minute, once because Abu Mustafa couldn't get leave from the university and once because of Umm Mustafa's declining health.

Mustafa's mother had been dead three years by the time he saw Fadwa again. He'd just finished college and started working at Halal. He'd heard Fadwa's family was back in Iraq—her father's American job a casualty of the Gulf War—but still he was surprised to get a letter from her, an invitation to her brother's wedding. He almost didn't go. He was on assignment that weekend, a stakeout in Samarra, but at the last moment he got Samir to cover for him and drove south to the village where his mother had been born.

Fadwa had grown into a beautiful young woman. Mustafa spent most of the wedding party hovering around her, and late in the day the two of them went for a stroll through the village, visiting their childhood haunts. Little about the place had changed, with the exception of the broad irrigation canal that now ran through the fields to the west. Numerous signs proclaimed the canal a "gift" of the Baath Labor Union.

Fadwa told Mustafa that her father was thinking of joining Baath. "He doesn't want to—he doesn't like or trust Saddam Hussein—but he's had a terrible time finding work since we got back from America."

"He is right not to trust Saddam," Mustafa said, going on to explain that the canal-building project, pushed through the state legislature with a series of bribes, was really an elaborate revenge plot. "The Shia smuggler gangs along the Persian border refused to join Saddam's syndicate, so as punishment he's draining the marsh out from under them." As for the many innocent marshlanders whose ancient way of life was being destroyed, Saddam didn't care about them. Neither did the federal government, unfortunately. "My boss has been trying to get the Environmental Protection Agency involved in the case—they actually have more power than Halal when it comes to this sort of thing. But Iraqis apparently don't qualify as an endangered species."

"So it falls to you then," Fadwa said, smiling at his seriousness. "You'll have to get the old gangster yourself."

"Well, I am going to try," said Mustafa, smiling back.

Several months later, Mustafa's sisters and aunts met formally with the women of Fadwa's family to hammer out the details of a marriage contract. Once that was taken care of, the men got together and had a barbeque. Mustafa and Fadwa's wedding was in June. With money from Mustafa's family, they got a starter house in the suburban district of New Baghdad.

That first year of their marriage was a happy one, though to Mustafa looking back later it often seemed like something that had happened to another person. Those were the days when he once more strove to be a proper Muslim: praying regularly, giving to charity, fasting during Ramadan. Much of what he did, he did to please Fadwa, just as he'd once done it to please his mother, but pleasing her gave him a sense of fulfillment that felt very much like righteousness. The sense of fulfillment carried over to his work. People sometimes referred to Halal agents as "God's policemen" because they enforced purity laws; Mustafa preferred to think of his job as protecting the weak against exploitation by the wicked, but either way you looked at it, it was a banner year for the God squad. They seized a lot of contraband and locked up a lot of bad people, and even the old gangster Saddam seemed, for a time, tantalizingly within reach.

The trouble began the following year, when Fadwa's family came to visit them in Baghdad during the Festival of Sacrifice. Fadwa's mother commented repeatedly on the fact that Fadwa wasn't pregnant yet. What were they waiting for? Was there some problem? Mustafa, figuring these were the pro forma expressions of concern that mothers-in-law were supposed to make, paid them little mind. Fadwa was badly shaken, though. After her parents went home, she broke down and confessed to Mustafa that she'd been keeping a family secret from him. One of her maternal grandmother's sisters had been divorced by her husband after she proved incapable of bearing children. Not only did he literally kick her out of the house, he blamed her infertility on immoral behavior, a vile accusation that she denied, but that so shamed her she ended up committing suicide.

Mustafa listened gravely to this story but failed to take it as seriously as he should have. Family honor was important and memories were long, but the events Fadwa described had occurred before either of them had even been born. More importantly, Mustafa had come to take his own good fortune for granted, seeing the past year's joy as a natural state of affairs rather than a blessing that might not last. This arrogance blinded him to the depth of Fadwa's fear.

"Your great-aunt's husband sounds like a monster," he said when she'd finished. "And what happened was a tragedy. But it's got nothing to do with us."

Fadwa looked at him warily. "What if I can't conceive?"

"Don't be silly. You will. Of course you will."

"What if I *can't*?"

"Fadwa, come on." He cupped her face in his hands. "You know I would never put you out."

She closed her eyes and nodded and pretended to be reassured. But after that day things were different between them. Fadwa began demanding sex more often—in itself, nothing to complain about, but the act was tainted by an aura of desperation that grew stronger over time. In matters of faith, Fadwa became a scold, chastising Mustafa for any sign he was shirking his obligations.

Six months later Fadwa still wasn't pregnant and Mustafa conceded that there might be a real problem, though he felt sure it was temporary, some biological speed bump that medical science could cure. He told Fadwa to make a doctor's appointment. She did, but the appointment kept getting rescheduled. After several months of delays, Mustafa placed an angry call to the doctor's office and found out it wasn't the doctor who'd been postponing the exam.

Now it was Mustafa's turn to play the chastiser. "You need to stop being foolish and get this checked out, Fadwa," he said. "Whatever's wrong, we'll get it fixed."

The verdict, when it finally came, was devastating. "Premature ovarian failure." Mustafa repeating the doctor's words felt sluggish and dumb. "Premature ovarian failure, that's, what is that, early menopause?"

No, it wasn't; it was much worse. A woman in menopause knows she cannot have children. A woman with premature ovarian failure knows only that she is unlikely to. Between five and ten percent of women with the condition still managed to conceive, the doctor said; but because the underlying causes were still poorly understood, there was no way to predict who would be in that lucky minority. And while they could treat Fadwa for some of the related symptoms, about the condition itself there was nothing to be done.

"And you're sure that's what's wrong with her?" Mustafa said this several times, not so much because he doubted the diagnosis but because he needed time to get used to it, this new reality that was not at all what he had expected. Meanwhile Fadwa was sitting right beside him, watching him, absorbing his every word, every facial tic. If Mustafa had it to do over again, he would have insisted on meeting with the doctor alone, first—not the act of an enlightened husband, perhaps, but one that would have allowed him a chance to sort his own feelings in private. As it was, Fadwa suffered the double torment of hearing the bad news herself while observing Mustafa's reaction to it—and projecting, into that reaction, all of her worst fears. By the time Mustafa had collected himself enough to try to comfort her, it was too late.

Fadwa called her mother that night in tears. Within twenty-four hours, the whole family knew. Fadwa's father was the first to offer advice, saying that of course they mustn't put all their trust in one doctor. They needed a second opinion—at least!—and he knew just where to go for one: a hospital with a first-rate family planning clinic that had recently opened in Adhamiyah.

Mustafa knew the hospital he was talking about. It had been financed by donations from Baath and the Saddam Hussein Foundation, and was already under scrutiny by Halal for possible narcotics violations. But Fadwa's father, now a fully employed union member, no longer regarded Saddam as a bad guy, and when he offered to arrange an appointment at the clinic, Mustafa couldn't refuse without insulting him.

The Baath fertility specialist confirmed the original doctor's diagnosis but added a measure of optimism. There were a number of experimental therapies, he said, that might increase Fadwa's odds of conceiving.

Mustafa quite naturally suspected a scam. "If the treatment is experimental, I assume it's not covered by Blue Crescent. Will Saddam's foundation be paying the bill?"

"Ah, no, I'm afraid you'll have to bear the expense yourself," the doctor replied. "And I won't lie, these therapies aren't cheap . . . But really, how can one put a price on parenthood?"

"You seem unashamed to," Mustafa said. Then he felt Fadwa's hand on his wrist and knew he had been overruled.

The doctor knew it too: "Let me get someone to take your financials."

While they waited to see whether the clinic would deliver more than hope in exchange for their savings, Mustafa and Fadwa received other therapeutic suggestions from family and friends: folk remedies, charms, foods to eat and foods to avoid. Mustafa's uncle Tamir, with the authority granted him by the eight children he'd sired, said that getting a woman pregnant was mostly a matter of proper positioning during the sex act.

And there were religious therapies, too. In addition to her regular attendance at mosque, Fadwa began making weekly pilgrimages to an Armenian church dedicated to Umm Isa, the mother of the prophet Jesus. Mary, revered by Muslims as well as Christians, was believed by some to be able to intervene on behalf of the faithful; pregnancy issues were, for obvious reasons, one of her specialties. A few of Mustafa's Sunni cousins grumbled that this was idolatry, but Mustafa was more concerned that, like everything else they tried, it would prove ineffective.

"Fadwa," he said one evening, as she prepared for her visit to Umm Isa's house, "you know I'll never stop praying for you to be able to have a child, but if . . . if it doesn't happen, will we—"

She looked at him as if *he* were an idolater—or a blasphemer.

"How dare you say that! How dare you say that! God can do anything!"

"God can do anything," Mustafa agreed. "He can say no. If He does—"

But Fadwa didn't want to hear *If He does.*

Mustafa went to see his father. Alone among the relatives, Abu Mustafa had refrained from volunteering advice so far, but now Mustafa asked him the question that Fadwa refused to consider: "What if nothing works? What if we simply can't have children?"

"Do you love her?" Abu Mustafa asked.

"Yes," said Mustafa.

"And how will you feel if you never become a father?"

Mustafa had to think about it. Since the initial shock of the diagnosis, he'd been so focused on reassuring Fadwa, he was no longer sure of his own feelings. "I will be disappointed if that happens," he said finally. "Probably more disappointed than I can imagine now. But I believe I could learn to live with such disappointment. What concerns me is Fadwa. I don't know if she'll ever be able to accept it. Or trust that I have."

"A marriage without trust is a failed marriage," Abu Mustafa said. "There's a simple solution for that."

"No." Mustafa shook his head. "A divorce would crush her. It might even kill her. I won't do that."

Abu Mustafa smiled sadly. "So what is it you're asking me, then? How to live with a wife who can never be satisfied? You want my expert opinion on that?"

"Father," Mustafa said, abashed. "I don't—"

"No, it's all right. My answer is simple enough: Be kind."

Mustafa frowned. He'd been hoping for something more detailed. "Be kind . . . That's it?"

"If you can do it consistently, you'll be a better husband than I was," his father told him. "And Mustafa? If you can't be kind, be honest. The sooner the better."

He did what he could. He acceded without complaint to whatever baby-making regimens Fadwa proposed, no matter how hopeless or absurd they seemed. He cultivated patience, and kept his own frustrations to himself, and tried not to be drawn into arguments. But here already he wasn't being honest, and the problem only got worse.

To help pay for the experimental fertility treatments (all worthless, and each series more expensive than the last) Mustafa began volunteering for extra assignments at work, as much overtime as he could get. This meant being away from home a lot, something that Fadwa couldn't reasonably object to. She objected anyway, saying that Mustafa was running away from her, which he denied.

The denials weren't lies, at least not exactly. Yes, there were times when he needed to get away from Fadwa, but his ultimate goal wasn't escape, it was renewal. Whatever the discontents of his marriage, Mustafa continued to find fulfillment in his work. It wasn't as easy as it had once been—like many a drug warrior before him, Mustafa had become a cynic about prohibition—but bringing down a villain, avenging (or more rarely, saving) an innocent: These things still gave him a jolt of righteousness, a sense that he was contributing, in some small way, to God's plan. Sometimes the sense of righteousness was infectious: He'd go home after a particularly good day and Fadwa would smile and laugh and be almost like her old self.

These moments of grace never lasted, and in the long run, the idea that the joys of one sphere of life could compensate for the deficiencies of another was probably poisonous. But it kept Mustafa going for quite a while.

Then in the fifth year of their marriage, at the end of another failed series of fertility treatments, Fadwa fell into a depression that lasted for months. Mustafa went out and arrested Saddam's chief lieutenant in Anbar Province, catching him red-handed with a truckload of whiskey and convincing him to give up his entire distribution network in exchange for leniency. This was a major coup for Halal Enforcement—a career-making success—but it didn't improve Fadwa's mood in the slightest. Mustafa, unable to contain his feelings for once, ended up shouting at her: Why could she not be happy for him?

That night he lay awake, thinking about the wedding party where he and Fadwa had reconnected as adults, wondering what his life would be like if that day had never happened. What if Fadwa's letter of invitation had been lost in the mail? What if his car had broken down, or he simply hadn't gone? What if, what if. Of course it might not have made any difference. It could be that he was fated to marry Fadwa no matter what. But it was possible to imagine a world in which that wasn't so. What if, what if.

He began looking at other women, not in a sexual way (well, not *only* in a sexual way), but as emissaries from that other world. He tried not to be completely selfish about it: If he got to walk a different path, so did Fadwa, and so he always gave her a husband who was loving and patient and kind and who, most of all, had the wisdom Mustafa lacked, the knowledge of how to make her happy. That being stipulated, his most detailed fantasies all focused on his half of the equation.

A woman in line at the post office; the secretaries at Halal; a mother at the supermarket wrangling three healthy children . . . What if, what if. Or a woman he spied waiting for a bus, sixty if she were a day and obviously plain-looking even in youth, but just as obviously content with her life. What would it be like to be married to such contentment, to see it every morning and every evening, to share a bed with it? What if, what if. And as the fantasy continued to take shape: I wish, I wish.

Such wishing was harmless, he told himself, so long as he remembered it wasn't reality. He had the wife he had and not another. He wasn't going to leave Fadwa; he'd sworn that oath a thousand times already and he meant it, even if she didn't believe him. Nor would he become like Samir, who'd broken off two wedding engagements because of his freely confessed inability to stop womanizing.

But maybe he wasn't careful enough about keeping his fantasies to himself. Or maybe God wanted to test his resolve. One morning at breakfast Fadwa started telling him about the previous night's homily in church, which had concerned the prophet Ibrahim's wife Sarah and her servant, Hagar . . .

Mustafa was only pretending to pay attention, so it was the silence that followed Fadwa's words rather than the words themselves that caused him to look up. Fadwa was at the kitchen sink with her back to him, standing rigid as though awaiting a physical blow.

"What did you just say?" Mustafa asked.

"I said, maybe you should take a second wife. Then you could have children, and I—"

"My God," said Mustafa, his bewilderment turning instantly to rage. "My God, Fadwa, what sort of madness are those Christians filling your head with?"

He stormed out of the house. Fadwa followed, calling his name, but he was through the front door and into his car before she could catch him.

But he couldn't outrace the knowledge of who he was really angry at. Not Fadwa, for making the suggestion. Himself, for being tempted by it.

The dead man's name was Ghazi al Tikriti. He was a mid-level Baathist who managed a string of rat cellars and a semi-legitimate nightclub in Rusafa. On the evening in question he'd left his car in a no-parking zone for an hour while he went to have dinner; he returned to find a ticket on his windshield and a surprise package wired to his ignition.

Mustafa was dropping Fadwa off at Umm Isa's church when he got the call. "It's a murder," he told Fadwa. "I'll be home late. Can you—"

"I'll find a ride." She got out without kissing him goodbye.

Samir and a homicide detective named Zagros were already at

the crime scene. A group of Baghdad PD uniforms stood by the rope line, ogling the car—a brand-new Afrit Turbo—and holding a high-spirited debate about how much the corpse would affect its blue-book value.

Mustafa was surprised that the vehicle was still intact. "I thought you said he got blown up."

"He did," Samir replied. "Somebody replaced the air bag in the steering column with a pack of ball bearings and some extra propellant. Think shotgun."

"Clever piece of work," said Zagros, who was crouched by the open driver's door. "It looks like they unscrewed the dome light to keep him from noticing the tampering. Or maybe that was to get him to lean in closer when he put his key in . . ."

"What about the parking ticket? Have you tracked down the cop who issued it?"

Samir pointed to one of the smugger-looking bystanders. "He claims he didn't see anything suspicious. But wouldn't you know, he's also from Tikrit. We're running him through the computer now, to see how close a relative he is of Saddam's. And whether he's got any auto shop experience."

"Here's the victim's wallet," Zagros said, standing up. "The driver's license matches the registration, but we'll need to check fingerprints to be absolutely sure."

A slip of paper with a woman's name and phone number was tucked into the billfold. "Noor," Mustafa read. The paper smelled faintly of perfume. "What do you think, a girlfriend?"

"Or a prostitute," said Zagros.

"I recognize the phone exchange. It's the BU campus."

"So? A whore can't seek higher education? This is the city of the future, my friend."

Mustafa turned to Samir. "We should get an address and go talk to her."

"What for?" Samir looked over at the rope line. "Ten to one our killer's right here."

"Yes, and a thousand to one he never talks."

"You think the girl will?"

No, thought Mustafa, but it's a more diverting waste of time. And it will take longer. "Indulge me."

"My mother had one of these," Mustafa said, lifting the statue of Bastet—black kitty-cat with an ankh on its collar—from the knick-knack shelf on which it sat. "She brought it back from her honey-moon."

"Mine was a gift from my father," Noor said. "He told me he'd stolen it for me from Cleopatra's tomb." She smiled. "I was eleven before I realized the gold was painted on."

"Your father was an archaeologist?"

"An amateur treasure-hunter. Not a very successful one. He did better with abandoned storage lockers than ancient tombs."

"And you?" Mustafa said, returning Bastet to her shelf. "What are you studying at university?"

"Ah, nothing," said Noor, with the coy look of revealing a naughty secret. "I'm not a student."

"No? I thought this was student housing."

"It's cheap housing," Noor said. "I couldn't afford such a view off-campus." The apartment, a fifth-floor walk-up, had an unobstructed view across the river. Mustafa could see the twin towers in the distance, rising towards a full moon. "It's supposed to be a student apartment," Noor conceded, "but I have a special arrangement with Umm Banat."

"Your landlady?" Mustafa pictured the old crone who'd answered the buzzer downstairs. The building was not just student-only but women-only, and Umm Banat had looked upon Mustafa and Samir as potential despoilers of virtue; their Halal badges had only barely sufficed to gain them admittance. "If you convinced that woman to break the rules for you, you must be quite the charmer."

"Oh, I can be," Noor said. "When I want to."

She was tall. In heels she would have been as tall as Mustafa, and even in the silk slippers she was currently wearing, she had to tilt her head up only slightly to look him in the eye. She did look him in the eye, her gaze frank and open and relaxed, unintimidated by the presence, at this late hour, of two strangers in her home, policemen who had yet to state their business.

She wasn't a great beauty. Her face, a mix (he would later learn) of Egyptian, Berber, and Spanish features, was off somehow, but off in an interesting way. Returning her gaze, he had to struggle not to become distracted—by her look, her manner, and by rogue thoughts about what it would be like to embrace a woman nearly his size. Fadwa was short.

"So," he asked next, "where do you work?"

"Al Jazeera," she said, smiling again—either at his visible effort to stay focused or simply because she liked smiling. "I do story research for *Mesopotamia This Week*. And once in a while I freelance for FOX, if they have an out-of-town crew that needs a guide or a translator."

"Jazeera *and* FOX," Mustafa said. "I didn't know it was possible to work for both at once."

"Ah, it's like juggling two boyfriends," Noor replied. "You just have to be careful not to let them in the same room together."

"You have experience juggling boyfriends, do you?" said Samir— the first words he had spoken since their arrival. While Mustafa bantered with Noor, he'd made a slow circuit of the apartment, touching things at random, looking for incriminating evidence or some other antidote to his boredom. Now in the kitchen, less a separate room than an extension of the living area, he reached into the open cabinet above the gas range and brought down a pair of champagne glasses.

"Uh-oh," Noor said. "Now I'm in trouble. You've found my drug paraphernalia." A bit of current-events humor: Earlier that year, a junior POG House member had introduced legislation to ban drinking vessels "designed specifically for the consumption of illegal beverages." Although the bill had never made it out of committee, the press had gotten wind of it, and it had since become a running gag.

Samir, trying to come off as though it were no laughing matter: "If I keep looking, will I find a bottle to go with these?"

"I think I will choose not to incriminate myself by answering that," Noor said good-naturedly. Glancing sideways at Mustafa: "At least until I know you better . . . Now I don't wish to be rude to such charming gentlemen, but what is it you are here for? Not to search my pantry, surely."

"No, we're here about this," Mustafa said, holding out the paper they'd found in Ghazi's wallet. Noor's fingertips brushed his as she took it.

"This is my phone number," Noor said, "and my handwriting, but I don't remember . . . Oh."

"Oh?"

She bit her lower lip. "This is about the car, isn't it?"

"The car?" Samir said. He set the champagne glasses on the kitchen counter and turned towards her. "What car?"

"Well," Noor said, focusing on Mustafa. "This man—"

"Ghazi al Tikriti," Mustafa said.

"—yes, he came to Al Jazeera a few days ago to be interviewed, and while he was waiting to be called into the studio he chatted me up. While we were talking, I mentioned I was looking for a new car, something a little sporty—"

"Why would you mention that to him?"

She shrugged. "It just came up in the conversation. And he said, you know, he had some friends who could get cars, good cars, very cheaply . . ."

Samir let out a rude laugh, then covered his mouth to stifle a yawn.

"Did you know this man was a gangster?" Mustafa asked her.

"Well," Noor said. "He didn't introduce himself that way of course, but—"

"But you knew. So you must also have known, or suspected, that he was offering to get you a stolen car."

"I knew the deal would be no questions asked." She sighed. "And I know it was stupid, but I do really want a car, so I gave him my number . . . But how did you get it? Did you arrest him for something?"

Mustafa told her what had happened. Noor was taken aback—the more so when Samir jumped in with the details of just how Ghazi had met his end—but it was clear from her reaction that she'd not only had nothing to do with the murder, she was also telling the truth about having just met the man. Ghazi's death was not a personal loss to her, the way a lover's death would be.

She said: "It's a pity he got killed, of course—"

"Not really," said Samir.

"—but I don't know how I can help you."

"You say he came in to do an interview," Mustafa said. "Do you know what the interview was about?"

"No. You think it has something to do with why he was killed?"

"It's possible."

"I could give you the name and number of the producer who handled the interview."

"Please," Mustafa said. He pointed to the slip with her home number on it. "Why don't you just write it on the back of that paper?"

"Of course." Her lips curved in a knowing smile. "I'll give you my work number too."

"That would be most helpful."

She jotted down the two numbers and handed the paper back to him. Then her smile faltered and she asked: "Should I be worried? About my safety, I mean."

Samir said: "A woman living alone, who invites criminals to call her at home? No, I'm sure you'll live a long full life."

"I doubt the men who killed Ghazi would care about you," Mustafa said. "But here, take one of my cards . . . If anyone bothers you, you can call me." He should have stopped there—should have stopped sooner, in fact—but added: "Halal periodically holds auctions of seized property, including cars. The daughter of a treasure-hunter might find a bargain there. I could notify you of the next auction."

"Thank you," Noor said. "Yes, I would like that." Samir, now standing at the apartment door and anxious to go, cleared his throat noisily.

"Right then," Mustafa said. "Good night." But as he turned to leave he paused and stared into the kitchen.

"What is it?" Noor asked.

"There is a baby bottle on top of your refrigerator. You have a child?"

"Ah, no," Noor said. "My friend Hawwa left that here."

"Ah," Mustafa said. Then: "Do you want children?" The question just popped out of his mouth, and Mustafa, mortified, was aware of Samir shooting him a long strange look from the doorway.

But Noor was amused by the query. "Not tonight," she said laughing. "One day, certainly . . . But I am in no great hurry." She went on laughing, looking at him in that frank way she had, and Mustafa laughed too, shaking his head, feeling like the fool that he in fact was.

Samir cleared his throat again. "Can we go now?"

That night was the beginning of it, the end of it as well really, because although there were still many moments afterwards when Mustafa could have chosen to act differently, he had, on some fundamental level, made up his mind. The devil had whispered in his ear; he'd listened; the rest was just details. Even the surprise windfall from

Wajid's IPO offering, which Mustafa would willfully interpret as evidence that God wanted him to pursue this fantasy, was just another step on a path he had already started down.

Now, departing the House of Wisdom, he felt the old remorse tugging at him. Rather than return to headquarters with Samir and Amal, he told them to go on without him. "I'll be back later."

"Where are you going?" Amal asked, and Samir said, with far too much good humor, "To see a woman about a car, I bet."

"You know, Samir," Mustafa said, "you have a bigger mouth than Wajid sometimes."

"Mustafa . . ."

"Bah!" Mustafa flung up his hand in a rude gesture and stalked off.

The condominium he'd bought Noor as a bridal payment was in a building several blocks away. Mustafa had not been inside for several years. Noor had banished him, tired, she said, of being treated as an unindicted coconspirator in Fadwa's death. Mustafa didn't blame her, but neither could he bring himself to let her go. Instead of granting her the divorce she wanted, he'd allowed their marriage to continue on in limbo. Every now and again, when he was in the neighborhood and his conscience was preying on him, he'd come stand in her building courtyard awhile, trying to muster the words that would justify ringing the buzzer.

Today all the curtains in Noor's windows were drawn, a sure sign she was away—probably on assignment for FOX, which had hired her full-time.

"Your wife is not here."

Idris was sitting in a shady corner of the courtyard with a full tea service arranged on a table in front of him, his casual demeanor suggesting that he'd just happened to choose this spot for some late-morning refreshment. It was a nice bit of stagecraft, Mustafa thought; he recognized the tea set as having come from a café just across the street, but even so, Idris's people must have had to hustle to set this scene.

"Your wife is not here," Idris repeated. "Would you like to know where she is? And with whom?"

The appeal to jealousy not the best opener, though. "Is Al Qaeda offering marriage counseling now?"

"Mock if you wish. I've kept all my wives."

"High walls help with that no doubt." Mustafa took a seat and waited while Idris poured him a cup of tea. "I assume you are here to warn me off the investigation."

"We both know you can't drop it now that the president's involved," Idris said. "But you would be wise not to pursue it too diligently."

"Speaking of things we both know, that sort of wisdom isn't my strong point."

"Yes, I'd already concluded that threatening you would be counter-productive." Idris regarded him brightly over his teacup. "What were the other options, again? Delaying tactics, bribery, and extortion?"

Ah, thought Mustafa, now that really isn't smart. I already suspected the office was bugged, and confirming my paranoia does not impress me. But perhaps you're too prideful to realize that.

He said: "Try bribery. I'm curious to hear what inducement you would offer."

"A return to righteousness," Idris said instantly. "And the peace of mind that goes with it."

Mustafa smiled. "You can give me righteousness?"

"Do you remember how we met, Mustafa?"

"Yes, I remember it very well. We were in the schoolyard. You and your gang were picking on Samir and that other boy, the one with the stutter, what was his name?"

"Abd al Rahman."

"Yes."

"Yes," Idris said, "and you stepped up to defend them."

"For what little good it did. You beat up all three of us, as I recall."

"Of course we did. We were bigger and stronger. You knew we would beat you. But you stepped up anyway, without hesitation."

"And you find this admirable?" Mustafa said.

"To act without fear is an aspect of righteousness." Idris poured himself more tea, then went on: "You know, this theory of Farouk's, that guilt over the death of your wife has made you suicidal and reckless, I don't think it's true. I think you have always been reckless."

"I ask again: You find this admirable?"

"You have lost your way," Idris said. "You have taken a wrong turning and you are not now where you should be. You know this in your heart. But to return to God's path is a simple act of will, and you have a strong will. You could be a formidable holy warrior, if you chose. We could help you."

Mustafa shook his head in disbelief. "You are inviting me to join Al Qaeda?"

"This surprises you?"

"It confuses me."

"Why?"

"You say, because I once stood up to you in your wickedness, you now wish to be my mentor in righteousness. I find your reasoning . . . counterintuitive."

"I'm not the bully I was when you first met me," Idris said. "I have grown. Afghanistan changed me. Working with Senator Bin Laden has changed me even more. You really should meet him, Mustafa. He is a great man, a true soldier of God. He has plans for Arabia."

"I am sure he does," said Mustafa. "But I rather doubt there is a place for me in those plans."

"Mustafa—"

"Let us return to earth for a moment and talk about another holy warrior."

"Which one?"

"Gabriel Costello."

Idris frowned. "He was not a holy warrior."

"You know what happened to him."

"Yes." Unable to suppress a small grin, Idris said: "He killed himself."

"I think we both know that's not true," said Mustafa. "Costello was murdered."

"I know no such thing. Even if he didn't take his own life, the man was an enemy of God. To kill such a person is not murder."

"I disagree."

"Do you?" Idris said. "Was it murder when you shot that Lutheran?"

"Martin Hoffman posed an imminent threat to an innocent woman's life," Mustafa said. "Gabriel Costello was an unarmed prisoner, at the mercy of his killers."

"The man deserved to die."

"Did you kill him because he deserved it, or to shut him up?"

"I," Idris began, and then caught himself. "I do not understand you. How can you even care about these terrorists?"

"I have been asking myself the same question lately," Mustafa said. "I think the answer is that it's not really the terrorists I care about; I care about a world in which murder becomes a commonplace. You are correct, of course, that I've lost my way. But if you consider the nature of my transgression, you'll perhaps understand why I am wary of mistaking human passion for the will of God. So, no," he concluded, "I don't think I'd make a good Qaeda recruit."

"Then I return to my first point," Idris said, "which is that you are unwise to go against us. This is not a threat but a promise: If you push this investigation too hard, it will end badly, for you and anyone with you."

"We must both do what we think is right," Mustafa said. "How it ends is in God's hands. But remember, Idris, you are not God. Neither is your master." He stood up. "Peace be unto you."

THE LIBRARY OF ALEXANDRIA
A USER-EDITED REFERENCE SOURCE

Temporary Marriage

> This page contains **unverified legal claims**. Readers are urged to consult appropriate authorities before accepting such claims as definitive.

Temporary marriage is a marriage with a pre-set, limited duration. Upon the expiration of the initial marriage term, the husband and wife have the option to extend it for an additional limited term, or to convert it to a permanent marriage; if they choose not to do either of these things, the marriage is automatically dissolved, with no need for a formal divorce.

LEGAL AND SOCIAL STATUS OF TEMPORARY MARRIAGE

Although it is recognized under the laws of the UAS, Persia, and many other Muslim countries, the practice of temporary marriage is highly controversial and can carry a significant social stigma, particularly for the woman involved.

Almost all religious scholars agree that temporary marriage was permitted during at least part of the lifetime of the Prophet Mohammed (peace be unto him). However, most Sunnis believe that Mohammed ultimately prohibited the practice. Most Shia, on the other hand, attribute the prohibition to the second Caliph, Umar al Khattab, whose authority they do not recognize; thus the Shia position is that temporary marriage remains lawful, if not necessarily wise . . .

Women's rights advocates are also divided on the subject. Some radical feminists see in temporary marriage a means of reconciling women's sexual liberation with traditional Islam. But more mainstream feminists typically regard temporary marriage, and the similar practice of traveler's marriage, as bad bargains. According to Senator Anmar al Maysani (Unity-Iraq), "The cause of liberation would be better served by strengthening women's marriage rights generally."

PRACTICAL CHARACTERISTICS OF TEMPORARY MARRIAGE

- The defining characteristic of temporary marriage is, of course, the built-in time limit, which is chosen at the outset. There is no minimum duration, so a couple could decide to marry for a matter of hours, or even minutes—a fact made much of by critics who compare it to prostitution.

- Beyond the requirement to pick a time limit—and specify a bridal payment—the couple have considerable freedom in setting the terms of the marriage, including the degree of physical intimacy. Non-sexual marriages are possible. A couple wishing to learn whether they are compatible before making a permanent commitment, for example, might agree to live together without engaging in intercourse.

- Unlike a permanent marriage, a temporary marriage does not require witnesses or formal registration. Many authorities hold that the permission of the woman's father is required, especially if she is a virgin, but in practice this rule is often ignored . . .

- A temporary wife does not count towards the limit of four wives that a man may have at a given time.

- Upon the dissolution of the marriage, the woman must undergo a waiting period to ensure that she is not pregnant before she can marry again. This waiting period is waived if the marriage was not sexual, and of course in any event, the man is free to remarry immediately.

- Any children born of a temporary marriage become the responsibility of the father.

Back at headquarters, Farouk's secretary caught up to Amal in the hallway and pulled her aside.

"What is it, Umm Dabir?" Amal said.

"A very insistent man named Abu Salim," Umm Dabir said, handing her a message slip with a phone number written on it. "He called on Farouk's direct line while you were out, asking for you. I almost forwarded the call to your cell, but I decided I'd better check with you first."

"Why? Who is he?"

"He claims he's your ex-husband."

"My ex-husband?" Amal shook her head. "My ex-husband's name is Hassan." Hassan was a Jordanian state policeman she'd met on a kidnapping case several years ago. Their marriage had been brief, with Hassan unable, despite his claims of feminist enlightenment, to accept a wife whose work took her all over the country while he remained in Amman. "He did remarry recently, but last I heard he and his new wife were expecting a daughter, not a son. Are you sure he didn't say Abu Salimah?"

"I'm sure," Umm Dabir said. "I asked him if he was Hassan Bakri and he got upset with me. Then he said no, he was your *first* husband . . ." Her eyes widened.

"Really?" Amal's own face betrayed nothing other than a bemused puzzlement. "Tell me, did this Abu Salim's voice sound anything like Samir's? Or Abdullah's perhaps?"

"No. I mean, I don't think so . . . What, you think it's a prank call?"

"Well, obviously. Come, Umm Dabir, you've seen my personnel file. If I were a two-time divorcée, you'd know it."

"Well yes, of course, but . . . What kind of a joke is that?"

"A little boy's joke." Amal shrugged. "You know how it is. I thought I'd gotten beyond this sort of hazing, but apparently not." She held up the message slip. "Can I ask you to do me a favor and not tell anyone about this? A rumor will only encourage them."

"Of course," Umm Dabir said, incensed now on Amal's behalf. "What do you want me to do if this 'Abu Salim' calls back?"

"He won't," Amal said. "I'll make certain of that."

If ever she wanted to blame someone, she could always say it was Saddam Hussein's fault.

The year Amal went away to college was the same year the federal government indicted Saddam's uncle, Khairallah Talfah. Talfah, the former Baghdad mayor who'd resigned under a cloud of scandal, had been out of the public eye for some time, but the feds hadn't forgotten about him. They'd been quietly building a racketeering case against him and had caught a break when Hussein Kamel, who was Saddam's son-in-law and Talfah's former aide, agreed to become a government witness.

In addition to Talfah, the indictment also named the current mayor, the chief and deputy police commissioners, and several high-ranking Baathists. Saddam himself was not charged—not yet—but with Hussein Kamel talking to the Attorney General, it was only a matter of time.

All of which put Amal's father, Shamal, in a difficult position. Shamal was a Baghdad police sergeant and a Baath Union officer. It was not possible to be either of those things without also being somewhat corrupt, but where some men embraced corruption willingly, others did only what they had to do. Shamal belonged to the latter group, and he and a number of like-minded friends had talked privately for years about banding together to clean up the police force.

Now suddenly it was more than just talk. In the shake-up following the indictments, Shamal was offered a promotion to police captain and a corresponding increase in his union responsibilities. If he took the offer, there could be no more fence-sitting: He'd either have to declare openly as a reformer and risk the consequences, or admit he lacked the courage and pledge his loyalty to evil men.

Amal, only sixteen, was told none of this, but she could tell by the way her parents and her older brothers were acting that something serious was going on. One night she was awakened from a deep sleep by her mother, who told her to get dressed—they had guests. When Amal came downstairs, her father was sitting at the kitchen table with Saddam Hussein and his son Uday.

The Baath Union president was famous for his late-night calls on friends and allies—or people he hoped to make his allies. In interviews, he ascribed this habit variously to insomnia, a busy schedule that made daytime socializing difficult, and a desire for honesty. "People are more open with you in the small hours," he said.

This was Saddam's first such visit to Shamal. He'd come bearing gifts: a silver-plated service revolver and a case of whiskey. Shamal struggled to project an appropriate combination of emotions—honor at the social call, gratitude for the presents, blasé disregard for the felony violation—while remaining respectfully noncommittal about the proposed alliance.

It was a tough juggling act to pull off at 2 a.m., and Amal didn't get to see how it turned out. She and her siblings were only in the room for a few minutes, just long enough to be introduced, before her mother hustled them back to bed. As Amal left the kitchen she looked over her shoulder and saw Uday staring at her backside with a smile on his lips.

Several days later, her mother sat her down to talk about college. Amal still had another year of high school to finish, after which she'd been hoping to attend BU, but now her parents had come up with an altogether different plan. Amal's aunt Nida was on the board of the University of Lebanon, which had an early admissions program for gifted students. Given Amal's high grades, she'd surely qualify. She could start as a freshman this fall.

"But I don't have my high school diploma yet," Amal said, bewildered.

"You'll have to pass a test," her mother explained. "That's no problem, though—Nida will put you up over the summer and provide you with a tutor. She's already agreed." Before Amal could raise any other objections, her mother added: "Your father and I think it's a wonderful opportunity. You *will* take it."

Early one morning a few weeks later, Shamal and Amal climbed into the family station wagon and headed west along the interstate. Amal was full of questions she knew she couldn't properly ask; as they drove across Anbar Province she tried to think of some magic phrasing that would allow her to ask them anyway, but every time she thought she'd come up with an opening she'd take one look at her father's face and forget what she was going to say. Eventually, exhausted, she slipped into a doze. When she woke again, they were in Syria.

They stopped to eat at a diner outside Damascus and had what was technically a conversation, about the classes Amal was thinking of taking during her first semester. But the talk was all surface, and once they got back in the car they didn't speak again until they reached Beirut.

They arrived at Aunt Nida's in the late afternoon. Though they'd been on the road for ten hours, Shamal announced he wouldn't be staying; he had work the next day and needed to get back to Baghdad. Amal sensed he was less concerned about missing work than about having to explain where he'd been.

Shamal set Amal's bags on the sidewalk and kissed her on the forehead. "Be good," he told her. "Make us proud."

Amal opened her mouth to say "I will," but what came out was: "You too."

Aunt Nida was a successful businesswoman who'd gotten involved in politics and was now planning a run for the House of Representatives. She was a member of the Unity Party, the liberal, secular, pan-Arab coalition party founded in the late 1950s by Gamal Abdel Nasser. In Lebanon, Unity was opposed by not just one, but *two* Parties of God: the conservative National POG, which was dominated by Sunnis and the House of Saud, and the ultraconservative Lebanese POG, which was run almost exclusively by Shia.

The political intrigue involved in playing the two POGs off against one another made for some fascinating war stories, but left Nida with little spare time to act as a chaperone, especially once Amal (who'd aced her high school equivalency test) moved onto the U of L campus. Nida assigned one of her sons to check in on Amal periodically, but for the most part she was left to look after herself, in a way that would have been unimaginable had she remained in Baghdad.

Her two roommates were Jemila and Iman, both arts majors but otherwise as different as could be. Jemila, a Beirut native who was studying theater, was what was known in the parlance of the day as a "modern" girl, a term that could mean either "sophisticated free spirit," or, said another way, "whore." Jemila had a steady stream of boyfriends, and it was the boyfriends who most often used "modern" in its second sense—with a smile when Jemila first met them, and with anger or tears when, inevitably, she dumped them.

Iman came from Khafji, an oil town on the Gulf coast. She was studying to be a documentary filmmaker. Iman was also a "ninja": Outside the dorm and the women's gym where she took her exercise, she wore a black abaya with a niqab veil that left only her eyes visible. "Ninja," like "modern," was a term with multiple connotations, but anyone who assumed from her style of dress that Iman was a sheltered hick soon learned otherwise.

When Amal professed her ambition to become a cop like her dad, it was Iman who suggested she apply to the Bureau. "The ABI is more open to women than most local police forces," she said. "It still won't be easy, but you'll at least have a chance. And you'll get to chase bank robbers."

"It's not bank robbers I want to go after," Amal said. But the idea was a good one.

Iman took self-defense courses at the gym on Sunday afternoons. Amal began going with her. Then she heard about a West Beirut gun range offering an introductory women's pistol-shooting class, and on a whim decided to check it out. She turned out to be a natural with firearms.

Jemila meanwhile got the lead in a campus production of *Hair*. She convinced Amal to try out for a bit part in the play, that of an overzealous Halal agent. Amal wore a fake mustache and beard, and ran around stage during one of the musical numbers trying unsuccessfully to slip a burqa over Jemila's head.

On Friday nights when her mother called, Amal said nothing about these extracurricular activities. She felt a little guilty, but she also knew her mother wasn't telling her everything either. According to the national news, Baghdad was in an uproar: Thanks to the testimony of Hussein Kamel, Khairallah Talfah had been convicted on all counts, and the Attorney General was now talking openly about bringing charges against Saddam. This in turn led to a rash of Hussein Kamel jokes, like "What do Hussein Kamel and a migrating goose have in common? They're both found floating in the Tigris!"

Opening night of *Hair*, a student member of the Lebanese POG threw a smoke bomb onstage during the first act, and the theater had to be evacuated. As Amal stood outside with the rest of the cast waiting for the fire marshal to give the all clear, she noticed a handsome boy watching her from the edge of the crowd. He was laughing, and at first she thought he might be a friend of the smoke-bomber, but then he drew a finger across his upper lip and she realized the source of his amusement was her costume-mustache, which she still wore. Then she laughed too and he came over and introduced himself.

His name was Anwar. He was a senior, majoring in government. His family was originally from Iraq, but his father was a diplomat, so he'd spent most of his youth in Riyadh or abroad in Persia. It was while living in Tehran that he'd discovered a passion for the arts, not just theater and music but poetry. In fact he and some of his friends had an informal poetry club that met at a café on Tuesday and Thursday mornings. Perhaps Amal would like to drop by sometime and hear some of their verses?

She accepted his invitation, dragging Jemila to the café with her for moral support. She tried to get Iman to come along as well, but Iman declined, saying she didn't go on dates. When Amal insisted that it wasn't a date, just a "social gathering," Iman said, "I especially don't go on dates that aren't acknowledged as dates."

The poetry, most of which was in Farsi, wasn't very good—or if it was, Anwar's whispered Arabic translations didn't do it justice. Soon enough Jemila pronounced herself bored and left, but Amal stayed, enjoying the tickle of Anwar's breath in her ear, even though the words he spoke weren't that interesting. Afterwards he walked her to her next class and asked if he could see her again. She said yes.

They began meeting regularly, going on dates that weren't acknowledged as dates: picnics on the seawall that bordered the university; long walks through the city center, which after a decade-and-a-half-long recession was finally undergoing an economic revival, new buildings springing up daily. Amal met more of Anwar's friends, including a number of Americans—funny, good-natured people with hilarious accents. Years later, in the buildup to the invasion, she'd remember them and wonder if they were OK.

Anwar told her about his adventures as a diplomat's son and Amal shared some of Aunt Nida's political war stories. About her parents she was more circumspect, but she did eventually let on that her father was a Baghdad cop. Partly as a test, she told Anwar about her intention to become an ABI agent. She could tell from his reaction that he thought this was an odd career choice, but he didn't dismiss it. "Perhaps you'll visit me at the State Department when you come to Riyadh," he said smiling.

She invited him to come shooting with her. Anwar was *not* a natural with firearms, but he was a good sport, applauding as Amal hit the center of the target repeatedly while he largely failed to hit it at all. On the way back to campus from this outing, they stopped at a magazine shop. While Anwar bought cigarettes at the front counter, Amal wandered back to the shelf where they kept the out-of-state newspapers. That was where she saw the picture of her father, in uniform, on the steps of Baghdad city hall with a dozen other police captains. STANDING UP AGAINST CORRUPTION, read the headline on the *Baghdad Gazette*. SADDAM INDICTMENT EMBOLDENS REFORMERS, added the *Daily News*. The *Post's* headline was more sinister: THESE ARE THE ONES.

"Amal?" Anwar said, coming up beside her. "Are you all right?"

"Yes, I'm fine!" She pulled him away before he could see what she was looking at. It was the first time she'd ever taken his hand—and she didn't let go, even after the shop was far behind them.

In the days that followed there were other firsts. And so it happened that not long afterwards, on a morning when they both should have been in class, Amal found herself at their favorite picnic spot on the seawall listening to Anwar read a new poem, a proposal in verse. The key word in the poem—*sigheh*—was not one of the handful of Farsi terms she'd already learned from him, but from the context and the passionate way in which he spoke, she assumed he was asking her to marry him. And he was, sort of.

"Temporary marriage?" The concept, essentially a love affair with God's blessing, was straight out of a trashy romance novel. It also fell squarely into the category of things no smart or self-respecting girl would even consider.

Amal didn't know what to make of Anwar's proposal. It was as though he'd used an epithet whose meaning was ambiguous. Did he take her for a fool? Did he think she was a whore? Or was he really, in his own strange way, trying to be sweet? Anwar meanwhile interpreted Amal's dismay as a sign that he'd mortally offended her, and tried to take his words back. "Please," he begged, "forgive me! Forget I said anything!"

But Amal—recalling his breath in her ear, the touch of his hand—wasn't so sure she wanted to forget it. She needed to think it over some more.

She considered going to the campus Shia mosque for advice, but the place was a POG hangout and thus not exactly welcoming. Instead, she talked to her roommates.

Jemila was dismissive: "Don't be ridiculous, Amal! If you want to sleep with him, just sleep with him." At first Amal thought this was just Jemila being modern, but then she realized there was more to it than that. Jemila was Sunni, and Sunnis believed that temporary marriage was forbidden. Of course Sunnis like all Muslims also believed that sex outside of marriage was forbidden, but Jemila apparently made a distinction between sins she liked and sins she found distasteful. "I mean really, it's kind of gross if you think about it. Like being an actual prostitute."

"What are you saying, Jemila?"

"Well . . ." Jemila grew defensive, recognizing she was on shaky ground. "It's just, to make a formal bargain . . . It's like you're renting yourself out . . ."

Amal stared pointedly at the gold bracelet on Jemila's wrist. "So says the girl who expects gifts from all her boyfriends."

"Those are *gifts,* not contractual obligations!"

Iman wasn't surprised by Jemila's attitude towards temporary marriage. What surprised her was that Anwar didn't share it. "Isn't he a Sunni, too?"

"He's Sunni, but his grandmother is Shia."

"My grandmother is a Jew," Iman said. "But you don't see me celebrating Yom Kippur."

"Anwar knows I'm Shia," Amal said. "And he respects me, so—" She stopped, because Iman was laughing. "Fine. You think he just wants to have sex with me, is that it?"

"If he were Shia, I would definitely think that. And I still think it's the most likely explanation, but there's a difference: A Shia boy who proposes temporary marriage to get sex may honestly believe he's following God's law. A Sunni boy knows he's being cynical."

"I'm glad you think so highly of Anwar."

"It's not the only possible explanation. I can think of other reasons why a Sunni might propose temporary marriage, but they're all worse."

"What other reasons?"

"He might be an idiot," Iman said. "Or mentally ill."

"Oh, wonderful. Anything else?"

"The worst reason of all: He might be in love with you. Maybe what he's really after is a permanent marriage, but he's afraid you're not ready, so this is his way of easing up to it."

"You call that the *worst* reason?" Amal said. "How could Anwar loving me be a bad thing?"

"Because you don't love him," said Iman. "I've listened to you talk about him, Amal. You *like* Anwar. You enjoy his company and the attention he pays you. He distracts you from worrying about your family. But you don't love him, and I don't think a temporary marriage—or an affair—is going to change that."

"Well, it doesn't matter anyway," Amal said. "I mean, it's not as if I were going to say yes to Anwar's proposal."

"You haven't told him no yet, though."

"No, but I'm going to." And then, as if to demonstrate that there was an idiot here, but it wasn't Anwar, she added: "Don't worry, Iman. I know what I'm doing."

The number on Umm Dabir's message slip had a Baghdad area code rather than the Riyadh code Amal would have expected, and as she dialed she entertained the notion that this really was just a prank of some sort. But the voice that answered said "Al Rasheed Hotel," and when she asked to speak to Abu Salim bin Amjad she was put straight through. The next voice she heard was Anwar's.

He told her he was in town for a conference. He told her he needed to see her. He wouldn't tell her why, but he also wouldn't take no for an answer, and any impulse Amal might have had to hang up on him was checked by the thought that he'd just call Farouk's office again, or perhaps show up in person.

She named a restaurant a few blocks from the hotel and agreed to meet him that evening at half past six. She arrived early, and like a Bureau agent setting up a sting, parked her car across the street, facing the direction of his most likely approach.

She'd run his name on the office computer. Sure enough he was a federal employee, though not with the State Department as he'd always planned—his posting was in Commerce, in the Patent and Trademark Office. His wife, Nasrin, was Persian, the fourth daughter of a former trade delegate. They had two daughters of their own . . . and one son.

Abu Salim. Salim's dad. Of course it was the most natural thing in the world for a father to take the name of his firstborn son. But when the son is the product of a marriage that should never have happened and a woman who rejected you . . . Who does that? What does it mean? What do you want from me, Anwar?

Amal had been in the fifth month of her sigheh when Aunt Nida found out. Amal never learned who tipped Nida off, though she suspected Iman, in an act of kindness, had made a phone call.

That day she'd gone to the seawall to walk and think about drowning herself. Even in her worst despair, suicide wasn't really in Amal, but another idea—of fleeing across the sea to some country where no one knew her—appealed more strongly, and if she'd come upon an unguarded boat she might have taken it.

Instead she went back to the dorm. A girl sitting in the lobby stared at her as she came in, and Amal walked by swiftly, drawing her abaya around her. To conceal her weight gain she'd been dressing more and more conservatively, but not even a burqa would hide her belly-bump much longer. Already there were whispers.

Anwar wanted to do more than whisper. "Let's declare our marriage openly and move in together," he said. "We're in love, what's the problem?" The problem? The problem was a future in which Amal ended up living in Riyadh, not as an ABI agent but as a suburban housewife. A future in which instead of helping her father chase Baath out of Iraq, she went shopping at the Hayat Mall. Oh, and they weren't in love. Anwar was insane, and Amal was stupid.

She opened the door to her room and Aunt Nida was inside, sitting on her bed and smoking a cigarette. Amal stopped short, in panic trying to come up with some lie to tell, but it was pointless; she could see on Aunt Nida's face that Nida already knew everything.

"Amal," she said. "I'm very disappointed in you." This mild rebuke, the only one Nida would offer, struck Amal like a blow to the head. She didn't pass out, not exactly, but the terror she'd just barely been holding in check rose up and cloaked the world in a haze.

When the haze lifted, Amal was sitting down and Nida was interrogating her.

"How many months?"

"One more," Amal said numbly. "The sigheh ends in thirty-four days."

"Not the marriage. The pregnancy."

"Oh." Amal reddened. "I don't know. It's been three or four months I guess."

"Three, or four?"

"I don't . . . Four. I think four."

"Ah." Tradition held that God gave a fetus its soul a hundred and twenty days after conception. In civil terms, this translated into abortion being legal during the first four months of pregnancy and expensive thereafter. "Does the boy know?"

"Anwar? Yes, he knows." She almost laughed. "He thinks it's great news."

"And you?" said Aunt Nida. "Do you want to stay with this boy, Amal? Raise a family with him?"

"No." No hesitation. "I want—" I want the last five months back. I want the future I had before I did this stupid, stupid thing. I wish, I wish. "No," she repeated.

"All right then," Nida said.

"All right?" Amal couldn't imagine those words applying to her.

"I'll talk to my friends in the capital, see who knows his family." At the mention of family Amal flinched, which Nida acknowledged with a nod. "I will have to tell your mother, too, of course."

It wasn't her mother Amal was most concerned about. "And father?"

"Shamal has other matters to deal with, as you know. Perhaps we need not distract him with this just now. No promises," Nida added. "We'll see what your mother says." Looking around the room: "OK, let's get you packed."

"Packed?"

"Of course. You can't stay here, looking like that."

"But . . . my studies . . ."

"Those will have to wait awhile." Nida had on her game face now, the expression she wore when she plotted against the POGs. You could almost see the stratagems queuing up behind her eyes. "Don't worry, we'll work something out . . ."

Amal spent the next week at her aunt's house, not going outside, not even looking out the windows. One day there was a loud banging at the front door; Amal hid upstairs and listened while Anwar argued furiously with Aunt Nida. He came back again the next day and that time Nida had her bodyguards deal with him.

A few days after that, she sat Amal down for a talk. "I've spoken to the boy's family. The father is a reasonable sort. He agrees it's best we pretend this whole thing never happened." Then the bad news: "The boy is being much more difficult. He is afflicted with a combination of rebelliousness and romanticism. Too much time hanging around artists in Tehran I suppose."

"Please," Amal said, fearing the worst. "Tell me I don't have to stay with him."

"No. The marriage is finished. Well, soon enough. But there is something else the boy wants. Something he is willing to defy his own father to have."

Amal, feeling a kick, dropped a hand to her stomach.

She couldn't give birth in her aunt's house. With Aunt Nida's election campaign gathering steam, her opponents would be trying to dig up any dirt they could. But Nida was owed favors in some unlikely quarters; she made a call and arranged for Amal to complete her pregnancy in a place the Party of God would never look.

The convent was on the coast, an hour's drive from Beirut. Amal never learned the name of the place or of most of the women who lived there. With the exception of a Sister Demiana who met her at the gate and showed her where she'd be sleeping, the nuns had all taken vows of silence.

Amal was given a room in the convent's north tower that faced the sea. The view was nice, but she could have done without the icon of Saint Mary, the irony of which was not lost on her. Umm Isa, Amal prayed that first day, my request is simple: Please stop staring at me. Later, as her confinement dragged on, she asked a different favor: Can we speed this up somehow?

The baby did arrive early, though Amal's labor lasted an entire night. Towards the end of it she grew delirious and imagined herself in two places at once: the clean bright hospital ward to which Sister Demiana had delivered her, and another, much dimmer and lonelier room, with not even a saint's portrait for company, just a flickering bulb that transformed itself into a tall and smokeless flame. "Push," said a voice—the midwife's, her own—and Amal pushed.

By September she was back at Aunt Nida's, filling out a stack of forms for her readmission to school. Anwar was gone. The baby, whose face Amal had never seen, was gone too. Amal had a strict curfew now and a paid chaperone to accompany her everywhere, but otherwise it really was as if the whole thing had never happened. Best of all, Amal's father had still not been told, and it seemed more and more likely he never would be.

Amal knew she should be grateful and she was. She was also terrified. Good fortune doesn't have to be matched by bad, but Amal very much feared this was one of those times when it would be. And it wasn't hard to imagine how the scales might be balanced.

On the eve of Saddam Hussein's trial, Hussein Kamel had disappeared. The rumor was that Kamel, faced with a lifetime in hiding, had decided at the last moment on an ill-advised attempt to reconcile with his father-in-law. He'd slipped the marshals assigned to protect him and gone to Saddam to beg forgiveness—with predictable results. Absent Kamel's testimony, the case against Saddam collapsed; federal prosecutors threw up their hands and retreated to Riyadh, leaving the local cops who'd defied Saddam standing naked and exposed, like the vanguard of an army of liberation that had never arrived.

"Father?" Amal said, speaking to Shamal by phone the day after Hussein Kamel's body was found. "Father, are you OK?"

"Yes, we are all fine here!" He had to shout over the background noise. He was calling from a pay phone, no longer trusting their home line. "It's so good to hear your voice!"

"Father, are you coming to see me?"

"Your mother will be visiting you soon," Shamal said. "Your brothers too. I don't think I can get away right now . . ."

"No, father, you have to come too!"

"I have things I have to do here, Amal. I will see you when I can. I miss you."

"I miss you too, father," Amal said, and began to cry.

. . . and now she was crying again, in this other world, the city of the future where her father was no more.

Sunlight flashed off a passing car and she saw Anwar across the street. He hadn't seen her yet, and as he made his way along the sidewalk checking signs for the restaurant, Amal hurried to compose herself. The man from my past, she thought, stepping out to call his name. Just not the right one.

"You're looking well," Anwar said.

They sat in a back corner of the restaurant, untouched menus and water glasses on the table between them. Already Amal regretted the choice of meeting place, with its implication of a long and leisurely conversation. She just wanted to find out what Anwar was after—what it was going to take to make him go away—and then get out of here.

Anwar for his part seemed equally uncomfortable. His smile was forced and there was a pained rigidity to his posture, as though a mild electrical current were passing through the chair in which he sat. But rather than hurry to come to the point, he insisted on making small talk.

"So," he said, trying another gambit, "you actually did it. Became a federal agent, I mean."

"Yes," Amal said.

"That's great!" A waiter passed by, carrying food to another table, and Anwar reached for his menu. "Are you hungry? Should we—"

"Anwar," Amal said sharply.

"Right." He dropped the menu and lifted his hands in a gesture of surrender. "OK."

"Please tell me what this is about. You call my office, my *boss's* office—"

"I'm sorry about that," Anwar said. "That was stupid, I know. I was afraid you wouldn't talk to me."

"So you decided to call my boss? Did you think embarrassing me would make me more willing to speak to you? Or was it supposed to be a threat?"

"No! No, I . . . I don't know what I was thinking. But this is important, Amal. I needed to see you."

"Well, here I am," Amal said. "Now what is this about?"

"It's about our son." He looked at her in sudden defiance, daring her to challenge him on his choice of pronoun. "*Our* son . . . He's done something very foolish, something I can't undo on my own."

"What has he done?"

"I think he's trying to follow in your footsteps."

"What does that . . . Anwar, you didn't—"

"No." Anwar shook his head. "He knows nothing about you. He thinks Nasrin is his mother, and she, she loves him very much. But there must be something of you in his blood. From the time he first learned to talk, he's wanted to do something exciting with his life, something dangerous. As a boy he would go on about how he was going to be a test pilot, or a deep-sea diver, or a police detective. Then, after November 9, he came up with a new career goal: soldier. On his thirteenth birthday, he told Nasrin and me how he was going to go to America to fight for his country, bring democracy and Islam to the Christians. We tried to talk him out of it. We told him if he really wanted to make the world a safer place, he should become a diplomat like his grandfather." He smiled ruefully. "A hopeless argument . . . Nasrin and I consoled ourselves with the thought that the war would be over by the time Salim was old enough to enlist, and anyway he'd probably grow out of the idea. And he seemed to, or at least he stopped talking about it.

"Then last year he turned eighteen and left for college. I was so proud when he chose U of L, it never occurred to me the real reason he wanted to go to Beirut was because the Marine training center is there. The friend who was supposed to be Salim's roommate played along, taking phone messages and forwarding his emails, so we wouldn't realize he was at boot camp. Nasrin did get suspicious when Salim came home for winter break—he'd lost weight, and his hair was very short—but he told her he'd joined the wrestling team. Then in May, after he'd finished his advanced training and was about to deploy, he sent us this letter . . ." He drew two wrinkled sheets of paper from his suit jacket. "You should read it," he said, setting the letter on the table, but Amal made no move to take it. "Salim apologizes for misleading me and for not being the person I wanted him to be." Anwar looked at her. "His choice of words is . . . very familiar."

Amal closed her eyes. "Anwar," she said, "I am sorry if my blood caused your son to act against your wishes. But I don't see—"

"Salim is in Washington now. Posted to the Green Zone. They say it's relatively safe there, but no place in America is truly safe. Not for a Muslim boy who craves excitement."

"What is it you want from me, Anwar? What is it you think I can do?"

"Get Salim transferred back to Arabia, of course."

"How?"

"Your mother is a senator."

"My mother!" Amal laughed. "Do you know what my mother will say if I tell her you came to see me?"

"You don't have to mention me at all. Ask her to do this as a favor to you. It's a small thing."

"Why don't you ask your father, then? Surely an ex-diplomat has friends who can do such favors."

"I did ask him," Anwar told her. "And he is trying, but his friends all supported the invasion, and those who still have influence are worried about the appearance of hypocrisy . . ."

"Maybe they should be worried about that," Amal said.

Anwar's face reddened. "How can you be so selfish?"

"Selfish? Do not speak to me of selfishness!"

"I know what you think of me, Amal," Anwar said. "You think that when I insisted you give birth to Salim, it was because I thought it would make you stay with me. Well, you are right: At the time, I did think that. But that wasn't my only reason. I believed then, as I know now, that Salim was a human soul who deserved to be born for his own sake . . ."

"An easy thing for a man to say."

"An easy thing for a father to say," Anwar countered. "Salim is a good boy, Amal. I have tried to be a good father to him. You don't know, I've made sacrifices . . . And I would do it all again, and more if I could . . .

"I don't ask you to feel the same way," he continued. "Regard Salim as the stranger he is to you. A stranger's life is still worth protecting. Isn't that what you do in Homeland Security, save the lives of people you don't even know? Do that, then. Save one more."

"And if I can't?" Amal said. "Or won't?"

"Then peace be unto you," Anwar replied. "If your answer is no, I'll go my way and trouble you no more. Perhaps my father can still do something . . . But please, Amal. In God's name, I beg of you, don't just say no. Look into your heart first. God willing, you'll find some mercy there. A little mercy for our child, that's all I ask."

He stood abruptly, trembling on the verge of tears, and walked away, barreling past a waiter who was just then coming to check on them. The breeze of his sudden departure lifted the pages of the letter that he had left behind on the table. Seeing this, Amal started to call him back, but he was already at the door and anyway she thought better of it. She watched him go out, watched through the restaurant window as he marched off, head bowed, back the way he had come.

"Ma'am?" The waiter, a Pashtun, stood beside the table with his hands folded, looking embarrassed for her.

"It's all right," she said. "Can you get me some coffee?"

"Of course . . ." Amal watched him hurry away too.

Then she picked up Salim's letter and began to read.

The Library of Alexandria
A USER-EDITED REFERENCE SOURCE

Failed search result

You searched for: "Gay rights movement"

There is no article with this title. If you are a **registered user,** you may create one.

PARTIAL MATCHES:

<u>Sodom and Gomorrah</u> – 91.5%

<u>Crimes against nature</u> – 78.9%

<u>Feminism</u> – 65.2%

<u>European monastic orders</u> – 42.3%

<u>Honor killing</u> – 22.4%

I he young woman sat before the imam with her head bowed. "My uncle is no longer my uncle," she said. "He stays out all night at jazz clubs, gambling and drinking alcohol. He is cruel to my aunt—he won't go to the mosque anymore, and mocks her when she does. He's stopped praying . . ."

"Sadly, what you describe is not unfamiliar to me," the imam said. "These days, all too many children of Islam have been seduced by the modern world."

"No!" The woman looked up suddenly, eyes wide. "No, you don't understand! My uncle would *never* abandon his faith!"

"But . . ."

"The man living in our house, pretending to be my uncle, is *not my uncle*. He's someone else. Perhaps . . . some *thing* else."

Poor doomed girl, Samir thought, as this scene played out on the break room TV. By the time the imam next saw her, she'd be a pod person, worldly and soulless, her chaste headscarf exchanged for a decadent '50s hairstyle. The imam would fare little better: Locked in the muezzin's tower of his own mosque, fighting sleep, he'd leap to his death rather than be turned. And so it would be left to the imam's son—a dissolute jazz saxophonist, played by an improbably young Omar Sharif—to defeat the alien menace. Returning to his faith in the last reel, he'd load up a truck with explosives and drive through the gates of the dockside warehouse from which the invaders were preparing to infect all Arabia.

Samir could remember staying up late to watch *Invasion of the Body Snatchers* with his father when he was just six years old. He'd huddled close to his father's side and covered his face during the scary parts, then cheered as the tide turned against the invaders. Good times.

The film had been remade in color in the late 1970s, with the Israeli actor Leonard Nimoy playing the part of the doomed imam. The remake had attracted controversy for its more explicit sexuality— which made the "worldliness" of the original *Body Snatchers*' pod people seem quaint—and also for its more pessimistic ending. In the new *Body Snatchers,* the attempt to stop the invaders failed. The closing shot showed the imam's son marching in a crowd, emitting the characteristic shriek of a pod convert. The implication, that aliens could actually conquer Islam—that God would *allow* that—struck a number of real-life imams and sheikhs as blasphemous. There were calls to ban the film and demonstrations outside some theaters that showed it.

Samir caught the remake several years later, at a midnight showing on the BU campus. He didn't care for it. By then he was struggling with his own alien invasion—physical and emotional impulses that he'd long been aware of, but could no longer deny. The movie's theme cut too close to home, and the downbeat ending upset him as much as it had the clerics.

He still loved the old black-and-white version, though.

Abdullah came in the break room in search of coffee just as Omar Sharif was preparing his final assault on the invaders' warehouse stronghold. "Hard at work, I see."

Samir held up his cell phone. "I'm waiting on a call from an informant."

"Uh-huh." On screen, Sharif finished wiring up the explosives in the back of the truck and got behind the wheel. "Wow," Abdullah said. "Talk about a movie that plays differently now."

"Nah, Sharif's a good guy," Samir said. "And he's no suicide bomber."

"Are you sure? I thought he sacrificed himself to kill the aliens."

"No, he jumps out of the truck at the last second. Here, watch . . ."

The truck crashed through a barricade and accelerated along a pier towards the warehouse. Then the film hit a splice and they were looking at a long shot of the warehouse blowing up.

"Wait a minute," Samir said.

Abdullah laughed. "Edited for television."

"No, that's not right. It must be a defective copy or something. Just wait—he's in the water, and he comes out of the surf and Faten Hamama is waiting for him . . ."

It didn't happen. The destruction of the warehouse went on and on, the same explosions looping several times while martial music played, and then the words THE END appeared.

"That's not right," Samir said. "Omar Sharif survives. He gets the girl!"

"Yeah, well." Abdullah shrugged. "It's just a movie, dude."

"But that isn't how it ends!"

His cell phone rang.

Abdullah, in no hurry to get back to whatever task was keeping him here after dark, followed Samir to the elevators. "So you're going to meet with the guy?"

"What guy?" Samir said.

"Your informant."

"Ah. No. Turns out it was a waste of time. He just called to say he couldn't find out what I needed."

"Well if you're not busy then, you want to go grab some dinner? Or maybe"—Abdullah looked hopeful—"hit a club? I'm supposed to be babysitting a wiretap, but now that Farouk's gone home I was thinking I'd put the machines on automatic for a few hours."

"You know I'd love to," said Samir. "But I'm actually not feeling too well. I'm going to go home and get to bed early for once."

Samir's "informant" was actually Isaac, his former colleague from

Halal Enforcement. Isaac was still at Halal; these days he headed a task force that was conducting a probe of the Baghdad PD's vice division. Between his monitoring of the vice squad's activities and his knowledge of Halal's own operations, Isaac was able to predict with near-perfect accuracy which of Baghdad's rat cellars, brothels, and other illegal establishments were liable to be raided on any given night. Earlier today Samir had forwarded his old friend an email joke—their prearranged signal that he was planning to go out. Once Isaac had the night's vice raid schedule, he went to a pay phone, called Samir's cell, and, without identifying himself, recited a list of target neighborhoods to avoid. Isaac did not ask, and Samir did not tell, what sort of illicit entertainment he'd be seeking. But Samir was pretty sure Abdullah wouldn't be into it.

He drove home to the Kadhimiyah district apartment where he'd been living ever since his divorce. He showered and changed clothes, then pulled all of the ID out of his wallet, lingering for a moment over a snapshot of his twin sons, Malik and Jibril. The boys, ten years old now, lived with their mother in Basra.

Samir left the snapshot with the pile of his ID and grabbed a driver's license with a fake name. The phony license was primarily a good luck charm—if he got into trouble tonight, the thing most likely to get him out was cash. He made sure he had plenty of that, too.

He slipped out of the apartment building through the back door, walked to a Baghdad Transit stop several blocks away, and caught a bus across the river. At Antar Square in Adhamiyah he switched to the subway. Descending into the station he glimpsed a funhouse reflection of himself in a security mirror. Past the turnstile, the darkened glass of a smoke shop presented him with another reflection; though less distorted than the first, the image still seemed like that of a stranger. It was the way he was carrying himself, he knew: Along with his identification, Samir had left behind his usual swagger.

He boarded a southeast-bound number 6 train, choosing a car

whose only other occupant was a long-haired BU student reading a biology textbook. Samir sat across from him and waited, smiling, to see if he'd make eye contact. But the boy only burrowed deeper into his book.

The door at the far end of the subway car slid open and a transit cop entered. As he came down the car, rapping his nightstick against the empty seats, Samir straightened up and put on his day-face for a moment. The cop gave him a look but walked past without saying anything.

At the Muadham Gate station three men boarded the train together, all wearing the black uniform of the Mahdi Army's Guardian Angel street patrol. The transit cop, making another pass through the car, pulled up short and raised his nightstick; but when all three Angels turned towards him, he reconsidered his options and stepped off onto the platform just as the train doors were closing. Samir, not quick enough to disembark, instead stood up and moved to the next car. Looking back, he saw the Angels approach the long-haired student, one of them reaching out to flick the locks brushing his collar.

Two stops later, the conductor announced the transfer point for the Sadr City El. When the subway got underway again, Samir took another look back into the adjoining car. The Angels and the student were gone, but the textbook lay on the floor, broken-spined. Samir watched it shuddering with the motion of the train.

He might have become a sailor if he weren't so afraid of drowning.

Samir's Uncle Zuhair—actually a cousin of his father's—had been in the merchant navy. No one ever called him Sinbad, but like David Cohen he was a handsome man, so it was something of a curiosity that he never married. Whenever he was asked about this, Uncle Zuhair would say that he was married—to the sea. If the questioner was male, he might add a ribald joke about the hundreds of "ports" he had visited in his career.

Even now, knowing firsthand how far a man will go to hide his true nature, Samir had a hard time believing that his uncle was anything but an itinerant heterosexual who happened to love the smell of salt air. It would have been a fantastic cover. But Samir's sole experience with deepwater travel, during a high school field trip to Kuwait City, had been a nightmare: The tour boat that was taking the class out to Failaka Island had gotten caught in a storm, and with the waters too rough for safe docking, they'd been forced to ride it out. Samir had thought for sure they would capsize, and when they finally made it back to port he swore he would never go through that again.

If he couldn't share Uncle Zuhair's profession, he could still adopt other aspects of his lifestyle. For most of his youth, Samir had been overweight, but towards the end of high school he began to work out, and his new physique, along with the rough sense of humor he had developed as a defense mechanism, proved attractive to a certain kind of girl. At BU, Samir cultivated a reputation as a ladies' man. It wasn't a complete charade, but he routinely exaggerated his exploits, at times recklessly endangering the reputations of the women involved. He felt bad about that, but he was terrified and desperate to hide what he was—at first from himself, and then later, when self-denial became impossible, from his friends and his family.

For a while he lived two lives, in two separate worlds. He knew he couldn't go on playing a womanizer forever: As a man of the land, not the sea, he was expected to get married. The prospect wasn't entirely unpleasant. He liked kids and thought he'd make a good father. As for the husband part of it, well, the movies and soap operas he relied on for advice in this matter all suggested that a good wife could work miracles of transformation. Samir doubted that even a great wife could make him truly enthusiastic about women, but he hoped that she could at least curb his lust for men.

In his senior year he got engaged to a fellow student, a chemistry major named Sabirah. Their betrothal, rather than magically curing him of his vice, only made it worse: As the wedding date neared, Samir began acting like a glutton taking his last pass through an all-you-can-eat buffet. When Sabirah confronted him about the fact that he was never home at night when she called him, he lied, confessing that he'd been seeing other women. He begged for another chance, but his lack of conviction was evident and Sabirah broke it off with him.

He tried again a couple of years later with Asriyah, a Halal switchboard operator. Asriyah, while perhaps not as smart as Sabirah, was a good deal more perceptive, and guessed the truth about Samir's infidelities. She could have ruined him but chose to be merciful, supporting his public explanation of their breakup.

After two spoiled engagements Samir had a new reputation, one that made it much easier to remain unmarried without raising suspicion. Sometimes friends and relatives would take pity on him and try to fix him up with women who, for various reasons, couldn't afford to be choosy about their prospects, but through a practiced obnoxiousness, Samir managed to keep even these women at bay.

He met Najat around the same time Mustafa met Noor. She was a new tenant in his building, and he got to know her after helping carry some packages up to her apartment. Najat was a Gulf War widow whose husband had been killed by friendly fire on the outskirts of New Orleans. She'd been alone since his death, but was thinking of getting married again. The way she said this—"I'm thinking of getting married again"—as though contemplating a business deal or a career move, piqued Samir's interest. Marriage as a formal arrangement rather than a romantic adventure: That might suit his needs. But he wasn't able to bargain in good faith, and Najat showed glimmers of the same perceptiveness Asriyah had had, so he didn't pursue it.

Two things eventually changed his mind. The first was a holiday visit to see his sister Johara. Johara and her husband had just had a baby boy—their third—and holding the infant in his arms awakened Samir's paternal longing. Johara's husband, seeing his expression, said, "You really should marry, Samir. You could be a daddy too."

The other factor was Mustafa's announcement that he was going to marry Noor. This was a crazy decision, as even Mustafa seemed to recognize, and it was even crazier that Samir would allow it to influence his own behavior. But the night he heard the news, Samir had a dream in which he was being questioned before a grand jury. His inquisitor, who bore a resemblance to his old grade school nemesis Idris Abd al Qahhar, wanted to know why he was still single. "Your best friend has two wives," the inquisitor said, "while you have none. What is the meaning of this riddle? What defect are you hiding?" Samir looked over at the section of the seating area reserved for upcoming witnesses and saw Asriyah, her eyes full of secret knowledge. He woke up gasping.

The next day he ran into Najat in the elevator and asked her if she was still thinking about getting married.

A week before Samir and Najat's wedding day, Halal raided the home of a bookkeeper in Adhamiyah. The bookkeeper, who unwisely decided to test his quick-draw skills against the agents who broke down his door, did not survive, but they managed to get his laptop computer intact.

Back at headquarters, it took Isaac all of half an hour to guess the laptop's password—the bookkeeper's father's name, followed by the bookkeeper's mother's name, followed by the bookkeeper's own birth date, backwards—and another hour to go through the files. By then most of the other agents had gone out for a post-raid dinner; only Samir, who'd gotten hung up booking some other seized items into evidence, was still around.

"What's wrong?" Samir said, seeing Isaac's expression as he came out of his office. "Don't tell me the encryption defeated you."

"No, I got in," Isaac said. "I found a list of payoffs to Baghdad PD officers—including that patrolman you suspect in the Ghazi al Tikriti murder."

"Well, that's great, man! Why the long face?"

Isaac pulled up a chair beside Samir's desk. "I found another file as well," he said. "Payoffs to federal agents. Including Halal."

"Ah," Samir said, feeling the same nervous flutter he always did when the subject of corruption came up. Though he'd never taken a bribe, like every Halal agent he'd committed other infractions— sampling the wares of the bootleggers they arrested, now and then taking a bottle home with him, or when they found cash, letting a few bills stick to his palms on the way down to evidence. In fact at this very moment he was sitting on five hundred riyals that had, until a few hours ago, been in the dead bookkeeper's wall safe. A little wedding bonus. "So who's on the list?" he asked Isaac. "Anyone I know?"

"No one on our team, thank God," Isaac said. "But you know Habib Murad?"

"Yeah, sure." Habib worked upstairs, in the department that handled confidential informants. Samir actually knew him quite well— and not just from work.

Isaac ran a hand through his hair. "I fucking hate this. You know I'm a team player, right? And it's not like my own hands are spotless. With small stuff, I'm happy to look the other way. But if a guy in the CI's office is taking Saddam's money, he could be getting people killed. I can't look away from murder."

"No," Samir said. "Of course not."

"Right, of course not." Isaac laughed, then sighed. "All right," he said, standing up, "let me go report this before I lose my nerve."

Samir watched him walk out. Then he got up himself, and went to find a pay phone.

The following evening Samir stopped on his way home to drop off a check at the hall where the wedding reception was due to be held. As he was getting back into his car, Habib Murad drove up alongside him and gestured for him to follow.

They drove to a nearby parking garage. Habib went all the way to the top level, which was deserted at that hour. By the time he turned off his engine and opened his door, Samir was already coming around the car. He dragged Habib out by the collar and began pummeling him.

"Hey!" Habib shouted, putting his arms up to block the blows. "Knock it off! I just want to talk! Hey! *Hey!*"

Samir shoved him back and drew his pistol. "What the fuck are you doing here?" he demanded. "All of Halal is looking for you."

"I know, I got your message . . ." Eyeing the gun warily: "It's not just Halal. Saddam knows you have the bookkeeper's list and he's cleaning house. Anybody on there who's not already in custody is due to have a bad accident. They'd have got me already if not for your warning."

"Why are you here, Habib?"

"To thank you for saving my ass."

"To thank me! You think I did it for you?"

"No, I can see that was too much to hope for," Habib said, with a trace of bitterness. "But if you did it to protect yourself, you're a fool. Go ahead, threaten me, but it's true! What were you afraid I was going to do, out you as a faggot to the DA as part of some deal? How paranoid do you have to be to think they'd even care about that?"

Samir shrugged. "Who knows what you might try, if you get desperate enough? A guy who'd throw in with Saddam—"

"Yeah, and if I wanted to screw you over, that's who I'd betray you to. Halal would kick you out for being gay. Big deal. But Saddam? If he knew? He'd put you to work, just like he put me to work. Yeah, that's right, smart guy," Habib said nodding. "That's why I did it."

Samir took a step back. "When?" he said.

"A few months ago. Right after you broke up with me, as a matter of fact." He looked away. "I went home with the wrong guy. They got pictures. They said they'd tell my parents if I didn't play along."

"But the bookkeeper's list . . . They're paying you!"

"Of course they're paying me. They pay everybody—and once you take the money, they've got that to hold over your head, too. I tell you what, I'm actually glad this happened. I'd been thinking of running anyway. Of course I'd hoped to have a bit more cash saved up before I did it."

"So that's why you've come to me? You want money?"

"No," Habib said, and once again there was bitterness in his voice. Then, saying, "Don't shoot me," he reached into his jacket for a blue envelope marked POSEIDON LINES. Inside the envelope were two ferry tickets from Haifa to Piraeus; the departure date was three days from now.

"What is this?" Samir said.

"An invitation."

"A—"

"I still like you, Samir," Habib said. "I know it's a long shot, but it'd be nice to run away with someone I like, and I thought, maybe you didn't warn me *just* for your own sake . . ."

"Are you insane?" said Samir. "Did you really think for one second that I would throw away my whole life, to—"

"We could have a life in Greece. A better one, in some ways. You still have to be discreet, but they won't hound you like here. I've heard the same is true of Paris, but I like the water . . ."

"Well I don't." Samir threw the tickets back at him. Habib caught one, but let the other fall to the ground. "You go to Greece, or Paris, or wherever the hell else you want that's not here," Samir said. "I'm staying in Baghdad and getting married."

"Yes, I know, you've told me," Habib said. "You'll have a wife, and children you adore, and you'll live happily ever after. The part about the children I almost believe. But the wife? The happiness? That I don't think will last."

"It'll last longer than you will if you don't get the fuck out of here."

"OK, OK, I'll go," said Habib. "But if you change your mind before Saturday, I'll see you on the boat."

He got in his car and a minute later he was gone. Samir put away his pistol and remained standing in the empty garage, looking down at the ticket on the ground at his feet.

Madness, he thought. Madness. How wrong in the head must the guy be, to think there was even a chance I'd say yes? It isn't possible. It's totally not even within the realm of the possible. Well yeah, of course. But what if . . . What if—in some other world, not this one— what if it were possible? What if that, or something like that, could really happen, and work out? Hah! Right! If only . . . If only . . . I w—

No.

No. It *wasn't* possible. It wasn't even conceivable.

That isn't how the movie ends.

He rode the number 6 train to the end of the line. The last stop was aboveground, the elevated station heavily graffitied and lit by harsh fluorescents that made it much brighter than the neighborhood below, where most of the streetlamps were out. As always at this point, Samir thought about crossing to the far platform and heading for home, but with no wife or children waiting for him there, the thought was only a formality.

He descended to the street of shadows. Along the curb near the base of the station steps, a pile of rubbish had been set ablaze. At the edge of the firelight two women loitered in an open doorway. Samir moved swiftly past them, trying to project the lawman's sense of immunity he was no longer even close to feeling. In the next block more rubbish piles were burning, and in the next. He passed more open doors, each offering some hint or glimpse of depravity within; in front of one, a very young boy serving as a tout tried to latch on to his sleeve, but Samir pulled free and quickened his pace.

A half kilometer from the station he turned left into an alleyway, bracing himself as he did so, for predators sometimes lurked here. Tonight the alley was empty. He followed it to where it dead-ended at a blank iron door. A bulb in a wire cage was socketed into the wall above the doorframe and a security camera was mounted beside it. The camera, Samir knew, was there to warn of incoming police raids and wasn't normally set up to record, but all the same, he was careful not to look up as he rang the door buzzer.

The door opened and Samir stepped inside, into soft red light and the thump of disco music. The doorman was new. He was handsome in a rugged sort of way—his chin and cheeks were rough, and it looked as though he'd cut himself several times while shaving. He smiled a welcome, nodding in gratitude at the twenty-riyal note Samir offered him. He placed a hand in the small of Samir's back and propelled him gently forward, then turned to shut and bolt the door.

A beaded curtain separated the entryway from the club proper. As Samir passed through it, more hands reached out from either side to catch him above the elbows. Iron grips crushed his biceps, lifted him up, and pitched him headlong into the center of the room.

The music stopped. The lights came up. Samir pushed himself to his knees and stood, eyes adjusting to the brightness. The club had been gutted: The bar that had just three nights ago taken up the entire right-hand wall of the room was gone, ripped out, leaving only a few bent nails and bits of broken mirror and bottle-glass. All the tables and chairs were gone too, except for a single high stool at the center of the room on which a man sat perched like a dark-eyed bird of prey.

His identity at least was no surprise.

"Idris." Samir let out a sigh, more dazed than frightened at first, some part of him clinging desperately to the hope that this was all a bad dream. He turned to see who had thrown him to the floor. There were four of them, all rugged types like the doorman but with their beards intact. They stood in a line, blocking his escape, and Samir noted with dismay that they were all holding bludgeons of some sort: a wooden plank; a steel reinforcing rod; a splintered chair leg; a crowbar.

"Idris," he repeated, this time with panic edging into his voice. "Please—"

"Be silent, sodomite," Idris said. "I did not come to listen to you beg." A braver man might have challenged that assertion. Looking him in the face, Samir saw the same Idris he had known and feared back in grade school: a religious thug who claimed to love God, but who also loved bullying—and therefore loved sin, as a pretext to violence. *You disgust me,* his expression said. *I'm so glad you disgust me. Now I can hurt you with God's blessing.*

"I offered Mustafa a chance to work with me, but he refused," Idris continued. "He is proud and he is not afraid of dying. So I am forced to deal with weakness and perversity instead." He waved a hand at the blank wall where the bar should have been. "This is overkill no doubt. You are a coward, and cowards break easily. But Senator Bin Laden has instructed me to make certain you understand how serious we are, and what lengths we are willing to go to, to destroy you, if you don't do exactly as you're told."

The doorman appeared beside Samir, holding a stack of photographs. Like a sorcerer weaving a magic circle, he began walking counterclockwise, peeling photos off one by one and dropping them at Samir's feet. Samir looked down to catch a glimpse of himself in an embrace with another of this club's patrons; then he shut his eyes.

"For what you are you deserve to be put to death," Idris said. "And you know I will gladly do this. But understand, if you give me cause,

I won't just kill you. I will bury your memory in shame. Everyone who knows you, everyone who has ever called you friend, or spoken a single kind word about you, will learn precisely what sort of person you are. Everyone. I swear it."

Samir opened his eyes again as the doorman finished his third and final circuit. The doorman held up the last photo from his stack, a blow-up of Samir's wallet snapshot: Malik and Jibril, smiling, happy, maybe a little sad too that their father no longer lived with them—but innocent, thank God, as to the reason why.

"Everyone," Idris said.

THE LIBRARY OF ALEXANDRIA
A USER-EDITED REFERENCE SOURCE

Republic

A **republic** is a <u>government</u> whose <u>chief of state</u> is not a <u>monarch</u>, and which is to some degree answerable to its <u>citizens</u>. The term was coined by the <u>Christian philosopher</u> <u>Niccolò Machiavelli</u> from the <u>Latin</u> phrase *res publica*, "a matter for the people . . ."

Like "<u>democracy</u>" and "<u>freedom</u>," the word "republic" is sometimes used by <u>tyrants</u> to create the suggestion of limited government without its substance. Thus the phrase "people's republic," which at first glance appears redundant, but is in fact an example of <u>reinforcing a lie through repetition</u>.

The Israelis were bombing Vienna.

Over the weekend, Roman Catholic guerrillas had attacked an IDF patrol along the border west of Salzburg, capturing two soldiers and carrying them back into Austria. The hills around Salzburg were riddled with tunnels and fortifications, and so many hidden rocket launch sites that the region had been nicknamed Peene-münde South; Israeli troops attempting to rescue the kidnapped soldiers came under heavy fire, and as they pressed the attack the Von Brauns up in the hills began lobbing terror bombs at Jewish settlements in Bavaria.

The Israeli Air Force blasted Salzburg and its environs for two days without letup, but the rocket attacks continued. On the third day the prime minister in Berlin decided to adopt a new strategy, holding the Viennese parliament and the Austrian people collectively responsible for the guerrillas' misbehavior. Israeli bombers began hitting infrastructure targets all over the country: highway bridges and tunnels, railroad yards, river ports, as well as any vehicle that looked like it might be transporting rocket parts. Now the capital had made the target list. Vienna's airport was a cratered ruin, and the bridges over the Danube were all heavily damaged or destroyed, cutting the city in half.

"Samir," Mustafa said. "Are you all right?"

"What?"

They were in the black van, driving west on the BIA Expressway at dawn. For the entire ride Samir had been staring out the window with a scowl on his face.

"What's eating you?" Mustafa said. "You've been like this for days."

"It's nothing," Samir said, forcing a smile. He nodded at the radio.

"I'm just bummed I won't be able to go skiing in the Alps this winter."

"Samir . . ."

"Also, I heard the Israelis blew up that hotel where they make the chocolate cakes with the apricot filling. I always wanted to try one of those."

"Seriously, Samir. Is it something to do with Najat? Or your boys?"

"Najat hates me, which as we know is perfectly normal. And the only problem with Malik and Jibril is that I haven't seen them in months."

"So what is it, then? Are you still worried about Idris coming after us?"

Samir sighed. "And what if I was, Mustafa? What would you do about it, threaten to beat him up for me?"

"Samir—"

"Please, just drop it. I'm OK, really."

Baghdad International Airport was just ahead. Mustafa took the exit lane marked FREIGHT TERMINAL and followed the signs to the Arabian Parcel Service hub.

The man at the customer service counter was reading a Syriac New Testament. He greeted Mustafa and Samir warmly but turned hostile when he saw their Homeland Security IDs. "Is this about a missed delivery?"

"No sir," Mustafa said. "We're here to intercept a package containing evidence that pertains to an investigation. I spoke about this on the phone to a supervisor named Abd al Shakur. He—"

"Abd al Shakur is not here. Do you have a legal warrant for this package?"

Samir, happy to have a focus for his own ill humor, leaned forward across the counter. "Why, are you a lawyer?"

"My daughter is a lawyer," the man said. "She works for the ACLU. Should I call her?"

"No need for that," Mustafa said, placing a hand on Samir's shoulder. "We're not looking to persecute any Christians, brother."

"Ah, so it's a Muslim's civil rights you want to violate. And I'm supposed to smile and say OK then? What kind of Christian do you think I am?"

"I'll tell you what kind of Christian you are," Samir volunteered.

"Please, brother," said Mustafa. "Your respect for the Constitution is admirable, but this is a case where even a good Christian should want to help us."

"Even if I believed you, there's nothing I can do," the man replied. "If Abd al Shakur had set aside a package for you, it would be behind this counter, but as you can see there's nothing here. That means it's on a truck, and most of the trucks have already left."

"Well then, you'll just have to call them back, won't you?" said Samir.

"That I cannot do, even if I wished to. The trucks have no radios."

"I thought they were all linked by computer," Mustafa said.

"They are, but it's a one-way link. When a delivery is made, or attempted, the system sends a notification so that paying customers— *not* government thugs—can check the status of their shipments. But there's no way for me to send an outgoing message."

"And in an emergency? What do you do if there's a bomb on the truck?"

"Trust to the mercy of Almighty God, whom all good men believe in."

Mustafa found himself liking this guy despite his uncooperative attitude. "In the spirit of God's mercy, then," he said, "can you at least tell us for certain whether the truck has left yet?"

The man looked at him sourly, but because Mustafa had been polite he relented. "I suppose I could do that . . . Do you know where the package is going?"

"Adhamiyah," Mustafa told him. "The Republic of Saddam."

Amal meanwhile was in the reception area of her mother's Baghdad office. The senator had flown in from Riyadh the night before to attend a fund-raiser and was due back in the capital this afternoon for an important vote. She'd squeezed fifteen minutes out of her morning schedule for her daughter, but as usual, she was running late.

The wall across from where Amal sat waiting was hung with the obligatory Unity portrait of Gamal Abdel Nasser. This iconic image was what Aunt Nida had always privately referred to as the pre-assassination photo. If only Nasser had had the good grace to be martyred in the early '60s, Nida said, the Party would have been spared the embarrassment of his second presidential term: the scandals, the abuses of power, the long, drawn-out impeachment process that had revitalized the Party of God and set the progressive agenda back decades. Still, embarrassment or no, Nasser was the Party patriarch, and respect had to be paid.

To the right of Nasser's beaming mug, almost as large, was a copy of The Moment. Other scenes from her mother's life and career were displayed around the room, Amal herself appearing in some of them. She'd chosen her seat to avoid having to look at the most painful of these, a shot of her parents attending the ceremony where she'd been sworn in as an ABI agent.

It was not an event her father had expected to live to see. If Saddam Hussein had been a real king, he surely wouldn't have. But Saddam was only a king of the underworld, and even the fiercest mobster couldn't slaughter police captains with impunity. Which is not to say he forgave and forgot. Of the men who stood with Shamal as leaders of reform, four later died in suspicious accidents. Another six were ensnared—framed, they all said—in a corruption scandal of their own; of these, three committed suicide, one went into hiding in Europe, and the remaining two were murdered in prison.

Shamal, through a combination of caution, luck, and God's grace, managed to avoid both accident and indictment, but within the police force he became a pariah, a marked man nobody wanted to get close to. The constant tension ate at him; by the time of Amal's swearing-in ceremony, his hair had gone gray and his face was lined and careworn.

Four months later while driving into work, Shamal had happened across a burglary in progress. Two men lugging a television out of a house whose owner was on vacation had been confronted on the street by an elderly neighbor. Shamal drove past just as one of the burglars backhanded the old woman. He screeched his car to a halt and jumped out, pistol in hand. The burglars drew their own guns. Shamal killed them both, but was shot several times in return and died on the way to the hospital.

What appeared at first to be an unplanned tragedy became something more sinister when the burglars were identified as natives of Tikrit, Saddam's hometown. Then when Amal went to reinterview the neighbor who'd interrupted the burglary, she couldn't find her. Other neighbors said she'd moved away, though no one knew quite where: Some said Jordan, some said Kuwait. Some said Mauritania.

Amal petitioned the Bureau to open an official investigation into her father's death and was turned down. Her superiors acknowledged that she had reason to be suspicious, but still felt that the whole thing was most likely a coincidence. After all, as Amal herself had told them, her father had varied his route to work every day precisely in order to avoid being lured into a trap. Amal wanted to agree with this logic—a coincidence was easier to live with—but she also knew that the likelihood of a setup depended in part on just how patient the killers had been willing to be.

Amal's mother never doubted that Saddam was responsible. At the funeral she rose to give a speech—seemingly spontaneous, but in fact carefully crafted with the help of Aunt Nida—in which she asked those in attendance whether they really wanted to go on living in a climate of fear. In the following weeks she gave more speeches, in front of larger and larger crowds. Though she did not denounce Saddam Hussein by name, her listeners got the message loud and clear, and eventually so did Saddam, who sent some of his men to disrupt one of the speeches. The result was another photo, almost as famous as The Moment: Amal's mother on stage, pointing towards a Baathist heckler in the process of being mobbed, the heckler's expression shifting from arrogance to terror as he realized just how badly he'd misjudged the mood of the crowd.

It was a nice bit of theater, enough to get Amal's mother, after a few more twists and turns, elected to the mayor's office. But whatever good works she'd been able to accomplish there, and whatever good works Amal had accomplished as a fed, two things remained unchanged: Saddam Hussein was still a free man; and Shamal was still dead.

The outer lobby door opened and Amal's mother came in, accompanied by Amal's brother Ali, who was her chief of staff, and Amal's brother Haidar, her head of security. As they crossed the room Amal's mother spotted Amal, nodded, smiled, and gestured for her to follow, all without breaking stride or interrupting her ongoing conversation.

A moment later they were in the inner sanctum. Ali and Haidar both excused themselves, Ali saying "Ten minutes," and winking at Amal as he stepped back out of the office.

"So," Amal's mother said. "I've been hearing good things about you lately. I'm told you saved another agent's life."

"Yes, I did," Amal said.

"And shot a terrorist."

"Yes."

"But there's been no press release," her mother noted. "No public recognition of your heroism."

"There were some problems with the mission."

Her mother translated: "Somebody else screwed up and you saved his ass . . . All the more reason you should be lauded. Nobody needs to be embarrassed by it—they can leave the mistakes out of the official statement."

"I am being recognized," Amal said. "In-house."

"'In-house.'" Her mother rolled her eyes. "I know what *that* means."

"Mother, please. It's not that I don't want a public commendation, but—"

"Well that's good then, because you're getting one."

"But this isn't what I came here to talk to you about. I—"

"Just let me put a note in my PDA. I have a meeting with the Deputy Director of Homeland Security on Wednesday, so—"

"I got a call from Anwar."

Her mother paused, a hand on her purse. "Sadat, I hope," she said.

Amal told her the story. By the time she finished her mother was standing with her arms crossed, shaking her head.

"Why would you agree to meet with him?"

"He practically begged me to."

"So?"

"Well, I didn't want him showing up at the office."

"If he shows up at the office, you have security turn him away. My God, Amal . . ." Her eyes narrowed. "Who chose the restaurant?"

"I did, why? . . . What, you think it's a blackmail scheme? Hidden cameras? Anwar wearing a wire?"

"It's not a joke, Amal," her mother said. "I've got the vote on the marriage bill coming up soon. And now, out of the blue, this man you had a sigheh with a lifetime ago decides to get in touch to ask a favor?"

"You're wrong," Amal said. "The timing must be a coincidence."

"There are no coincidences in politics. Trust me on this."

"You didn't see him. The way he talked about Salim . . ."

"Oh, I'm sure it was heartfelt. He may not even know he's being used, you know. It could be that some friend of his in Riyadh, someone he confides in, suggested that he contact you."

Some friend of his in Riyadh . . .

"Bin Laden," Amal said.

"What?"

"Osama bin Laden . . . Would Anwar's father know him?"

"I don't know," her mother said. "It's possible. You think Senator Bin Laden might be behind this?"

"If he is," said Amal, "then you're not the one they're trying to get to."

"I would love for you to explain that statement to me."

"It's probably better if I don't." Then she said: "So what about Salim?"

"I'm sorry, there's nothing I can do for him. If the *Post* publishes a Page Six exposé about my daughter's temporary marriage, that's embarrassing, but not really damaging. But if they run a story about how I used my influence to get my daughter's son out of America, while other sons—beloved sons—are still fighting and dying there . . ."

"The *Post*." Amal made a face. "You can stay a step ahead of Tariq Aziz, surely. You used to run rings around him."

"You know, when you try to flatter me I fear the worst . . . Tariq Aziz is one thing, Osama bin Laden is another. What have you gotten yourself into, Amal?"

"I'm honestly not sure yet," Amal said. "But will you do this for me, please? Whatever favor you were going to call in to get me a commendation, use it instead on Salim's behalf."

Her mother shook her head again. "You don't even know the boy, Amal."

"I know. But I don't need to know him, to show him compassion. Anwar was right about that much."

They called it the Republic of Saddam: a patchwork of estates and commercial properties that collectively formed an outlaw nation, a separate country within the UAS. Most of it was in Iraq, but there were scattered outposts throughout Arabia—villas in Alexandria and Tunis, a hotel in Abu Dhabi, a gambling den in Casablanca, rat cellars everywhere.

The Republic's capital was of course Baghdad, where Saddam

owned houses in each of the city's major districts, with the notable exception of Sadr City. Back when Mustafa and Samir had
worked for Halal Enforcement, Saddam had split his time between
the Mansour lake estate that adjoined the Baghdad Airport and the
downtown mansion in Karkh that many Baghdadis regarded as a
shadow city hall.

After 11/9, increased security around the airport had made the
Mansour estate less attractive—the TSA really had a bug about
people firing rifles into the sky. Then in 2003, a mysterious fire
gutted the mansion in Karkh; rumors of the cause ranged from
faulty wiring to Uday. Saddam had been trying to rebuild the place
ever since, but the Baghdad City Planning Commission, on orders
from a certain mayor-turned-senator, kept delaying the necessary
permits, and in the interim squatters had invaded the property, turning it into a palace of the homeless.

While Saddam's lawyers tried to cut through the commission's red
tape, he had relocated the headquarters of his Republic to his compound in Adhamiyah. The walled estate occupied three hectares of
prime riverfront property and had its own dock and helipad. It was
patrolled night and day by a uniformed security force known colloquially as the Republican Guard.

Having raced across town, Mustafa and Samir were now parked
at the end of the street that led to the estate's main gate. The package they were hoping to intercept had been sent standard overnight
delivery, which meant that in theory it could show up anytime between now and 6 p.m., but Mustafa doubted they'd have to wait long.
"Think about it: If you were a deliveryman and Saddam Hussein was
on your route, would you keep him waiting until afternoon?"

"I see your point," Samir said, "but by that logic, couldn't we already have missed him?"

"Let's give it an hour. If the truck hasn't showed by then, we'll give
that helpful fellow at the airport another call."

They passed the time by speculating about the occupants of a jeep parked half a block behind them. Mustafa thought he'd seen the same vehicle at the APS hub; Samir was sure he had, but feigned uncertainty. "Who do you suppose they are?"

"Al Qaeda, most likely," Mustafa said. "Unless the Mukhabarat has taken an interest in us." Mukhabarat was a nickname for the network of Iraqi private investigators who donated free labor to the Baath Union in exchange for police favors, in effect serving as Saddam's personal intelligence bureau. "What do you think, shall we go introduce ourselves?"

"You go right ahead."

Mustafa shot him another concerned look, but didn't push. "All right," he said. "You stay here, I'll go talk to them."

But even as he opened his door, a brown truck rounded the corner, a familiar trademarked question on its side: WHAT CAN AL ARABI DO FOR YOU? Mustafa flipped out his ID and hurried to flag it down.

"Your mother cannot help you."

There was a sculpture park adjacent to Amal's mother's office building. It was a popular open-air lunch spot, but at this hour of the morning it was empty except for a pair of elderly backgammon players and a few women pushing strollers.

Amal sat on a bench alongside an enormous bronze jug. A hole had been cut in the jug's side, making a window onto the miniature city within. The city's outline and the river that bisected it suggested Baghdad, but a Baghdad from an alternate universe: The sort-of-familiar landmarks were all in the wrong place and the streets were laid out differently.

Amal switched on her cell phone. She had two missed calls, both from Mustafa. She was about to check messages when a ninja sat down beside her and began speaking in Gulf Arabic. It took Amal a moment to realize the woman's words were addressed to her.

"I beg your pardon?" Amal said.

"I said, your mother cannot help you." The woman raised a hand and pointed to another of the park's sculptures. "You see that globe over there? It models the world as the Abbasid cartographers knew it. If you walk around to the other side, where the Western Hemisphere should be, there's nothing. No Americas. The lines of latitude and longitude don't meet. From this angle, though, it looks almost whole. A tourist might even mistake it for the Unisphere." The woman chuckled. "Your mother's authority is like that. Hollow and incomplete. A trick of perspective . . . A mirage."

Amal slipped her cell phone into her pocket and turned to face the woman fully. "Who are you?"

"A servant of a true servant of God. Someone whose power is real. Someone who can guarantee your son's safety."

"Osama bin Laden," Amal said nodding. "And should I take it as an insult or a compliment, that he sends a woman with his message instead of Abu Yusuf?"

"It is a sign of respect." The ninja sniffed behind her veil. "Perhaps you are unfamiliar with proper decorum."

"Perhaps *you* are unfamiliar with the penalty for threatening a federal agent."

"I do not threaten. I speak the truth. Salim bin Anwar will not be saved by Anmar al Maysani—or by Amal bint Shamal. But the man I serve can remove him from harm's way."

"In exchange for what?"

"Nothing."

"Nothing?"

"Do nothing. Mustafa al Baghdadi has chosen a path to self-destruction. Do not follow him. Do not help him. Do not interfere."

"You expect me to just sit on my hands?"

"Ask to be taken off the investigation. Your mother's name is good for that much, at least."

"That's your idea of nothing, is it?" Amal laughed. "And once I've made it clear to my colleagues that I can no longer be relied upon, then what? Just wait and see whether the senator holds up his end of the bargain?"

"Give me your word that you'll ask to be reassigned and Salim will be on his way home in forty-eight hours."

Amal fell silent, still skeptical but also not wanting to believe it.

"Here, let me show you something." The ninja took out her own cell phone. "The other day on your computer you looked up Abu Salim's file, but you didn't look up the boy's. That's understandable, but before you decide his fate you really should see his face." She passed the phone to Amal, who accepted it reluctantly. "He is a handsome boy," the woman continued. "A good Sunni Muslim, strong and intelligent. He should have a bright future, if—"

But Amal, suddenly livid, cut her off: "Is this a joke? Are you mocking me?"

"Mocking you?" The woman glanced at the cell phone's screen. "That is Salim bin Anwar. What—"

Amal interrupted again, this time by drawing her pistol. "What are you doing?" the woman said.

Amal leveled the pistol at the woman's face and flicked off the safety. "You say your master has power. Can he raise the dead?"

The woman shook her head. "You are making a mistake."

"No, the mistake is yours," said Amal. She understood now, but understanding did not lessen her fury. "Go back to your master. Tell him I don't need any favors from him." She gave it another ten seconds, then put away the gun.

But the woman didn't leave.

"We're done," Amal said. "Why are you still here?"

The ninja held out her hand. "My phone."

"Any guesses?" Mustafa said, gazing at the tiny parcel in his palm. It was slightly larger than a cigarette pack. The return address was a shop in Israel, Hillel's Curios of Frankfurt.

Samir shrugged. "An antique mezuzah case?"

Mustafa laughed. "Yes, I'm sure Saddam collects those."

The jeep was gone, Samir having waved it off discreetly while Mustafa spoke to the APS deliveryman. But now they had other observers. Their interception of the truck had been noticed by the Republican Guard, and when the driver went to deliver the rest of Saddam's packages he must have told them what Mustafa had taken. Binocular lenses flashed from behind the gate; their license plate number was doubtless being forwarded to the Mukhabarat.

Untroubled by the attention, Mustafa picked at the tape seal on the package. "Do you have a box cutter?"

"Sorry, I left mine at the airport."

Mustafa used the van's ignition key as a crude knife and managed to get the package open. Inside, in a slim plastic case, was a deck of playing cards. Each card bore a picture of a man's face, captioned with an English transliteration of his name and a job title. Mustafa recognized many of the names and faces—almost all of them were prominent Baath Union members—but the job titles were whimsical.

Here, for instance, the five of clubs: Barzan Ibrahim Hasan, Saddam's half brother, who was said to have come up with the idea for the Mukhabarat. The card caption called him a "Presidential Advisor." Or the eight of diamonds: Hikmat Mizban Ibrahim al Azzawi, a Baathist long suspected of running Saddam's money-laundering operation. His caption read "Finance Minister."

The eight of spades: Tariq Aziz. "Deputy Prime Minister?" Samir let out a snort as Mustafa translated. "What, is he moonlighting as a member of the Persian government?"

Mustafa shuffled through the deck, looking for the aces. The ace of diamonds was Abid Hamid Mahmud, Saddam's publicist, identified here as "Presidential Secretary." The ace of clubs was Qusay Hussein. The ace of hearts was Uday: "Olympic Chairman," Mustafa read.

"Yeah, chairman of the bookmaking division, maybe," said Samir.

The ace of spades was Saddam himself: "President." Not "Baath Union President," just "President." There should have been another joke here—the biggest joke of all—but Mustafa's sense of satire suddenly abandoned him.

A folded sheet of paper had been enclosed in the package with the cards. It was a printout of a private eBazaar auction page, the same one Wajid Jamil had forwarded to Mustafa late last night. The item description was short and cryptic: "From beyond the mirage, Lot #157. Interest tags: Iraq, Saddam Hussein, Baath Party, U.S. invasion." The winning bid, placed by eBazaar user **King_Nebuchadnezzar,** was fifteen hundred riyals.

Mustafa's cell phone rang.

"Hello, Amal," he said. "Nice of you to check in . . . No, it's OK. We do have a lead, though." He told her where they were. "How soon can you get here? . . . Fifteen minutes, excellent. Samir will be waiting in the van." He hung up.

"Samir will be waiting?" Samir said. "Where will Mustafa be?"

"Making a delivery." Mustafa slipped the cards and the paper back into the package. "Fifteen hundred riyals is a pittance for King Nebuchadnezzar, but something tells me he'll be anxious to get this."

"You think he'll talk to you?"

"It can't hurt to try. And I must admit I'm curious to see the inside of that house."

"As long as it's not the last thing you see."

"Ah, that's where you and Amal come in," Mustafa said. "If I'm not back out in an hour, you come rescue me."

"And is there some particular way you'd like us to do that, or should we just blow the gates in?"

"Improvise." Mustafa smiled. "But please ask Amal not to shoot the Olympic Chairman unless it's absolutely necessary."

Nebuchadnezzar II

Nebuchadnezzar II (reigned 605 – 562 BCE) was a king of the Neo-Babylonian Empire. His historical feats include the construction of the Hanging Gardens of Babylon and the conquest and destruction of Jerusalem and its temple. He is mentioned in several books of the Hebrew and Christian Bibles, most notably the Book of Daniel . . .

NEBUCHADNEZZAR AND BIBLICAL PROPHECY

Daniel chapter 2, verses 31–35 describes a dream in which Nebuchadnezzar saw "a great statue . . . The head of that statue was of fine gold, its chest and arms of silver, its middle and thighs of bronze, its legs of iron, its feet partly of iron and partly of clay. As [the king] looked on, a stone was cut out, not by human hands, and it struck the statue on its feet . . . Then the iron, the clay, the bronze, the silver, and the gold, were all broken in pieces . . . But the stone that struck the statue became a great mountain and filled the whole earth." As interpreted by Daniel, the statue's golden head represents Nebuchadnezzar's own kingdom, and the other parts of the statue represent three other kingdoms that will come after it; the mountain that arises from the stone is a fifth and final kingdom that will rule over all the earth, forever. Although this fifth kingdom is generally understood to be the Kingdom of God, the identity of the fourth kingdom and the nature of the stone that will shatter it is a subject of heated debate among Christian eschatologists . . .

MODERN LEGACY

Nebuchadnezzar remains a popular figure in the UAS, particularly in the state of Iraq. The Iraqi city of Al Hillah, located near the ruins of

ancient <u>Babylon</u>, has numerous Nebuchadnezzar-themed tourist at-
tractions, including the <u>Six Flags Hanging Garden Waterpark</u>.

Nebuchadnezzar is also a favorite among aspiring politicians. A
survey conducted by *Riyadh Week in Review* found that of the historical leaders to whom Arabian presidential candidates compared themselves, Nebuchadnezzar was second in popularity only to the holy
warrior <u>Salah al Din</u>.

While the Republican Guardsman patted him down, Mustafa contemplated the Baath Labor Union motto, painted on the arch above the gate: ACT NOW, TALK LATER.

Words to live by. It occurred to him that he ought to be at least a little nervous, but the only thing that concerned him at the moment was keeping his balance. Shuffling through the cards in the van, he'd felt his vertigo starting, and the giddiness had intensified during the walk to the gate. Now, standing on the border of Saddam's Republic, whatever apprehension he might have felt was swallowed by that same giddiness, leaving him unsteady on his feet but otherwise serene.

The first Guard finished his pat-down and a second stepped up to repeat the procedure. Mustafa's pistol, wallet, Homeland Security ID, and cell phone had already been taken from him, along with Saddam's package, and all of these were being carefully scrutinized as well. A Guard who appeared to be the leader of the gate detail recited Mustafa's name and federal employee number into a walkie-talkie.

Several minutes passed. Mustafa looked up the drive towards Saddam's mansion and saw a keeper walking a lion on a leash. The big cat stopped to sniff the tire of an armor-plated limousine that was parked at the turnaround. Then a bird flew by overhead and the lion took off after it, pulling its keeper along behind.

The front door of the mansion swung open and the ace of clubs emerged. Qusay, the "good" son: sober and self-controlled, far less likely than his brother to shame the family with a tabloid headline, and for that very reason more apt to be trusted with jobs requiring discretion. The consensus among Halal and Bureau agents was that

Qusay had many more murders to his name than Uday did. This morning he did not appear to be in a good mood. Perhaps Mustafa's arrival had interrupted his breakfast.

The leader of the gate detail handed Mustafa's Homeland Security ID to Qusay. Qusay glanced cursorily at it, then said: "What is it you want here?"

"I would like to speak with your father about his recent online purchase." Mustafa nodded at the package. "And about any other similar items he may have acquired."

"I don't know what items you are referring to, but a conversation with my father is impossible."

"I understand your father is a busy man and not especially trusting of government agents. But if I may appeal to him directly . . ."

"You may not."

"Then please tell your father for me that I am on a special assignment for the president, who will be grateful to anyone who assists me."

Qusay didn't blink. "And if my father isn't interested in the president's gratitude? What then?"

"Please," Mustafa said. "I make no threats, only a respectful request for help. If your father says no, I'll leave and trouble him no further."

"Just like that, eh?"

"Hey." Mustafa waved a hand at the land outside the gate. "It's a free country."

It was the kind of really big house that seemed designed to make you remark, repeatedly, on how really big it was. The ungodly nature of the excess, the awful tackiness of the furnishings and décor that also begged for comment—those were perhaps less deliberate.

Baath-affiliated artists had been drafted into the decorating effort. The mansion's grand reception hall featured a painting of Saddam and his wife Sajida dressed as heads of state of some antique kingdom (Babylon, judging by the ziggurats in the background). That portrait wasn't so bad actually, but another, which cast Saddam as a knight of jihad defending Jerusalem against Richard the Lionheart, struck Mustafa as a bit much. And a third painting, showing Saddam as the Spartan King Leonidas holding the line against Xerxes' Persians at Thermopylae—that had to be either a gag or a loyalty test: Look at this without snickering and you may have a future as a citizen of the Republic.

"This way," Qusay said. He led Mustafa through an archway into a hall lined with statues. More historical figures, each carved or cast with the same mustached face: Saddam as Hammurabi the Lawgiver; Saddam as Gilgamesh; Saddam as Shalmaneser, as Sargon, as Sennacherib; Saddam as Ramesses the Great . . .

The hall ended in a circular domed chamber with one last statue at its center. This ultimate king stood seven meters tall, and sunlight streaming through windows in the dome made the monarch's head glister like gold. But when Mustafa, unable to resist, gingerly rapped a knuckle on one of the royal feet, what he discovered was neither gold nor a mix of iron and clay, but the hollow ring of tin.

"Wait here," Qusay said, leaving Mustafa in Nebuchadnezzar's shadow. "My father will join you shortly."

As Qusay's footsteps faded into the distance, Mustafa heard a low droning sound. Following it to another archway, he gazed into a side room where a boy sat playing with a fleet of toy trucks. The boy was European or possibly American and looked about five years old. There was something forlorn about the way he pushed the same dump truck back and forth, making listless *vroom-vroom* noises.

A woman who sat minding the boy looked up at Mustafa looking in. Mustafa nodded to her, then turned to see the real-life king of the Republic coming up behind him.

The prosecutor at one of his trials had described Saddam Hussein as "a village thug in city clothes." He was a big brute of a man, tall and thick, like the monument he longed to become. He swam laps daily to keep himself in shape and dyed his hair and mustache to hide his age. Informants said he had back trouble and often limped when out of the public eye. But there was no sign of that now—as he approached Mustafa he kept his stride confident and even, channeling whatever agony this cost him into an air of affable menace, like a cunning old lion strolling out to see what had wandered into his den.

"Welcome to my home!" Saddam said. As he reached out to shake, his sleeve pulled back to reveal an old gang tattoo on the back of his wrist. His grip was strong and he squeezed Mustafa's hand to the point where it almost became painful, sizing him up as he did so. Mustafa, still too giddy to feel fear, did his own counter-assessment and decided that the way to play this was to be respectful but straightforward.

"Mustafa al Baghdadi," Mustafa said. "Thank you for seeing me."

"It's my pleasure to be of service. I trust I need no introduction, but in answer to your next question, you should feel free to refer to me as either Saddam, or Uncle. Many of my union brothers prefer the latter."

"'Uncle' would be awkward for me, I'm afraid. I'm not a member of Baath."

"But you are an Iraqi," Saddam said. "I consider all Iraqis honorary Baathists."

"Yes, well," said Mustafa, "as I suspect you've already been told, I'm also a former Halal agent who spent nine years trying to bust you. So you really shouldn't do me that particular honor."

"Ah, Halal." Saddam smiled. "An amusing organization . . . Did we ever meet, during those nine years? You look familiar to me."

"I attended a couple of your trials," Mustafa told him. "And I was part of the team that executed the search warrant against the

Hakum factory. I tried to speak to you on that occasion but your lawyers wouldn't allow it."

"A pity. I could have told you you were wasting your time. But I suppose you found that out on your own."

"We surely did." The Hakum Seltzer-Water bottling plant, located outside the city of Musayyib, had been identified by several trusted informants as a secret distillery producing thousands of liters of hard liquor, but a two-day search had failed to turn up so much as a drop of alcohol. The incident had been a major embarrassment for Halal, and a lawsuit by the plant's management had resulted in the firing of one of Mustafa's superiors.

"And now you work for Homeland Security," Saddam said. "A much more satisfying career, I'm sure . . . And my son tells me you're working for the president?"

Mustafa nodded. "A special assignment."

"And you need *my* help?" Saddam raised his eyebrows, as if amazed that a humble palace-owner such as himself could have anything to offer.

"I believe you can assist my investigation, yes."

"Then I shall be glad to. Come, let's go to my office."

"If I may ask . . . ," Mustafa said.

"Yes?"

"That boy in there. Who is he?"

"His name is Stuart. He's the son of an Englishman I'm doing some business with. He's staying with me until the deal is completed, to make sure everything goes smoothly."

Mustafa blinked. "The boy is your hostage?"

"My honored guest," Saddam Hussein said. "Don't worry, he's being looked after. He's getting his milk." He paused, and a shadow of uncertainty crossed his face. "You there!" he called, to the woman minding the boy. "Is he getting his milk?"

"Yes, Saddam!" the woman replied.

"There, you see?" Saddam said to Mustafa. "He's getting his milk. Nothing to worry about!"

Saddam's office resembled a war room, with wall maps of Baghdad and other Iraqi cities, each map decorated with a constellation of pushpins. "Would you like to take some cell phone pictures?" Saddam asked, noting Mustafa's interest in these. "I'm sure your old Halal colleagues would be fascinated."

"They would," Mustafa said. "But I'm not here for that."

"Good. Very good." Saddam opened a drawer in his desk and brought out two glass tumblers and a bottle. "You like whiskey? I know it's early . . ."

"Ah, no thank you."

"I insist. Before we talk business, you must have a drink with me."

"I really can't," Mustafa said.

"Of course you can. Halal agents drink all the time, ex-Halal agents all the more so . . ."

"I'm a Muslim."

Saddam chuckled. "So am I!" he said. "I'm not a saint, though, and I don't trust men who act as though they are." He poured a finger of whiskey into each tumbler and pushed one across the desk. "Come. Share a small sin with me, so I can relax. God will forgive you."

The whiskey was bitter on Mustafa's tongue and it made his eyes water, which Saddam found funny. "That's good stuff. You should appreciate it!"

"I guess I'm not a sophisticate," Mustafa said.

"Ah, but you are well informed." Saddam placed a hand on the package containing the cards. "Who told you about this? Your friend Wajid Jamil I suppose."

"I see I'm not the only one who's well informed." Mustafa set down his tumbler, which still had half a finger of whiskey in it. "You should know Wajid wasn't spying on you, specifically."

"No?"

"I asked Waj for help researching something we're calling the mirage legend. One of his keyword searches turned up several eBazaar auctions, including that one. When he saw the mailing address attached to the winning bidder's account, he contacted me."

"Ah, the mailing address . . . Qusay warned me about that. 'Rent a PO box,' he said. But it's a hassle, for something that's not even illegal."

"Your eBazaar account name isn't exactly subtle, either," Mustafa noted.

"Well, that I couldn't resist. I've always been an admirer of Nebuchadnezzar."

"So I gather."

"I dedicated my first novel to him . . . He was a great leader. A great *Arab* leader, unlike Salah al Din, who had the misfortune to be born a Kurd." Saddam's expression grew distant as he sipped his whiskey. "You know, the Jews say Nebuchadnezzar went mad. For seven years. Exiled from his rule in Babylon, forced to live like a lesser person . . ."

"Like a beast, actually," said Mustafa, who'd been reading the Book of Daniel as part of his research into rapture theology. "'You shall be driven away from human society, and your dwelling shall be with the wild animals.'"

"But the story has a happy ending," Saddam said. "At the end of the seven years, the king returned to his right mind, and to his throne."

"Yes." Mustafa glanced at the whiskey bottle. "After he submitted to God and became a righteous man . . ."

Saddam seemed to mull something over. Finally he reached under the edge of his desk and toggled a hidden switch. The section of wall on which the map of Al Hillah was mounted gave a shudder and began to swing inwards.

"Finish your drink," Saddam said. "I want to show you something."

"I call it my alternate-reality room," Saddam Hussein said. "You know this expression, 'alternate reality'? It's a new media thing." He waggled his hands in the universal gesture of the over-fifty trying to get a grip on the Internet Age. "My daughter Hala explained it to me. They do this thing now, to promote movies and new TV series, sometimes video games as well. They plant clues and hints in cyber-space, so it's like this mystery for people to solve, but really it's an advertisement."

"They?" Mustafa said.

"Bollywood. The Hindus invented the practice. But now film com-panies here are doing it too, and in Israel. Some of the cutting-edge alternate-reality productions are very elaborate, not just stuff on the web, but live-action events with props. Hala, who is very interested in new media, got wind of an alternate-reality campaign that seemed to be about me. Now you know there's going to be a movie version of *Zabibah and the King*—if my producer ever gets off his ass—so at first I thought it was connected to that. But nobody at the production house knew anything about it. So I had my people do some investi-gating, and they started finding these items, these—"

"Artifacts."

"Yes. Like pieces of a puzzle. As you can see, someone is quite fixated on me."

The room was like a small museum whose focus was the same as the vanity art in the rest of the house. On the walls behind glass were many newspaper and magazine clippings, all featuring Saddam's image. Most of the clippings seemed to be from English-language publications, or ghost publications—Mustafa spotted several *New York Times* front pages.

Display cases in the center of the room held other types of arti-facts. Mustafa lingered beside a tabletop display of a war game. The playing board showed North America, divided into sectors; an inva-sion force of brightly colored plastic tanks and troops had landed on the east, west, and Gulf coasts and was pushing into the heartland.

Mustafa was confused as to how this fit with the general theme of the room, but then he saw the art on the game box lid—the face of the invaders' leader—and he understood.

"So what does it all mean?" Mustafa said. "If this is a puzzle, what's the solution?"

"I'm still working that out," Saddam Hussein said. "But these objects tell a story about another world, an Arabia and an Iraq with a different history."

"And you are the hero of this story?"

Saddam spread his hands and smiled, as if to say, Who am I to argue with my fans? "Every legend needs its champion."

"What about the other characters?" Mustafa said. "Who else is in the story?"

"Various celebrities, politicians mostly." Smirking: "That clown Al Gaddafi, though I think he's the comic relief."

"Osama bin Laden?"

"Ah, that one." Saddam shrugged. "He might have a role I suppose. But you know, I don't even find him interesting in real life. He's too stuck up, like a Saud without the pedigree."

"And America?" Mustafa looked down at the game board. "What's America's role in the story?" He looked up again to find Saddam nodding.

"That's what you're here for, isn't it?" Saddam said. "Something to do with the Americans."

"It seems this alternate-reality campaign, or whatever it is, has caught the attention of a number of crusaders," Mustafa told him. "But they think it's a true story."

Saddam chuckled. "Americans . . . Always confusing fantasy and reality."

"Tell me where you get these items," Mustafa said. "Are they all from eBazaar?"

"I have various sources. Lately though, yes, a lot of items have been turning up on eBazaar. The auctions are typically private, but there's an email notification list for people known to be interested in such things . . . By the way, as long as your friend Wajid Jamil is giving away personal information about his customers, I would love to know who has been bidding against me. That game, for instance, that cost me almost ten thousand riyals."

"Ten thousand?"

"I wanted it," Saddam said, sounding defensive. "But some bastard tried to snipe it out from under me at the last minute."

"Do you know the source of these items?" Mustafa asked next. "The return address for the deck of cards—"

"A shop in Frankfurt, yes. It's a front. All the return addresses are—I've checked them out. The ultimate source of the items is elsewhere."

"Do you know where?"

"Let's say I have an idea. If I'm willing to pay ten thousand riyals for a board game, what would a clue about the game's maker be worth?"

"You want money?"

"If you were a banker I might ask for money. As a servant of the president, there are more important things you can do for me."

"Like help you with a legal problem?" Mustafa guessed.

"There are rumors of a new indictment being prepared against me by the IRS. If the president could shut that down, it would go a long way towards earning my gratitude."

"A long way, or the whole way?"

"Perhaps one other small favor as well," Saddam said. "You're not the only one intercepting my deliveries. Recently I had a private shipment that was stolen on its way into Baghdad . . ."

"That sounds like a matter for the local police. Surely you've got that covered."

"Ordinarily that would be true. But the thieves come from a neighborhood where police influence is . . . weak."

Sadr City, Mustafa thought. "The Mahdi Army stole a package

from you? Does that mean Muqtada al Sadr is playing the alternate-reality game too?"

"No, no," Saddam said. "This is nothing to do with that. It's a different kind of shipment."

"If it's alcohol or some other drug—"

"Please. If it were that, the Mahdis would just have set fire to the truck. Who knows, maybe that's what they had in mind. But the shipment is an antique, something whose value would be obvious even to ignorant Shia bandits. So they took it."

"And you want me to get it back?"

"I could do it myself," Saddam said, "but you know I hate to disturb the peace. And if I send my men into Sadr City . . ."

"Right." Blood in the streets. More importantly from Saddam's perspective, there was a good chance his men would never be heard from again. "What is it you expect me to do, send in the real army?"

"The method I leave to your discretion. But if the president's servant can't get my property back, who can?"

Mustafa frowned. "I can't promise anything now."

"Of course not," Saddam said. "You go check back with the president—about the IRS thing too, don't forget—only don't take too long. If the Mahdis decide to destroy my property, or sell it to someone else . . ."

As they returned to Saddam's office, there was an urgent knock on the outer door. "Come," Saddam said, and Abid Hamid Mahmud—the ace of diamonds—entered looking flustered. "What is it, Abid?"

"I'm sorry to disturb you, Saddam, but there's trouble at the main gate. A crazy woman. She says she's Anmar al Maysani's daughter, and says if we don't let her in, she'll have the estate reduced to rubble."

Saddam Hussein looked at Mustafa.

"A friend of yours, perhaps?" he said.

THE LIBRARY OF ALEXANDRIA
A USER-EDITED REFERENCE SOURCE

Mahdi Army

This article is about the contemporary, Baghdad-based Mahdi Army. For other Armies of the Mahdi throughout history, please see the disambiguation page.

The **Mahdi Army of Iraq** is a Shia community relief organization whose stated mission is to provide security, charity, and other services to poor neighborhoods that have traditionally been ignored or under-served by government agencies. Based in Baghdad's Sadr City district, the Army has established chapters in other parts of Baghdad and in other Iraqi cities such as Najaf and Kufah.

The Army's founder and leader is Muqtada al Sadr.

ORGANIZATION HISTORY

In 1959 the Baghdad city council, faced with a huge influx of poor Shia workers from southern Iraq, voted to build a public housing project called Revolution City in northeast Baghdad. Much of the money allocated to the project ended up in the pockets of corrupt city and union officials. The new housing was shoddily constructed, and Revolution City quickly gained a reputation as a slum.

This was hardly the last insult the neighborhood would suffer. In the decades that followed, Revolution City's residents complained of being shortchanged on all manner of public services, from health-care access to street repair. Law enforcement was a particular sore spot—within the RC district, the Baghdad police often acted more like an armed gang, shaking down legitimate businesses while allowing criminals to run free. For their own protection, citizens formed militias, often organized around local mosques; while these militias did provide a semblance of order, they also fought one another for control, or were broken up by police when they became too powerful.

The cycle of corruption and anarchy continued until the late 1990s, when the election of Baghdad's first Shia mayor, Anmar al Maysani, brought a brief period of hope for change. Unfortunately, Al Maysani's sweeping reform program did not fare well against the reality of Baghdad politics. Crime remained a serious problem, and matters reached a crisis point after the RC district's most prominent resident, the Grand Ayatollah Mohammed Sadiq al Sadr, was murdered. When police announced they had no suspects in the case, Revolution City—now renamed Sadr City—exploded in protest. At a rally attended by an estimated 50,000 men, the Grand Ayatollah's son, Muqtada, called for the formation of a new super-militia to fulfill the promise of peace and justice the occupants of city hall had failed to deliver on . . .

CONTROVERSY AND CONFLICT

Although the Mahdi Army's vigilantism is excused by some as a necessary evil, it has also come in for a lot of criticism. In addition to its well-publicized attacks on muggers, burglars, drug dealers, prostitutes, blasphemers, and homosexuals, the Army is accused of targeting innocent Sunnis who wander onto the Army's "turf."

The Mahdi Army has also clashed repeatedly with the Baghdad police force. The police have often come off the worse in these encounters, with the result that patrolmen are now said to be reluctant to enter Sadr City and other Mahdi Army strongholds without large amounts of backup. Al Sadr's spokesman insists that such animosity is not the Army's fault: "We don't hate all cops, just the bad ones. Unfortunately, finding a good cop in Baghdad is rather like finding a righteous man in Sodom."

The Mahdi Army is also believed to be involved in a recent rash of assaults on members of the Baath Labor Union. Although Baath has long been implicated in the corruption afflicting Sadr City, there is speculation that the real motive for the attacks is a personal <u>vendetta</u> against Baath Union President <u>Saddam Hussein</u>, who some suspect of having ordered the murder of Muqtada al Sadr's father. Whatever the truth, Baathists and their allies give Sadr City an even wider berth than the police do . . .

Mustafa called his cousin Iyad.

Iyad was the son of Fayyad, the uncle who treated God like one of his creditors. Partly in reaction to his father's impiety, Iyad had been intensely religious as a young man, even studying for a time to become a Shia cleric. Ultimately more like his dad than he liked to admit, he'd dropped out of seminary without completing a degree and gone to work driving a cab. He stayed on good terms with his old classmates, though, and when the Mahdi Army took over Sadr City, Iyad became one of a select group of Baghdad cabbies allowed to operate in the district. A few Army big shots kept him on speed dial, and once or twice—so he claimed—he'd even given the Ayatollah's son a ride.

Iyad did other jobs for the Mahdis as well. A few years back he'd been arrested for vandalizing a betting parlor that had opened shop too close to Sadr City. Mustafa had intervened with the police on that occasion and was able to get Iyad released with no charge and no penalty other than the beating he'd already received.

So Iyad owed him, and Iyad was family, but even so Mustafa knew better than to tell him what he wanted over the phone. Instead he had Iyad come by the apartment while Abu Mustafa was out and explained the favor in person, trying to make it sound like it was no big deal.

Iyad wasn't buying it. "You want me to help you rip off the Mahdis for Saddam?" He cocked his head to stare at the stitches on Mustafa's neck. "I heard you'd been injured, cousin, but I didn't know there was brain damage."

"I'm not looking to rip anyone off," Mustafa said patiently. "I want to strike a bargain with the Mahdis."

"For something Saddam wants. You think you can bribe them into overlooking their blood feud?"

Mustafa did think that, actually, but saw no point in saying so. "I'll be bargaining on behalf of Homeland Security. The Mahdis' vendetta against Saddam doesn't come into it."

"The Mahdis may not agree," Iyad said. He frowned. "I'm not even sure I do. What about your own oath to put that monster in prison? And now you're working as his errand boy?"

"I'm no one's errand boy," Mustafa said. "But I have a mission, and Saddam has information I need. This is a one-time deal."

Iyad looked skeptical—and reproachful. "So what is it anyway, this stolen property of Saddam's? Drugs? A weapon of some kind?"

"An antique battery," Mustafa said.

"A *what*? You mean like for an old car?"

"More antique than that. It's from an archaeological site, near Al Hillah. Saddam didn't have any pictures, but I was able to find a sketch of a similar artifact on the Library of Alexandria."

Mustafa showed him the printout. "That's a battery?" Iyad said. "It looks like a vase."

"It's a clay jar, about fifteen centimeters tall. There's a cap with an iron rod attached to it, and a copper cylinder that goes around that, and you fill the jar with acid—vinegar or grape juice—and the iron and copper generate a current."

"And then what? You attach it to the headlamps on your war chariot?"

Mustafa shrugged. "The Library said something about electroplating. Or maybe Nebuchadnezzar's court magicians used it to do tricks, who knows?"

"What sort of tricks does Saddam want to do with it?"

"He claims he wants it for his private art collection. My own guess is he means to sell it on the black market."

"*Which* black market?" Iyad sniffed. "Grape juice . . . It's probably full of heroin."

"If it is, we're dumping it in the Tigris," Mustafa said. "I already promised Saddam as much, and I'll promise you too. But if it's just a stolen antiquity, I'm willing to let Saddam have it in exchange for his cooperation. We can always confiscate it later."

"You really want this thing? Let me put a bomb inside. Then I'll get it for you gift-wrapped."

"Sorry, no bombs . . . Now are you going to help me, or not?"

Iyad sighed. "I suppose I can make some calls, see which faction of the Army has this thing. But if it's possible to get it at all, it's going to be expensive."

"I can get money."

"You'll need a good cover story, too. And a better front man wouldn't hurt."

"What do you mean?"

"The Mahdis don't trust feds any more than they do the Baghdad PD. I'll vouch for you of course, but if they get the notion that cutting off your head might ruin Saddam Hussein's day, well . . ."

"Ah," said Mustafa. "I would like to avoid that."

Iyad looked at the stitches again. "I hope that's true, cousin, for both our sakes . . . In any event, I think it would be safer to have someone else play the buyer. Do you know anybody with a public grudge against Saddam?"

"I believe I can find someone who fits that description," Mustafa said.

Several nights later Iyad picked the three of them up outside head-quarters. Mustafa and Samir wore matching suits, while Amal had gone full ninja, donning an abaya and niqab she'd acquired some years ago for a Bureau assignment in Medina. Something about Amal's costume—maybe just the self-possessed way she moved in it—caused it to have the opposite effect it was supposed to. As she approached the taxi, several men passing on the sidewalk turned to look at her.

"Nice hijab," Iyad said archly. But then he chuckled and held up the copy of the *Baghdad Gazette* he'd been reading. "Nice PR stunt, too." The front page of the paper had a picture of Amal's face, unveiled, under the headline SENATOR'S DAUGHTER RECOGNIZED FOR HERO- ISM IN ANTI-TERROR FIGHT. After her mother pinned a medal on her, Amal had spoken movingly about how her late father's stand against evil had inspired her own career; it was this invoking of Shamal, the *Gazette* speculated, that had motivated a mysterious assailant crying "Saddam! Saddam!" to take a shot at her as she left the stage.

"So who's the mystery shooter?" asked Iyad.

"Abdullah al Hashemi," Mustafa said. "A colleague. We were just going to have him throw a shoe at Amal, but he decided a cap pistol would be more dramatic." The senator's security detail, overplay- ing their own part in the charade, had dislocated one of Abdullah's shoulders in the course of subduing him. "It got a little out of hand."

"Well, the Mahdis ate it up," Iyad said. "You could get a meeting with Muqtada al Sadr himself now, if you wanted to . . . Although for the guys we're actually going to see, it was probably overkill."

"Who are we going to see?" Amal asked.

"A bunch of wannabes. Not proper Army, more like junior aux- iliaries. The sense I got from the one I talked to is that they were freelancing when they hijacked the truck—which is good for us, be- cause it means they're anxious to fence the goods. God willing, the deal should go down quickly." He looked at the briefcase Mustafa was carrying. "You have the cash?"

"Yes." The riyals in the case had been requisitioned, by presiden- tial order, from a larger stash of drug money recently seized by Halal. It was rough justice, the ransom for Saddam's property to be paid with Saddam's own ill-gotten gains.

"Good. Let's get going, then."

Samir cleared his throat. "Right," said Mustafa. "Samir would like the address of our destination, so we can leave word of where we're going." In fact, Samir had been pestering him nonstop about this.

Iyad regarded Samir with suspicion. "Who do you want to leave word with?" he asked. "Your mother?"

"Yes," Samir deadpanned. "If something goes wrong, I'd like her to know where to pick up the body."

"If it comes to that, you can trust the Mahdis to dispose of your body properly," Iyad said. "But don't worry, we'll be fine."

"One other thing," Mustafa said, making a quick check of the other vehicles on the street. "There's a possibility we may be followed. Not by our people," he clarified. Or by the Mukhabarat, whom Saddam had promised to call off. "By agents of Al Qaeda."

"Al Qaeda, trying to enter Sadr City?" Iyad chuckled again. "If only God were that generous . . . Now come on, let's not stand here all night."

On maps it didn't look like a neighborhood that would be hard to get into: a five-by-six kilometer rectangle extending northeast from the canal that ran like a moat between it and Rusafa. What the maps didn't show, but what could be glimpsed in satellite photos on the Internet, were the clusters of black-clad Guardian Angels who stood watch all along Sadr City's borders, on every thoroughfare and side street, profiling the incoming traffic. More Angels flocked on the El train platforms, ready to help as well as hinder. The station elevators rarely worked, but a wheelchair-bound El rider could count on being carried down to the street—unless the Angels pegged him as a Baath spy in cripple drag, in which case he'd make his descent even more swiftly, and headfirst.

The most closely watched entry points were those along the City's northwest boundary, which it shared with the Adhamiyah district. Angels assigned to that border were especially vigilant, and they were matched on the Adhamiyah side by a neighborhood watch of off-duty cops and Baathist street thugs. The two groups of border guards catcalled one another across Safi al Din al Hilli Street, and these exchanges of verbal insults sometimes escalated into physical fights or even full-blown riots.

Iyad approached Sadr City from the southeast, detouring through the New Baghdad suburb and coming up Jerusalem Boulevard. At Habibiya Circle, where the boulevard crossed Port Said Street, the Guardian Angels were encamped on the central traffic island, at least three score men in black sitting on or standing around the civilian-model Humvees they used as interceptors. Inbound traffic entering the circle tended to slow down, the drivers hoping to avoid being singled out, but Iyad kept the cab rolling at a steady speed and waved at the border guards. Several waved back, including one particularly brawny Angel who'd traded his uniform top for a T-shirt that said MAY I READ YOU YOUR RIGHTS, OFFICER?

The taxi continued along the boulevard, passing two cars with out-of-state plates—one from Jordan, one from Qatar—that had been pulled over, probably on suspicion of Driving While Sunni. Farther down the block, a rented camper with a Danish flag on its antenna had been cut off by a Humvee after ignoring a signal to stop. Now the three passengers were being made to stand in the street while the vehicle was searched for contraband. As the cab drove by, an Angel emerged from the back of the camper waving a stack of comic books as if it were pornography.

"Idiot tourists," Iyad muttered. Samir eyed the unhappy Danes and began fidgeting in his seat, and Iyad, catching this in the rear-view, said: "Dude, I told you, we'll be fine. But if you don't quit acting nervous it's going to cause problems."

"Sorry," Samir said, and forced himself to sit still.

Mustafa, feeling like a tourist himself, stared out at the boulevard, comparing it to his memories from the early '90s when Halal had had regular business here. No question, the Mahdi Army had improved some things. Though the district was still ailing from decades of coming in dead last in every city budget allocation, the Army had worked overtime to patch the crumbling infrastructure, filling potholes, repairing sidewalks, shoring up dilapidated buildings, and organizing garbage collection and other services that most of Baghdad took for granted. There was a heavy smell of diesel in the air from the thousands of generators brought in to bolster the unreliable power grid, the fuel to run them being siphoned from Baath-owned tanker trucks and Baath-controlled oil depots.

Traditional street crime, once rampant, was practically nonexistent now. But here and there were glimpses of the price paid for that, the dark side of the new order. Among a row of well-tended shops Mustafa spied a grocery whose front window had just been busted out. The Angel who'd done the deed was still standing there, slapping his palm with a wooden club while the grocery's tight-lipped proprietor used a push broom to sweep up the glass.

"What's that about?"

"Don't stare, cousin," Iyad said. He shrugged. "Guy must've broken a rule. Maybe he stayed open during prayer time or tried to sell something he shouldn't. Or it could be he didn't pay his dues."

"Dues," Mustafa said, and Iyad shrugged again.

"You think your buddy Saddam doesn't charge the shopkeepers in his territory for protection? At least here, you actually get the security you pay for."

At the next corner they stopped for a red light and Mustafa looked up at a pair of billboards on the side of the El tracks just ahead. One billboard carried the ubiquitous AL SADR FOR GOVERNOR poster. The other was an ad for a local cell phone company, with a map of Iraq contrasting its superior coverage area with that of its competitors, the multicolored overlay giving the state a fragmented look that reminded Mustafa of the grocer's window. He shifted in his seat, and Iyad, thinking he'd caught Samir's case of nerves, said: "Dude, seriously. Chill out or I'm turning us around."

The helicopter orbited at eight hundred meters, the camera on its belly automatically tracking the progress of the cab.

Six Al Qaeda commandos sat in the helicopter's cargo compartment. For tonight's mission they had dressed in paramilitary uniforms of the Badr Corps—another super-militia, based in Najaf, that was currently disputing the Mahdi Army's right to represent Iraq's Shia downtrodden.

Idris Abd al Qahhar was in the co-pilot's seat. While the pilot focused on maintaining line-of-sight with the taxi, Idris reviewed the rules of engagement with his men. "Retrieval of the object is your top priority," he said. "All guards and bystanders are expendable. Remember the neighborhood is hostile and any commotion is likely to bring armed reinforcements."

"What about the Homeland Security agents?" the lead commando asked.

"If you can spare their lives without compromising your main mission, do so. But if you can't, make sure you kill all three of them, and also any witnesses. Set incendiary charges on your way out of the building. One last thing—this goes without saying, but you are not to allow yourselves to be captured alive."

"Understood," the commando said.

The pilot, watching the camera feed, spoke next: "The taxi just turned off the boulevard. I think they are approaching their destination."

In front of a mosque at the corner of a block of tenements, a group of kids were playing in the water from an open hydrant. An imam's assistant with a wrench stood watch from the sidewalk; despite his efforts to come off like a stern lifeguard, Amal detected a certain wistfulness, as if what he really wanted was to throw off his robes and join in the splashing.

Iyad drove another block to a vacant lot surrounded by more tenements and a small factory that had been turned into an auto shop. A sign said FAWZI'S CAR REPAIR, but the true nature of the business was hinted at by the stripped chassis littering the lot.

A gang of young men, too motley to be Angels, loitered outside the chop shop's garage entrance. As the taxi approached they came alert, brandishing an assortment of firearms.

Iyad parked next to the rusted carcass of a minibus. "Wait here until I signal you," he said. He walked up to the garage and spoke to a fellow whose AK-47 had what looked like four ammunition clips bound side-by-side with duct tape. "Somebody must like war movies," Amal observed. "Or maybe he's just compensating for something."

"Yeah, that's great," said Samir. The guy with the AK-47 was nodding now. He sent one of the other gang members into the garage and Iyad turned towards the taxi and raised a hand.

Mustafa and Samir exited the cab first, Mustafa coming around to open Amal's door. After she got out, they fell in step beside her, making like bodyguards, Mustafa doing the better job of projecting professional menace.

Not that it mattered much: The gang members only had eyes for Amal. As she neared the building she heard a whistle and glanced up to see two teenage boys peering out a window on the factory's second floor—and almost directly above them, another guy with a rifle leaning over the parapet of the roof. Amal resisted an impulse to wave.

The group in front of the garage door parted to make way for their boss. He was older than the others but still young, at least five years Amal's junior.

"Fawzi bin Taymullah al Walid," he introduced himself. "At your service."

"Amal bint Shamal," Amal said. She undid the lower half of her niqab so he could see it was really her, the sudden exposure of her face causing the gang rank and file to collectively drop their jaws.

You Sadr City kids, Amal thought, you really need to get out more. "Thank you for agreeing to meet with me."

"The honor is mine," Fawzi said. "Please, come inside."

In the large open space beyond the door, four different cars were in the process of being cannibalized. The mechanics all put their tools down to gawk at the visiting celebrity. One guy with a lit blowtorch on the ground by his feet held up a copy of the *Baghdad Gazette* and waved it like a groupie hoping for an autograph. Amal politely ignored this, her attention drawn instead to the only intact vehicle in the chop shop, a sedan with a bar of flasher lights mounted on its roof.

"Our secret weapon," Fawzi said grinning. He didn't elaborate, but Amal could figure it out for herself: Out on the highway at night with its flashers on, the sedan would easily be mistaken for a police car. This must be how they got their inventory. Amal wondered what sort of arrangement these guys had with the Mahdi Army, and how much of their gross they had to pay in protection money.

"This way, please," Fawzi said. The back half of the ground floor was a warren of industrial shelving. The shelves nearest the chop shop were filled with auto parts, but those deeper in were stacked with consumer goods—electronics, small appliances—that must have come from hijacked trucks. The boxes on one shelf carried the mark of the Red Crescent and were labeled ANKARA EARTHQUAKE RELIEF. Of these, Fawzi quipped: "Could I interest you in some cheap medical supplies?"

A space at the center of the warren had been furnished as a parlor: stolen carpets and chairs, a sheesha pipe, even an espresso machine. Fawzi, Amal, and Iyad sat down, while Mustafa, Samir, and Fawzi's lieutenant with the AK-47 remained standing.

"So," Fawzi said, after an abbreviated exchange of pleasantries, "I understand you're interested in something I may have in my possession."

"Actually, it's my mother who is interested," Amal said.

"Oh? Not that I'm not flattered, but I wonder how such an important senator would even know about my business here."

"My mother has many friends in the intelligence community. As a personal favor, they keep tabs on certain people for her. One of these people has been doing a lot of talking on unsecured phones lately about an item that was stolen from him. He's a very unhappy man."

Fawzi shrugged, as if it were no big thing to be an object of Saddam Hussein's displeasure. "Not all unhappiness is a curse."

"My mother agrees wholeheartedly," Amal said. "She'd like to increase this man's unhappiness. So she asked me to see if I could track down the missing property. With my local contacts, it didn't take long."

"Well, we aren't exactly hiding out here," Fawzi said, a hint of unease breaking through his cool. "And of course, *you* are welcome in Sadr City . . . So the unhappy man, I assume he's looking, too."

"Oh yes," Amal said. "High and low. But he's still a few steps behind me, and my hope is to take the object off your hands before he gets any closer."

"And then what? Your mother will let him know she has it?"

"That's the plan."

"And what will your mother do with the object? Destroy it?"

"She considered that. But once she heard the item was an antiquity, she decided it would be more fitting to donate it to a museum."

"A museum?"

"Yes, in Persia," Amal said. "Or perhaps Kurdistan . . ."

"I see," said Fawzi. "And once it's behind glass in Tehran or Kirkuk, what, you wait for the unhappy man to come visit it?"

"If only God were that generous . . . But my mother will see that he gets an invitation and let him know that a warm welcome awaits him if he accepts."

Fawzi was grinning now. "I like how your mother thinks. And

I believe we can do business." With a measured note of regret, he
added: "Of course, since it is business, I'll have to ask for payment."

"Of course," Amal said. "I'm ready to pay a reasonable price. May
I see the item?"

"Absolutely." Fawzi turned to his lieutenant. "Shadi. Go get the
crate."

The guard on the roof was listening to Green Desert's "I Pray by
Myself" on a pair of headphones, snapping his fingers and swaying
to the music. The helicopter, now in whisper mode, had descended
almost to the rooftop before he noticed it, and what drew his attention was not the muted *shuss*ing of its rotors, but the downdraft,
which made the smoke from his cigarette dance as if it too had
caught the tune.

When the guard looked up, a Qaeda commando shot him between the eyes with a silenced submachine gun.

"Right side clear," the commando said.

"Left side clear," said another.

"Go," said Idris. The helicopter touched down on the roof just
long enough for the six men to jump out; then the pilot increased
power and took it back up to five hundred meters. The commandos
sprinted across the roof to the stairwell.

A hallway ran the length of the building's top floor. A man was
just coming out of a bathroom near the middle of the hall, adjusting
his belt as he walked, when the lead commando reached the bottom
of the stairs. The silenced SMG made a flat sound that might have
been mistaken for a cough; the fall of the corpse was louder and
more distinctive.

"Ali?" a voice called, through an open door midway between the
bathroom and the stairs. "Did you trip over your pants again?" This
was followed by laughter. The commando stepped quickly to the
doorway. Inside the room, three men sat around a card table. The
commando killed them all, then paused, listening. When no one

else called out or came into the hallway to see what was going on, he returned to the stairs and exchanged hand signals with his men.

They began a careful sweep of the entire floor. At one end of the hall, a commando opened a door on a roomful of machine tools and saw a teenage boy standing in front of a row of windows. Rather than shoot him immediately, which might have broken the glass and alerted others outside, the commando gestured for the boy to put his hands up. The boy did so, and the commando made him come closer to the door and kneel down facing the wall. Then he shot him in the back of the head. As the boy slumped to the floor, the commando made a quick visual scan of the room, but he didn't actually walk around the machines, so he didn't see the second boy, down on one knee behind a lathe, his trembling fingers gripping the laces of an untied sneaker.

The commandos completed their sweep, killing three more people in the process. They regrouped at the top of another stairwell. The lead commando keyed his headset and spoke to Idris in the helicopter: "Top floor is secure. We are ready to go downstairs."

"Proceed," Idris said.

"Is there a problem?" Fawzi said.

Amal was frowning. "Are you sure this is the right object?"

"But of course." Fawzi picked up the lid of the little wooden crate and showed her the attached label, which bore the crest of the University of Iraq at Al Hillah. Scrawled by hand beneath this—rather haphazardly, Amal thought—were the words PARTHIAN BATTERY, 2ND C. BCE. "There, you see?"

"Yes, I see. It's just, this doesn't look like what I was told to expect."

Instead of a terracotta urn, the object Fawzi had pulled from the crate was a crude brass bottle, about fifty centimeters tall. The vessel was a flattened sphere with a long tapered neck; its surface, unadorned by any decoration or pattern, was pitted and tarnished, thickly encrusted with grime, except for one small area where someone had tried to rub it clean, exposing a dull shiny spot the size of a half-riyal coin. The bottle mouth was open and the vessel was empty. Amal had a hard time seeing how it could function as a battery.

"You're sure this was the only object?" she said. "There weren't any other crates?"

"Not like this one." Fawzi snorted laughter. "Not unless the Parthians also made home theater systems." Sobering, he continued: "I hope you aren't suggesting I would try to cheat you."

No, never, Amal thought. She wanted to consult with Mustafa, but knew that that might spoil their charade.

But then Mustafa spoke up on his own: "Was there a stopper?"

"What?" said Fawzi. Amal turned around. Mustafa was staring at the bottle with a hypnotic intensity; he was also leaning heavily on Amal's chair, as though to keep himself from falling.

"Was the bottle sealed?" Mustafa said. "Was there anything inside it?"

"Inside it?" Fawzi gave another snort. "Like what, a double-malt whiskey?" Mustafa didn't answer, but after a moment he looked at Amal and gave a firm nod.

"Very well," Amal said. "Let's talk about payment . . ."

But now Fawzi was frowning. "I'm sorry, I am confused," he said. "I thought I was dealing with you."

"You are," said Amal.

"And this man? Your bodyguard? He's an antiquities expert as well?"

"As a matter of fact, yes."

"No." Fawzi shook his head. "No, I don't think so. I don't think he's a bodyguard, either. He looks stoned. And this one"—turning to Samir—"this one looks scared." He focused on Iyad next, saying nothing, only staring, then looking back at Mustafa as he noticed the family resemblance. "What is going on here?"

"What's going on here is, we're making a deal," Amal said. "Come,

Fawzi al Walid—whatever unfounded suspicions you have about my men, you know who I am. And I am ready to meet your price, so—"

"Let's not rush things," Fawzi said, easing back in his chair. "Let's talk a bit more, about what your real interest in this object is."

The stairs came down at the rear of the storage area. The commandos surprised another gang member there, killed him and stashed his body. They paused again to listen. The leader sent three of his men to circle around to the chop shop while he and the other two entered the warren of shelves. They followed the sound of voices until they were right outside the inner sanctum, with just a meter of boxes between them and the chair where Fawzi was sitting. To their left was a gap in the shelves through which they could see Shadi leaning on his AK-47.

"Let's not rush things," Fawzi said. "Let's talk a bit more, about what your real interest in this object is."

The lead commando slung his weapon and took out a flash-bang grenade. There was a final exchange of hand signals. The commando pulled the pin on the grenade and cocked his arm back, even as a wild-eyed teenager came darting around the shelves behind him holding a machine pistol taken from a dead man. One of the other commandos saw the boy coming and snapped off a shot, but the boy tripped over his own shoelaces and the bullet only grazed his ear. Then the boy cried out "Al Sadr!" and pulled the trigger on the machine pistol.

The machine pistol's ammunition clip held thirty rounds. Twenty-six hit nothing of consequence; three struck the commando who'd just fired, killing him; and one caught the lead commando in the throat, which, among other things, caused him to lose his grip on the flash-bang. As the unwounded commando pivoted towards the boy, the grenade went off.

Fawzi, Amal, and the others were shielded from the blast by the wall of boxes, but the sudden close explosion of sound stunned them all anyway. The boy continued shouting, his battle cry of "Al Sadr!" replaced by a warning: "Badr! Badr!" The blinded and deafened commando staggered into Fawzi's parlor. Shadi reacted first, raising up his AK-47, but even the legendarily reliable Russian Orthodox weapon was no match for misapplied duct tape, and it jammed. The commando's SMG coughed out a bullet that flicked Mustafa's collar and sent Samir and Iyad diving to the floor. Amal leaned forward in her chair. There was a crack of a pistol shot and the commando fell dead.

A moment of stillness, as smoke curled from the muzzle of the gun in Amal's hand. Then the gang members running in from the front of the building were ambushed by the other three commandos and a massive firefight broke out in the chop shop. Shouts of "Al Sadr! Al Sadr!" mingled with "Badr! Badr!" and then "God is great!" as the Qaeda men realized they might be outgunned.

Fawzi was staring at the body on the floor and trying to figure out what the hell was going on. Concerned that this thought process would end badly for her and her colleagues, Amal put her own confusion aside and seized the initiative. "It seems I was wrong about being ahead of the competition," she said. "I wouldn't have thought the Badr Corps would join forces with Saddam, but I guess it's true what they say about the enemy of my enemy." When Fawzi didn't respond, she continued: "Let me take this cursed object off your hands, Fawzi al Walid. I believe Iyad said your asking price was ten thousand riyals."

This deliberate lowballing broke through to him. "The asking price was *thirty* thousand," Fawzi said, glaring at her. "And that was before—"

"*AL SADR! AL SADR!*"

"Let's say twenty thousand and be done," Amal suggested.

"Thirty thousand."

"Twenty-four."

"*Thirty.*"

A stray round passing above the shelves struck a light fixture directly over their heads. Amal managed not to flinch but recognized that she was running out of time and luck. "I'll tell you what," she said. "We'll call it twenty-eight thousand—and two thousand more for your man Shadi here to show us where the side door is."

"*—other men are down and I am cut off. I cannot—*"

"*Al Sadr! Al Sadr!*"

"Abu Musab?" Idris said. "Abu Musab, are you there?" Static in the headset. On the camera feed, he saw Mustafa, Amal, Samir, and Iyad come around the building and run for the taxi. Idris told the pilot: "Take me down there."

But the pilot, noting the black line of a power cable suspended over the lot, and guessing there might be others he couldn't see, said: "I don't think—"

"Take me down!"

So the helicopter began to descend, and Idris took off his headset and unbuckled his seat harness. As he got up to go back into the cargo compartment, there was a loud *crack!* and a hole appeared in the right side of the cockpit windshield.

Idris and the pilot both turned their heads in time to see the second muzzle flash. The shooter was in the tower of a nearby mosque. A Guardian Angel on night watch perhaps, or the muezzin himself, up in his roost after hours and doing what any good Sadrist would do upon spying a black helicopter hovering over the 'hood.

"Son of a bitch!" the pilot cried, blood running down his cheek where he'd been cut by flying glass. His trigger finger twitched on the control stick, but it was an empty gesture. The helicopter was unarmed.

And unarmored. The next muzzle flash had a different shape, the shooter switching his aim towards the tail of the aircraft. A red lamp lit on the control panel, and a recorded male voice began warning of damage to the hydraulic system.

"Take me *down!*" Idris repeated.

But the pilot, in sudden panic at the thought of crash landing amidst a million Shia, shook his head. "No," he said. "We must abort!" As Idris continued to yell at him, he increased throttle and yanked the control stick hard to the left. The chopper flew away into the night, trailing smoke. The last image on the camera feed before line-of-sight was lost was of the taxi speeding away as well, Iyad laying rubber to escape before the Mahdis could close down the streets.

The Library of Alexandria
A USER-EDITED REFERENCE SOURCE

Scheherazade

Scheherazade is the master storyteller in the classic Arabian folk tale collection *One Thousand and One Nights*.

In *One Thousand and One Nights'* framing story, King Shahryar of Persia is driven mad with rage when he discovers that his wife has betrayed him. Not only does he execute her, he vows to take a new wife every night and have her strangled the following morning. These executions are carried out, reluctantly, by the king's grand vizier, until the vizier's eldest daughter, Scheherazade, comes up with a plan to put an end to the cruelty.

Scheherazade marries the king. On her wedding night, she asks permission to say farewell to her sister Dunyazad. Dunyazad is brought to the king's chambers, where, in accordance with Scheherazade's plan, she asks Scheherazade to tell her a story. Scheherazade begins the tale but is forced to break off at the coming of dawn. The king, entranced, grants her a one-day stay of execution so that he can hear the end of the story. The following night Scheherazade finishes the first tale and begins a second, earning another stay of execution. This continues for a thousand and one nights until at last King Shahryar, transformed by love, lifts Scheherazade's death sentence and makes her his queen . . .

In the small hours of the morning, Saddam Hussein descended to the deepest cellar of his Adhamiyah estate.

West of the main house, in back of the outbuilding that abutted the lion enclosure, was a plain-looking steel door secured by an electronic keypad. Past the door, a circular stairway descended to a guard room staffed by a half dozen of Saddam's most trusted men. Two of the men wore the standard Republican Guard uniform and were armed with riot guns. The other four were dressed as if for a heavy contact sport: chest, shoulder, and thigh pads; knee, shin, and elbow guards; groin cups and throat protectors; reinforced gloves and boots; and helmets with face shields that they lowered into place as Saddam entered the room.

The four-man extraction team preceded Saddam and the two gunmen through a long cellblock. The cells were empty and had been for some time, but bloodstains were still visible on some of the walls and a search of the floor would have turned up the occasional tooth or fingernail among the rat droppings.

At the end of the cellblock was another flight of stairs and another security door, beyond which was a brightly lit antechamber containing two chairs. One was a throne-sized easy chair with a matching ottoman; the other was a steel-backed restraint chair that had been bolted to the floor.

The antechamber also contained a liquor cabinet, and Saddam helped himself to whiskey while the gunmen positioned themselves to either side of him and the extraction team continued on through a final security door. From beyond the door came sounds of a man being tackled and pummeled into submission.

The extraction team returned with the prisoner. He was a blond American in his early thirties, tall and muscular. He wore camou-

flage fatigue pants and a gray ARMY T-shirt; a skull in a green beret
was tattooed on his upper right arm.

The prisoner was limp and unresisting as the guards carried him
out, but as they approached the restraint chair he abruptly came
alive and began to fight again. This was an old trick and the extraction team were ready for it. They kept hold of him, and with
some joint-twisting, a bit of head trauma, and a few hard taps to the
solar plexus they got him into the chair and strapped down. Saddam
picked up a small remote from atop the liquor cabinet. There were
electrical contacts inside the chair's wrist and ankle straps, and by
pressing a button on the remote he could deliver painful shocks.

The extraction team had stepped away from the chair and were
looking at Saddam expectantly. A flexible black cable tipped with a
large alligator clip dangled from the seat of the chair between the
prisoner's legs. This was an optional attachment that could be used
to deliver current directly to the prisoner's genitals, but to put it on
him, they'd have to remove his pants or at least cut a hole in the
crotch—a delicate procedure.

"No," Saddam said, to the unspoken question. "We won't need
that tonight, I think. Leave us."

His men went back up the stairs. Saddam rested a forearm on the
back of the easy chair and sipped his whiskey. The prisoner watched
him, grinning despite a bloody nose and a black eye; probably he was
thinking about what he would do if his restraints were removed.

"You know, these displays of defiance are unnecessary," Saddam
said. "No one here questions your manhood. But you are alone and
powerless. You can't escape. You can't kill me. There's no shame in
accepting these facts."

"Thank you for the advice," the prisoner said. "I appreciate you
acknowledging my manhood. But you know I don't have that much
else to occupy me, so I might as well *try* to kill you."

Saddam smiled. "Your Arabic is improving. You must be studying
very hard."

"Like I say, I don't have much else to do. I couldn't even follow the TV, without it."

"So you're happy with the television? The screen is big enough?"

"Yes."

"And that Xbox thing I got for you—you like that?"

"I do," the prisoner said, truthfully. "I could use some more games for it."

"I'll see what I can do. I want you to be happy. Anything else you'd like, just ask . . . Are you sure you don't want a woman?"

"No, and we've been over that. I'm not interested in Helen Keller, and if she can see me or hear me she can tell people about me, and that means you'll kill her, after. I don't want that on my conscience."

"This world is full of people who are already as good as dead," Saddam Hussein said. "I could find you a woman like that, a beautiful woman. There'd be nothing for you to feel bad about."

"No thank you."

"Or we could keep her here as your guest. Someone to play Xbox with, how would that be?"

The prisoner considered it. "No," he finally said. "Trapping a woman in this place wouldn't be much better than killing her." Thinking of Uday: "Maybe worse, in some ways."

"Very well," Saddam said. "But if you change your mind . . ." He freshened his drink, then took a seat in the comfy chair. "And now I would like some entertainment. You have a story for me?" His eyes narrowed. "A *good* story, this time?"

The prisoner smiled. "You didn't like that last one, huh?"

"No I did not."

"What part didn't work for you? It was the ending, right? Where the Mahdis stretched your fucking n—*uuhhhhhhhh!*"

Saddam kept his thumb on the button of the remote while he took a long sip of whiskey. When he finally let up on the current, the prisoner sagged forward, gasping.

"That was four," Saddam said, indicating the remote's numbered dial. "Would you like me to remind you what ten feels like?"

The prisoner was too busy catching his breath to answer.

"Now I want to hear a story," Saddam continued. "It doesn't have to be perfect—I know you're not a professional—but it needs to be inspirational, something that acknowledges *my* manhood. No more of these ridiculous fantasies about military defeats, or spider-holes, or . . . guilty verdicts. I want a tale I can believe in. Are you ready to give me that?"

The prisoner had recovered enough to fix his captor with a look of absolute hatred. For a moment it seemed as though he might spit, but Saddam held up the remote, turning it to show the numbers on the dial. The prisoner held out a moment more, then lowered his eyes and capitulated.

"Yes," he said. "I'll tell you what you want to hear."

"You'll tell me what I want to hear, what?"

"I'll tell you what you want to hear . . . Mr. President."

The call to dawn prayer had just ceased when Saddam came back up out of the cellar. His son Qusay was waiting for him.

"What is it?"

"Mustafa al Baghdadi," Qusay told him. "He's inside. He has the object."

Saddam smiled. The day was starting off well: He'd enjoyed the prisoner's story very much, and now this.

"The senator's daughter is with him," Qusay continued. "And the other agent, Samir, the one the Mukhabarat say is reporting to Al Qaeda."

Better and better. "So Bin Laden will hear about anything we say." Saddam nodded. "We'll have to make sure he gets an earful, then . . . You had them all searched?"

"Yes." Qusay hesitated. "There was a problem with the senator's daughter. Uday tried to pat her down himself, instead of calling a woman from the house to do it. She reacted violently to the insult."

"Tell me that idiot didn't hurt her."

"*She* is fine. Uday I think is very lucky she'd already surrendered her weapon."

Saddam reddened. "Where is your brother now?"

"Out. I told him to go for a long drive."

"When he gets back, I want to speak to him . . . What about the object? Where is it?"

"The Guard are taking it to your office."

"Bring Mustafa and the others there, too."

"Do you want me to exclude the senator's daughter?"

"You are sure she's not armed?"

"Positive. Still, she has reason to wish you dead, so perhaps to be absolutely safe—"

"No, that's fine. Let her in. She's welcome to stare daggers at me all she likes." Saddam rubbed his hands together. "But the only one getting his wishes granted today, is me."

Amal *did* stare daggers at him. But the sharpness of her gaze was tempered by a small smile, the latter inspired by knowledge of the .22 pistol, hidden in a fold of her abaya, that both Uday's clumsy pat-down and the more thorough search that followed had failed to discover. The gun was single-shot and not very accurate, but Amal was confident of her ability, if she chose, to put a bullet in Saddam Hussein's brain.

Of course she would die too, then. On another day she might have at least considered making the trade, but now, like Mustafa, she had other priorities. It was enough to know that she could have done it—that Saddam was vulnerable. She could always come back and shoot him later.

Though his face didn't show it, Samir was also thinking about shooting Saddam. But he didn't have a hidden weapon and he definitely didn't want to die. That was the problem: Idris had been very insistent about acquiring Saddam's prize for himself, and while the botched commando raid wasn't Samir's fault, he knew Idris would hold him responsible anyway. So while Amal stared at Saddam, Samir cast side glances at the submachine gun slung over the shoulder of Saddam's nearest bodyguard. He thought: Grab the gun, take down both guards, take down Saddam, take down Qusay, grab the battery, and run, run, run . . .

Yes, and if he were super-spy Jafar Bashir he might have pulled it off, might even have made it out of the mansion before being cut down by the rest of the Republican Guard. Samir Nadim would be lucky to get out of the room alive . . . assuming he had the heart to try, which he did not.

Mustafa, the only one of them not contemplating murder, focused his attention on the brass bottle. He'd examined it as carefully as he could in the moving taxi. It contained nothing but a few grains of sand and a faint odor of incense: Sniffing at the bottle's opening, Mustafa detected an undertone of sulfur. The smell sparked no special memories, but the weight of the bottle in his hands was weirdly familiar.

Mustafa had offered Iyad a chance to examine the bottle as well, but Iyad was no longer interested. As soon as they were clear of Sadr City, he pulled the taxi over and told Mustafa and the others to get out. "And next time you need a favor, cousin, try calling the Mukhabarat." Mustafa didn't argue with him, only nodded solemnly and said, "Peace be unto you, Iyad."

As Iyad drove off, Samir suggested with forced casualness that they return the bottle to headquarters and "have it checked out."

"Checked out for what?" Amal asked. "It's empty."

"Well, yeah, there's nothing in it, but what if the thing itself is . . . I don't know, radioactive or something."

Amal laughed. "If it's radioactive, I say we get it into Saddam's hands as soon as possible."

Mustafa had sided with Amal, so they'd hailed another cab and gone directly to the Republic. And now they stood waiting while Saddam's antiquities expert verified the authenticity of the "battery." The expert, a diminutive Kurd whom Saddam had introduced as Mr. Rammal, acted more like a fortune-teller than an archaeologist: He laid both hands on the bottle, closed his eyes, and muttered under his breath. When this incantation, or whatever it was, was completed, he looked over at Saddam and nodded.

"Excellent!" Saddam said.

"Are you sure?" said Mustafa, who'd found himself hoping incongruously that the bottle would fail the test.

"Of course we are sure," said Saddam. He glanced at the Kurd, who repeated his nod. "If Mr. Rammal is satisfied, so am I. And so should you be."

"It's just that this object isn't what I was expecting. There's no iron bar inside, no copper cylinder . . ."

"Copper cylinder?"

"To generate the electric current. If it's really a battery, it's a broken battery."

"Mustafa al Baghdadi, you think too hard," Saddam Hussein said. For a moment his good humor lifted like a veil, exposing a more dangerous emotion underneath.

Then he was smiling again. "Come! Let me give you your reward!" Saddam turned to the wall map of Samarra and pulled it down to reveal a hidden safe. He opened the safe and took out an index card which he handed to Mustafa.

"'V. Howell Industries,'" Mustafa read from the card. "This is the source of the mirage artifacts?"

"It's as close to the source as I've been able to get," Saddam told him. "My agents have traced several of the items in my collection

to V. Howell. Whether they're the origin or just a link in the chain
I can't say."

"And this address: 1145 Jefferson Davis Pike, Herndon, Virginia . . ."

"It's a small office park."

"In Fairfax County?"

"Yes. A section that the Marines didn't burn down. From the outside it looks like a low-security facility, but every spy I've sent in for
a closer look has failed to report back."

"So this is the big lead?" Samir said. "An office park in America?"

"It's more than you had," Saddam said. "It's more than Bin Laden
has. Al Qaeda would give a lot for that address, I'd bet. Though
whether they'd be able to do anything with it . . ."

"But you think we can?" said Mustafa.

"If you're working for the president as you claim. You can have
the Marines escort you while you make your inquiries. I imagine
they'd be only too happy to help convince V. Howell Industries to
cooperate."

"And if we end up disappearing like your spies?" Amal said. "I'm
sure you'll shed a tear for us from the safety of Baghdad."

Saddam shrugged. "I promised information, not immunity from
danger. I think it's more than a fair trade. But here, I'll sweeten the
deal . . ." He reached into the safe again and pulled out a sheet of
paper. "This information is less exclusive, but still quite valuable."

The sheet contained a list of names. "Who are these people?"
Mustafa asked.

"Candidates for my own deck of cards," Saddam Hussein said.

"I'm sorry?"

"I believe you would call them 'persons of interest.' If you can find
them and get them to talk, they should have many fascinating things
to tell you." He added: "I'd like to interrogate one or two of them
myself, if I could. In fact I would pay for the privilege. Handsomely."

"But you don't know where they are?"

"At least some of them should be living in or around the American capital," Saddam said. "A few others may be in Texas. They will probably be people of influence, well respected, but however much power they have, it won't be what they feel they deserve." His expression clouded. "They'll be . . . frustrated. Eternally frustrated."

"You are talking in riddles," Mustafa said, "and I'm afraid after being up all night I have no head for it . . . Who are these people? How did you get this list?"

"I can't tell you where the list comes from."

"Somehow I thought that would be your answer." Mustafa sighed and stared at the paper. "What kind of name is 'Condoleezza'?"

"A woman. A black lady. She's less interesting to me than some of the others. The names higher up the list, those are the ones I really want."

The top two names on the list were almost identical. "A father and son?" Mustafa asked.

"Yes," Saddam said. "Those two I would very much like to have as my guests."

"You would like . . . So is this list for our benefit or yours?"

"There's no reason why we can't all benefit. If you should find any of these people, and if, after questioning them, you decide to pass them along to me, I will of course show my gratitude. Get me the father and the son, and you can have anything that is within my power to give . . . But please, don't say yes or no now. Just keep my offer in mind."

Mustafa ran a hand through his hair. He looked from the paper to the card and back again, then took another long look at the brass bottle. "Very well," he said finally, "I'll thank you for this information and see where it leads us. Enjoy your 'battery.'"

"Oh, I will," Saddam Hussein said. "And you, Mustafa al Baghdadi . . . Good hunting."

Book Three

The Glory and
the Kingdom

The Library of Alexandria
A USER-EDITED REFERENCE SOURCE

Lyndon B. Johnson

> This page is currently **protected** from editing to deal with **repeated acts of vandalism.** To suggest changes, please **contact an administrator.**

Lyndon Baines Johnson (August 27, 1908–December 30, 2006), a Protestant of the Disciples of Christ sect, was president of the Christian States of America (CSA) from November 22, 1963 until April 9, 2003. He seized power in the wake of the Kennedy family assassinations and was deposed during the Arabian invasion of America.

EARLY LIFE

Johnson was born in Stonewall in the Evangelical Republic of Texas. His father was a government official whose fortunes declined after he incurred the wrath of a powerful Baptist senator. In 1929 the entire family was forced to flee into exile in America.

RISE TO POWER

Little is known of Johnson's activities over the next quarter century, but by the mid-1950s he had become a member of the Department of Justice (DOJ), the American national police bureau charged with maintaining internal security. In 1958 Johnson uncovered a plot by a former naval officer named Richard Milhous Nixon to assassinate then-president Joseph P. Kennedy. Two years later, when Kennedy abdicated in favor of his son John, Johnson was put in charge of the DOJ's Secret Service branch.

On November 22, 1963, during a state visit to Texas, John F. Kennedy was shot and killed by a sniper. Back in Washington, D.C., Johnson ordered the Secret Service to round up the rest of the Kennedy clan and take them to a safe location. That evening, Johnson went on television and announced that the plane carrying the Kennedys to Hyannis Port had blown up in midair. "For the good of the country," he said, he would assume the powers of the executive himself. He then declared martial law . . .

While he solidified his grip on power, Johnson also began laying the groundwork for the conquest of his birth country.

"FOR THINE IS THE KINGDOM . . ."

Under interrogation following his capture by Coalition forces, Johnson's senior advisor Henry Kissinger revealed that since at least the 1960s, Johnson had had a recurring dream in which an angel recited to him the closing line of the Lord's Prayer: "For thine is the kingdom, and the power, and the glory, forever and ever." In the dream, Johnson understood "the kingdom" to be a reference to the Republic of Texas, while "the glory" was America; "the power" was Johnson himself, destined by God to unite the two nations—and ultimately, the entire North American continent—under one rule.

In September 1964, Johnson publicly accused the Texas CIA of masterminding the Kennedy killings. Among other evidence, he cited the suspicious death, in custody, of Dallas sniper Lee Harvey Oswald—murdered, Johnson said, to prevent him from revealing on whose orders he had acted. The Texas government formally denied Johnson's charges. Johnson put his armies on alert and prepared America for war.

Both Kissinger and military strategist Robert McNamara recommended a naval blockade of the Texas coast followed by an amphibious assault. But Johnson, inspired by another dream, decided to attack over land. As Texas and America do not share a border, this meant going through another country—either the Pentecostal Gilead Heartland, or the independent kingdoms of Mississippi and Louisiana.

Johnson chose to go through Gilead. He manufactured a *casus belli*, claiming that American patrol boats on Lake Erie had been fired at by ships of Gilead. On November 1, 1964, he launched a three-pronged ground assault west out of Appalachia. The attack went smoothly at first, but on November 3, an early blizzard blanketed the Midwest and halted the advance. Pentecostal militias, undaunted by the snow, counterattacked the Americans' supply lines; by the time the weather cleared two weeks later, Johnson's troops were starving and running out of fuel and ammunition. They staged an emergency retreat to the mountains, but were forced to abandon much of their equipment, which the Gileadites then seized . . .

The Heartland War raged on and off for eight years. Gilead's eastern plains were devastated and the cities of Detroit, Columbus, and Nashville were all but destroyed, but Johnson's troops were never able to gain a decisive advantage. America's technological and industrial superiority was matched by the fanaticism of the Gileadites, who pioneered the use of suicide bombers as a military tactic. The Mormon and Rocky Mountain tribespeople, fearing they would be at risk if Gilead fell, also joined in the fighting. Texas sent military aid and advisors.

The 1973 Algiers Peace Accords officially ended the war. Johnson's forces withdrew to the Appalachians for the last time. Although America had suffered little physical damage during the conflict, its economy was in shambles and its people were on the verge of revolt. Johnson would spend the next two decades coping with civil unrest and other domestic crises, but he never gave up his dream of conquering Texas. By the 1990s, he was ready to try again.

1991: THE MEXICAN GULF WAR

In June 1990, following a palace coup, the Kingdom of Mississippi allowed itself to be annexed and became America's eighteenth state.

Henry Kissinger flew to New Orleans and invited Louisiana's leaders to join the CSA as well; they declined.

On August 2, American troops invaded Louisiana. By August 6 much of the Louisiana Armed Forces had surrendered or fled into Texas. LBJ christened Louisiana the nineteenth American state and began massing his forces along the east Texas border.

Texas successfully appealed to its fellow OPEC members for help. On August 8 the UAS and Persia began airlifting troops into Houston and Dallas–Fort Worth, while the Venezuelan Navy established a defensive cordon along the Texas coastline . . . On January 17, 1991, the Coalition launched a massive air campaign. A ground assault followed on February 23, and in just 100 hours of fighting, Louisiana was liberated . . .

Although the Americans had suffered a humiliating military defeat, Johnson declared the Gulf War a great victory. Johnson's preening only added to the sense among many of the war's critics that, by allowing LBJ to remain in power, the Coalition had failed to finish the job. This in turn set the stage for the final act in the dictator's career . . .

They had landed in Tripoli to refuel. Looking out the window beside his seat, Mustafa could see, through the heat-shimmer rising off the tarmac, a broad tract of eucalyptus trees abutting the airfield. A sign identified this as CARBON SEQUESTRATION TEST PLOT #11.

By North African standards Tripoli was a lush city, its parks and gardens well irrigated by one of the governor's most successful public works projects, the Great Manmade River, which had tapped into the vast fossil water aquifer beneath the Sahara Desert. These eucalypti were part of an even grander Al Gaddafi scheme to fight global warming by turning the desert into a forest. Test plots like this one had been established throughout Libya, some two hundred hectares in all; the final plan called for the planting of a billion hectares, with over a trillion trees. It was going to take a while. But then the Internet hadn't happened in a day either.

Mustafa, Samir, and Amal had left Baghdad in the early morning, catching a commuter flight to Riyadh, where a military jeep had been waiting to transfer them to Al Kharj Air Force Base. At Al Kharj they had boarded this massive cargolifter. Although the occupation of America was supposed to be winding down, you'd never guess it by the amount of matériel crammed into the plane's cargo bay. An airman led them forward between the pallets of ammunition, medical supplies, and food rations, and up a stairwell to the passenger deck. There was relatively little human cargo; the handful of occupied seats were taken mostly by flight attendants and other crewmembers not directly involved in flying the plane.

The cargolifter's scheduled travel time was fifteen hours. Mustafa had brought plenty to read: lots of background material on America, and some classified documents obtained for him, with minimal re-

dactions, by the president's staff. Samir and Amal had similar reading packets.

"Ready for takeoff," the pilot announced.

A peculiarity of the cargolifter was that the passenger seats,
unlike those in a civilian airliner, were fixed facing backwards, so
as the plane lifted off Mustafa was easily able to look out and watch
first the eucalyptus tract and then the dusty green patchwork that
was Tripoli recede into the distance. Soon they were gone from view
and the plane proceeded westward over a tan landscape, the rocks
and sand of the great forest yet to be.

Mustafa returned to his reading.

The report, authored by the Political Science Faculty of the University of Sudan at Khartoum, was titled "Colorblind: The Role of Race
in the American Insurgency." It began with a brief recap of the history of black-white relations in 20th-century America. For the first
two-thirds of the century, the CSA had practiced a form of racial
apartheid—openly in the southern states, and more covertly in the
north, where, according to the report, "white citizens wanted the
benefits of racial preference without the culpability."

A Civil Rights Act banning race discrimination had been drafted
by the Kennedys and signed into law by LBJ during the first year of
his rule. "Statements made by Johnson and his closest aides suggest that in this, as in the attempted conquest of Texas, he believed
he was carrying out God's will. His enemies accused him of more
cynical motives. In the south, particularly, the Civil Rights Act was
seen as a pretext for expanding federal power and curtailing 'states'
rights.'" Several attempts at insurrection had to be crushed by federal troops. The Department of Justice rounded up political trou-
blemakers—black as well as white—and shipped them off to the
front lines of the Heartland War. "While Johnson succeeded at dis-
mantling the American apartheid system—the one truly admirable

achievement of his reign—he did not eliminate American racism. Rather, he drove his subjects' ethnic hatred underground, where it festered for decades, waiting for a chance to spring forth again. That chance finally came in 2003. The Coalition invasion of America crippled federal control over the states. It also created a situation in which open expression of prejudice against darker-skinned people was considered not just politically acceptable, but patriotic . . ."

Enter Boulos al Darir, a favored son of the National Party of God and the man chosen to oversee the reconstruction of America during the crucial first year following the invasion. He was a disaster, issuing a series of unpopular decrees that killed whatever small chance there might have been of a peaceful transition to democracy.

The most infamous of these decrees was Order Number 2, which disbanded the Minutemen—the American National Guard— thereby throwing half a million heavily armed Christians out of work. Order Number 3, a purge of all Christian Democrat Party members from the Federal Civil Service, created another hundred thousand unemployed. "Because many of these civil servants, as well as many of the Minutemen stationed in the Washington, D.C., area, were African-American," the report stated, "these Orders were widely interpreted as an attempt by the occupying forces to ally with the white majority against the black minority. Had this in fact been the case, Administrator Al Darir's policy decisions might have been defensible on practical if not moral grounds. However, it appears in hindsight that he acted in ignorance, creating enormous racial animus to no purpose."

Any favor that Al Darir had incidentally earned with white Americans went out the window with Order Number 5, the decree banning the manufacture and sale of alcoholic beverages. The idea that prohibition could be made to work in what was still a war zone was farcical at best; outside the occupied capital, the ban had little effect on Americans' drinking habits. But there were other consequences.

In suddenly dry Washington, a thriving black market sprang up, giving out-of-work Minutemen a new way to make a living—and a new reason to fight for territory. The Coalition forces, meanwhile, became an army of untrained Halal agents. Troops that should have been helping to reestablish stability were instead sent on search-and-destroy missions for breweries and distilleries. Sometimes they found them. Sometimes they made mistakes and destroyed other targets instead: medical supply factories; food warehouses; schools. News of the worst outrages spread throughout the country, causing more unrest.

At an emergency meeting, some of Al Darir's aides tried to convince him to repeal the Order. He refused. Then, making the single most regrettable statement of his career, he suggested that if Americans wanted to relax at the end of the day, they should try smoking hashish; the climate of the southern states in particular, Al Darir noted, ought to be excellent for the cultivation of cannabis.

Perhaps he was trying to make a joke. Perhaps he was being overly candid about his own habits. No one ever really knew for sure, and once the remark was leaked to the public by Al Darir's enemies, he refused all further comment. Morally, of course, the suggestion made no sense: The Quran condemns all intoxicants, not just alcohol. But a much bigger problem was that it displayed, yet again, the administrator's complete ignorance of American racial sensitivities.

Like cocaine and opium, cannabis had long been illegal in the CSA—not for religious reasons, but out of a belief that its consumption inflamed the lust of black men. In many white communities, Al Darir's "let them smoke hash" comment was interpreted as an incitement to mass rape. This did not go over well.

It was only a week later that a white mob in Langley hanged the bodies of four Arab civilian contractors from a highway overpass. For Boulos al Darir's superiors, it was the last straw; as the Marines went into Fairfax County, the administrator was recalled to Riyadh, and his pending Order Number 9, which would have outlawed pork products, was quietly shelved. But the damage had been done, and on one issue at least, white Americans and black Americans were now in total agreement: The Coalition Authority had outstayed its welcome.

Mustafa got up to stretch his legs. He noticed Amal laughing at something from her own reading packet and asked, "What is it?"

"Our tax dollars at work," Amal said. She showed him a pamphlet, *Thirteen Simple Rules for Dealing with Americans*, designed for first-time visitors with short attention spans.

Rule #1 was DON'T EXPECT THANKS: "Americans are a proud people. Though their civilization is still in its infancy, they consider themselves equal, if not superior to, older and more established cultures. The fact that they had to be liberated by outsiders is a source of great shame to them, and while the vast majority are grateful for the gift of freedom, they are extremely reluctant to show it.

"You may feel that Americans complain too much. Try to ignore this. Pointing out the many ways in which their lives have improved will only make them complain more. *Never* tell an American that they 'ought to be thankful.' In American culture this is considered a grave insult and may lead to violence."

The accompanying cartoon illustration showed a tank parked on the lawn of a house. The tank driver stood beside his vehicle, smiling and holding out a hand of friendship, but the owner of the house, a sullen black man in a tri-cornered hat, had his arms crossed. In the background a woman could be seen peeking out the house's front window, looking frightened—as well she might be, Mustafa thought, with a cannon pointed at her living room.

"Isn't it brilliant?" Amal said. She indicated the byline on the pamphlet's back cover. "The American Culture Initiative, I remember my mother showing me the budget earmark for this. They got three million riyals just for research. Three million riyals, to figure

out that people won't say thank you if you drive a tank into their yard.
That's money well spent, don't you think?"

"It might have been," Mustafa said, "if anyone in the Coalition
had paid attention."

Two hours later they crossed the Moroccan coastline. As the cargolifter headed out over the Atlantic, Mustafa opened a folder
marked TOP SECRET. Inside was a summary and partial transcript of
the interrogation of Lyndon Baines Johnson.

The Coalition had not planned on taking the American president
alive. The opening move in the "shock and awe" campaign had been
an attempted decapitation strike: Arabian stealth bombers based out
of Houston had targeted the White House, the Capitol Building, and
seven command bunkers scattered throughout the District of Co-
lumbia. The attacks on the Capitol and the bunkers had been successful, but the smart bombs dropped on the White House had all
either missed the target or failed to detonate—a statistical unlikeli-
hood that verged on the miraculous and convinced the Coalition air
commander not to bother with a follow-up strike.

LBJ must have seen the hand of God in the White House's sur-
vival as well. Rather than go into hiding once the invasion started,
he remained in the executive mansion until ground forces arrived
to apprehend him. Two different stories were told about his capture. In one version, reported by FOX News and dismissed by the
Arab government as propaganda, a defiant Johnson was waiting in
the Oval Office when the UAS Army Fourth Infantry entered the
White House. The president saluted the soldiers, then thwacked his
cane against the unexploded thousand-kilo bomb that had crushed
his desk, asking, "Did you gentlemen lose this?"

In the other version, as told to Al Jazeera by an Army corporal
who claimed to have been there, Johnson was found upstairs, cow-
ering in the Lincoln Bedroom. Frightened and confused, he had
seemed unable at first to comprehend the presence of foreign troops

in his home. "What are you doing here?" he demanded, over and over again. Mustafa had always suspected that this version of events was propaganda as well, the notion of a senile dictator fitting too neatly with the official rationale for the war. But according to the folder in his hands, the story was accurate, except for one detail: The question Johnson asked his captors was not "What are you doing here?" but "What am *I* doing here?"

The Coalition's leaders debated what to do with LBJ now that he was in custody. The consensus was that he should be turned over to the Americans for trial—once the country had a functioning legal system again—but before that happened there were some questions that needed answering, about 11/9 and about the elusive WMDs. A few hardliners advocated sending him to the Chwaka Bay detention camp on the island of Zanzibar, but that plan was rejected for fear that the ninety-four-year-old Johnson was too frail to survive the trip, let alone the standard interrogation process. Instead he was flown by helicopter to Cape Cod, to the old Kennedy Compound. There, attended by a team of Navy doctors, he slept in a real bed and ate decent food. He was permitted books, music, and DVDs, though he was denied newspapers and live television. Twice daily if he wished he was allowed to go for walks on the beach, frogmen in the surf making sure he didn't try to drown himself.

With this gentle treatment, his physical and mental health improved, as did his mood. By the time an intelligence officer named Abd al Rahim al Talib arrived to interview him, Johnson was ready to talk.

AL TALIB: Please tell me if you would, Mr. President, what is the Domino Theory?
JOHNSON: An idea of William Westmoreland's. Kissinger and McNamara weren't enthusiastic about getting involved in a land war, but Westmoreland was all for it. His theory was that each piece of territory we took on the way to Texas would be like a domino fall-

ing, helping us knock down the next one, and by the time we got to Austin we'd have built up so much momentum that we could just keep going, all the way to the California coast. Bring the whole country under one roof like God intended.

AL TALIB: The whole country? Don't you mean the whole continent, Mr. President?

JOHNSON: The country and the continent are one, Mr. Al Talib. That's destiny.

AL TALIB: It would seem many of your would-be countrymen didn't agree.

JOHNSON: You mean the Pentecostals? It was a mistake to pick on them first. People who believe the Holy Spirit grants them magic powers are inclined to be stubborn. Still, I wouldn't be too sure about what they do or don't agree with. You're a man of faith, Mr. Al Talib. Don't you find yourself fighting hardest against those things you know in your heart to be true?

AL TALIB: Yes. But the struggle you are alluding to is not one that can be won with violence. At least I don't believe so.

JOHNSON: I regret the violence. I know history will regard me as a warmonger and that was never my intention. Everything I did was to defend my country.

AL TALIB: But you do feel remorse?

JOHNSON: Of course I do. How could I not? I have the blood of thousands of Americans on my hands. I'm going to have to answer to God for that, and soon, and I am not looking forward to it.

AL TALIB: And what about Arabian blood, Mr. President? What about the thousands killed in Baghdad and—

JOHNSON: There you lose me, sir.

AL TALIB: Do I, Mr. President? As you say, soon you must answer to God, from whom nothing is hidden. Why not make a full confession now?

JOHNSON: I can only confess to my own sins, Mr. Al Talib, just as I can only acknowledge my own faults. One thing I am not is a fool.

AL TALIB: I'm not suggesting you're a fool, Mr. President.

JOHNSON: That's exactly what you're doing, when you accuse me of attacking your country. Why would I do that?

AL TALIB: As revenge for the Gulf War, of course. We stopped your dominoes from falling. Surely this made you angry?

JOHNSON: Yes, it did. And when I get angry at someone, I call him a son of a bitch. I don't burn down his house and start a feud with his whole family. Especially a feud I know I can't win.

"The prisoner remains adamant that he had no involvement in 11/9," Al Talib wrote to his superiors in Riyadh. "When I suggested that the mountain Christians who claimed responsibility for the attack were too backward to have carried it off without help, LBJ replied that it wasn't long ago that 'the Ay-rabs' were 'riding around on camels,' and yet only a bigot would argue that we were incapable of 'both great and terrible deeds.' I then asked him to speculate: If it wasn't the mountain men, who might be responsible? He reminded me that the hijackers were all traveling on Texas passports and noted that the Evangelical Republic's leaders were obviously pleased to see him out of power. 'I'm not saying they did it, but that's what I'd look for in a culprit: Someone who wanted to start a war, or a jee-had as you call it.'

"As to the other matter, I regret that I've made no better progress, though here the problem isn't denial but rather the inability to have a coherent conversation. Johnson as you know suffers from incipient dementia. Though generally lucid, he has episodes in which he becomes delusional and believes that his dream of 'uniting America' has already come to pass. These episodes are typically random, but they can also be triggered, and the subject in question appears to be one of the most potent triggers."

AL TALIB: I am sorry, Mr. President, but once again I must raise the subject of the WMDs.

JOHNSON: WMDs?

AL TALIB: [Sighs.] Yes sir, weapons of mass destruction. Nuclear, biological, and—

JOHNSON: Nuclear? You're asking me whether America has nuclear weapons?

AL TALIB: Yes.

JOHNSON: Of course we do. What do you think a superpower *is,* son?

AL TALIB: And where are these weapons, Mr. President?

JOHNSON: Out west.

AL TALIB: West of the capital?

JOHNSON: No, *west* west. Wyoming, Montana, the Dakotas—

AL TALIB: Montana? In the Rocky Mountains?

JOHNSON: —and Missouri.

AL TALIB: But how could that be, Mr. President? Missouri is Mormon territory, is it not?

JOHNSON: Mormons? What do the damn Mormons have to do with it?

At no point during the interrogation or in any of his communiqués with Riyadh did Al Talib give any sign that he thought Johnson's "delusions" might reflect a broader mythology shared by others, nor was there any explicit mention of the mirage. But perhaps in response to the "triggers," Johnson's mental state began to deteriorate again, and as his statements became more cryptic and oracular, gaps appeared in the transcript.

The last interview took place following a five-day period during which Johnson was ill with a fever. The Riyadhis, having accepted by this point that they were not going to get a confession, and fearful of having LBJ die in their custody, decided to terminate the interrogation process after one final exchange.

AL TALIB: How are you today, Mr. President?

JOHNSON: [Inaudible.]

AL TALIB: "Bushed"? You are tired? Here, have some water.

JOHNSON: Thank you.

AL TALIB: I won't stay long today.

JOHNSON: No, it's all right. Sit down, sir. I know we're running out of time. Or rather, I am.

AL TALIB: Has someone told you something, Mr. President?

JOHNSON: The Almighty and I have been in consultation.

AL TALIB: God spoke to you?

JOHNSON: After a fashion. Would you like to hear about a dream I had?

AL TALIB: If you wish.

JOHNSON: I was back in Stonewall, in a one-room schoolhouse.

AL TALIB: This is the school you attended as a boy?

JOHNSON: The schoolhouse itself was a set, from the LBJ Library in Washington. But in the dream it had been moved to Stonewall, and because there was no roof I could look up and see the sky that I was born under.

I was alone, sitting in a pupil's desk. There were ten desks in all, arranged in three rows of three, with the last desk in the middle of what would have been the fourth row. I was directly in front of that one, in seat number eight. And at the front of the room was a blackboard with ten digits written on it, one through zero . . . Your English is so good, Mr. Al Talib, I assume you're also familiar with how we Americans write our numbers?

AL TALIB: You call them Arabic numerals for a reason, Mr. President.

JOHNSON: Oh yes, of course. Well, I was sitting there, looking at the numbers on the blackboard, and the sky above got very dark and there was an . . . earthquake, I guess, only more than that, as if God had picked up the whole planet in His hands and was shaking it. My desk stayed put, and I myself couldn't move, but most everything else went flying. The blackboard came right off the wall and went tumbling end over end, whirling around the room. Even when it went behind my head, though, I could still see it, as though it were reflected in a mirror.

Now numbers, when you do reflect them in a mirror, you know what happens to most of them? They look different. You can still recognize them for what they are supposed to be, but they become strange, alien.

AL TALIB: But not the number eight.

JOHNSON: No, not number eight. You can turn it on its head, write it backwards or forwards, it stays the same.

AL TALIB: Also zero. And one, if you write it with a single stroke.

JOHNSON: Yes, but one is God's number. And zero, you can guess who that belongs to. Eight, however, eight could be a man, or aspects of man.

AL TALIB: And how do you interpret this dream, Mr. President?

JOHNSON: Some things don't change. The world could be turned upside down and still some things would remain exactly as they are. The Almighty Himself, of course. Good and evil. The creed of God's disciples.

AL TALIB: And the person of Lyndon Baines Johnson?

JOHNSON: I am who I am.

AL TALIB: And the transformation of the world, what is that an allusion to? The invasion of your country?

JOHNSON: A week ago I would have answered yes. Now . . . Now I think my reversal of fortune is only a piece of a larger whole.

AL TALIB: What is the larger whole?

JOHNSON: You wouldn't believe it if I told you. But it all makes sense now. I understand what I'm doing here. It's about continuity.

AL TALIB: Continuity, Mr. President?

JOHNSON: God wanted to keep a Texan in charge. He upended everything else, but He still wanted that: a Texan, with something resembling a brain, to lead America in her darkest hour. And really, who else are you going to get to fill that role?

AL TALIB: I don't understand.

JOHNSON: That's all right, Mr. Al Talib. You will, in God's own time. Peace be unto you, sir.

During the second refueling stop, in the Azores, some of the crew came off the plane to pray and Mustafa joined them. Afterwards he noticed something about the way they'd been facing, and realized that since leaving UAS airspace they'd crossed another invisible boundary. He spoke to one of the airmen, who confirmed that he was right.

"From here, the direction of the Qibla is eighty-six degrees, slightly north of east. It's an effect of the earth's curvature," the airman added, used to dealing with civilian officials whose grasp of world geography was poor. "Mecca is closer to the equator, so on a flat map it looks as though you ought to pray facing southeast. But if you plot it on the surface of a globe, you see that the shortest distance to Mecca is actually a great-circle route, which—"

"I know what a great circle is," Mustafa said gently, picturing a younger version of himself standing at the front of a classroom.

"The effect is more pronounced in America," the airman said. "In Washington, the Qibla direction is fifty-six degrees. And should you continue on to the west coast of the continent, you'd be facing almost due north when you prayed. Of course the cannibals in the Rocky Mountains would probably eat you before you got that far . . ."

When they were airborne again, the pilot announced they'd be at Andrews Air Force Base in another five hours, around 9 p.m. local time. A flight attendant described the special landing procedure. To minimize the threat from ground-based missile attacks, the plane would stay above ten thousand feet until it was directly over the airfield, then spiral down quickly to the runway. "Especially in darkness, it may seem like we are out of control and about to crash, but God willing we'll be fine, so please don't panic."

Mustafa had more reading to do but decided to rest his eyes for a few minutes first, and fell into an uneasy sleep that lasted for the rest of the flight. When the cargolifter began its terminal dive, he dreamed he started awake to find the plane packed with Americans. In the seat beside him a woman was reciting a rosary in terror, and when Mustafa stood up and looked about the now strangely enlarged passenger cabin, he saw other frightened faces—some praying, some crying, some whispering covertly into cell phones. None of these people seemed able to see him, but that could change in a heartbeat, and he did not think it would be healthy to become the focus of all that fear.

Struggling to keep his balance in the steeply angled aisle, he made his way to the front of the plane. Two Arab men in civilian dress stood guard outside the cockpit door, and with the certainty of dream Mustafa knew they were no more his allies than the Christians in the back. He passed ghostlike into the cockpit, where another Arab sat hunched over the controls.

They were very close to the ground. It was morning, not night, and Mustafa could clearly see the American capital across the river ahead. He also saw an airport off to the right, but they weren't turning towards it. Instead they were headed straight for a large pentagonal building on the near side of the river. This was deliberate. The pilot had the plane under control and he was calm, smiling like a man on his way into paradise.

"Hey, moron!" Mustafa shouted at him. "You're going to murder us all, what's wrong with you?"

The pilot gave no answer, just dipped the nose of the plane a bit farther. Mustafa made a grab for the controls and woke for real aboard the cargolifter even as its wheels bumped the runway at Andrews.

Across the aisle, Amal let out a sigh of relief and then laughed. "Now that's a landing!" she said. Samir, tearing at his armrests in the next row forward, added: "Already I hate this country."

Green Zone

The **Green Zone** is a heavily fortified region of Washington, D.C., that served as the headquarters of the Coalition Provisional Authority. It measures roughly 10 square kilometers and is surrounded by a blast-proof concrete wall topped with electrified razor wire. Entry into the Zone is only possible via helicopter or through one of seven tightly controlled checkpoints.

The Green Zone includes the National Mall, a large open park space lined with monuments and government buildings that is claimed by some sources to have been the original inspiration for the Zone's name. By 2004, however, with the American insurgency in full swing, "Green Zone" was understood to be a reference to the fact that this was an oasis of relative safety in an increasingly dangerous area. The rest of Washington—and America—became, by extension, "the Red Zone."

In January 2009, control of the Green Zone passed from the Coalition Authority to the newly installed American government. Many of the Coalition troops have since withdrawn to bases outside Washington. However, a sizeable garrison of UAS Marines remains within the Zone to safeguard the Arabian, Persian, and Kurdish embassies, and to help American security forces defend against the continuing insurgent attacks.

NOTABLE SITES IN THE GREEN ZONE

· The White House

· The Capitol Building (undergoing reconstruction)

· The Washington Monument

· The CSA Treasury Building

· The Smithsonian Creation Science Museum

· The Watergate Complex

Mustafa woke again, from a dream of smokeless fire. He was lying on a four-poster bed with an embroidered canopy. Samir was a snoring lump on a second bed to his left, and to his right was a massive oak chest of drawers. A sign atop the chest, just legible in the faint glow of a nightlight, claimed that all three pieces of furniture were the onetime property of Pope Urban II. As for the room, it had originally been an office; looking between the bedposts Mustafa could see a windowed door, the words ASSISTANT CURATOR painted in reverse on the glass.

He sat up, remembering a helicopter ride from the airbase and a hasty meet-and-greet with a Marine Colonel Yunus who had been assigned to act as their host. Mustafa estimated he'd gotten to sleep between eleven and midnight. His watch now said 11:30, which, whether a.m. or p.m., seemed unlikely.

He got up and slipped out quietly. The hall outside the office brought him to a room painted with a mural of a deluge. Three of the walls showed only clouds and rain and wind-tossed waves; inset against the fourth was a scale model of an ark. A bearded white patriarch stood at the ark's stern, gazing towards the center of the room, where a jagged pedestal like the tip of a drowning mountain jutted up from the blue carpet. The skeleton of a dinosaur with sickle-shaped claws on its hind feet was set on the pedestal, poised as if it were about to take a leap at the ark, but the placard at the pedestal's base suggested it would not make it. "*Velociraptor antirrhopus*," the placard read. "Extinct, 2349 B.C."

A doorway in the wall opposite the ark led to a gallery containing the bones of many more of the Flood's victims. The gallery had a skylight as well, and looking up Mustafa saw stars.

Wandering farther through the museum, he came upon Colonel Yunus in a room that looked like a tourism ad for Giza. "Good morning," the colonel greeted him.

"So it is morning, then," Mustafa said.

"Yes, about half past four. Were you able to sleep at all?"

"Some. The accommodations are quite comfortable." Thinking of the velociraptor: "And unusual."

The colonel smiled. "I don't know how much you remember from our conversation last night, but this building really is a storehouse of wonders. During the initial occupation a large number of troops were housed here, in part to prevent looting. Now that the Americans have retaken control the museum is mostly unoccupied, but a few of us have been allowed to remain as unofficial caretakers until the new government has the money to reopen the place."

"Thank you for sharing it with me."

"You are welcome. I was just about to pray. Would you like to join me?"

"I would, thank you."

"And your friend?"

"Samir is not observant, I'm afraid."

"Ah. Well," the colonel said, pointing, "there's a washroom that way, and you'll find some spare prayer rugs tucked behind Pharaoh's palace."

"You pray in here?"

"Sometimes, yes." Smiling again: "I have a theory that a Muslim helped design this room. It turns out if you draw a straight line from the Sphinx to the part in the Red Sea over there, it corresponds almost exactly to the Qibla direction."

"Interesting symbolism," Mustafa said.

"Yes, there's a lot of that in the Green Zone. It's a weird place."

Amal woke among lionesses.

At last night's meeting with the colonel she'd been sufficiently alert to understand that Mustafa and Samir were being given VIP accommodations while she was being relegated to women's quarters, which annoyed her until she realized which women she'd be bunking with.

The Women's Combat Support Unit, aka the Lionesses, had been formed in 2007 as part of the broader counterinsurgency strategy known as the Surge. In addition to their reluctance to show gratitude, most Americans had a deep-seated cultural aversion to having their homes ransacked, but research had found that a feminine presence could help moderate this. Lionesses were assigned in pairs to accompany Marines on patrol in the Red Zone. When a house was searched for weapons or insurgents, it was the Lionesses who interviewed the occupants, preserving the honor of the women and keeping the men calm; they could often get answers where a male interrogator would be met by stony silence, or violence. The Red Zone being the Red Zone, violence did still sometimes occur, but as their nickname implied, Lionesses could also fight, and with a ferocity that took insurgents by surprise.

They lived along with the Marine garrison troops in the former residential and business complex adjacent to the Arabian embassy. Most of the male Marines occupied apartments in the Watergate East and South buildings; the Lionesses were housed on the top two floors of the Watergate Hotel, which had been turned into a high-security women's dorm.

It was like college, but with more guns. Amal shared a room with a girl from Nablus named Zinat. Barely nineteen, Zinat had followed her six brothers into the military in order to earn a scholarship and pursue an engineering degree. When Amal asked what sort of engineering she was interested in, Zinat said, "Cars. Fast cars."

Zinat kept a picture of her family taped above her bunk. A second photo showed Zinat and several other Lionesses gathered around the Persian war correspondent Christiane Amanpour, who'd done a special report on the women's unit earlier this year. Zinat stood to Amanpour's right, cradling a .50-caliber sniper rifle that was almost as big as she was. "Do you bring this weapon on patrol?" Amal asked.

"No, that was just for the photo," Zinat said, sounding a bit wistful. "We were at the combat range and I talked the gunnery sergeant into letting me pose with it . . . If you'd like, I could probably take you over there for some practice shooting." She raised an eyebrow. "They've got flamethrowers, too."

"That sounds like fun," Amal said, less interested in flamethrowers than in locating Salim. But perhaps this girl could help her with that. As for what she would do once she actually found her son . . . Well, Amal was still working on that. One step at a time.

Reveille for the troops was a muezzin's call piped through the Watergate intercom system. After washing up, Amal followed Zinat to the top-floor lounge that served as the women's prayer room. Attendance at prayer was voluntary, but it looked as though most of the Lionesses, save the few who were Christians or Jews, were there. The majority were Zinat's age, but among them were a number of older career Marines.

The Lionesses' commander was a fifty-two-year-old from Yemen named Umm Husam, who also served as the women's prayer leader. As the last of her charges entered the room, she turned to face the northeast wall and raised her hands beside her head.

"God is great," Umm Husam began.

The main banquet room in the Watergate Hotel was now a Marine chow hall. A portion of the seating area had been reserved for the Lionesses, and during Christiane Amanpour's visit that section of the hall had been cordoned off by folding screens. Today, with no reporters present, the screens had been exchanged for orange traffic cones, and even these were largely ignored, the women and men fraternizing openly with only an occasional disapproving glance from Umm Husam.

At a table just on the men's side of the divide, Mustafa, Samir, and Amal took breakfast with Colonel Yunus, Zinat, and two male Marines. Mustafa asked a question about the African-American civilians working the serving line; like the iconic homeowner in Amal's pamphlet, they were all wearing tri-cornered hats.

"The tricorne is a symbol of the Minutemen," Colonel Yunus explained. "Most of our support staff are former National Guard. We give them jobs to discourage them from taking up arms against us. The hats are a touchy subject—insurgents like to wear them, too—but we're trying to win hearts and minds so we don't make a fuss about it."

"What kind of Christians are they?" Mustafa asked next. "My reading suggested that black Americans are more often Protestant than Catholic, but it didn't say what denominations they favor."

"I'm afraid I know nothing about Protestant denominations," Colonel Yunus said. "But these men aren't all Christian. Some of them are Muslim."

"Muslim?" said Samir.

"Yes. Islam is still a minority faith in America, but it has made inroads, particularly among the marginalized."

"Which sect of Islam?" Mustafa wondered. "Sunni or Shia?"

The colonel seemed disappointed by the question. "Surely that's of no consequence. Islam is Islam."

"I agree," said Mustafa, "but still I'm curious."

The colonel shrugged. "If it were considered polite to inquire, I imagine most would answer Sunni."

"That's interesting," Amal said, guessing at Mustafa's train of thought. "If they're Sunni Muslims, that would make them eligible for membership in Al Qaeda, wouldn't it?"

"Al Qaeda!" Zinat snorted laughter. "What fantasy is this?"

Samir looked alarmed. "You really think Bin Laden would recruit Americans?"

"If I might change the subject a moment," Colonel Yunus said, clearly uncomfortable with this turn in the conversation. "I'd like to talk a bit about your mission here . . ."

"Of course," said Mustafa.

"I've discussed the matter in some depth with Lieutenant Fahd." The colonel indicated one of the other Marines at the table. "The address you are interested in visiting is about thirty kilometers from here. There are insurgents in the vicinity—they've been quiet lately, but we know they are still there, and if we try to secure the area in advance it might just encourage them to mount an assault. Lieutenant Fahd proposes instead that we dispatch you with a light reconnaissance force—four Humvees, plus air support—and try to get you in and out before the insurgents can react. Do you know how much time you'll need on site?"

"It depends what we find there," Mustafa said. "Obviously we won't stay any longer than necessary."

"Very well," Colonel Yunus said. "I'll reserve some additional forces in case it does become necessary to secure the area—or in case there's trouble. This will take another twenty-four hours to arrange. I suggest you spend today resting, and be ready to leave tomorrow after breakfast."

"Thank you. That will be fine."

"If you'd like some diversion, I can have one of my men give you a tour of the Green Zone. Or if you don't mind waiting while I take care of a few matters, I can show you around myself."

"Sir," Zinat said. "Amal has expressed interest in visiting Potomac Park. With your permission I'd be happy to take her."

"The combat range?" The colonel gave Amal a quizzical look, but then shrugged. "Of course . . . If that's what you wish."

He said something else but Amal didn't hear it. She was staring at the chow line, where the ghost of her father was bantering with a black man in a tri-cornered hat.

The ghost was not Shamal as she had known him. This was the young Shamal, a newly minted BU grad working off his ROTC scholarship, still a year or two away from meeting the ambitious woman from Maysan Province who would become his wife. The uniform was wrong—he'd been an Army cadet, not a Marine—but other than that he might have stepped right from the family photo album, so uncanny was the resemblance. Likewise his mannerisms—the way he stood, the way he tilted his head to listen, the easy way he laughed, which would become less easy as time and Saddam wore him down—were all just as Amal remembered.

Zinat saw the ghost too. While Amal sat motionless, fearful of dispelling this vision with a careless gesture, the Lioness stood up, cupped her hands to her mouth, and called out: "Hey! Salim! Over here!"

"Target right!"

This Minuteman was a white American, with big teeth and a big nose, angry eyes, and slashing eyebrows beneath a tricorne that looked a size too small for him. Like the restaurant in whose window he had so suddenly appeared—a painted stage flat adorned with golden arches—he was also two-dimensional. And he was armed with a revolver, which made him a bad guy: Amal pulled the trigger on her rifle and put three bullet holes in a tight grouping between his eyes. The Minuteman continued to glare at her for another full second before succumbing to his wound and dropping out of sight.

A chime sounded and Amal walked another ten paces down "Main Street"—actually an indoor lane lined with fake buildings. Her next target swung out sideways from behind a building marked KRISPY KREME. He had the same exact face as the Minuteman, but instead of a tricorne he wore a jersey with the word REDSKINS on it.

"Target left!" Amal said. But the man was holding a soda cup, and after double-checking that the straw wasn't really a lit fuse, she held her fire. After three seconds, the man ducked back into cover.

The rules of the game were simple. There were four kinds of targets—Minuteman, sports fan, woman, child—each holding one of four objects—revolver, pipe bomb, daisy, or soda cup. The goal was to shoot only those targets holding weapons. Hit three unarmed adults or one unarmed child, and you lost. Miss even one target holding a gun, and you lost. Miss a target holding a pipe bomb, and everyone on the shooting course lost.

Two of the course's four lanes were down for maintenance, so Zinat sat out while Amal and Salim played. To keep from shooting each other, they advanced side-by-side and announced the appearance of each new target before deciding whether to pull the trigger.

"Target left!" Amal called out again, as a woman in a cocktail dress appeared in one of the windows of the Krispy Kreme. The woman was holding a daisy, but Salim had just called a target of his own and was firing, so Amal imagined she saw a revolver cylinder and put a three-round burst in the woman's ample bosom. A buzzer sounded and an X appeared on the scoreboard at the end of Amal's lane. It was her second strike.

"Damn it," Amal said.

"You're doing fine," Salim told her. "Stay cool, we're almost at the end."

There were only two buildings left in Amal's lane, a house and a hospital. She watched the windows, and got two Minutemen in quick succession, one—"Target right!"—with a revolver, whom she killed, the other—"Target left!"—with a daisy, whom she (just barely) let live. In his lane, Salim shot a Redskins fan with a pipe bomb, and then a final chime sounded and the voice of the gunnery sergeant said, "Course completed. Please clear your weapons."

Amal removed the magazine from her rifle and emptied the cham-

ber, calling out "Clear!" once this was done. Salim called out "Clear!"
as well and a long buzzer sounded, indicating that the course was,
for the moment, safe.

"You did well for a first-timer," Salim said as they walked back
down Main Street.

"I don't think those two poor innocents I shot would agree with
you," Amal said. But she was pleased with her performance. Earlier
at the sniper-rifle range she'd been a bundle of nerves, barely able to
focus on the target.

She was beginning to get used to him. Thank God he didn't sound
like her father. The timbre of his voice was more like Anwar's, and
while Anwar's voice in young Shamal's mouth was unnerving in its
own way, at least she didn't feel as though she were talking to the
dead.

Zinat had been joined by another Lioness. "Do you mind if we
have a go?" Zinat asked, nodding at the course.

"Please," said Amal. She and Salim turned in their weapons, and
then, at Amal's suggestion, stepped outside to have a smoke.

Before the invasion, East Potomac Park had been LBJ's private
golf course, and you could still get in nine holes down by Hains
Point. But the Marines, on the pretext of securing the Tidal Basin,
had turned the upper part of the peninsula into a carnival of violence. East of the blockhouse that contained the indoor target range
was a great earthen berm, erected around the sniper's range to stop
stray rounds from traveling into Southwest D.C. To the north was
the grenade toss, and to the right of that in a concrete pen, hand-
held sprayers belched fire at asbestos-clad mannequins. West was
the Potomac, with Marines and other Green Zone refugees sunning
themselves on the riverbank, while patrolling gunboats kept watch
for waterborne suicide bombers.

Salim bent close to light Amal's cigarette. She glimpsed her father's ghost again and shivered.

"So where did you learn to shoot?" Salim asked.

"Beirut."

He was surprised. "You're Lebanese?"

"Baghdadi," Amal said. "But I went to college at U of L."

"Huh! Me too!"

She played it coy: "Really? Forgive me, you don't look old enough to be a graduate."

"Ah, I'm not—I was only enrolled for about a week." He looked around. "I didn't want to miss this."

"Doing your part for the War on Terror," Amal said. "Your parents must be very proud."

He frowned, and she worried she'd been too forward. But then he said: "My dad, you know, he's not *entirely* happy with me . . ."

"Oh?"

"He's a conservative," Salim explained, loyalty and resentment warring on his face for a moment. "He loves me, but he doesn't want me to take any risks."

"And your mother? What does she think?"

This time there was no conflict: He just looked guilty. "She's scared for me. In her last letter . . ." He trailed off, took a drag on his cigarette. "But I've promised her I'll be OK."

"Well then," Amal said, eyeing one of the gunboats on the river. "As long as you promised."

He laughed. "It's only a seven-month deployment! In no time I'll be home again, and bored . . . So what's it like to work for Homeland Security?"

"Exciting," she said. "More exciting than I expected, actually. And before this I worked for the Bureau, which was also pretty cool. You get to chase bank robbers. Of course," Amal added, "for either job you need to finish college."

"Yeah, I know," Salim said. "I promised my mother I'd do that, too."

They tossed their cigarette butts and went back inside the target range, where Zinat and her friend had just finished. "What's wrong?" Salim asked, seeing their faces. "Don't tell me you lost!"

"*I* didn't," Zinat said. "But Tamara shot a kid with a soda cup."

"A fat American child," Tamara sniffed, handing her rifle back to the gunnery sergeant.

"It's well-known that soda's no good for your health," Salim offered.

"Speaking of unhealthy sweets," said Amal, "what is that about?" She pointed to a dish of hard candies that sat on the counter in front of the gun storage area. The candy dish, which had been fashioned from a piece of a mortar shell casing, had a steel tab sticking up from its center, to which a crude skull and crossbones had been welded. Just in case this wasn't clear enough, a little cardboard sign had been taped beneath the skull, reading FORBIDDEN! Amal had noticed a similar candy dish at the sniper range, although that one had contained toffees.

"That," said the gunnery sergeant, "is an object lesson about the importance of following rules."

"And of the long-term effects of testosterone on one's sense of humor," Zinat added. The gunny scowled at her, but she smiled back sweetly until he turned away.

"They're not really poisoned, though," Amal said.

"Oh yes," Salim said, "with cyanide." He explained: "There's a Christian holiday here, called Halloween—the Eve of the Saints— where it's traditional to give away candy to strangers. Last year, the chow hall got an anonymous gift of Halloween candies."

"Did anyone die?"

"No Marines did. There was a stray dog that hung around behind the Watergate kitchens, begging for scraps. One of the cooks gave it a sweet, and that's how they found out about the poison. The candies were supposed to be destroyed, but as you can see, some were kept as souvenirs. And as good luck charms, of course."

"Good luck charms," Amal said. "Because no one died."

"Except the dog," Salim said. Smiling, he took one of the candies from the dish and gave it to her. "Here. To keep you safe while you're in America."

Amal stared at the candy, which was wrapped in a twist of green cellophane. "Thanks," she said. "I think."

"Just don't forget and eat it by mistake," he told her.

Samir spent the morning trying to hide from Al Qaeda.

Just before leaving Baghdad, he'd gotten a message from Idris saying that a Qaeda agent would contact him in America with instructions. Samir had no idea what he was going to be ordered to do, but he assumed that it would be something dangerous, possibly fatal, almost certainly illegal, and likely a betrayal of both his country and his friends.

He also knew that he couldn't say no. But during the night a desperate strategy had occurred to him: If he couldn't refuse the agent's orders, perhaps he could avoid receiving them. The Green Zone was big enough that it ought to be easy to make himself scarce for the day. In the evening he'd have to return to the Smithsonian, but that was a pretty big place too; maybe he could sleep in a closet, or find a diorama of an empty tomb to curl up in.

All he had to do was make it through the next twenty-four hours. Tomorrow he'd be out in the countryside, and God willing if the insurgents didn't get him by tomorrow night he'd be on a plane bound for home. Then when Idris asked, "Did you do what my man told you to?" he could say honestly, "What man?"

And Idris would accept that answer. Sure . . . But Samir would worry about that later.

Of more immediate concern was the discovery that it wasn't just his own countrymen he needed to steer clear of. As he sat with Mustafa in the Watergate's lobby, waiting for Colonel Yunus to finish up his business, Samir regarded each new black or Arab face that

came into view with a mixture of fear and suspicion. When a group
of Somali Marines burst through the lobby doors in a cacophony of
laughter, he nearly jumped out of his chair.

Mustafa lowered the *Washington Post* he'd been perusing. "Too
much coffee at breakfast, Samir?"

"I'm fine," Samir replied. His attention shifted to a coal-skinned
maintenance man who was up on a ladder replacing some bulbs on
the lobby chandelier. To a casual observer he would have seemed
completely absorbed by this task, but because he wore a white knit
prayer cap, Samir became convinced that the guy was casting sideways glances at him.

"You know what," Samir said, "I think I'm going to skip the tour
of the White House . . ."

"Are you sure?"

"Yeah. I'm exhausted, so I think I'll just hike back to the museum
and take a nap."

"You should at least let the colonel get you a ride," Mustafa said.
"It's a long walk."

"Nah, the fresh air will be good for me."

The maintenance man, done changing bulbs, was coming down
the ladder now. Samir stood up quickly, ignoring Mustafa's perplexed
look, and bolted for the nearest exit.

Passing through a set of double doors he found himself in the adjoining office building at the intersection of three hallways. A group
of Arab Marines approached along the left-hand passage, and two
black men in suits were having a conversation in the hallway straight
ahead; to his right he saw only a Hispanic woman vacuuming the
carpet. Samir went right, his heart skipping a beat when the woman
greeted him with a hearty, "Peace be unto you!"

Two minutes and several multicultural encounters later he was
out on the sidewalk. A bus idled beside a sign that read FREE SHUT-
TLE in both Arabic and English. Samir boarded, not bothering to ask

where the bus was headed, and slouched across two seats so that no one could sit next to him.

The doors closed. Just as the bus started moving, someone came running up alongside of it, banging furiously for admittance. Samir tensed, but when the bus driver opened the doors again, the late-comer turned out to be a white man with a silver cross pinned to his lapel.

The bus proceeded along its route, the driver calling out stops: State Department, Department of the Interior, various other agencies of the new American government, some of them still more hoped-for than real. Samir stared dully at the passing scenery while the bus was in motion. When new passengers got on, he lowered his eyelids and pretended to doze. When the driver announced "White House!" Samir slumped down below the level of the windows and remained that way until the executive mansion was far behind him.

He got off at the Hoover Building stop. The bus driver didn't say what government agency was headquartered there, but from the look of the place—a boxy, concrete structure hinting at kilometers of filing cabinets—Samir assumed it was something stodgy and ul-trabureaucratic, the Department of Weights and Measures, maybe. He thought about sneaking inside and finding an empty office to hole up in.

Instead he picked a random direction and started walking. The sun rose higher in the sky; the morning got hot, and humid. Samir stopped to take a drink at a water fountain. He noticed a Christian church across the street. Its front doors were propped open, and a sign proclaimed in multiple languages, ALL SOULS WELCOME.

The church's interior was cool and dim. There was no service in progress, and despite the open invitation the place was almost de-serted. As Samir sat in a pew near the back, he could see only one other person, a gray-haired Chinese woman. Her head was bowed, and at first he thought she was praying, but then he heard her snores.

He looked up at the altar and was relieved to see that it was decorated with a plain cross rather than a crucifix. The Christian habit
of depicting the prophet Jesus's tortured body was objectionable on a
number of levels, and while Samir wasn't personally offended by the
practice, he did think it was creepy. The empty cross, however much
it had come to be associated with terrorism in recent years, seemed
far more civilized.

The hairs on Samir's neck prickled as someone slid into the pew
behind him. He told himself to stay calm. But then a hand gripped
the back of his pew and a voice said in Arabic, "Aren't you one of
Lut's friends?" which was the code phrase Idris had told him to be
alert for.

Samir let out a sigh of despair. He turned around. Sitting behind
him was the white Christian from the bus. The silver cross on his
lapel—definitely a symbol of terror in this context—shined faintly
in the churchlight.

"You?" Samir said. "You're Qa—"

"Shut up," said the Qaeda man. "Follow me outside."

There was a pocket park adjacent to the church. Something about
the way it was laid out—the configuration of the benches, perhaps—
reminded Samir of a park in Kadhimiyah where, not long ago, two
gay men caught in a tryst had been beaten by a mob.

The Qaeda agent led him behind a hedge at the back of the park,
then rounded on him with his fist clenched. "Take this!"

Samir raised his arms to ward off the blow. "Wait! Wait!"

"I said take this!" The Qaeda agent slapped a cell phone into one
of his upraised palms. Samir fumbled and nearly dropped it, then
held it out in front of himself as though it were contaminated.

"What . . . What's this for?"

"It's for tomorrow. When you go out on patrol with the Marines,
you're going to bring it with you."

Samir was shaking his head even before he thought of an argument: "I'm not supposed to have a phone with me. They told us—it's a security risk."

"Never mind the rules," the Qaeda agent said. "The Humvee you'll be riding in will probably be equipped with a broad-spectrum radio jammer, so an ordinary cell phone wouldn't work anyway. This one's been modified to transmit on an unblocked military frequency."

Samir kept shaking his head. "You want me to make a call from a vehicle full of soldiers?"

"The speed dial on this phone is very simple. You don't even need to take it out of your pocket, just leave it turned on, and then when you get the signal push two buttons. I'll show you."

"What signal?"

"There'll be a billboard by the side of the road with a white cross painted on it. As soon as you pass the billboard, you'll hit the speed dial and let it ring."

"And what happens then?" Samir asked.

The Qaeda man showed him a picture of Malik and Jibril. This was not the same photo Samir kept in his wallet. It was a photo he'd never seen before, the boys playing in their bedroom in their new home in Basra. The picture taker, whoever he was, had been standing outside the bedroom window, at night, looking in.

"What happens then?" the Qaeda man said. "Your sons get to grow up, that's what happens then."

The White House was something of a letdown. Mustafa would have liked to meet the new American president, about whom he'd heard good things, but a scheduling conflict made that impossible. Absent its chief occupant, the building was just another palace, albeit more tasteful than the Hussein residence. The rose garden was pretty.

From the White House they took a driving tour of some of the Zone's other sights, eventually circling back to the center of the Mall, where they proceeded on foot to the base of the Washington

Monument. Colonel Yunus drew Mustafa's attention to a series of pockmarks in the obelisk's north face. These were, he explained, the result of insurgent mortar strikes, the Monument having become a target after rumors spread that Boulos al Darir was planning to use it as the gnomon for a giant Islamic prayer clock.

"False rumors?" Mustafa asked.

"Rumors," said Colonel Yunus. "Speaking of prayer, it's almost noon. Shall we stop back at the museum before lunch?"

They walked east along the Mall. The colonel pointed to a castle-like building which he said was another branch of the Smithsonian, dedicated to Christendom's wars. "LBJ's misadventures feature prominently, but there's also quite a lot about the original crusades. It's rather interesting to see them portrayed from the antagonists' perspective."

"Is the crusaders' wing where my guest bed came from?"

"Yes." The colonel smiled. "I rather doubt it belonged to Pope Urban, though."

Ahead in the distance they could see the half-completed dome of the new Capitol Building. A low-flying cloud passing behind it made the dome seem momentarily whole. Mustafa's inner ear went crazy. He stumbled and would have fallen if the colonel hadn't caught him.

"Careful," Colonel Yunus said. "You have dizzy spells?"

"I do get vertigo sometimes," Mustafa told him. "But I think this is just jet lag."

"Chronic vertigo is common here. It's a symptom of what the doctors call Gulf Syndrome."

"Gulf Syndrome? Like the Gulf War?"

"Yes, but also gulf in the sense of a void, a gap between the way things are and the way instinct says they should be. The sense of dislocation is difficult to describe exactly, but once you've felt it—"

"I have felt it," Mustafa said. "I think my father has, too."

The colonel nodded. "I'd heard that there were cases of the Syndrome back in Arabia. Here though it's much more pervasive. Almost everyone experiences it to some degree."

"What do you do for it?"

"Valium helps, supposedly. Also certain antihistamines. For myself I prefer a more natural remedy."

"And what is that?"

"Devotion to God, five times a day," the colonel said. "Not quite as potent as benzodiazepine, perhaps, but it has other benefits."

Mustafa snuck another look at the Capitol, and this time when his balance wavered, he knew it wasn't jet lag. Forcibly shifting his attention, he said: "It really is different here, isn't it? So many trees, Gaddafi would be jealous." Glancing up at the sun: "Even the summer heat feels different."

"I'll tell you something funny, it's not the climate or the country I find alien, it's the war." The colonel shook his head. "I really should be used to it by now. This is my fifth tour of duty. I've been here so long, when I think about Arabia, it's not just like another lifetime, it's like I was never there at all."

"Maybe you should take a leave," Mustafa suggested. "Go back home, get reacquainted with the place."

"No, I'm here for the duration, now . . ." A tremor went through him that he did not seem to notice. "You know, I have these dreams sometimes, very vivid, you'll probably get them too if you stay here long enough."

"Dreams about what?"

"About being an American citizen . . . This one dream in particular, I have it over and over. I dream that I'm a civilian only pretending to be a soldier. It's outdoors in a big field, at a place called Manassas. I'm there with other Americans, professionals mostly—doctors, lawyers, defense contractors . . . We dress in these costume uniforms, some blue, some gray, and stage mock battles, 'fight' for freedom. Then at the end of the day we go to a tavern and drink beer—mine is nonalcoholic. And then I get in my car and drive back to Alexandria . . ."

"A long drive," Mustafa said.

The colonel laughed. "Alexandria, Virginia, not Egypt . . . It's right across the river, just south of here. In the dream I have a house there, a big yellow house by the water. I live there with my wife and four children. It's nice . . . And then I wake up and I'm here in the house of war, not a citizen but an invader. And my head spins . . . But prayer helps."

They'd reached the museum. A drowned tyrannosaur welcomed them back.

The colonel asked: "Have you been to Mecca, Mustafa?"

"You mean on hajj? Yes," Mustafa said. "My wife Fadwa insisted on it . . . What about you?"

"I want to go," the colonel said. "When I am done here . . . I've spoken to other Marines who've gone, and they all seem very grounded, in a way I would like to be."

"Grounded?"

"At peace," the colonel said. "Mecca is peace."

"What about Alexandria?" asked Mustafa. "Have you ever gone across the river to look for your dream house?"

"No. That would not be wise."

"Really? I would be tempted."

"I am tempted," the colonel said. "But it's the Red Zone. Not a good place to go chasing after dreams. You should remember that on your foray tomorrow."

"You're not coming with us, then?"

"No, I have business here. But I'll ask God to look out for you." Then he smiled, for even as he spoke these words they entered a hall decorated with another mural, showing the prophet Daniel standing untouched in the den of the lions.

"Thank you," Mustafa said, looking from Daniel's calm expression to the frustrated snarls of the beasts. "I would appreciate that."

THE LIBRARY OF ALEXANDRIA
A USER-EDITED REFERENCE SOURCE

T.A.B.

T.A.B. is an abbreviation of the English-language phrase "That's America, baby." During the reign of Lyndon Johnson, it was common for American citizens to say "T.A.B." in response to bad news, particularly bad news that the government was in some way responsible for, a usage captured in this protest song by Jewish folk singer Robert Zimmerman:

> *Power's out in the city tonight . . . T.A.B.*
> *Shelves at the co-op store are bare . . . T.A.B.*
> *Gas lines stretching out of sight . . . T.A.B.*
> *LBJ don't seem to care . . . T.A.B.*

Following the Coalition invasion of America in 2003, the expression took on a new meaning of defiance towards the occupying troops. "T.A.B.!" became a popular chant at protest marches and a rallying cry for insurgents; Coalition soldiers have reported finding it scrawled on the side of unexploded roadside bombs. In July 2005 an attempt by the Coalition Authority to discourage the use of T.A.B. as a graffiti tag led to a gun battle in the Anacostia neighborhood of Washington, D.C., in which 17 Coalition soldiers and at least 400 Americans were killed.

The church was located in the town of Herndon, in western Fairfax County. The men of the militia began assembling there after midnight, arriving singly or in pairs and dispersing their vehicles throughout the surrounding neighborhood so that their gathering would not be noticed from the air.

By 2 a.m. there were sixty men in the pews. The church lights were kept low and there was no music or singing, just the soft voice of the preacher reading from the climax of the New Testament: "The sixth angel poured out his bowl on the great river Euphrates, and its water was dried up to prepare the way for the kings from the East. Then I saw three evil spirits that looked like frogs; they came out of the mouth of the dragon, out of the mouth of the beast, and out of the mouth of the false prophet . . . They gathered the kings together to the place that in Hebrew is called Armageddon."

The sermon that followed was long and full of assertions that a more critical Bible scholar might have taken issue with. But the men of the militia, many of whom expected to die this coming day, listened attentively and without objection.

Sitting alone in a pew at the back of the nave was a man with a plain silver cross in his lapel. He was the militia's chief strategist and he had provided the intelligence that had resulted in this gathering being called, although he had lied about where his information had come from.

The strategist's Christian name was Peter Lightfield. He claimed to be a descendant of Thomas Jefferson; in truth he knew nothing of his ancestry, having been raised in a series of foster homes. To his secret masters in Al Qaeda, he was known as Ibn Abihi, "his father's son," and Ibn Abihi was also how he thought of himself, though for reasons of personal amusement he preferred the Aramaic rendering: Bar Abbas.

Bar Abbas sat through the reading of the scripture and the first few minutes of the sermon, but got up before the preacher could start blaspheming against Islam. If anyone had asked, Bar Abbas would have said he was going to check on the progress of the bomb-laying team, which was true—but first he had a different call to make.

He stepped out into the narthex and went downstairs to the church basement, which was divided into three rooms. The front room contained mostly paper: old church newsletters, handbills attacking the Coalition Authority and threatening retaliation against collaborators, and stacks and stacks of comic-book tracts that explained, using crude images and semiliterate prose, the connection between the Antichrist and the Arab and Persian governments.

A padlocked door gave access to the church armory. As was the American custom, every weapon carried a scriptural reference—either an actual Bible verse or a coded citation. The sights of the assault rifles racked along the front wall were all engraved with the legend JER50:14 ("Take up your positions around Babylon, all you who draw the bow. Shoot at her! Spare no arrows, for she has sinned against the LORD."). The grip of a .45-caliber handgun was stamped PSA110:5 ("The LORD is at your right hand; he will crush kings on the day of his wrath") and the stock of a machine gun read JDG15:16 ("Then Samson said, 'With a donkey's jawbone, I have made donkeys of them. With a donkey's jawbone, I have killed a thousand men.'"). The lid of a crate of hand grenades had been stenciled with the words of 1st Samuel, chapter 17, verse 45: "David said to the Philistine, 'You come against me with sword and spear and javelin, but I come against you in the name of the LORD Almighty, whom you have defied.'" And a case holding the militia's prize possession, a Scorpion man-portable surface-to-air missile launcher, was painted with a verse from Revelation chapter 12: "Satan was hurled to the earth, and his angels with him."

The third room was a disused janitor's closet that now held random junk. Sitting on a chest-high shelf was a dusty laptop; it looked like it hadn't been touched in a long time, but its battery was fully charged and it started up immediately when Bar Abbas pressed the power button. While the operating system loaded, Bar Abbas retrieved a webcam from behind a box of crèche figurines and plugged it into the laptop. He opened a videoconferencing window and entered a series of passwords. There was a burst of sand-like static, and then he was staring into the face of Idris Abd al Qahhar.

"You are late," Idris said.

"I had to wait until the service started." Bar Abbas glanced at the armory's outer door, which he had bolted behind him. "We're less likely to be interrupted this way."

"Did you locate Samir Nadim?"

"Yes," said Bar Abbas. "I gave him the cell phone and told him what to do. But I don't know if he'll go through with it."

"You told him what would happen if he didn't?"

"Yes, and from the way he reacted, it's clear he loves his sons' lives more than his own. But that may not be enough when the moment comes. He seems . . . weak-willed."

"He is a coward," Idris said sternly. "You have a contingency plan?"

Bar Abbas nodded. "I'll be there to set it off if he doesn't."

He might have asked, Why involve this Samir at all? but Idris would likely regard such a question as impertinent. Bar Abbas assumed it was a subterfuge of some kind: Military investigators would find the modified cell phone on Samir's body, and Idris would use that fact to cast him and his colleagues as traitors, and discredit whatever government agency had sent them on their mission to America. Hearing the way Idris said "He is a coward," Bar Abbas decided there might be a secondary motive, as well: Perhaps Idris, for personal reasons, wanted Samir's last hours to be filled with fear and torment. This was not professional behavior for an Al Qaeda leader, but Bar Abbas, who had tortured a number of his own enemies in the past, was in no position to pass judgment.

"What about the other matter?" Idris said next. "Have you investigated V. Howell Industries?"

"I took a squad of men to the address you gave me," Bar Abbas told him. "The offices were abandoned—but recently. It looks like they cleared out in a hurry."

"They knew you were coming."

"If they did, it wasn't any of my people who warned them. There wasn't time."

"And you found nothing?"

"There were some artifacts in one of the rooms. Books, mostly."

"Books about what?"

"The history of Arabia," Bar Abbas said. "The real history, I mean."

Idris's face expanded on screen as he leaned forward. "What did you do with these books?"

"Burned them in a dumpster behind the facility." Or most of them. Bar Abbas had saved a few volumes for himself.

"And the other men who were with you . . ."

"They were curious, but nobody read anything they weren't supposed to. Anyway," he couldn't resist adding, "it doesn't matter. Once God lifts the mirage, everyone's going to know the truth."

"Yes, but until that day, there are certain truths we don't want widely known . . . What else did you find?"

"A Texas state flag. That was in another room that was being used as a dormitory. There were some empty pill bottles in a wastebasket."

"What kind of pills?"

"The bottles weren't labeled, but I'd guess Valium or some other sedative," Bar Abbas said. "Almost everyone takes something to sleep here."

"What else?"

"Just some personal effects. Somebody must be a Green Desert fan—I found a copy of the *Son of Cush* CD under one of the dormitory beds."

"*Son of Cush?* What is *Son of Cush?*"

"Alternative punk rock," Bar Abbas explained, which judging from Idris's expression didn't clarify matters. "Don't worry, none of the songs are about Osama bin Laden."

"If it's music, you should destroy it anyway."

"Already done." Bar Abbas lied. He looked up, hearing a board creak overhead. "I should go. I still have preparations to make."

"You'll contact me again when it's accomplished?"

"If I can," said Bar Abbas. "If you don't hear from me, it's because God had other plans."

At that same hour not far away, two disciples crouched on a wooded ridge overlooking the Jeff Davis Pike.

The lead disciple's name was Timothy. He was tall and thin, and paler than any man who ever sat at the foot of the living Christ. He wore a pair of night-vision goggles and was using them to spy on a trio of Christian militiamen as they planted an IED in a culvert beneath the roadbed.

He could not help but admire the militiamen's bravery. They were dressed in the reflective jackets of a legitimate road crew and had a Dominion Water & Power truck parked on the median, but while that might fool passing civilian drivers (or at least give them an excuse to play dumb), it would be no protection at all against a military patrol. In the early days of the insurgency, when Army snipers sat on D.C. rooftops with orders to shoot anyone carrying a shovel or a toolbox after dark, Washington utilities employees had suffered a horrible death toll. After years of entreaties from the citizenry, the capital's defenders were a little less trigger-happy now, but out here in the Virginia suburbs it was still open season on potential saboteurs—and rather than a quick clean bullet through the head, you were likely to get a shower of explosive shells from a helicopter gunship, leaving you torn up and dying in slow agony beside your burning vehicle.

As the militiamen ran a wire from the bomb to an antenna on the back of a mile-marker post, a clatter of rotor blades echoed from the east. The militiamen didn't stop working or even look up. More bravery, or maybe it was just fatalism: If the chopper pilot had spotted them, they were as good as martyred already. But minutes passed with no deadly hail of shells, and the sound of the rotor blades gradually faded away. Not long after that, the job was finished; the militiamen got back into the truck and drove off.

"All right." Timothy stood up and peeled off his goggles. "Let's do it."

The other disciple made no move to rise. "I don't know about this, Tim," he said.

"There's nothing to know. You heard the director's orders."

"What if that chopper comes back?"

"It won't. You heard the director. We're protected from on high."

"Yeah? If the director's so sure about that, how come he's not here?"

A crunch of leaves as Timothy half turned towards him: "We're doing this, Terry. You're doing it."

After so much time in the dark, Terry didn't need night-vision goggles to see the expression on his companion's face. He shuddered, trying in vain to summon up the nerve to tell Tim to go fuck himself. But there was a reason Timothy was a leader while he was only a sidekick.

"OK," he said, ducking his head in submission. "OK." Then: "Fuck it."

Mustafa opened his eyes around 4 a.m., disturbed by silence. Samir had been tossing and turning most of the night, but now the other bed was empty. Mustafa got up and went to use the restroom. Samir wasn't there either, but the toilet stall smelled strongly of vomit.

He found Samir in the deluge room, seated on the "mountaintop" beside the velociraptor skeleton. The 'raptor remained poised to leap at Noah's ark, but Samir looked like he'd already tried that and failed: His face and neck were damp, and his hair was plastered to his skull.

"Samir?" Mustafa said. "Are you ill?"

"I suppose I am," Samir replied, his voice thick like a sleepwalker's. "Many would say so."

"Do you want me to get a doctor?"

"No. It's not that kind of sickness." Then: "Is it time to go already?"

"Not just yet. But listen, Samir, if you're unwell, perhaps you shouldn't go at all. Amal and I can—"

"No!" Samir came suddenly alert, looking alarmed and then angry. "I'm not a coward!"

"All right," said Mustafa. "I'm going to go find Colonel Yunus, to pray. Would you like to join us?"

Samir's face had gone slack again, and he took so long answering that Mustafa became convinced that he really was still asleep. Finally Samir said: "No. If God has no time for me, I have no time for Him . . . Come get me when you're finished."

A covered foxhole had been dug into the hillside by some previous group of partisans, abandoned and forgotten, then rediscovered by Bar Abbas as he scouted the highway for ambush sites. He crawled inside just before dawn. Twenty other militiamen were dispersed along the top of the ridge, lying belly down in the dirt with their weapons beside them.

The foxhole's observation slit gave a view of the Davis Pike, hazy now in the dawn mist. On the ledge of packed earth that formed the base of the slit, Bar Abbas laid out a pair of binoculars, a pack of cigarettes, a coffee thermos, and last but not least, a remote-control box.

The green lamp on the remote control lit as soon as Bar Abbas switched it on, and when he pressed the test button the lamp flashed, indicating that the detonator circuit on the IED was live. A red lamp would let Bar Abbas know if and when Samir pressed the SEND button on his cell phone. After that, he wouldn't have to do anything; the bomb would use the cell's GPS to decide when to detonate. But the remote control also had a second button, under a safety catch, that would allow Bar Abbas to detonate the bomb manually if the red lamp failed to light.

Bar Abbas's own cell phone vibrated silently in his jacket. It was a text message from a confederate in the Green Zone: SARACENS WILL DEPART 0700. Assuming normal traffic, drive time from the Green Zone to this kill zone should be about thirty minutes, so he had roughly two hours to wait.

There was room in the foxhole for at least three men, but Bar Abbas had insisted on privacy. While his subordinates shivered in the open air, he poured himself coffee and took a book from a satchel at his feet. In the gray dawn half-light he studied the title and author on the book's cover: *The Osama bin Laden I Know,* by Peter Bergen.

A truck rumbled by on the highway below. Bar Abbas lit a cigarette and began to read.

The four Humvees were lined up in front of the Watergate Hotel. Three of them were what the Marines called "luxury models," with bolted-on side and rear armor plating, bulletproof windows, and an armored turret surrounding the roof-mounted .50-caliber machine gun.

Mustafa, Samir, and Amal were each assigned to one of the armored Humvees. Mustafa would ride in the lead vehicle with Lieutenant Fahd. Humvee number two was the unarmored model.

Amal was assigned to Humvee number three with Salim, Zinat, Umm Husam, and a Sergeant Faris. Zinat offered to drive, but Sergeant Faris insisted on taking the wheel himself, and since Lionesses were not allowed to operate heavy weapons except in emergencies, that put Salim on the .50-caliber. "Ah well," Zinat said, after Umm Husam claimed the other front seat, "at least we'll have a nice view." She tried to show Amal how the gunner's sling would dangle Salim's buttocks directly before their eyes, but Amal's attention was focused on the turret armor, which struck her as inadequate. Salim's head and upper torso would still be exposed, especially to a shooter firing from an elevated position.

Samir was assigned to the fourth Humvee, which had a sign mounted between its taillights reading AMERICA, TAILGATE AND WE WILL KILL YOU.

They had been issued helmets and flak jackets. Samir found the body armor constricting and pointless, so he stripped it off while he had a last smoke and then, when the order came to get into the vehicles, tried to leave it behind. The Marines were looking out for him, though, and one of his Humvee-mates, Private Dimashqi, patted him on the shoulder and handed the flak jacket back to him. "I know it's a pain in the ass," the private said, "but we really do want to keep you safe, sir."

"Thanks," Samir said glumly.

Colonel Yunus came out to see them off. He made eye contact with Mustafa and pressed his palms together in front of his chest. Mustafa smiled and returned the gesture, and the colonel nodded to Lieutenant Fahd.

"OK, let's roll," the lieutenant said.

Their air escort, a Shaitan missile-equipped helicopter gunship, was hovering over the Kennedy Arts Center. As the Humvee convoy rounded the Arabian embassy and entered the on-ramp for the Theodore Roosevelt Bridge, the pilot dipped the chopper's nose in acknowledgment and flew out over the Potomac ahead of them.

Lieutenant Fahd, playing tour guide, explained that the bridge was named for the first American president to pay a state visit to the UAS. Teddy Roosevelt had spent little time in Arabia itself; instead he and Ibn Saud had gone down the East African coast for six weeks of big-game hunting in Kenya.

The bridge passed over an island in the middle of the river. The island too was named for Roosevelt and prior to the invasion it had been a nature preserve. Unfortunately the forest cover had attracted insurgents, and after a pair of former Minutemen had been caught laying dynamite under the bridge piers, Army engineers had been dispatched to the island. They'd chopped down every tree and shrub within two hundred meters of the bridge and used flamethrowers on the rest. Looking ahead, Mustafa could see that similar measures had been employed on the Virginia shoreline—and not just on the foliage. Many of the high-rises in downtown Arlington were blackened husks, and those that hadn't burned were heavily damaged by artillery and rocket fire. "Is that from the 2004 assault?"

"Some of it," Lieutenant Fahd said. "Some of it dates back to the initial invasion, and some is more recent—Arlington has always been a trouble spot. Despite how it looks, we do try our best to minimize collateral damage, but there are limits to how surgical you can be with high-explosive munitions in a built-up area like this."

The road circled north and west around the urban core. The Humvee gunners kept their weapons trained on the broken skyline and watched for snipers. Zinat, ogling Salim's butt, gave Amal a nudge as his hips swiveled along with the turret. Amal ignored her. Like the gunners she was focused on the tall buildings, appalled not by the destruction but by the number of viable sniping perches that remained among the wreckage. Minimizing civilian casualties was all well and good, but if you were going to raze a city anyway, why not do a more thorough job?

For the first kilometer no one attacked them. Then they drove past a housing subdivision that had been blasted flat during an encounter between the Virginia Sons of Liberty and the Seventh Marine Regiment. A gang of little kids were playing Patriots and Muslims in the rubble-strewn field, darting from cover to cover and shooting one another with rifles made from sticks.

Lieutenant Fahd keyed his radio. "Hold fire, hold fire," he said. "These are noncombatants."

The Humvee gunners held their fire. The kids, being kids, showed less restraint. When Salim snapped a mock salute at one mini-patriot in a newspaper tricorne, the boy threw a rock at him. The kid had a good arm; the rock struck the lip of the turret armor and bounced up, nearly catching Salim in the face. "You little shit!" Salim said—a sentiment echoed by Amal inside the Humvee. But Salim was laughing, and he kept the .50-caliber aimed safely skyward, even as the other kids started throwing rocks too.

"What's that phrase they're chanting?" Mustafa asked.

"'Sand nigger,'" said Lieutenant Fahd. He added drily: "It's a term of endearment. They are comparing us to the noble slaves who built this country."

Mustafa got the joke, but he didn't laugh. He didn't wish to be a spoilsport, and he really did believe that the military had done the best it could here with the tools available. Nevertheless, as the convoy continued on its way, passing more and more scenes of devastation, the thought was inescapable: On the Day of Judgment, whatever other achievements might be credited to the Coalition, nation-*building* wouldn't be one of them.

The rising sun had burned off the fog and there was enough light inside the foxhole now that Bar Abbas could read without squinting. He'd paused to light a fresh cigarette and pour the last of his coffee when his cell phone vibrated again.

He had two incoming text messages. One was from the secondary ambush team, confirming that they were in place, ready to finish off any Marines who managed to escape this kill zone.

The other message was from a watcher along the route: SARACENS ON PIKE @ FALLS CHURCH. EXECUTING DIVERSION.

"Excellent," Bar Abbas said, and sent a text of his own: SARACENS INBOUND. ALL MAKE READY.

Samir was trying to hypnotize himself.

He'd recalled all that he had ever heard about how suicide bombers prepared themselves mentally—the ritual prayers and recitations of faith, the visions of heavenly reward waiting beyond the pearly gates—but none of it was any use to him. He didn't know the words of the Nicene Creed and didn't believe in Saint Peter. Maybe if he'd had a ball of hashish to eat, like one of Hassan Sabbah's assassins— or better yet, a good stiff drink.

He concentrated on the drone of the Humvee's motor, hoping that combined with his exhaustion it would put him in a headspace where he could push two buttons without thinking. It worked too well: His head drooped until his chin touched his chest, and then the sound of an unmuffled motorcycle passing on the other side of the road made him jolt upright again, saying, "Where are we? Where are we? Did I miss it?"

"Easy," Private Dimashqi said, chuckling along with the other Marines. "We aren't there yet."

"How long was I asleep?"

"A minute or two at most. You didn't miss anything, I promise you."

They were passing through another burned-out urban pocket. Samir pressed his face against his door window and tried to look back, to see if there were any billboards on the road shoulder behind them, but it was no use. Fretting, he dropped a hand to his thigh and felt for the cell phone in his pocket. As he touched it, an explosion thundered in the distance.

"What was that?" Samir looked out the window again and saw black smoke rising to the north. "What the hell was that?"

In the lead Humvee, Lieutenant Fahd was asking the same question in more measured tones. "Looks like a truck bomb," the helicopter pilot radioed down. "Somewhere in McLean . . . Yeah, citizen's band is reporting an insurgent attack on the main fire station."

The lieutenant hissed in disgust. "You see?" he said, looking over his shoulder at Mustafa. "This is what these fucking people are like. They kill their own first responders, and then they blame *us* when their neighborhoods go up in smoke."

The radio crackled. It was the helicopter again: "Insurgents are hitting the McLean police headquarters now. The attackers have a mortar and the cops are asking for help taking it out."

"Yeah, yeah, go," Lieutenant Fahd said. "We'll call if we need you."

Samir watched the helicopter fly away and understood. He hadn't missed anything. The sign he'd been commanded to watch for was still ahead, but now that their escort had been lured off, he wouldn't have long to wait. He abandoned his attempts at mesmerism and fell back on fatherhood, taking the snapshot from his other pocket and cupping it in his hands. Malik, he thought, Jibril, I'm sorry I couldn't be the dad you deserved. But now I'll do this thing, for you, and pray Idris keeps his part of the bargain.

"Are those your sons?" Private Dimashqi said.

Samir gritted his teeth. "Yes," he said.

"Handsome boys." The private held out a snapshot of his own. "These are my daughters. That's Faiza and Basilah, and the baby is Aisha."

"Adorable." Shut up. Please shut up.

"Yeah . . . I haven't actually met Aisha yet. But my tour's up in a month, so I'll finally get to hold her . . ."

OK, God, Samir thought. I get it. I'm a sinner and I'm going to hell. Well, to hell with you too. Pressing the photo of Malik and Jibril to his chest, he stared at the roadside in grim silence while Private Dimashqi prattled on about his daughters.

This seemed to be the last of the devastated zones. They drove under a crumbling highway overpass, passed a sign that read LEAVING TYSONS CORNER, and entered a green suburb of mostly intact housing developments. There was still plenty of evidence that battles had been fought here—a roadside church missing its steeple; a pair of American tanks, sans turrets, sitting in a field overgrown with brambles—but no more scorched earth.

"We're close," Lieutenant Fahd said, consulting the electronic map on his dashboard. "Another five kilometers."

A moment later, hearing approaching sirens, he called a halt a hundred meters from a road junction. A line of emergency vehicles—two fire engines, an ambulance, another fire engine—came racing along the crossroad, bound for McLean or some other trouble spot. The gunner on the lead Humvee tracked each vehicle in turn. After the last of them had passed by, the convoy continued to sit, while Lieutenant Fahd scanned the terrain ahead with a pair of binoculars.

Beyond the junction, the land to the left of the pike rose up to form a wooded ridge. The land on the right was flat woods, the trees serving as a screen for a cluster of houses. The pike itself—four lanes, two on either side of a broad grassy median—ran straight and level for about a kilometer before turning sharply to the right.

"Do you see something?" Mustafa asked.

"No," Lieutenant Fahd said. "Just a funny feeling . . ."

While the lieutenant scanned the woods again, Samir stared at the billboard that stood at the southwest corner of the junction at the base of the ridge. The ad, which showed a bare-chested Oded Fehr caressing an Uzi while Natalie Hershlag pouted beneath silk sheets, was for an Israeli action film Samir knew he had seen—twice—but whose Arabic title he could not, just now, recall. Vandals had given Fehr a yarmulke and horns, and put a swastika on Hershlag's forehead. These additions, like the ad itself, were weathered and faded, but the white cross spray-painted on the billboard's lower right corner was fresh and unmistakable.

"All right," the lieutenant said, still uneasy, and regretting his decision to let the helicopter go. "Proceed."

As the convoy started forward, Samir slipped his hand into his pants pocket, struggling a bit because of the flak jacket, and also because of the numbness that flooded his body. In grasping the phone he pushed the first button without meaning to. Then dread paralyzed him.

The lead Humvee rolled past the marked billboard. The second Humvee. The third. Samir closed his eyes.

He forced them open again. He turned his left hand palm upward, looked down at the faces of his sons. Malik, he thought, Jibril. God help me.

He pressed SEND.

A final text message had alerted Bar Abbas to the convoy's arrival at the junction. He picked up the remote-control box and pressed the test button. The green lamp flashed reassuringly. Then, as he lifted the safety catch on the detonator button and looked out at the kill zone, the red lamp came on.

"Good for you, Samir," Bar Abbas said. "I guess Idris and I were wrong about you."

He crouched to shield himself from the coming blast and the sound of music filled the foxhole. Bar Abbas had had Green Desert on the brain for several days now, so it was a moment before he realized that the tune wasn't in his head. He looked down at the wooden planks that lined the foxhole's floor. He'd assumed there was nothing beneath them but dirt, but apparently someone had hidden a CD player under there and queued up track 17 from *Son of Cush,* "Good Riddance (Enjoy the Virgins)"—a catchy, sarcastic ballad about a suicide bomber.

The ballad was almost to the end of its first verse, counterpointed by the sound of the approaching Humvees, when Bar Abbas figured out it wasn't a CD track he was listening to.

It was a ringtone.

On the morning of 11/9, Mustafa and Samir had rushed to Ground Zero along with every other cop, firefighter, and EMT in Baghdad. But because they were Halal and not true first responders, there was never any chance they'd be ordered into the towers, something that Samir had always been secretly grateful for—and secretly ashamed of. He sometimes wondered, if he had gotten such an order, whether he would have been able to obey it.

The other thing he thought about, when he thought about that day, was the jumpers: the victims trapped on the upper floors who'd plummeted to their deaths, many not so much leaping as falling as they climbed out broken windows to escape the heat and smoke. But some of them really had jumped. Samir remembered one old man in particular, up in the Windows on the World restaurant, clasping his hands in prayer as he surrendered to gravity and God. There too, Samir wondered what he would have done, and what it would feel like to knowingly step into a hundred-story void.

Now at last he had an answer. The first seconds after he pressed the SEND button were pure freefall, the Humvee seeming to roll straight down rather than forward. Now, Samir thought, as he waited to hit bottom. Now . . . Now . . . Now . . .

Around the sixth or seventh Now he panicked and tried to tell the Humvee driver to stop, but the hiss of air that escaped his fear-constricted throat didn't even qualify as a whisper. Now . . . Now . . . The Humvee hit a bump in the road and Samir opened his mouth again and screamed out *"STOP!"* but no one heard him, because the bomb had gone off.

The blast was near the top of the ridge, and the main force of the explosion was directed straight up in the air, but the pressure wave that rolled down the ridge and across the pike was still powerful enough to rock the Humvees sideways on their suspensions. The exposed gunners got the worst of it, feeling, to a man, as if they'd been swatted with a brick wall. A shower of debris followed: dirt and mud, stones, tree branches. The gunner in the unarmored Humvee was knocked cold by a hunk of timber from the foxhole's roof that glanced off the top of his helmet.

"Stop!" Samir screamed, again, as debris continued to pelt the Humvees. "Stop!"

"Go! Go!" Lieutenant Fahd commanded his driver. It was the first rule of the Red Zone: You don't stop in the middle of an ambush. But the splintered trunk of a Douglas fir had fallen across the Humvee's hood, and the startled driver had thrown the engine into reverse, stalling it. While the driver wrestled with the starter, the lieutenant impatiently opened his door and got out to move the Christmas tree.

The air had cleared enough now that the Marines could see the blast crater up on the ridge. Incredibly, men were moving along the edge of the crater and in the wreck of foliage that surrounded it. Because they had been lying flat, most of the militiamen had survived the blast, though those closest to the foxhole were bleeding from their ears and noses and staggering like drunks.

The Humvee gunners, more than a little punch-drunk themselves, spent the first few seconds just gaping at the scene. Then Salim noticed the rifle rounds plinking off his turret armor and his training took over. "Chris-*TIANS!*" he shouted, bringing his gun up to fire. The gunners on the lead and rear Humvees followed his example.

The Barad .50-caliber machine gun had an effective range of two kilometers and could destroy even lightly armored targets. At close range against unarmored personnel it was murderous, not so much shooting the targets as exploding them. With three such weapons aimed at the ridge, firing at anything that moved, the number of surviving militia fell rapidly.

One of the last Minutemen standing tried to aim a rocket-propelled grenade launcher with one hand, his right arm having been shattered by blast debris. A machine gun cut him in half at the waist, and as his torso toppled backwards, his finger squeezed the trigger. The grenade flew up in a high parabola, arcing over the pike and landing in the woods on the far side, where it exploded harmlessly. But a Marine in the unarmored Humvee, scrambling up to take the place of the unconscious gunner, heard the explosion and assumed that a second wave of ambushers was attacking from the north. While his brothers continued to fire on the ridge, he swung his gun around and opened up on the woods—and the houses beyond. His first burst hit a propane tank, blasting the roof off a bungalow and sending a ball of fire into the air.

Mustafa had gotten out of the Humvee to help Lieutenant Fahd with the tree. When the lieutenant saw that Mustafa had left his helmet in the vehicle, he was furious. "Idiot!" he shouted. "You want to get shot in the h—"

Thunk! The lieutenant's own head jerked sideways and his eyes rolled up. Mustafa caught him as he fell. The lead Humvee gunner zeroed in on the sniper a half second later and vaporized him. The driver, having restarted the motor, shouted at Mustafa: "Get in! Get in!"

Having run out of targets on the ridge, the gunner in the rear Humvee rotated his turret to check on the road behind them. A few cars were coming up the pike on the far side of the junction, but when their drivers caught sight of the firefight, they all made hasty U-turns.

Then a truck rig rumbled into view along the crossroad. The driver had his radio cranked, so he didn't hear the shooting, and distracted by the U-turning cars on his left, he didn't see the Humvees until he'd already begun his own right turn onto the pike. By then, the Humvee gunner's attention had been drawn to the long silver tank that trailed behind the rig like a bomb.

"Fuck that," the gunner said, taking aim. "No tailgating!"

Just up the road and out of sight around the bend, the members of the secondary ambush team listened to the explosions and the gunfire and watched the rising fireballs and smoke. Because they knew God was on their side, they concluded the initial ambush had been a great success and the Marines were being slaughtered.

Their feelings about this were mixed. They wanted to see God's enemies destroyed, of course. But that was just it: They wanted to *see* God's enemies destroyed, and take part in the destruction. What was the point of being a soldier of Christ if you didn't get to do battle?

So instead of thanking God for granting them victory, they asked Him for another favor: Please Lord, they prayed, lips moving silently as they watched the road. Please, don't let them all die. Save some Muslims for us.

God, they soon discovered, was in a generous mood.

Mustafa had loaded Lieutenant Fahd into the back of the Humvee so that the corpsman who occupied the other rear seat could tend to him. The sniper bullet had put a deep dimple in the lieutenant's helmet, and while the slug had failed to penetrate the Kevlar, the impact had concussed him. A dark bruise was forming beside his temple, and when the corpsman tried to get his attention, his eyelids barely fluttered.

Mustafa sat up front and listened to the radio chatter. A Marine in one of the other Humvees was trying to call back their air support. But the gunship was having its own problems: After taking out the mortar, it had been fired on by a surface-to-air missile. It wasn't clear, from the frantic transmission, whether the helicopter had actually been hit or was just maneuvering to get a shot at the missile launcher.

The convoy rounded the bend in the road. Just past the turn, the woods to their right gave way to a strip mall, the string of shops extending to a gas station at the corner of another crossroads up ahead. On the left side of the road, still slightly elevated on the back end of the ridge, was a single long box-structure building, its windows painted over and covered with OUT OF BUSINESS signs; individual letters running along the concrete lip of its roof spelled the words PIGGLY WIGGLY next to a smiling hog face.

A roadblock had been set up at the crossroads. A pair of Dominion Water & Power trucks were parked nose to nose on the pike's eastbound side. And on their side of the median, just pulling into place across both lanes, was a big yellow school bus.

The lead Humvee driver eased up on the throttle. Knowing how insurgents thought, he was inclined to be highly suspicious of vehicles, like those used to transport children, that a Marine might be reluctant to shoot at. "Talk to me, Abu Azzam," he called up to his gunner.

The gunner was already looking through a pair of field glasses. This was no ordinary school bus. Sheet steel had been welded onto its side, in a poor man's imitation of the Humvee's armor kit. As he scanned the windows, he saw no little kids' heads inside, only big heads in tri-cornered hats, and gun muzzles, and—

"RPG!" the gunner shouted. The driver swerved to the right, as did the driver of the second Humvee. The third Humvee was just a little too slow, and the grenade struck it on the left side above the rear wheel well. The explosion was deafening and the tire instantly went flat, but the armor plating prevented any shrapnel from entering the passenger compartment. Amal, ears ringing, looked up at Salim, but he seemed to be OK too—he was standing firm in the turret, already returning fire at the school bus.

All of the Humvee gunners were firing at the school bus, whose improvised armor proved far less effective than the Humvee's. The bus became a sieve.

More militia appeared atop the Piggly Wiggly. They had rifles, another RPG, and a machine gun that set up directly above the pig's head. Most of them began shooting at the convoy, but one Minuteman whose rifle was loaded with incendiary rounds took aim at the gas station.

"Don't stop, don't stop," the lead Humvee driver chanted to himself, machine gun fire rattling against his door as he raced along the strip mall parking lot. Mustafa looked ahead, and had just noticed that the blacktop around the gas station pumps was soaking wet when the air itself seemed to ignite and the station disappeared beneath a massive bloom of flame. The driver slammed on the brakes; they jerked forward in their seats and then back as the second Humvee rear-ended them.

The third Humvee, which had fallen slightly behind, tried to brake more gently, but the friction shredded the damaged tire. The Humvee fishtailed, caught a pothole, and began to tip sideways. Its right wheels left the ground and it tilted to a forty-degree angle and hung there for an instant as if considering the matter, before the added weight of the turret armor and an inadvertent nudge from the fourth Humvee carried it all the way over. "Salim!" Amal cried. She tried to grab him, but his legs abruptly vanished as if God had yanked him up on a string.

The Humvee came to rest on its side. Amal, who had fallen against Zinat, immediately pushed herself up, grabbed Zinat's rifle, and started crawling through the turret opening. "Wait," Umm Husam called to her, but Amal didn't wait.

Salim had landed on his back a few meters from the Humvee. He wasn't seriously injured but the tumble had left him punch-drunk again. Rifle rounds were ricocheting off the parking lot surface all around him but instead of seeking cover he sat up slowly. A bullet grazed the shoulder of his flak jacket and he frowned, swatting at the spot as if it were a mosquito. Then he shrugged and started to get up, and a bullet whined off the asphalt directly behind him and ricocheted upwards and a red cloud puffed out of the top of his right thigh. He fell back, hard, onto his tailbone, and stared at the bleeding hole in his leg and said, sounding exactly like a little boy: "Ow."

Amal, in a crouch, raised the rifle to her shoulder and sighted on a bobbing tricorne. She killed the Minuteman who'd shot Salim, and another man next to him. This got the attention of the Minuteman with the machine gun, who began swinging his weapon around, meaning to ventilate Amal and the Humvee behind her. "Target right," Umm Husam said, appearing at Amal's side. She fired, and the machine gunner's head disappeared in a red sunburst.

The lead Humvee, having recovered from its fender bender, backed up to give them some cover, while the unarmored Humvee ranged back out onto the pike to offer itself as a moving target. Hunks of concrete began flying off the lip of the Piggly Wiggly's roof as the Humvee gunners went to work.

In the back of the rear Humvee, Samir sat through all of this in numb detachment, feeling as though he were encased in a bubble. He'd thought for sure he'd died in the roadside bombing, and even now a part of him wondered whether that might not be so, and the chaos around him just the normal process of entering into hell. The prospect didn't frighten him. The gunfire, the explosions, even the flames, all left him unmoved.

What did finally move him, and begin dragging him back to the world of the living, was the sight of the wounded Marine, Salim. Samir had missed seeing Lieutenant Fahd get shot, so Salim was his first glimpse of the human cost of his betrayal—something he had not counted on surviving to witness. He got a good close look, as the Humvee he was riding in tucked in behind the lead Humvee to form an armored screen for the exposed Marines.

Salim was not the worst of it. The worst was Amal, the expres-

sion on her face as she tied her headscarf around Salim's leg to try
to stanch the bleeding. From her fear and her rage, one might think
the Marine were family, rather than just some guy she happened
to be riding with. Watching her, Samir felt a horrified pang in his
heart. I'm sorry, he thought. I'm so sorry, Amal, but my sons, I had
no choice . . .

Mustafa and the corpsman both got out of the lead Humvee to
help Amal. An RPG round flew by too close for comfort, punching
through the plate glass of a minimart in the strip mall and making
everybody duck. Samir, suddenly sure he was about to see his friends
get killed, looked away. Looked up. His gaze lit on the sign above the
minimart, which to his tear-blurred vision appeared to read 9/11.
He turned his head to the right, towards the roof of the Chinese
restaurant next door.

There was another Minuteman up there. He had crept in a crouch
to the corner of the roof, unnoticed by the Marines. He was holding
a bottle filled with amber fluid and trying to use a balky lighter to
ignite the rag stuffed in the bottle's neck.

"No," Samir said. And once more he was in freefall, but this time
the fear was galvanizing rather than paralyzing. Like an acrobat in
midair, he twisted and reached, drawing the .45 automatic from the
leg holster of Private Dimashqi beside him, turned again, shoved
his door open, stepped out, and aimed up. Samir's first three shots
missed, but the fourth hit the bottle even as the Minuteman got the
rag alight. The Minuteman became a burning man with a blazing
three-cornered crown.

Samir fired the pistol until it was empty. Then he ducked down
beside Mustafa and Amal and Salim and the startled corpsman. "I'm
sorry," he said, weeping. "I'm sor—"

The ground shook. All the windows in the Piggly Wiggly blew
out, and the roof, suddenly fluid, bulged upwards, flinging Minutemen into the air. "Shaitan!" one of the Marines cried, thinking that

the helicopter gunship had returned. But this was no missile strike; it was another bomb, detonating inside the store—or rather, in the parking level below it.

The roof fell back in and with a long rumble the outer walls collapsed, spilling a last few screaming Christians into the rubble. After that a stillness fell, a stretch of calm during which even the roar of the gas station blaze seemed muted. When half a minute had passed with no more shots being fired, the Marines began to relax.

A voice called out: "Mustafa al Baghdadi!"

Heads—and guns—turned towards the sound. Forty meters back along the parking lot from where the Humvees were stopped, a pale man had appeared, standing out front of a greeting-card store with his arms in the air. His hands were open and empty, and he'd unbuttoned his shirt to reveal a scrawny chest to which no bombs or weapon holsters were strapped.

The unarmored Humvee drove up beside him. Marines jumped out and shoved the pale man to his knees.

Mustafa stood up. "Hey!" Umm Husam said. "Your helmet!" Mustafa nodded and got his helmet and then walked down the parking lot to the unarmored Humvee. When he got there, one of the Marines was staring through the open door of the greeting-card store; just inside, another Minuteman lay dead with a loaded RPG launcher beside him.

Mustafa turned his attention to the pale man. "I am Mustafa al Baghdadi," he said. "Who are you and what do you want with me?"

"My name is Timothy McVeigh," the pale man replied. "I'm an agent of the Texas CIA and I was sent here to find you—to protect you." His eyes flicked briefly to the dead man, and then to the pile of rubble across the pike, before returning to Mustafa. "The director would like to see you, sir."

The Library of Alexandria
A USER-EDITED REFERENCE SOURCE

Christian Intelligence Agency

(Redirected from **CIA**)

The **Christian Intelligence Agency**, or CIA (sometimes also referred to by its members as "Christ in Action"), is the primary <u>espionage</u> arm of the government of the <u>Evangelical Republic of Texas</u>. According to the public version of its charter, the CIA's function is to collect and analyze intelligence on foreign governments, organizations, and individuals. However, it is believed that the agency also engages in domestic spying and acts as a <u>secret police force</u>, detaining, torturing, and assassinating political dissidents.

The CIA's headquarters are located in <u>Crawford</u>, about 15 kilometers west of the city of <u>Waco</u> . . .

"No," Umm Husam said firmly. "I cannot permit this."

They were standing in the parking lot of another strip mall on the far side of the crossroads. More Humvees and a tank had arrived, and the road was now blocked off in all four directions. The only nonmilitary vehicles that had been allowed through were a couple of fire engines, whose crews, under the watchful eye of Marine riflemen, were working to put out the gas station. Two helicopter gunships now circled overhead, and a medevac chopper had just landed. With Lieutenant Fahd heading back to base still unconscious, Umm Husam was the senior officer on site.

"I understand your reluctance to allow me to go with this man," Mustafa said. "But if he wanted to kill me, I think he would have done so already."

"If he kills you he cannot kidnap you," said Umm Husam. "Do you know the term *Verschärfte Vernehmung*?"

"'Sharpened interrogation.' It's a Lutheran euphemism for torture."

"American Protestants call it *enhanced* interrogation. The latest version is what's known as crucifixion: The victim is tied spread-eagle to the hood of a car and driven around at high speed. Road debris pelts the front of the body, while heat from the engine block causes burns to the back."

"I don't believe he intends to crucify me, either."

"If you are wrong, you won't be the only one who pays." Umm Husam shook her head. "I am sorry, but I don't wish to risk more Marines on a rescue mission."

Mustafa looked at McVeigh, standing just out of earshot with a pair of Marine guards. "He predicted this would be your reaction."

"That hardly makes him a seer."

"He asked me to give you this." Mustafa held up a gas station map of the county, backfolded to show a portion of Herndon village. "A gesture of good faith, he says. He's marked the location of a house that he claims is the current headquarters of the leader of the militia that attacked us."

Umm Husam chuckled. "You want to know who really lives there? Someone this man has a grudge against. Perhaps someone he owes money to."

"Here I would be inclined to agree," said Mustafa, "except for one thing . . ." He showed her what was written on the map beside the circled address. "Do you recognize this name?"

"No."

"So it's no one famous, then?"

"Not that I am aware of. Why?"

"Before I left Baghdad, I was shown a list of people who were in some way connected to my investigation here. This name was on that list."

Umm Husam remained skeptical. "What list is this? Who showed it to you?"

Before he could answer, Amal appeared beside him. She'd been helping load Salim into the medevac chopper, and the hand she grabbed the map with was still sticky with her son's blood.

She said to Mustafa: "Find out what the house looks like."

McVeigh's co-disciple Terry Nichols drove up in a silver van with a guitar logo and the words MESSIAH PRODUCTIONS painted on its side. The Marines let him through the roadblock, and McVeigh opened the van's rear doors and bade Mustafa get in. "You'll have to sit on the floor," he said apologetically, "but it won't be a long ride."

"It's fine," said Mustafa. "Do you need to blindfold me?"

"Not for this part of the trip, no." He glanced up knowingly at the helicopters overhead. "It'd be pointless."

Samir, who had not been invited, stood by waiting to see if McVeigh would wave him aboard at the last moment. Umm Husam, in the midst of a planning session with Amal and several Marines, looked over as well, her expression making it clear that she still wasn't happy about this. Mustafa nodded to them both, mouthing, "God willing." Then McVeigh shut the doors.

The ride, as promised, was brief, their immediate destination a railway underpass just off the Davis Pike. As they entered the underpass and eased to a stop, Mustafa raised his head up and saw a second van, with identical markings, driving away out the far side: a decoy for the helicopters.

"Now we wait awhile," McVeigh said. "Go ahead and stretch your legs, but stay under cover."

They all got out. Nichols went to urinate behind a pillar. McVeigh lit a cigarette and offered one to Mustafa. As they stood smoking, Mustafa looked around the underpass, his attention drawn to a phrase—T.A.B., HAJJI!—spray-painted on the far wall. A shallow pit dug into the embankment beneath this graffito held the remains of something that had been doused in gasoline and burned. Mustafa drew deeply on his cigarette and tried not to think too hard.

Eventually a car came. The driver, a gray-haired white man with the beard and sun-leathered skin of a Rocky Mountain tribal warrior, got out and nodded to McVeigh and Nichols. "Keys are in it, Randall," McVeigh told him, and the man nodded again and got into the van and sat behind the wheel with the engine off. Nichols got into the front passenger seat of the car.

McVeigh turned to Mustafa. He pulled a cloth hood from his pocket and said: "If you don't mind . . ."

This next part of the trip was longer. With the hood over his head Mustafa couldn't see the road, but the cloth was thin enough that he could still judge light from dark, so when they stopped again he could tell they were outside in the open. McVeigh helped Mustafa out of the back of the car and led him, still hooded, across a gravel-covered expanse.

"Two steps up, here." They pushed through a thick plastic curtain. "OK," McVeigh said, and Mustafa pulled the hood off.

They were inside a building that was still under construction. The outer plywood walls had been attached, but the windows were open holes covered with plastic sheeting and the interior was bare studs and concrete. The studs were furry with dust, as if construction had halted some time ago.

"This way," McVeigh said.

The building was long and modular, each of its several sections consisting of a cluster of rooms surrounding a central corridor. Each section was more finished than the last—drywall appeared, then paint, fixtures, and carpeting—and the repetitive nature of the floor plan gave Mustafa the sense of a single office suite assembling itself around him as he walked. The final section had power. The sudden blast of air-conditioning caught Mustafa by surprise and he reacted as his father might have, clutching at the gooseflesh on his arms. "The director likes it cold," Timothy McVeigh said.

A door at the very end of the hall was adorned with an official-looking seal that on close inspection proved to be hand-painted. It showed an eagle with a lone star on its chest and a scrap of parchment in its beak; one claw held a cross and the other a Bowie knife. The motto around the circumference was a quote from the Gospel of John: "You shall know the truth, and the truth shall make you free."

McVeigh knocked and opened the door. The office inside, like the building, was a work in progress. To the right as they came in were a mismatched sofa and chair that might have been collected off a street corner, along with a knee-high plastic table. To the left was a small pile of boxes. At the far end of the room was a desk, its top bare except for a massive leather-bound book that Mustafa assumed was a Bible, though which one he couldn't say; stuck all around the edges of its pages and adding to its thickness were numerous slips of colored paper covered in writing.

A man stood behind the desk with his back to them. He faced a window as if contemplating a view, but the glass was still covered with a protective film that rendered it opaque.

"Sir?" McVeigh said. "I've brought Mr. Baghdadi, like you requested."

The man turned slowly around. He was dressed in jeans and a denim shirt with the sleeves rolled up. He had thick, curly brown hair and brown eyes behind gold-rimmed aviator glasses. His dark stubble beard was fading to gray. Mustafa placed his age at around fifty.

"Mustafa al Baghdadi," the man said. "Thank you for coming. My name is David Koresh."

"Can I have Timothy get you anything, Mr. Baghdadi?" David Koresh asked. "Coffee? Tea? Ice water? We have beer too, if you indulge, but my understanding is you don't."

"No thank you, I'm fine."

"All right . . . You can leave us now, Tim."

"Yes sir," McVeigh said. "I'll be waiting outside." He left the room.

"So, Mr. Baghdadi . . . May I call you Mustafa?"

"Please."

"Thank you, Mustafa. Please call me David."

"David," Mustafa said. "And 'Koresh'? That is a Hebrew name too, is it not? Your family is Jewish?"

"No." Koresh laughed. "My family name is Howell. Vernon Wayne Howell, that's my birth name. I changed it to David Koresh after my anointing, when I realized God's plan for me."

"Ah. I see." David for the prophet who slew Goliath, presumably. And Koresh—Cyrus—that would be the king who conquered Nebuchadnezzar's empire. Mustafa pictured Koresh's face on a statue, a hall full of statues. "I should tell you, David, if you seek the throne of Babylon, you're going to have competition."

"Saddam Hussein, you mean?" He laughed again. "We're not in competition. Mr. Hussein is a creature of the world. I'm not interested in earthly rewards or titles. Not anymore."

"Saddam is interested in you."

"I know. He's the one who pointed you in my direction, isn't he?" Mustafa nodded, and Koresh said: "He's a clever man, in his way. Evil too, of course, and an egomaniac, which makes certain truths impossible for him to grasp, but still. He knows as much about the mirage as any other Arabian, and no one has done a better job at following my trail of breadcrumbs."

"You are talking about the artifacts?"

Koresh nodded. "He's hardly the only interested party, but no one else has come as far in tracing the source. Gaddafi's people, they're still chasing false leads in Europe. Al Qaeda too, until very recently . . ."

"So it's true, then. You are the creator of these objects? And of the mirage legend itself?"

"It's no legend," David Koresh said. "And I'm not a creator, just a messenger."

"Will you tell me what you know?"

"Of course. It's why I had you brought here. But it's a long story." Koresh gestured to the couch. "You should make yourself comfortable. Are you sure you don't want anything to drink?"

"Perhaps some hot tea, if it's a long story," Mustafa said. "It's chilly in here."

"Agent McVeigh said you were CIA," said Mustafa. "He called you the director."

"And you're wondering, if that's true, what's the head of the Texas CIA doing hiding out in Virginia?"

"Yes."

"Well you know," David Koresh said, "it's traditional for both sides in a church schism to claim they represent the true religion."

"There was a schism in the CIA?"

Koresh nodded. "Between what you might call the Crawford faction and the Waco faction. My side—the Waco faction—lost, so we had to leave. But we still think of ourselves as the real deal, the *true* Christ in Action, wandering in the wilderness of America." He stirred milk into his tea before continuing: "I'm no stranger to life on the road. I started out as a musician-evangelist. I had my own touring band and Bible study group. We went all over Texas, spreading the Word. Then one night at a revival meeting I met a CIA recruiter named Lee Atwater. He brought me in to work as a scriptural analyst for the Company's theology division—and to jam with him on the weekends."

"Scriptural analyst?"

"Part of CIA's unwritten charter is to provide biblical support for the government elite in Austin," Koresh explained. "If they need justification for a new policy, or an explanation for something like mad cow disease, they turn to the Company. That was my job, for seven years. Then after the Mexican Gulf War, I was promoted and put in charge of a new Company research facility called the Mount Carmel Center, in Waco.

"Texas at that time was experiencing the first epidemic of Gulf Syndrome. The war created all kinds of headaches—even though we weren't invaded, the knowledge that we could have been, *would* have been if not for the help of the Muslims, led to a huge crisis in confidence. Insurrection was up. Heresy was up. And people—including some really senior people—were having nightmares and hallucinations about a secret American takeover. The mayor of Galveston announced on live TV that Texan independence was a myth and we'd actually been part of the CSA all along. A dozen officers in the Texas Air Guard resigned their commissions on grounds of mental instability. They said they kept having dreams that they were American pilots, flying sorties against targets in what appeared to be West Texas.

"Rumors circulated about a mind-control project infecting people with LBJ's vision. I know there were other CIA research teams that looked at that as a literal possibility, some sort of virus engineered to affect the subconscious. But our focus at Mount Carmel was on mystical explanations. We were told to evaluate the dreams as prophecy—or as evidence of demonic possession.

"We brought in volunteers with especially severe cases of Gulf Syndrome. We conducted sleep studies, tested the effects of different stimuli on their dreams. We used prayer, hypnosis, fasting, drugs, sensory deprivation, exorcism, electroshock. Anything and everything we could think of, that might crack the doors of revelation a little wider."

"And what did you learn?" Mustafa asked.

"Nothing," David Koresh said. "I mean, the content of the dreams was fascinating, but we didn't know how to interpret what we were getting. The answer was too straightforward, that was the problem—we were expecting parables. Then when we asked God to please speak more plainly, He just gave us more of the same.

"I was frustrated by the lack of progress, but the folks at the main office didn't seem bothered by it. Eventually I realized they'd already made up their minds that Gulf Syndrome was a product of mass hysteria. The Mount Carmel Center, the other research initiatives, all of that was just bureaucratic butt-covering. They weren't concerned with results.

"Then after a while, they forgot about us. The crisis passed, but our program was never shut down." He laughed. "I stopped filing reports and nobody in Crawford even noticed. Meanwhile I still had access to Company funds with no oversight, and you know, the flesh of a man is weak . . .

"I started making personnel changes, kicking out anyone who didn't see eye-to-eye with me and bringing in more loyal recruits to replace them. A lot of people who'd come to Mount Carmel as research subjects ended up on staff. The 'research' got more and more self-indulgent. Lee Atwater had died a few years earlier, so I hadn't jammed in a while, but one day I decided to put a new band together, in-house, 'to explore the effects of Gospel rhythm-and-blues on REM-sleep alpha-wave patterns.' That's what I wrote on the sign-up sheet, anyway . . . I dropped two hundred grand in government funds on instruments and a recording studio. We even had our own label.

"And there were other indulgences. I organized 'fact-finding' trips all over the world, anyplace that had some vague connection to sleep research, or religious prophecy, or music. In December 1999 I took the whole Mount Carmel staff to Jerusalem to celebrate the new millennium in the Holy Land.

"Jerusalem was strange," David Koresh said. "I mean, we had a great time, but from the moment we landed at Nashashibi Airport, I couldn't shake the feeling that I'd been there before. On Christmas morning we went to the Old City to visit the Holy Sepulchre, and there was another tour group there. They were just outside the church, gathered around a man who was standing up on a stone, preaching about Revelation and the prophecy of the Seven Seals. I recognized that preacher. He was *me,* maybe ten or fifteen years younger . . . And I looked at him, and he looked back at me, and then I had this fit, like an attack of—"

"Vertigo?"

"—epilepsy. I fell down thrashing, hit my head. By the time I recovered, the preacher was gone, and when I asked about him, no one else knew what I was talking about." He shook his head. "Gulf Syndrome. That was my first personal experience of it. But not my last.

"After we came home from that trip, I went through an especially self-indulgent patch. The best way I can think to describe it, I'd been given a glimpse of my true destiny and my inner Adam was rebelling against it. I was already treating Mount Carmel like my private amusement center, but now I really started acting out. I did things, decadent things I'm not proud of . . .

"Then 11/9 happened and the country went crazy again. That's what finally put Mount Carmel back on the Company radar. The video of the planes hitting the towers triggered an avalanche of new Syndrome cases. Austin wanted answers, and when CIA started organizing a new research initiative, they realized they still had an active facility in Waco that hadn't made a progress report in years.

"I would have been in hot water no matter what, but what made it worse, since the last time I'd checked in, the Company had appointed a new director. A nasty piece of work . . ." Koresh uttered a name that Mustafa recognized from Saddam Hussein's list. "His nickname was the Quail Hunter," David Koresh said. "Texas humor. The joke is, if you've got an enemy you want to get rid of, you invite him out shooting and mistake him for whatever game you're after. The Quail Hunter had actually done that once. And he'd stepped over a *lot* of bodies, climbing the Company ladder.

"So this was the man I now had to justify myself to. He sent armed agents to haul me over to the Crawford campus. They took me to his office and he showed me a stack of accounting records and ordered me to explain what the hell I'd been spending all that money on.

"I lied. I told him we were still following our original research mandate, looking into dreams. I told him we were close to a major breakthrough with serious national security implications. All we needed was a little more time. Six months, a year.

"He gave me two months. He took a bullet out of his breast pocket and put it on his desk blotter. He told me that in sixty days, one of two things would be true: Either there'd be a report about this major breakthrough sitting where the bullet was now, or the bullet would be in the part of my brain that controlled bowel function. He also told me that I was under house arrest; if I tried to leave Mount Carmel before the report was ready, I'd get the bullet early.

"His centurions took me back to the Center. I called the staff together, and we formed a circle and prayed to God for my salvation. Then we dusted off our old research notes and got to work.

"For forty days and forty nights, we got nowhere. Every morning I got down on my knees in the chapel and said, 'Please, God, forgive me my pride and throw me a bone here,' and He heard me, He answered, but I still didn't understand. Nightmares," Koresh said. "We all started having nightmares, the *same* nightmare, about being trapped in a burning building surrounded by armed men." He tugged at his collar and closed his eyes a moment, breathing through his nostrils while the air-conditioning hummed in the background. "I thought it was just stress . . ."

"And what was it really?" Mustafa asked.

But Koresh only shook his head. "By the time we were down to three weeks, it had gotten so bad nobody could sleep anymore, which is a problem if you're trying to study dreams. Of course we had plenty of conventional sedatives on hand, but I decided to call psychopharmacology at Crawford and see if they'd cooked up anything new since the last time we'd done drug trials. They sent over a variety pack of experimental hypnotics. The first one we pulled out of the box was Elefaridol tartrate, a non-benzo sleep aid with some very interesting side effects. It turned out to be the breakthrough we'd been praying for."

"Why?" said Mustafa. "What did it do?"

Koresh stood up. "This part's easier if I show you."

They entered the basement through a room containing several large portable generators. The noise of the machines' operation, reflected off bare cinderblock walls, was deafening, but at least it was warmer than Koresh's office.

One generator had stalled. Terry Nichols, now wearing a tool belt, had detached the generator's exhaust hose and was examining it. The faint haze of diesel smoke in the air seemed to alarm David Koresh, who went over and shouted something in Nichols's ear. Nichols responded with a gesture that might have meant, "Don't worry, I've got this," or possibly, "Nothing you can say will make me more miserable than I already am."

The new sleep lab was in another, quieter, part of the basement. There were no bed frames yet, just a score of mattresses, arranged in two rows of ten along the room's longer walls. Each sleeping figure was attached by a web of electrodes to a battered EEG, and blankets had been drawn up over them, though these seemed more ceremonial than practical; the bodies, flushed and feverish, were throwing off more waste heat than the generators had.

Mustafa scanned the sleeping faces. They were of various races and ranged in age from early teens to late middle age, but they were all women. "Division of labor," David Koresh said, when Mustafa asked about this. "I don't know if it's body chemistry or the predilections of the Holy Spirit, but we get more consistent results with female subjects." He smiled. "Aren't they beautiful?"

Like a harem in a mad scientist's bomb shelter, Mustafa thought. "What is it they do, exactly?"

"I'll show you." Koresh went over to the room's only other waking occupant, a man in a long-sleeved cardigan who was leafing through a Scofield Reference Bible. "Hey, Steve," Koresh said. "Anyone close?"

Steve nodded towards a young woman whose red hair had spread in a fan on her pillow. "Lily's thetas and gammas have been spiking for a while."

Koresh sat down on the edge of the mattress and lifted the woman's right hand from the blanket. "What have you got for me, darling?" he said, in an exaggerated drawl. He bent his head, pressed his lips against her knuckles, and then reached up to brush his thumb beneath the electrodes on her forehead.

The woman's eyes flicked open. Mustafa, already discomfited by Koresh's display of intimacy, took a half-step backwards. Then the woman started speaking Arabic and Mustafa's arms broke out in gooseflesh again.

"Give me those two in the back," she said, in a deep, masculine voice with the accent of a native Iraqi. A pause. Then: "No, no! That one there, on the left! Yes . . . Yes, that's what I want!"

A woman on one of the other mattresses made a sharp clicking sound. Mustafa startled. Then another woman let out a honk, almost like a car horn. That seemed to get them all going, making clicks, rustling noises, whispers, shouts. The individual utterances seemed arbitrary and meaningless, but as they bounced off the walls and melded together, they began to paint a picture in sound, familiar-seeming background noise.

The red-haired woman went on speaking. "What's she saying?" David Koresh asked. "Do you know?"

"She is haggling," Mustafa said. "Bargaining over the price of something . . ." Then he realized what the background noise was: a souk. An open-air market, possibly in Baghdad.

The red-haired woman was sitting up. The EEG wiring stretched behind her and the blanket slid to her lap. She plucked her hand from Koresh's grip and began to reach forward, focused on something that only she could see. She extended her arm slowly, as if reaching through a curtain or into a stream. Her hand rotated, palm upward, and her thumb and forefingers came together, grasping nothing.

Grasping something. A flicker, a flicker, and then a limp violet rectangle appeared between her fingers. A scarf, Mustafa thought at first. But it was too small for that, and it was made of paper. A banknote.

"Good girl," David Koresh said. He laid one hand on her forearm and with the other prised loose the bill. As she lost contact with the object, the woman's eyes fluttered closed and she sank back onto the mattress. The other women fell silent. Koresh held up the banknote and inspected it.

"Speak of the devil," he said, laughing. "Looks like someone's following you . . ."

He showed Mustafa the banknote. Saddam Hussein's face was printed on the front. On the back was an engraving of what looked like hieroglyphs and the legend CENTRAL BANK OF IRAQ, TWO HUNDRED AND FIFTY DINARS.

"Not legal tender in this reality," David Koresh joked. "And not worth much in any."

It was a big white Colonial Revival house, on a three-quarter-acre lot surrounded by a high brick wall. The lot was at the end of a dead-end street half a mile from the Herndon church.

The other houses on the street were more modest, but they were all well maintained, their lawns and gardens well tended, the cars in their driveways shiny and new. An observer standing lightheaded at the turn-in might have mistaken it for the *other* America, the one glimpsed only in dreams.

Now and then the war intruded. Earlier that morning, the street's residents had heard the distant echoes of explosions on the Davis Pike, and the assaults on the McLean police and fire stations had made the mid-morning news (thirty-nine confirmed dead so far, including all of the attackers). But with the approach of noon, the illusion of peace had returned.

Sprinklers hissed gently on several of the lawns. A cat rubbed itself against the slats of a white picket fence, while a little boy in a coonskin cap pedaled his tricycle along the sidewalk. The guard at the gate in front of the Colonial house watched the boy and stifled a yawn.

The wind shifted. The boy stopped pedaling and coasted to a stop. He swung his head around, listening. A flock of birds exploded from the woods that ran behind the houses. That got the attention of the gate guard, who unhooked a radio from his belt and raised it halfway to his lips.

A moment passed. Another. The birds settled back to their perches. The guard relaxed and put his radio away, and the boy resumed pedaling. Only the cat wasn't fooled: Tail held high, it raced away up the street in the direction of the church, like a sinner who'd just gotten a two-minutes' warning of the Judgment Trump.

"So this was your breakthrough." They were back in Koresh's office and Mustafa was turning the Iraqi banknote over in his fingers, half expecting it to dissolve back into the ether. "You discovered how to conjure these objects. Out of your dreams."

"It was a pretty awesome trick," David Koresh said. "A miracle. Of course we had no idea how it really worked, or how to control it. Eventually we did learn how to steer the dreams, a little, to bring back specific kinds of objects, but that was later. In the beginning, we just took whatever God gave us." He went over to his desk and lifted the cover of the great Bible. Pressed between the leaves of Genesis was a photograph, which he handed to Mustafa. "This was one of the first artifacts we recovered."

The photo showed Koresh standing beneath the Jaffa Gate into Jerusalem's Old City. He looked to be in his mid-twenties—too young for the picture to have been taken during his 1999 visit. "This is your ghost double," Mustafa guessed. "The one you saw preaching at the Holy Sepulchre."

Koresh nodded. "As soon as I saw that, I finally understood what the dreams were about. God wasn't sending us coded messages. He was showing us another world, a world as real as this one. Maybe more real."

"And how did that other world fit into your Christian theology?"

"Well, that was obviously the next big task," Koresh said. "To make sense of that, and square it with the scriptures. But first I had to get my head off the chopping block.

"By the day I was due to deliver my report, we'd retrieved twenty-seven objects. I packed them up along with some videotapes of the dream sessions and a few PowerPoint slides, and got an escort over to the Crawford campus.

"The presentation didn't go well. Usually I'm a natural as a speaker, but that day in the Quail Hunter's office I was as nervous as Moses going in front of Pharaoh for the first time. The loaded revolver on the desk might have had something to do with that . . . Also, I could see in his face that he wasn't buying a word of what I was saying. Half the time I was speaking, he looked at me like I was crazy, and the other half, like I was pulling his leg.

"It was the latter reaction that carried. When I finally got done, he put the revolver away in a drawer and I breathed a sigh of relief. But then he said, 'No, Mr. Howell, don't relax. I don't know what possessed you to think you could come here and mock me in my own house, but you've made a very grave error in judgment. A bullet is too good for you, sir.'

"He called in the centurions and they took me away to the interrogation wing. They beat me black and blue and gave me a waterboard baptism. After I passed out they threw me in a cell.

"I fell into a dream. I was in the burning building again, trapped and alone, but then God came and lifted me up and whispered my new name to me. He told me I was going to live. When I woke up in the dark, I wasn't afraid anymore.

"The staff at Mount Carmel got word of what had happened to me, and they *were* afraid, but they didn't give up. They kept working in the sleep lab, and on the second day of my captivity God sent them another artifact. The bravest of them volunteered to deliver it to the Crawford campus. The Quail Hunter was still in a foul mood, so he had the deliveryman tortured and issued orders to have the rest of the staff rounded up—but he also looked at the artifact, and that night, I think, he had a dream of his own.

"In the morning, he sent for me."

"What was the object your man brought him?" Mustafa asked.

"A newsmagazine, called *Time*," David Koresh said. "In the politics section, there was a picture of the Quail Hunter with a caption describing him as America's Vice President. Not *this* America." Koresh waved a hand at the room. "The America of manifest destiny. The superpower." He smiled. "I only wish I could have been in the room to see his face when he finally got it. He thought he was such a great man, a mover and a shaker in the kingdom of Texas. But now he saw how tiny that kingdom was, and how insignificant his office compared to what might have been . . . The shock of the realization must have nearly killed him. And when it didn't kill him, it drove him insane.

"So he got me out of the hole. He shoved the magazine in my face and said, 'What is this, Mr. Howell? What does it mean?' He questioned me for hours—about what I knew, what I believed, what I suspected might be true—but it was just like the investigation into Gulf Syndrome: I could tell he'd already made up his mind what the answers were. If there really were two worlds, then the one where he was a heartbeat away from being the most powerful man on earth had to be the true one. And *this* world—the world where he was a glorified secret policeman in a dinky backwater country—this one had to be false. A cheat. A mirage."

"His idea, then," Mustafa said. "Not yours."

Koresh shrugged. "It's not that I disagreed, necessarily. I'd experienced the Syndrome too, remember, and that feeling, that sense that this world wasn't right, it was very powerful—especially around the artifacts. Where I started to have doubts was with the Quail Hunter's program for what to do about it."

"He wanted to go back to the other world, of course," Mustafa said.

"He believed it was his destiny to go back—and God help anyone who stood in the way," said David Koresh. "I thought God might have other plans. If the mirage was a judgment, which seemed likely, then it stood to reason that judgment had something to do with the behavior of the leaders of that other world—that some sort of atonement was in order. But the Quail Hunter couldn't conceive of having anything to atone for. We're talking about a man who viewed torture and murder as legitimate tools, not just of statecraft, but of self-expression. What would count as sin to such a person?

"To the Quail Hunter the mirage was evidence of a crime, not against God, but against *him*. Someone was denying him his rightful place in history. The obvious thing to do was track down the guilty party and beat on them until the natural order of the universe was restored." He shrugged again. "It wasn't a coherent plan so much as a gut reaction."

"But you didn't try to argue against it," Mustafa said.

"No, I didn't," said David Koresh. "God had already gone to some trouble to keep me alive, and there was no reason to make Him work even harder. I thought I could see how this was meant to play out: If the Quail Hunter wouldn't repent, then like a wicked prince he would have to be brought down. Then someone else could step into his place and redeem God's people from their exile."

"Someone else," Mustafa said. "A Cyrus, perhaps?"

Koresh spread his hands in a gesture of ersatz humility that reminded Mustafa very much of Saddam. "If that was what God was calling me to do, of course I would do it . . . So I pretended to go along. I told the Quail Hunter he could count on my full support and he put me back to work as if the whole waterboarding-and-imprisonment incident had never happened.

"Our first order of business was to learn as much as possible about how the world had changed. Then, by looking at who'd benefited most from the changes, we could start compiling a list of potential suspects. So we started conjuring more artifacts, but it was a slow process—like I said, the selection was random at that point, and for every news clipping or map or videotape we brought back, we got a slew of less informative items. Still, we were able to identify one glaring geopolitical anomaly very quickly."

"The United Arab States," Mustafa said.

"Yeah," said David Koresh. "Of course that only narrowed the suspect list down to 360 million people, but it could have been worse. It could've been China. And it was enough for a start.

"The other big CIA project at that time was something called Operation Curveball. Ever since word had gotten out that the 11/9 hijackers used Texas passports, the powers in Austin had been worried about retaliation. Even after the World Christian Alliance claimed responsibility for the attacks, there were concerns that the UAS might not be satisfied with slaughtering mountain men in Aspen. What if you decided to blow up a real country as payback? Regime change in Texas would show the world you were serious about not tolerating even the suspicion of terrorism. Plus there'd be one less dissenting vote at the next OPEC meeting.

"So because of this fear, CIA had been tasked with finding an alternate target for Arabia to vent its rage on. The Company forged evidence of a link between LBJ and the Alliance, and bribed an expat engineer—Curveball—to make phony claims about America's WMD program.

"That was the officially sanctioned part of the operation. But now the Quail Hunter added his own twist. Once it became clear that Arabia had taken the bait, he sent Company agents into America to make contact with militia groups and start laying the groundwork for the post-invasion insurgency.

"The idea was to create a proxy army," Koresh explained. "The Quail Hunter hadn't told anyone in Austin about the mirage, and even if he had, there was no way they were going to authorize violent

action against Arabian citizens—they were trying to *avoid* a war between the UAS and Texas! But the Quail Hunter realized he could
use Americans to do the job for him—it's not like they'd need much
encouragement to take up arms against occupying troops. He'd let
them bleed the Arabians for a while, and be bled in return, and then
once he figured out which specific Arabs had stolen his birthright,
he'd have a legion of battle-tested crusaders with no direct connection to him . . . It was a cunning plan."

"And what were you doing while this cunning plan was taking
shape?" Mustafa asked. "Playing in your sleep lab?"

"Labs, by that point," Koresh said. "Mount Carmel was still my
base of operations, but the Quail Hunter had converted a spare
building on the Crawford campus over to artifact production as well.
I traveled back and forth between the two sites and met with an
in-house think tank whose job was to collate information from the
objects we recovered. I kept the Quail Hunter informed of our progress.

"But what I was really doing, of course, was working on my
scheme to bring the man down. His perversion of Operation Curveball alone was enough to get him removed from power—if I could
get proof to the right people. And that was hardly the only abuse he'd
committed: The Quail Hunter ran the CIA the way I'd used to run
the Center.

"Of course he was extremely paranoid about security breaches,
but the reign-of-terror mode he operated in didn't exactly breed loyalty. A lot of people at Crawford hated his guts, and I managed to
recruit some of them to the Waco faction. They told me secrets and
stole documents for me.

"By mid-2004 I'd collected enough hard evidence to burn the
Quail Hunter for sure. All I needed was someone high up in the
government to report him to. I didn't know anyone in Austin, but I
had a few names. In particular there was this one elder statesman,

H., who Lee Atwater had been friends with and who he'd always spoken very highly of."

"H.?" said Mustafa.

"One of his middle initials," Koresh explained. "People called him that to distinguish him from his oldest son, who was a family embarrassment. I'd never been introduced to H., but I knew if I could show him what I had, he'd be able to help me. The problem was getting to him. He wasn't the sort of man you could just drop by and see, and I was afraid if I tried to make an appointment the Quail Hunter would find out somehow.

"Then one day an Austin dignitary named James Baker made a surprise visit to Crawford. Baker was another name I knew from Lee Atwater; he and H. were supposedly close. When Baker showed up, I was giving the Quail Hunter a report on the latest crop of artifacts. Instead of dismissing me, the Quail Hunter had me wait in his outer office. One of Baker's aides was cooling his heels out there too, and we struck up a conversation.

"The aide's name was Irving Liebowitz. While we made small talk, I tried to work up the nerve to slip him a note to pass to Baker. Then the Quail Hunter's secretary got called away for a minute, and as soon as we were alone I just blurted it out: 'I need you to get your boss to get me a meeting with H.' 'What about?' Liebowitz said. 'I can't tell you here,' I said, and nodded towards the inner office door, 'but it's a matter of national security. Please.' Then the secretary came back and I couldn't say any more, but Liebowitz gave me his card and told me to call him the next time I was in the capital.

"A few days later I had the Mount Carmel staff cover for me while I drove down to Austin. I called Liebowitz from a hotel and he agreed to come see me on his lunch hour. The deal was, I'd show him what I had, and if he agreed about the implications, he'd take my evidence to Baker and set up a meeting between me and H.

"I told him everything. I was worried how he'd react to the stuff about the mirage, but I'd brought some artifacts with me, and they made enough of an impression that at least he didn't dismiss me as a nut. And he was very interested in my documents about Curveball and the other operations the Quail Hunter had subverted. 'You were right to come forward with this,' he said finally. He told me his boss had suspected for some time that the Quail Hunter was up to no good, but until now there'd been no way to pin anything on him.

"I wanted to go back with him to see Baker, but he said that wouldn't work, he needed me to stay in the hotel room and wait for his call. 'Don't worry, it'll only be a few hours,' he promised. 'Then I'll send somebody to take you to H.' I was so relieved, I almost cried. 'Thank you, Mr. Liebowitz,' I said. 'Please,' he said, 'call me Libby. All my friends do.'

"So I waited, but he never called. I started getting nervous again. To calm myself I got out a Bible, but it slipped out of my hand and when it hit the floor it opened to Matthew 26—the chapter where Judas Iscariot conspires with the high priests. My blood ran cold when I saw that. I picked up the Bible and closed it and flipped it open at random. Luke 22: Judas and the high priests.

"I didn't need a third warning. I walked out of the hotel and got in my car and laid rubber for Mount Carmel. I'd already worked out an exodus plan with the staff in case the worst happened, and now I called them on my cell and told them to be ready to go as soon as I got back.

"I stopped for gas outside Troy. Another car pulled in while I was using the restroom, and when I came out I recognized the driver as one of the Quail Hunter's centurions. Then before I could react three other men blindsided me. They grabbed me, tasered me, and threw me in the trunk.

"If they'd taken me to Crawford I'm not sure how I would have escaped. But after we left the gas station I could tell from the sound the tires made that we weren't following the main highway. I figured we were probably headed out into the county and the centurions' orders were to dispose of me in some farmer's field."

"What did you do?" Mustafa asked.

"The only thing I could do," David Koresh said. "I took a nap. I didn't have any Elefaridol on me but I thought this once God would let me work the trick without it. I closed my eyes, started reciting, 'Now I lay me down to sleep,' and by the time I got to 'pray my soul to take,' I was back in the burning building. Not trapped this time. Searching. Looking for a room where guns were kept . . . I found it just in time. Picked up a rifle, gripped it tight. Then the car stopped, the centurions opened the trunk, and I woke up and became death.

"One of the centurions managed to draw his own gun before I killed him." Koresh placed a hand on his abdomen. "He got me here, same place Jesus was wounded. I was bleeding pretty bad, but I stayed conscious long enough to get back to the highway. I called the Center again and told them what mile marker I was at. Then I passed out.

"I woke up a day later in a caravan headed north. We'd already crossed the border into Oklahoma Territory and the staff told me everything was fine—we'd made a clean getaway. I knew that wasn't true, though. While I was out, God had sent me another dream, a detailed prophecy. During the first stage of our exodus God had confounded our pursuers, made them think we'd gone south, but they'd realized their error now and the Quail Hunter was determined not to let us get away. His centurions were screaming up the road behind us with orders to kill us all . . . But God had arranged some reinforcements for us in Oklahoma City. I knew just where to go. And that was how we met Timothy."

"What was he?" Mustafa asked.

"A freedom fighter," Koresh said. "Oklahoma Territory, you know, it's like New Mexico and Coahuila—Texas claims it as a dependency, but the residents beg to differ. Timothy was a demolitions expert for the rebels. He agreed to help us deal with the centurions on our tail. Afterwards, he and some of his friends decided to join us.

"From Oklahoma we made our way east through Gilead, following a path God laid out for me in my dreams. Eventually we crossed the frontier into America, and we've been living underground here ever since. The Quail Hunter is still looking for us, but God keeps us one step ahead of the centurions, and we've sabotaged a lot of the Quail Hunter's links to the insurgency. To the extent that they weren't sabotaged already." He arched an eyebrow. "Turns out the Quail Hunter isn't the only foreign power using Americans as pawns."

"And V. Howell Industries?" Mustafa said. "What is that about?"

"It started as a way of supporting ourselves," Koresh said. "When we left Texas we didn't have much cash, but we did smuggle out a bunch of mirage artifacts, along with a lifetime supply of Elefaridol. Then as we made our way across the Heartland, we discovered that to people with Gulf Syndrome, those artifacts were like pieces of the True Cross. We used them to barter for goods and services and to recruit new allies. Once we got here, we established a trade network with some local entrepreneurs God told us we could trust, and eventually expanded the business onto the Internet. The money's not great—not after all the middlemen and cutouts take their share— but as you see, we live pretty cheaply. And in the end it's less about commerce than evangelism: As the artifacts spread further around the globe, awareness of the mirage spreads with them."

"So your business plan is to infect the whole world with Gulf Syndrome?" Mustafa said.

Koresh acknowledged the criticism in Mustafa's tone with a crooked smile, but he said: "It's what God wants."

"To drive other men mad, as your Quail Hunter was driven mad? As the crusaders have been driven mad?" Mustafa shook his head. "I thought you wanted to redeem God's people. How does plunging the world further into chaos accomplish that?"

"That was the hardest part to understand," David Koresh said. "When I found out what kind of people were collecting the artifacts, when I thought about what that knowledge might inspire them to do, I asked the same question. I prayed about it: How can this be the road back from exile, Lord? As usual, what made the answer so difficult to see was that it was just too simple. But it had been there all along, from my very first vision." He got up and went over to his desk and opened the big Bible again. Post-it notes fluttered from the margins as he turned to the back of the Book. He found the verse he was looking for and read aloud: "And when he had opened the fourth seal, I heard the voice of the fourth beast say, Come and see. And I looked, and behold a pale horse: and his name that sat on him was Death, and Hell followed with him." Koresh looked at Mustafa. "Death," he repeated. "I am become Death. You see? You get it?"

"No," said Mustafa.

"Koresh. The name of my anointing. It means Cyrus, but it also has another meaning, a secret meaning. It means death."

"In what language?"

"The language of the Seven Seals." Koresh pressed his hand against the page of scripture. "*This* is what the mirage is. A period of chaos and tribulation, when the world turns upside down and then keeps on tumbling. I was wrong: It's not *a* judgment, it's *the* Judgment, and my job isn't to find a road back from exile, it's to prepare the way forward, to the Last Day. To break the seals, and blow the trumpets, and pour out the bowls.

"It's going to be terrible," Koresh said smiling. "Not everyone will make it through the final storm. The Quail Hunter won't. Not Saddam Hussein either, or any of the other walking dead . . . But those of us who are blessed, washed in the blood of the Lamb, will meet up again after the End, in a new world, the golden city of God's kingdom." His smile broadened and he looked off as if he could see what he spoke of, shining on a distant horizon.

Madman, Mustafa thought, and recalled the words of Lieutenant Fahd: These fucking people. "And what about me?" he said.

"You?" Koresh blinked, drawing back from his reverie. "You could still be saved. Any living man can be, if he accepts Christ."

"That's lovely to hear," said Mustafa, "but I was thinking more of my role in your apocalypse. From your story, it sounds as if most people who come looking for you either don't find you, or meet bad ends. Saddam told us all of his spies had disappeared. I doubt they converted."

"Oh," Koresh said. "No. We killed them all."

"But not me," Mustafa said. "You saved my life to bring me here and tell me all this. Why?"

Koresh seemed momentarily nonplussed by the question. Then he shrugged and said: "It's what God wanted. He doesn't always explain His reasons to me . . . But if I had to guess, I'd say He intends you to do battle with the false prophet of the east."

"False prophet?" Mustafa said.

Koresh nodded. "I told you, the Quail Hunter's not the only one using Americans as pawns. Arabia has its own wicked prince." He hesitated. "And there's something else. You remember I told you about the think tank at Crawford?"

"The one that was collating information about the artifacts?"

"Right," said Koresh, "to help refine the list of suspects. And of course, speculating about *who* caused the mirage leads naturally to speculation about *how* they caused it . . ."

"Naturally."

"The Quail Hunter was never that interested in the mechanism. I guess because when violence is your answer to everything, the only question that really matters is, 'Whose face do I stomp on next?' But the members of the think tank were more intellectually curious. One of them, a Company Orientalist named Hank Wessells, came up with what he called the magic lamp theory, which is just what it sounds like: a theory that somebody somewhere in Arabia made a wish that changed the world.

"It wasn't a serious idea—it wasn't Christian—but Hank made the mistake of writing the Quail Hunter a memo about it anyway. The Quail Hunter hit the roof."

"Why?" said Mustafa. "Because the theory was heretical?"

"Probably the Quail Hunter thought Hank was making fun of him," Koresh said. "That was usually what set him off. Or it could be he was worried that if the theory was true and it was just some anonymous Arab who stumbled over a magic lamp, we'd never be able to find the guy. Whatever the reason, the Quail Hunter fired off a memo of his own, warning the members of the think tank to stop wasting resources on 'unproductive lines of inquiry.' Hank got called to the interrogation wing and didn't come back. After that, nobody ever mentioned magic lamps again.

"But sometime later, we got an artifact in the Mount Carmel sleep lab that reminded me of Hank's theory. I never showed it to the Quail Hunter. I put it with a secret stash of other artifacts that I'd held back for one reason or another. And last week, when I dreamed you were coming here, I dug it out." He reached into his desk drawer.

It was another photograph. The scene was an excavation, somewhere in the desert. Two grinning men stood in a shallow pit with their arms over each other's shoulders. One of them was a blond in a gray ARMY T-shirt. The other was Mustafa, or a version of him, with a red, white, and blue bandanna tied around his head.

In the foreground at their feet, a blanket held an array of objects: a small clay urn; a jumble of pottery shards; a rusted artillery shell casing; another rust-pitted artifact that might have been an old bayonet; and on the far right, set slightly apart, a stoppered brass bottle.

"Does this ring any bells?" David Koresh asked. Mustafa didn't answer; he'd dropped the photo in his lap and was gripping the sofa cushions with both hands. "Well," Koresh continued after a moment,

"I've got some other things to give you. Let me go get them, and then I'll have Timothy take you back to the Green Zone."

"What?" Mustafa looked up, still holding on to the couch for dear life. "Wait. I have other questions . . ."

"I'm sure you do," David Koresh said. "But don't worry. God's got you covered."

The boy on the tricycle had stopped to listen again. This time the sound—diesel engines, approaching fast—was one that even adult ears could hear.

A Humvee swung into the street. Mounted on its front end was a wedge-shaped steel plow like the cow-catcher on a Gilead locomotive. Two more Humvees with roof-mounted .50-calibers followed behind it. Then a troop truck pulled sideways across the street entrance and Marines with rifles began jumping out.

The boy on the tricycle watched in awe as the Humvees roared past. The gate guard spoke frantically into his radio and then reached for his gun, but a .50-caliber cut him down before he got a shot off. The front door of a house halfway down the street banged open and a man came running onto his porch. A burst from an assault rifle knocked him back through the doorway.

A loudspeaker on the troop truck began blaring a recorded message: "STAY IN YOUR HOMES! . . . STAY IN YOUR HOMES! . . . THIS IS A POLICING ACTION! . . . STAY IN YOUR HOMES!" The Marines fired warning shots at a couple of the other houses.

The lead Humvee crashed through the gate and drove onto the lawn of the Colonial house. The other Humvees pulled in and flanked it, the machine gunners killing two more guards on the balcony above the Colonial's front door.

As the Marines deployed from the Humvees, other militiamen began shooting at them from the second-floor windows and the dormers on the roof. The militiamen tried to duck in and out of cover, but the Colonial's wood siding might as well have been cardboard for all the protection it offered, so they generally only got off a shot or two before being killed. Still, there were a lot of them, and the Marines were being careful—because they hoped to take prisoners, they could not simply rake the building with fire from end to end. They picked their targets and lobbed tear gas grenades in between gun volleys.

While his men gave their lives to delay the Marines, the militia leader fled out the back of the house. The attack had caught him in the shower and he came out wrapped in a damp bathrobe, his gray hair tucked under a blue shower cap and water beading his glasses. His bodyguards formed a protective circle around him and they made for a wooden gate in the wall at the rear of the yard.

The Marine snipers hiding in the trees behind the wall let them get most of the way there and then killed all the bodyguards at once. The militia leader stopped short, scowling at the suddenly dead men as if their mortality were proof of incompetence.

The firefight at the house ended moments later. A Marine leaned out of an upstairs window, stripping off a gas mask and calling out, "All clear!" More Marines appeared around the sides of the building.

The wooden gate opened. Umm Husam, Zinat, and Amal stepped through. Amal marched straight up to the militia leader, who still stood glowering amid the circle of corpses.

"Mr. Rumsfeld," Amal said. "The mothers and daughters of Baghdad would like a word."

THE LIBRARY OF ALEXANDRIA
A USER-EDITED REFERENCE SOURCE

Jinn

A **jinn** is a supernatural being. According to Holy Quran and Hadith, God created jinn from smokeless fire, as He created human beings from clay and angels from light. Like humans, jinn possess free will and thus are capable of both sin and submission to God: "There are among us some that are righteous, and some the contrary: We follow divergent paths." (Quran chapter 72, verse 11)

Jinn occupy a parallel universe hidden from human eyes—though they can see us, and may choose or be compelled to reveal themselves. Evil jinn may be enslaved by human masters, while good jinn may volunteer their service. The nature and magnitude of their powers is disputed, but they can do nothing contrary to the will of God . . .

JINN IN WESTERN MYTHOLOGY

In Christian Europe and the Americas, jinn are referred to as *genies*. The Western conception of the creatures comes primarily from adaptations of stories from *One Thousand and One Nights*, combined with elements of non-Arabic folklore such as the Greek myth of King Midas.

Western tales typically strip jinn of their moral agency, turning them into anthropomorphized wish-granting machines. The wishes invariably go wrong, resulting in tragedy or lasting humiliation for the wish-makers. Although commonly read as parables about the dangers of hubris, literary theorist Edward Said has argued that such genie stories also serve as propaganda reinforcing Western authoritarianism: "This message, that the natural order mustn't be tampered with, encourages blind deference to one's leaders—even as those same leaders show no compunction about imposing their own magical thinking on the world."

The flight home left Andrews Air Force Base in the early evening. After takeoff, Mustafa rested his head against the window and watched America drop away over the horizon.

Amal was in the cargo bay, interviewing the prisoner. By default this should have been Mustafa's job, but in his extreme annoyance at being apprehended, Donald Rumsfeld had revealed something he might better have kept secret: He spoke Arabic. Not well, and not willingly—but Amal had evinced a knack for goading him into talking and she'd wanted first crack at the interrogation.

The wounded Marine, Salim, was stretched out asleep in the rear of the passenger cabin. His presence on the flight was also Amal's doing, although Mustafa, who'd been elsewhere when Amal and Umm Husam had spoken to Colonel Yunus, didn't know the details.

Samir was sleeping too—or pretending to. Upon Mustafa's return to the Green Zone, Samir had tried to quiz him about his meeting with the CIA director, but Mustafa had put him off, saying he could read about it in the official report. Samir was startled at first by Mustafa's brusqueness, but then a sad understanding seemed to dawn in him and he nodded, saying, "Yes, perhaps that's best . . . Perhaps that's what I deserve." Since then he'd been withdrawn and uncommunicative, keeping his head bowed during the ride to Andrews, his expression recalling the one he'd worn on the trip into the Red Zone: the look of a condemned man.

When it was too dark to see anything more outside, Mustafa sat up and got out the new reading packet that David Koresh had given him. It contained three artifacts, dispatches from beyond the mirage.

Item number one was a file from the archives of the Jihaz al Mukhabarat al Amma—the General Directorate of Intelligence of the Republic of Iraq—concerning an Iraqi National Police officer named Mustafa al Baghdadi. Mustafa had read it several times already, but now he began again, reviewing the details of his other life: a life recognizable in its broad strokes, yet bound and shaped by a very different set of constraints.

As in this world, he'd been a cop, trying to do good. But "good," in the Republic of Saddam, was defined more by loyalty and submission to the Baath Party than by any normal measure of virtue. From a promising beginning—top marks in his class at the Baghdad police academy—he'd fallen swiftly. He was reprimanded repeatedly for being soft on suspects, using talk rather than more direct methods to obtain confessions and refusing to pursue cases against people he believed to be innocent. Then, in what should have been the end of his career, he'd attempted to arrest a Party official for the murder of a young girl. Mustafa had himself been arrested and held in Abu Ghraib for several months. Upon his release, he'd gone after the official again, this time turning up evidence not of murder, but of anti-government conspiracy—a much more serious crime. The official had been arrested by the Mukhabarat; Mustafa had received a personal commendation from Uncle Saddam, been restored to his former police rank, and warned to watch his step in the future. But the reprimands and brushes with Party authority continued.

The personal history ended in 2002, but attached to the file folder was a memorandum on United States Army stationery dated July 9, 2003. Written by a Captain Edward Lawrence, the memo requested that Mustafa al Baghdadi be cleared for work as a field translator, citing his strong language skills and "obvious anti-Baathist sentiment." The memo said nothing about treasure-hunting in the desert, but given the proximity of Al Hillah to Baghdad, it wasn't hard to imagine a scenario where Captain Lawrence and his translator, grown restless perhaps after several years of nation-building, decided to go off-mission. Mustafa also suspected—Koresh had hinted as much—

that if he kept this artifact near him, he might start to remember details. He wondered if he really wanted to.

The section of the file marked FAMILY listed only one spouse, Fadwa bint Harith. Mustafa wasn't surprised by this—he sensed that Saddam's Iraq didn't have many Internet IPOs, so an honest cop probably couldn't afford more than one wife. What he didn't know was whether that would have made him a kinder and more devoted husband, or a more bitter one. He wished he could believe it was the former.

The reading packet also contained a Mukhabarat file for Samir Nadim, another Baghdad cop who worked in the same precinct as Mustafa. Samir's police career had been less rocky than Mustafa's, though it appeared their friendship had gotten him into trouble on more than one occasion.

Like Mustafa, he'd had a second career, but not with the U.S. Army. From 1997 through 2002, Samir had been an informant for the Mudiriyat al Amn al Amma—the General Security Service, which, as best Mustafa could tell, was another arm of Saddam's secret police force that ranked somewhere below the Mukhabarat but still well above the ordinary street cops.

Samir had not volunteered to be a spy. A report included in the file explained what had happened: After an unnamed source had accused him of meeting in secret with "subversive elements," Samir had been placed under surveillance and followed on several late-night excursions to see whether the subversives in question were Kurds, Turks, Iranians, or dissident Iraqi Shia.

The answer, as the accompanying photographs showed all too clearly, was none of the above. The report concluded there was no treason here, but recommended that Samir and his fellow "subversives" be conscripted into the Amn's informant network. "To avoid public exposure of their vice, we expect they will be most obedient."

We expect they will be most obedient . . . Mustafa looked across the seatbacks to where Samir was once again tossing and turning in his sleep. He considered waking him, asking what his nightmare was about, asking some other questions too. Then he took another look at the photographs and decided that midair over the Atlantic wasn't the right place to broach this subject.

The last, and lengthiest, of the items in the packet was an August 2001 report by the Central Intelligence Agency's Bin Laden Issue Station titled METHODS AND GOALS OF AL QAEDA. David Koresh had affixed a Post-it note to the cover reading, "Not my CIA! . . . But a wicked prince in one world is a wicked prince in all worlds." Mustafa turned to the first page and began to make some notes of his own.

At the Azores refueling stop, the harshly lit tarmac had the bleak look of a gas station after midnight. No one got on or off the plane. Mustafa used the lavatory in the passenger cabin, then went back to the cargo bay to check on how the interrogation was coming. He stayed out of sight at the top of the stairs and listened to the high whining voice of Donald Rumsfeld. The man's accent was almost impenetrable; the only phrase Mustafa could make out was "majahil marufah"—"known unknowns"—which made no sense to him. But then Amal asked a follow-up question, her confident tone making it clear that she understood. Sensing he could only cause trouble by interrupting, Mustafa returned to his seat.

As the cargolifter taxied back onto the runway, he opened his wallet and took out the 250-dinar note. He studied Saddam's smiling face and saw, in his mind's eye, a stoppered brass bottle.

Known unknowns, Mustafa thought.

The sun reappeared as the cargolifter approached the North African coast. Mustafa was dozing, but the pink light reflecting off the seatback in front of him invaded his sleep.

In the dream, he was crossing the Sahara on foot. He had traveled a long way over a sea of sand dunes, but now the sea ended, giving way to a rocky plain that was pockmarked with blast craters. He knew without being told that this was Site Yarbu, the testing ground where the first atom bomb had been detonated, and where the military had continued setting off larger and more powerful devices throughout the 1950s and '60s. Located in a remote part of southern Algeria, Yarbu was named for the hopping desert rodents that were, according to the government propaganda of the day, the only living things endangered by the bomb tests. Of course that hadn't been true: Berber nomads occupied the fallout zone as well, as did a number of former French soldiers who'd remained in the Maghreb after the war. Comedians sometimes joked about this latter group, the *gerboises françaises,* Legionnaires who glowed in the dark.

Mustafa walked to the lip of one of the blast craters and looked down into it. It was surprisingly deep, so deep that its bottom was hidden in shadow. He wondered what kept it from filling up with sand, and in answer a wind devil started on the crater's far rim, vacuuming up loose grit as it moved. In the waking world, the cargolifter banked to change course and Mustafa's lolling head turned away from the window; in the dream, the wind devil circled the crater, gaining size and substance until it blotted out the sun.

Then Mustafa was walking again, through a haze of blowing sand. All about him was formlessness and void, but soon enough the sand began to condense into the trunks and crowns of eucalypti. He passed a sign: REALITY REORGANIZATION TEST PLOT #99.

In a clearing beyond the trees lay a hybrid shrine, an amalgam of Cairo's Nasser Memorial and one of the monuments Mustafa had visited on his tour of the Green Zone. Shallow steps mounted to a platform on which burned a guttering Flame of Unity. Behind this, a half-circle of fluted marble columns supported a curved slab chiseled with the words I TREMBLE FOR MY COUNTRY WHEN I REFLECT THAT GOD IS JUST.

Another wind devil started, seizing hold of the Unity Flame and drawing it up into a twisting pillar of blue smokeless fire. Then the fire vanished, and in its place stood a figure in a white tunic whom Mustafa recognized from another dream.

"Hello again," the jinn greeted him. "Have you sorted out your time zones yet?"

Mustafa held up the photo of the dig site. "Al Hillah," he said. "I found your bottle."

"Not mine," said the jinn. "It belonged to a prince of Babylon. So did I, for a time."

Mustafa heard a hiss of windblown sand and turned to find the eucalyptus forest transformed into a mighty metropolis, its skyline dominated by twin towers. New York, Mustafa thought, but already a second transformation had begun, changes cascading through the cityscape, turning it into Baghdad. And even though he watched it happen, once the transformation was complete and the Tigris and Euphrates towers were standing there so familiar, it was hard to imagine the scene had ever been different.

"Did I do this?" Mustafa said. "Was this my wish?"

The jinn seemed to ponder the question. "To remake the whole world would be an act of extraordinary pride. Does that sound like you?"

Mustafa looked at the photograph in his hand. "No," he said, surprised by his own answer. "No, it sounds like something an American would do . . ."

"I must have a touch of American in me as well then," the jinn said smiling. "To grant such a request. Ah, but I do love a challenge . . . And I was most grateful to be released from my confinement."

"What did I wish for, then? If not this . . ."

"Smaller things," the jinn said. "Harder things. Things I could not give you, grateful though I was." He gestured towards the cityscape, and Mustafa saw, through windows that opened in the sides of the towers, Fadwa in two aspects. She was riding a crowded subway train; she was also, in a parallel reality, home alone, praying for the return of her husband, who had walked out after their latest argument. Then the planes flew in over Baghdad, and Fadwa looked up, and looked up, and was no more.

"I could not bring her back to you," the jinn told Mustafa, whose cheeks were wet now with tears. "I tried, but God wouldn't permit it. Not her. Considering some of those He did allow back, perhaps that's a good sign . . ."

"And her misery?" Mustafa said. "If you could not spare Fadwa's life, could you not at least have done something about that?"

The jinn didn't answer.

"And Noor?"

"Ah, Noor," the jinn said, looking embarrassed. "A misguided attempt at consolation. I thought she would at least make *you* happier. But it appears I miscalculated."

"I would say so," Mustafa agreed. "You should not have given me a second wife. You should have given Fadwa a better husband."

"That would not have been her wish," the jinn said, "and I could not have granted it anyway. Look again at the city."

Mustafa looked. The skyline appeared to rush towards him, and the towers and skyscrapers which seemed so solid from a distance were revealed to be composed of tiny, discrete particles whirling through empty space.

"Sand," the jinn said. "So much of this world, sand, and easily reshaped, God willing. But not everything."

The city receded again. Mustafa, feeling as though he were reciting a line in a play, said: "Human beings from clay."

"Some parts softer than others," said the jinn. He laid a hand against his own skull, beside the seat of memory. "Pliable enough with the right touch. But the characters of men and women—their strengths and weaknesses, their passions and fears, the sins and vices they are prone to—those are made of iron, and steel, and brass.

Those I cannot alter. Oh, perhaps a detail here and there . . . But at your core, you are who you are. I cannot make you someone else."

"Well," Mustafa said, fresh tears starting. "Well, that's wonderful then."

"You should not weep," the jinn said. "I can't make you a better person, but God, who gave you both life and free will, can help you try to become one. Try honestly, and when you stumble, ask His forgiveness and try again."

"If only it were that easy," Mustafa said.

"It isn't easy. It is a struggle. But struggle is better than self-pity. You do not honor Fadwa by continuing to dwell on what cannot be undone. You only distract yourself from the good you still can do—and the evil you may still prevent. You are a sinner, Mustafa al Baghdadi, but you are not the only sinner. You are surely not the worst."

Something in his words made Mustafa look at the city again. Most of the skyline had faded away, leaving only the twin towers—two sets of them, side by side. Behind them loomed the shadow of a man, like a devil come to claim them. It was just a silhouette, but Mustafa thought he knew who it belonged to. How many other men were that tall?

"Iron and steel and brass," the jinn said. "A wicked prince in one world is a wicked prince in all worlds."

They landed at Al Kharj Air Force Base in late afternoon. The outside temperature was 121 degrees, and a curtain of heat haze made the hangars and control tower shimmer like protean objects that had yet to assume their final shape. Mustafa stepping out onto the tarmac wondered whether he might still be dreaming.

Amal helped Salim into a wheelchair. Mustafa watched them together and was suddenly struck, as he had not been before, by the resemblance between them. And not just between them: Staring at Salim in profile he flashed back on a magazine article Abu

Mustafa had shown him recently. The focus of the article had been Senator Al Maysani's career, but there'd also been a sidebar about Amal's father, Shamal, the corruption-fighting cop . . . Yes, Mustafa thought, I must still be dreaming.

A bright flash of light drew his attention back to the heat curtain. He held up a hand to shield his eyes and the light resolved into an ambulance with sun glaring off its windshield and front grill. A man in civilian dress was leaning out the passenger window, and before the ambulance had come to a complete stop he leaped out onto the tarmac, dashed up to the wheelchair, threw his arms around the young Marine, and began showering him with kisses.

"Father," a red-faced Salim said, several moments later, "this is my new friend Amal. She saved my life."

"Thank you," Anwar said, his eyes brimming with tears. He leaned forward as if he might embrace Amal too, but restrained himself. "Thank you."

Amal offered him a complicated smile. "It's what we do in Homeland Security," she said. Lowering her eyes, she added: "I'm sorry about the leg."

"What for, that wasn't your fault," Salim said, thinking this was addressed to him. "Anyway, I'll be up in no time. Come visit me in a month and I'll outrace you!"

Amal said: "You should go home now and see your mother."

"Yes," Anwar said nodding. "She is waiting for us." He looked at Salim. "We have many things to talk about."

"I know," Salim said. But then he smiled and handed Amal a slip of paper. "My email address is on there. Write to me!"

"You just take care of yourself and be good to your parents," Amal told him. She stepped back and Anwar got behind the wheelchair and pushed it towards the ambulance. He and the driver helped Salim into the back. Anwar waved solemnly at Amal and climbed in beside his son.

Amal stood beside Mustafa watching the ambulance drive away. "The boy looks a lot like his grandfather," Mustafa said—and then blinked, not having meant to speak the thought aloud.

Amal took it in stride. "He really does," she said. She looked at the slip of paper in her hand and then spread her fingers. An updraft caught the paper and carried it away into the sky.

Boots tramped on the cargolifter's loading ramp. An airman jumped down onto the tarmac and spoke into a radio: "All clear." A squad of military policemen brought the prisoner out of the hold.

The prisoner was hooded and shackled and still dressed in the bathrobe he'd been wearing when captured. He was also barefoot, and when Mustafa saw the MPs intended to march him onto the scorching hot concrete he called out: "Hey, what are you thinking? Get him some shoes!" The MPs hesitated. The airman, looking embarrassed, ducked back inside the plane and returned with a plastic pallet. He dropped this on the tarmac and the MPs sat the prisoner on it as though he were cargo.

Wavering black shapes like patches of oil appeared in the heat curtain. These too resolved into vehicles: a fleet of black SUVs. Unlike the sparkling-clean ambulance they were covered in dust, as if they'd driven a long way across the desert; instead of reflecting the sunlight they absorbed it.

Feeling eyes over his shoulder, Mustafa turned and looked up at the plane. He saw Samir, his face framed in one of the windows of the passenger cabin, staring nervously at the approaching vehicles. When Samir noticed Mustafa looking up at him, his face collapsed into shame and he vanished from the window.

The SUVs pulled up to the cargolifter. Idris Abd al Qahhar got out of the lead vehicle; the others disgorged bearded mujahideen who, but for the dark suits they wore, might have stepped straight off a battlefield in Afghanistan.

"Mustafa al Baghdadi," Idris said. "You have something that belongs to me."

"You are mistaken," said Mustafa, stepping forward to interpose himself between Idris's men and the prisoner. "This man is coming back with me for a proper interrogation at Homeland Security headquarters."

"Ah, I'm afraid there's been a change in plan." Idris pulled out a folded sheet of letterhead and presented it with a flourish. "The president, in consultation with Senator Bin Laden and several other members of the Intelligence Committee, has decided to classify this prisoner as a high-value detainee. We will be transferring him directly to Chwaka Bay."

Mustafa scanned the document, which bore the president's seal and his signature. "This isn't right."

"You are welcome to take the matter up with the president yourself," Idris said. "But I understand his schedule is quite busy today, so it may be some time before you are able to reach him. In the meantime . . ."

He signaled to his men. A group of four advanced towards the prisoner. "Wait!" Mustafa shouted. He turned to the MPs: "Stop these men!"

But before they could do anything, a man in an Army colonel's uniform got out of Idris's SUV. "Stand down," he told the MPs. "Do not interfere!"

The prisoner meanwhile seemed to have wilted in the heat. He was limp when the mujahideen seized hold of him. They hauled him up roughly and began dragging him, his bare feet trailing across the hot tarmac.

Mustafa took a step towards them and Idris said, "Go ahead. It's pointless, but if a beating will complete your day my men will be happy to supply it." The good humor with which he said this, more than the words themselves, convinced Mustafa that there really was nothing he could do.

The mujahideen bundled the prisoner's limp body into the back of their SUV. "I suppose," Idris said, disappointed that Mustafa had declined the beating, "there's no point in my asking what this man already told you."

"Nothing. I haven't interviewed him yet."

"Really." Idris looked skeptical. "Well, I'll know soon enough if that's true . . . And don't worry, I'll copy you a full report of my interrogation." Laughing at this joke, he signaled his men and they all got back in their vehicles and drove off.

"They won't get anything out of him," Amal said.

"You don't think so?" Mustafa looked at her. "You were with him for most of the flight. You're saying he didn't tell you anything?"

"No, he told me plenty: about America and Iraq, Saddam Hussein and Osama bin Laden . . . Strange stuff. Crazy stuff."

"Well if he told all that to you, why wouldn't he tell Idris?"

"Because I made a deal with him," Amal said. "He knew Idris would be waiting here to take him. Not Idris specifically, but someone like him, someone from Al Qaeda. He said he wasn't afraid to die, but he didn't want to be tortured—something about how he didn't feel the Golden Rule should apply to him . . . So I offered him a bargain. I told him if he talked to me, I'd make sure he wasn't tortured."

"And he believed you?"

Her hand was in her pocket. She brought it out and spread her fingers again. There was a green twist of cellophane in her palm: an empty candy wrapper. They both stared at it, and then the updraft caught it and carried it away as it had the paper.

"Amal?" Mustafa said. "What have you done?"

And Amal said: "That man tried to kill my son."

Book Four

The
Stone

The Library of Alexandria
A USER-EDITED REFERENCE SOURCE

Truther

A "**Truther**" is a <u>skeptic</u> who questions the official account of <u>the events of November 9, 2001</u>. Many Truthers belong to organizations such as the <u>11/9 Citizens Commission</u> and <u>Ulama for 11/9 Truth and Justice</u>. They hold meetings and rallies, petition for the release of secret government documents, and use the <u>Internet</u> to publicize their alternative theories about the November 9 terror attacks.

Almost all Truthers believe that the <u>UAS government</u> has suppressed important information about what really happened on 11/9, though they disagree about the nature and extent of the cover-up. Some Truthers claim that the <u>intelligence community</u> knew about the hijackings in advance, and some go even farther, positing that <u>government agents</u> participated in the planning and execution of the attacks.

Suggested motives for such government involvement in 11/9 include:

· To justify massive increases in military and intelligence spending.

· To create a pretext for the <u>War on Terror</u> and the <u>invasion of America</u>.

· To undermine the popularity of the <u>Party of God</u> and the <u>House of Saud</u> by making them appear weak.

· To halt the "<u>secularization</u>" of Arabian society and frighten people into embracing a new <u>Islamic Awakening</u>.

Government officials have been generally dismissive of the Truthers' claims, when they bother to acknowledge them at all. <u>11/9 Commission</u> spokesman <u>Mohammed Atta</u> called theories of government involvement in the attacks "offensive," adding: "There is no cover-up. No one denies that pre-11/9 anti-terror efforts were inadequate, but people need to accept that there's no deeper mystery here . . ."

Regarding the suggestion that the 11/9 attacks were an attempt to literally "put the fear of God" into people, the President's United Arab Fiqh Council has released a fatwa stating that the use of terrorism to spread belief in Islam would be a clear violation of God's law, citing as evidence Holy Quran chapter 2, verse 256 ("Let there be no compulsion in religion . . .") and chapter 5, verse 32 ("If any one slew a person—unless it be for murder or for spreading mischief in the land—it would be as if he slew the whole people") and also chapter 6, verse 151 ("Take not life, which God hath made sacred, except by way of justice and law"). "While we obviously cannot say that no one in government would do such a terrible thing," the Council concluded, "we can say that no true Muslim would."

Perhaps unsurprisingly, such statements have done little to dampen Truthers' enthusiasm for their theories. They continue to seek "the reality behind the mirage."

The crusader was staying on the ninth floor of the Zawra Park Hotel. His name was Joseph Simeon and he was the last surviving member of a five-man cell that had left Heidelberg two weeks ago.

Following a route common to both legal and illegal immigrants, the members of the cell had traveled by bus to Istanbul. There they'd met with a forger who was supposed to supply them with guest-worker ID cards and other documents, but when the cell leader insulted the man's Orthodox faith and tried to convert him to a more proper form of Christianity, he threw them out of his house. They were forced to turn to another counterfeiter, who charged three times as much for inferior work.

In fact it was worse than they knew. This second forger, having determined the crusaders had no Arabic, decided to play a prank on them. The Roman-letter portion of Joe Simeon's ID card gave his cover name as Thaddeus Schulman. But the accompanying Arabic text said he was Princess Jezebel and listed his occupation as "pole dancer." The cell leader's card identified him as a professional camel anus.

The crusaders continued on to Gaziantep, where they hired a guide to sneak them into the UAS. The guide got a look at their papers and realized they'd been taken for fools, but as they'd already managed to offend him too, he said nothing. He did what they paid him to do, smuggled them into Syria and delivered them to a workers' hostel in Aleppo. The manager of the hostel was highly amused by something but wouldn't share the joke.

ICE showed up in the middle of the night. Thirsty and unable to sleep, Joe Simeon had gone in search of a soda machine and wasn't in the room when the immigration agents kicked the door in. He heard shouting and then gunshots, and ran off into the darkness clutching a bottle of orange Fanta.

He thought about going home, but he was almost out of money, so even if he'd made it back over the border he'd have been stranded in Turkey. He decided to continue on alone to Baghdad, where additional conspirators were supposedly waiting, though he didn't know who they were or how to contact them. Praying to God for guidance, he went out to the highway and hitched a ride.

In Baghdad he found a cheap motel out by the airport. He was still using the Princess Jezebel ID, but the motel clerk, who'd lost a brother on 11/9, didn't laugh or crack a smile. He gave the crusader a room key and called the Homeland Security tip line.

An hour and a half later Joe Simeon woke to find a large Arab standing over his bed. "Get up," the man said. "The authorities are on their way to arrest you."

"Who are you?"

"You may call me Siraj al Din. I am a friend." He neglected to mention that he was a member of Al Qaeda and that he'd been sent here by Idris Abd al Qahhar.

Siraj al Din took Joe Simeon to the Zawra Park Hotel and got him another room. He told him to keep the DO NOT DISTURB sign on and the shades drawn. "Don't go out. Don't make any calls, not even to room service. I'll be back later with food and fresh clothing."

Joe Simeon crawled into the bed—much more comfortable than the one at the motel—and fell into a dead sleep. When he next opened his eyes, Siraj al Din was pushing a cart loaded with covered dishes into the room. "What time is it?"

"About eight o'clock in the evening. Come, eat something."

After the meal, he took the bag of clothes Siraj al Din had brought for him and went to shower. When he came back out the cart was gone, and a cardboard shirt box and a street map were lying on the bed. "What's that?" he said, nodding at the shirt box.

"First I must ask you, are you prepared to do what you came here to do?"

Joe Simeon had just been contemplating this very question. The answer seemed simple enough. By all rights he should be dead or in custody by now. That he wasn't was all the proof he needed that God wanted him to proceed. He would do what he was told, and then he would go to heaven. "I'm ready."

"Good," Siraj al Din said, picking up the map. "Your target is the Ground Zero Mosque. The city is close to breaking ground on the project, and tomorrow afternoon there will be a rally at the site. A large crowd is expected, and many politicians. Also lots of security—but I'll show you a path to bypass the outer ring of barricades and police. After that it's up to you."

"No," Joe Simeon said. "After that it's up to God."

Mustafa spent the night in Karkh General Hospital, sleeping at his father's bedside.

That morning, Abu Mustafa had gone out for a walk and not come home. Mustafa had divided his day between napping and abortive attempts to compose an official report of his meeting with David Koresh. By late afternoon, when his father had still not returned, he began to grow concerned. He was just about to get Uncle Tamir and the cousins and organize a search when he received a phone call from the Bunia Mosque.

It wasn't the first time he'd gotten such a call. His father often gravitated to places of worship when he got lost—Baghdad's holy sites, he said, being among the few things about the city that hadn't changed. But Al Bunia was across the river in Karkh, a long way for an old man on foot. "Is he all right?"

"I'm afraid not," the caller said. "He was dehydrated and having heart palpitations. We had to call an ambulance."

Mustafa and his aunt and uncle drove to the hospital. By the time they arrived, Abu Mustafa had responded to IV fluids and was sitting up, looking embarrassed. "I got on a bus," he confessed.

Mustafa understood immediately. Abu Mustafa treated much of Baghdad's mass transit system, especially the subway, as if it didn't exist; he acknowledged buses but rarely used them, since the routes almost never went where he thought they should. Today, though, having wandered a bit too far along Abu Nuwas Street, he'd tried to ride back, only to discover that the coach he boarded was an express that made no further stops before crossing the Tigris. He'd stayed on the bus for a while, hoping it would eventually turn around, but the increasing strangeness of downtown had overwhelmed him, until he spotted Al Bunia in the distance and decided to make for it.

"I don't understand," Aunt Rana said. "Why didn't you just hail a taxi?"

"Because I was confused!"

The doctor wanted to keep Abu Mustafa in the hospital overnight. Abu Mustafa wasn't happy about it but was too tired to argue, so Mustafa arranged to have an extra bed wheeled into the room. By the time that was taken care of, Abu Mustafa was already drifting off, but Mustafa stayed awake late into the night, thinking.

Farouk had phoned him at home earlier to give him a heads-up. "Idris is quite upset about Rumsfeld's suicide. He's blaming you for the security lapse that allowed it to happen, and he's asked that you be suspended pending a full investigation."

Mustafa was upset about the suicide as well, albeit for very different reasons. Still, he couldn't help observing: "Idris is only sorry that he didn't get to torture and kill the man himself. Even if it is my fault, I don't know that I can bring myself to regret denying him that."

"Regret it or don't, that's your business," Farouk said. "But I hope whatever you learned in America is good enough to compensate for this failure. My influence with the president only goes so far, and Idris and Senator Bin Laden are out for blood."

"Don't worry," Mustafa said. "I think the president will find my report most illuminating."

One thing he had yet to decide was what to do with the artifacts David Koresh had given him—particularly the second Mukhabarat file. Mustafa's first impulse was to destroy it and forget he'd ever seen it. But when he recalled how Samir had been acting lately, he was forced to consider that perhaps God had sent him the file for a reason.

He thought about Idris, turning up at Al Kharj with a presidential order already in hand. There were any number of ways Idris could have learned that they were bringing back a prisoner, but what if he'd been alerted by a member of Mustafa's own team? And what if that same team member had also given Idris advance notice of their expedition to Sadr City? And then there was the matter of the ambush on the Jefferson Davis Pike. According to Amal, Rumsfeld had claimed that his militia learned about the Marine convoy from an informant inside the Green Zone. Fine. But who told the informant, and who told the person who'd told him?

Are you ill, Samir?

At some point Mustafa slept. He woke to the dawn muezzin's call and found a prayer room on the hospital's ground floor. This morning he said extra prayers: for his father; for Colonel Yunus; for Amal and her son; and for Donald Rumsfeld, who though an enemy had still deserved the protection due any prisoner of war. Mustafa considered praying for Samir as well, but was too unsettled by his suspicions, so instead he ended by asking God to grant him wisdom.

When he went back upstairs, his father was awake, sitting up in bed and looking out the window. Mustafa paused in the doorway, distressed by his father's frailty, which the dawn light seemed to accentuate.

His father saw him standing there and gave a little grunt of annoyance. "I'm not dead yet," he said.

"I am glad," said Mustafa. He sat on the edge of the bed. "I could use some advice." His father laughed, and Mustafa said, "What?"

"Nothing," said Abu Mustafa. "I'm happy to help, but I think the last time you *followed* my advice was when you were eight years old." Another laugh. "Never mind, go on. What's the problem?"

Mustafa just said it: "I think Samir is a homosexual."

His father looked at him quizzically, then waited to hear if there was more. Finally Abu Mustafa said: "Well, that's not so big a surprise. Really, if you think about it, it explains a few things."

"What do you mean?"

"Do you remember when Samir got divorced?" Abu Mustafa said. "I was struck at the time by how eagerly he confessed his infidelities. In his shoes I think I'd have been more ashamed, and more discreet— unless I were trying to prevent speculation about some other problem with my marriage."

Mustafa blinked, feeling stupid. "You think Najat knows?"

"The mother of his children? Is that even a question?" Abu Mustafa chuckled. "But what troubles you about this, Mustafa? Are you worried he wants to do something improper with you?"

"What? No! . . . It's a sin, that's all."

Abu Mustafa shrugged. "Fornication with women is a sin too, last I checked," he said. "But you didn't get such a look on your face when you thought Samir was guilty of that. Is God's law really the issue here, or are you just being squeamish?"

Mustafa couldn't believe his reaction. "You're not shocked by this?"

"As a young man I might have been. But after forty years teaching university, it takes more than a little sodomy to shock me."

"Well, there is more. I think Samir is being blackmailed."

"That's not all that shocking, either. But it is serious."

"And now I'm trying to decide what to do."

"Surely that's not difficult," Abu Mustafa said. "Samir is still your friend, isn't he?"

"I don't know, father. I think he may have betrayed me in America."

"Are you still his friend?"

"I don't know that, either."

"Because he betrayed you, or because he's a different kind of sinner than you thought he was?"

"Both," Mustafa said. "Tell me what I should do."

"Let me ask a different question first. Of all the sins a man can commit, which do you think is the worst?"

"Murder," said Mustafa.

"I would say murder also. And if Samir were a convicted murderer, would you visit him in prison?"

Mustafa thought about it. "Yes. I believe so."

"Well then," said Abu Mustafa. "For one such as Samir, I imagine every day is like living in prison—all the more so if his secret shame has been discovered and is being used against him by his enemies. So if you ask what to do, I'd say go to him. Be his friend. And if his sin frightens you, remember your own conduct in this life has been far from perfect."

"All right," Mustafa said nodding. Reaching out, he took his father's hand. "Will you be all right alone here for a while?"

"Yes," Abu Mustafa said. "For a little while."

The alarm clock woke Joe Simeon at 9 a.m. A shaft of sunlight was coming through a gap in the window shades, and he marveled at it as if it were the divine light of heaven piercing the firmament. As the alarm continued to sound, he thought: Today I'll be in God's house.

He hadn't taken communion since leaving Heidelberg. He knew there were Christian churches in Baghdad but didn't know what kind they were or what sacraments they offered, and anyway he wasn't supposed to leave the hotel before it was time for his mission. So he made do in the room. He took a hunk of leftover bread from last night's meal and found a bottle of red fruit drink in the minifridge. He recited the words of the Last Supper as best he could recall them. Christ's body was stale, His blood more pomegranate than grape and not at all fermented, but still Joe Simeon felt refreshed, his sins washed away.

Just to be sure, he ran a bath, pouring in a handful of floral-smelling salts. He lay in the tub, pictured Jesus in the river Jordan, and holding his nose and mouth submerged himself completely.

He got out and dried himself off and opened up the shirt box. The suicide vest was heavy, in form very much like a flak jacket, but padded with plastic explosive rather than Kevlar. Strings of nails had been pressed into the squares of plastique to serve as shrapnel. The nails seemed like a crude touch, but the detonator and wire work were first-rate, and great care had been taken to minimize the vest's profile.

He slipped it on. There was a long-sleeved cotton shirt in the box as well, which he buttoned over the suicide vest, and a second, outer vest of dark cloth that he pulled on over that. He examined himself in a mirror, turning sideways to check: Does this make me look fat?

It didn't. He'd seen one other explosive vest, worn by a crusader in Bonn to blow up a busload of Israelis, and that one had been a lot bulkier, hard to conceal even under a winter parka. This one he thought might evade the scrutiny of even a trained observer, and he should be able to move in a civilian crowd without drawing suspicion. The hardest part would be not sweating to death in the midday heat.

It was ten o'clock. He still had a couple of hours to wait, so he undressed again, laying the vest carefully back in its box, and sat on the bed in his underwear. He was keyed up and giddy, feeling as though his soul had already begun the process of leaving his body. He picked up the TV remote and channel-surfed manically, unable to focus.

The image of a cross caught his attention briefly. It was a broadcast of a Coptic church service, an Egyptian priest reading from the Gospels: "But go and learn what this means: 'I desire mercy, not sacrifice.' For I have not come to call the righteous, but sinners . . ."

The words, unsubtitled, were just so much babble in Joe Simeon's ears. He changed the channel again and prayed to God to speed the hour of his death.

Samir was waiting in the tea shop near the Israeli embassy. He had a dark bruise on his cheek and a split lip on which the swelling had only begun to go down.

"Samir, what happened to you?" Mustafa said when he saw him.

"Najat's father," Samir told him. He touched a fingertip to his lip and checked it for blood. "I went to Basra yesterday to warn Najat to take the boys somewhere safe. Getting punched in the face wasn't part of the plan, but it did seem to convince her to take me seriously."

Mustafa pulled out a chair and sat down. "Idris threatened your children?"

"Among other things."

"Why didn't you say something? We could have—"

Samir bristled. "Why didn't I *say* something? You mean like, 'Mustafa, I think it's a really stupid idea to piss off the head of Al Qaeda?' Something like that?"

"I'm sorry," Mustafa said. "You're right, I'm an idiot."

"Yes, I've been thinking that too," Samir said. Then his anger deflated and he shrugged. "What the hell, it doesn't make a difference. That son of a bitch has had it in for me since grade school. Even if I'd walked away from this investigation—even if I'd convinced you to walk away—he still would have found a reason to ruin my life."

Mustafa nodded at the suitcase in the chair to Samir's right. "Is that from your trip to Basra, or are you going someplace else?"

"Keeping my options open," Samir said. "When I got home this morning, someone had been in my apartment. I was going to make myself a snack and noticed a thumbprint on the refrigerator door. Lost my appetite . . . So I threw some things together and got out."

"Where would you go? To be with Najat?"

"No, I don't know where she is going. It's better that way. I don't expect to see her again." His voice hitched. "Or Malik and Jibril . . . I was thinking I might go to Greece."

"What's in Greece?"

"A chance I was too cowardly to take." He smiled sadly. "I'm still too cowardly, really. Really what will happen, I'll slink around Baghdad for a couple of days until Idris catches up to me. Then my troubles will be over." He sighed. "Mustafa, I've got something to tell you . . ."

"Before you do," said Mustafa, "I've got something to ask you."

"Go ahead."

"Are you still my friend?"

"Not a very good one I suppose."

"The same could be said of me, the reckless way I've been acting," Mustafa pointed out. "And you did save me from being burned alive by that Minuteman."

Samir shook his head. "That doesn't count. You and I were supposed to be dead already, along with everyone else in the convoy."

"But we didn't die. God gave us another chance—and you made good use of yours. Now I would like to do the same. Tell me you're my friend and I can trust you, and whatever happened in America—whatever Idris forced you to do—it's behind us. Forgotten."

"Just like that, huh?" Samir barked a laugh, but then his throat hitched again and he began to cry. His shoulders shook as he wept, all the fear and shame that had been weighing on him releasing in a torrent. Mustafa took his hand and held it.

"Fuck, man," Samir said, when the storm had passed. He swiped water from his eyes, wincing as the heel of his palm pressed the bruise. "You know God didn't really give us another chance, don't you? Just a little reprieve. Idris is going to kill us both, Amal too probably."

"God willing, that is possible," Mustafa conceded. "But I choose to be optimistic."

"Remember what we were just saying about you being an idiot?"

"Yes," Mustafa said smiling. "Your idiot friend."

They were both laughing a few minutes later when Amal came in the tea shop. She approached the table slowly and asked Mustafa: "Do you need more time?"

"No." He gave Samir's hand a last squeeze. "We are good."

"Good." Amal nodded to Samir, noting the bruise but not saying anything about it. She sat down. "The coast looks clear outside. Or at least, if Al Qaeda is following us, they're doing a good job hiding the surveillance."

"We shall have to trust to God about that too," Mustafa said. "Now, speaking of Al Qaeda: Tell Samir what you told me, about Osama bin Laden."

The noon prayer had just ended and men and women were coming out of a mosque adjacent to Zawra Park, exchanging the blessing of peace as they headed off to lunch or back to work. Joe Simeon watched them from the back of an air-conditioned cab. He wiped condensation off the window to get a clearer view and stared at the mosque's entrance, wondering what it was like inside. Would they have stained glass, like a real church?

The cabbie mistook the nature of his interest: "You are Muslim?"

"What?" said Joe Simeon. "No. I'm a Christian." So there was no ambiguity: "I have a personal relationship with Jesus Christ."

"Christian, I thought so," the cabbie said nodding. "American?"

"Originally."

"'Originally,'" the cabbie repeated slowly, the word not in his lexicon. "This is your hometown, Originally?"

"Yeah," Joe Simeon said. "Originally, New York. It's just outside Manhattan."

"Manhattan I have heard of." The cabbie nodded again. "You know, the Muslims of Baghdad, we pray for the Christians of America, of Manhattan. Now that the war is over—now that you are free—we have very high hopes for you. That you will become, what is the word? Civilized!"

"Like the Arabs, you mean." The crusader's expression soured. "You really think we're going to turn into you?"

"With God's blessing, even the greatest miracle is but a trifle," the cabbie said pleasantly. "You'll see, my brother!"

Traffic began to back up as they got closer to Ground Zero. While Joe Simeon tracked their progress on his map, the cabbie switched on the radio, tuning in a flurry of Arabic that apparently constituted a weather report. "Shamal," he said.

"What?"

"Sandstorm."

Joe Simeon wiped off his window again. The sky overhead was blue and clear.

The cabbie chuckled. "Not yet. But it's coming."

"When?" A sandstorm, if it was anything like the movies, could disrupt the rally and screw up the plan. On the other hand, like the inside of a mosque, it'd be an interesting thing to see.

"A couple of hours," the cabbie said.

He'd miss it, then. Or on second thought, maybe he wouldn't— maybe he'd already be looking down when it happened. "OK," Joe Simeon said. "Let me off at this next corner, here."

"Are you sure? I can get you closer."

"No, that's all right, I'll walk from here. I don't want to be late."

"According to Donald Rumsfeld," Amal said, "in the real world Al Qaeda is a terrorist organization and Osama bin Laden is responsible for the September 11 attacks."

"This is what Bin Laden has been trying to cover up?" Samir said. "The Americans think he did to them what they did to us?"

"I suppose it might be a political liability, if anyone in Arabia could be made to believe it." Amal smiled. "Imagine the push-poll questions: 'Would you be more or less likely to vote for Senator Bin Laden if you knew he had an evil twin?'"

"Not a twin," said Mustafa. "The same man with a different history. Or the same history remembered differently."

"Would it really be a liability, though?" Samir asked. "Suppose he did kill a bunch of Americans in some other reality. So what? In this reality, which is the only one most people care about, the Christians attacked us."

"That is the official story," Mustafa said. "And given the blood-thirstiness of some Christians, it might well be true. But remember a key element of the mirage legend: America is the real superpower, while the individual states of Arabia are just that, independent nations. Weak ones. When a weak state is drawn into a fight with a superpower, what happens to it?"

Samir shrugged. "It gets its ass kicked."

Mustafa looked at Amal. "What did Rumsfeld say America did, in response to 9/11?"

"Invaded Iraq," she said. "His story about what happened to the Hussein family was heartwarming, but when I asked what the war did to the rest of us he pretended not to understand the question."

"Wait," said Samir. "So you're saying that in this alternate reality of Rumsfeld's, Osama bin Laden is an Iraqi?"

"No, he's still from Jeddah," Amal said. "A 'Saudi' Arabian."

"Then why the hell would America invade Iraq?"

"Because God put a Texan in charge," Mustafa said. "The point I am getting at is this: A terrorist who attacks a Christian superpower in the name of Islam knows he is setting up his fellow Muslims for slaughter, because that is how superpowers react when they are struck. Which raises the question: If in one version of history, a man is willing to murder thousands of innocent Muslims by proxy, is it not plausible that in another version, he might be willing to commit the same sin more directly?"

"So we're to become Truthers, now?" Amal said. "You think Osama bin Laden is responsible for the 11/9 attacks as well?"

"That is what I am suggesting."

"But the November 9 hijackers were Christians. That's documented—I don't care what the conspiracy theorists say. And Al Qaeda won't even recruit Shia Muslims, so how—"

"Oh God," said Samir.

Amal looked at him. "What?"

"There *are* Christians in Al Qaeda. Or at least people pretending to be Christian . . ."

"What are you talking about?"

"The ambush on our convoy in Fairfax County," Mustafa explained. "Al Qaeda was behind that."

"No, that was Rumsfeld's militia. I told you, he admitted to it. And Rumsfeld was *not* Osama bin Laden's ally."

"That does not preclude him from being Osama bin Laden's stooge. If anything, his fear and hatred of Al Qaeda would have made him easier to manipulate."

"To what end, though?" Amal said. "Why would Osama bin Laden want to provoke a war between Arabia and America, or between Islam and Christendom? What would he be hoping to accomplish?"

"I think," said Mustafa, "that he wants to turn the clock back. Undo modernity and the Republic, and usher in a new Caliphate." He brought out the CIA report David Koresh had given him and laid it on the table. Then he continued: "Imagine you are Osama bin Laden. A son of privilege, heir to one of the wealthiest men in Arabia. Like many a rich kid before you, though, you're not content to thank God for your blessings. You become disaffected, contemptuous of what you see as a decadent society and a corrupt political culture.

"Eventually you drop out, go to Peshawar and then Afghanistan. The harsh life of a holy warrior suits you, and your experiences on the battlefield lead you to a dark epiphany. The people of Afghanistan have never lacked for hardship and their suffering has only multiplied under the Russians, yet despite or perhaps because of this, the men you fight alongside practice what seems to you a much purer form of Islam, untainted by latter-day heresy. At some point you ask yourself what a dose of the same suffering might do for the state of the faith in your own country.

"Of course you can't turn Arabia into Afghanistan. But perhaps you don't need to. Modern living has made your countrymen so soft, maybe a hard shock to the system is all it would take to herd them back onto the righteous path. God willing, anything is possible; and if there's one thing being a holy warrior has convinced you of, it's that you know the will of God.

"So you go home, a hero. You pretend to make peace with the political elite of Riyadh, let them help you into a position of power. Behind the scenes you assemble Al Qaeda, the foundation of a new world order. You send scouts into Christendom to find the crusaders who will serve as your pawns, to make unprovoked war against Islam.

"And so November 9, 2001: The plan is set in motion and succeeds beyond your wildest dreams. Three planes out of four reach their targets. The carnage is spectacular. Even the downing of the fourth plane—the one you'd hoped would kill the young Saudi president—turns out to be a blessing. That same president, horrified by the destruction and his own close brush with death, declares a jihad against terrorism—the holy war you wanted, and then some. Political opinion tilts sharply towards the Party of God. Citizens return to the mosques in droves. God's will, as you've conceived it, is about to be made manifest.

"And then, somehow," said Mustafa, "it starts to unravel. The Republic trembles but does not fall. As the shock of 11/9 recedes, doubts are raised about the wisdom of some of the president's actions. And it's not just the die-hard secularists in the Unity Party asking questions. As the occupation drags on, as word of certain abuses is leaked to the press, fatwas are issued from some surprising quarters: fatwas condemning torture, condemning the erosion of civil liberties, condemning the persecution of Christians—condemning, even, the attack on America.

"To you, for whom devotion to God and devotion to liberal democracy are mutually exclusive, this must all be very baffling. Clearly the rot goes deeper than you realized. More shocks are needed. Fortunately the crusaders are ready to provide them. The Americans are spoiling for vengeance and the Europeans are happy to help. You don't even have to do anything, just sit back and watch them converge on Baghdad with their bombs and their scriptures. But the guardians of the homeland are alerted now, and a lot of these would-be martyrs are captured and interrogated. And they tell a very strange story.

"As head of the Senate Intelligence Committee, you are one of the first people in Arabia to learn about this peculiar legend the crusaders have latched on to. The parallels between the mythical September 11 and the real November 9 are alarming, to say the least. Some of these people are naming you as the architect of the attack, and even though they're talking about a different attack, even though they're madmen, that doesn't mean your secret won't be exposed.

"You need to bury this story. You put Al Qaeda on alert and start monitoring interrogation sessions. Crusaders who say the wrong thing are made to disappear, along with whatever artifacts they possess. In the course of this cover-up you become an expert on the mirage legend, and the more you learn the more familiar it all seems, like something from a half-remembered dream.

"Another world. A world in which America is the invading superpower, defiling the holy places of Islam. A world in which Arabia is broken up into minor principalities, in which men like Saddam Hus-

sein and Muammar al Gaddafi are not just criminals or the butts of
jokes but heads of state. A world in which the suffering of ordinary
Arabs is, correspondingly, multiplied.

"It's your turn to be shocked. You realize, if this is true, you've
been wasting your time, struggling inside an illusion, while the situation you were trying to create already existed. All you have to figure
out is how to restore it.

"And so, very late in the day, you have a new mission. It's the same
mission the crusaders are on, which ought to be ironic but really just
makes sense, since in your pride, you've invited the same person to
come whisper in your ear. In any case, that is your wish: To return to
a world of sorrow, to an Arabia whose people will be ripe to receive
your message, the word of God the All-Merciful and Compassionate as interpreted by the mass murderer Osama bin Mohammed bin
Awad bin Laden."

Mustafa paused and drank some tea. Samir was staring at him
uneasily, and Amal had picked up the CIA report and was flipping
through it.

"It's an interesting story," Amal said good-naturedly. "But even
with this"—she dropped the report back on the table—"you know
no one is going to believe it."

"No," Samir agreed. "If you go to the president talking like that,
he's going to think you're nuts."

"Oh," said Mustafa, "but I haven't even told you the crazy part
yet . . . Here. Let me show you a photograph."

Uday Hussein had come upstairs in pursuit of a maid. He'd been
stalking her on and off since she'd started work at the Adhamiyah
estate, following her through the house each time he caught sight of
her, each time letting her elude him, confident that he could corner
her whenever he wished. Today though he'd grown tired of the game
and determined to end it, and so he was very annoyed when he burst

into a bathroom where he was sure she was hiding, only to find it unoccupied.

He backed out into the hall, turning towards a gallery that over-looked the domed chamber containing the Nebuchadnezzar statue. A male servant was polishing the balustrade; sensing Uday's atten-tion upon him, he recalled another chore in a distant part of the house and hastened away.

Uday went the other direction, poking his head into rooms at random. In the westernmost part of the hall he paused in front of a massive wooden door banded in iron. The chamber beyond was off-limits but Uday decided to check it anyway, reasoning that if the maid were inside he'd have an excuse to punish her—not that he needed an excuse.

The door somewhat surprisingly was unlocked. Uday leaned into it and swung it wide, then spread his arms and cried "Aha!" No one tried to bolt past him. He lowered his arms again and stood just inside the threshold looking around.

The chamber was octagonal, ten meters wide. In the past it had been used as both a prayer room and an astronomical observatory, and its single broad window was oriented towards the Qibla. Its cur-rent focus, however, was neither Mecca nor the heavens, but the heart of the vast desert in the Arabian Peninsula's southeast quad-rant. Sand from that desert had been poured in a series of curving lines on the chamber floor, forming a pattern like a whirlwind viewed from above. In the whirlwind's eye the brass bottle from Al Hillah had been placed atop a mound of sand, its unstoppered mouth tilted towards the window. Incense burners and stands of bells and chimes were spaced around the whirlwind's outer edge, and other trinkets and talismans had been arranged within the swirls of sand according to some system Uday had not been schooled in.

The sight of it made him dizzy, and being dizzy made him angry. He approached the near edge of the whirlwind and nudged one of the smoking braziers with the toe of his boot.

"Do not disturb the pattern!"

Mr. Rammal, his father's sorcerer, stood in the doorway holding a set of iron shackles. Uday clenched his fists at the rebuke and for a dangerous second contemplated stomping through the whole design like a boy kicking apart a sand castle—and then maybe, for an encore, pistol-whipping Mr. Rammal until his brains came out his ears.

He resisted the urge. His father was home and not far away, and maids weren't the only ones in this house subject to cruel punishments.

Instead he glared at Mr. Rammal. "Who do you think you are talking to that way?"

"You mustn't disturb it," Mr. Rammal repeated. He came forward to make sure that it hadn't already been damaged, and Uday suppressed another impulse to violence.

"What's this supposed to do, anyway?" Uday said. "Suck the jinni into the bottle like a magic vacuum cleaner?"

"You should not refer so directly to the creature," Mr. Rammal cautioned. This time he moderated his tone. Though he knew he was under Saddam's protection, he also understood that there were limits to Uday's self-control—and standing this close, the younger Hussein's rage was palpable. "But to answer your question, no, this is only a lure. What it will do, if it works, is draw the creature into this city and compel it to reveal itself. Then while it is visible we must find it, and bind it." He held up the shackles. "To incant it back into the bottle will require a final ritual."

"Do you actually believe this shit you're spewing?"

"Your father believes it."

"I'll tell you what my father believes," Uday said. "My father believes in making examples of people who try to cheat him. When he realizes you're a charlatan—and he will—he's going to want you hurt. And guess who he's going to call on to hurt you." He bent his head close to the sorcerer's and exhaled sourly against his cheek. "Go ahead, guess."

A gust of air came through the window, causing several of the chimes to jangle. Uday reared back laughing at Mr. Rammal's reaction. "Praise God the All-Compassionate!" Uday said. "The wind is ringing the wind chimes! It's a miracle!"

Then the breeze ceased, but the noise didn't. It spread around the circle, an unseen hand gripping each stand, agitating the bells. The clean lines of smoke rising from the braziers twisted and dispersed. An incense burner near the window shot up a column of blue flame, as if a gas jet had been fired through the bowl; the flame rose to a height of a meter before flickering out. There was a pause, long enough for a heartbeat, or a whisper, and then another brazier spat fire, and another, and another—but only one at a time, as if it were really a single flame jumping playfully around the circumference of the circle. Uday, feeling as though the room were revolving, stayed rooted in place until the flame reached the brazier by his feet. Then he fell back shrieking all the way to the door, his spine fetching up painfully against the jamb.

Mr. Rammal remained where he was, observing the progress of the fire and listening to the rustle of the chimes. A cold smile bloomed on his lips.

"Go and get your father," he said to Uday. "If you please."

The rally was being held just south of Ground Zero Plaza, on a wedge of land where the World Trade Center Number Seven building had once stood. In 2002 this property, cleared of debris and converted temporarily into a park, had been used for the memorial services commemorating the one-year anniversary of the attacks.

The idea of erecting a mosque on the site had first been floated in April 2003 and had met with near-universal approval. The devil was waiting, as he always is, in the details, and soon enough a squabble had broken out between various Sunni and Shia factions over just who would be in charge of funding, planning, building, and admin-

istering the project. Public meetings called to discuss the matter
ended in acrimony, and closed-door sessions between city, state, and
religious officials fared no better; a visiting mullah compared the
atmosphere of the latter to Prime Minister's question time in the
Persian parliament, "only not so friendly."

The politicking and debate over the mosque had continued for another six years—culminating in an announcement five months ago
that a deal had finally been reached. Since then several deadlines
for fixing a start date for construction had been missed, and new
fault lines had appeared in the mosque coalition. Today's rally was
an attempt to get things back on track. Billed as a celebration, it was
really more an act of sympathetic magic, the idea being to get all the
principals together in public acting *as if* construction of the mosque
were going forward. Then, assuming they made it through the ceremony without the world coming to an end, maybe they could bring
on the builders and the cranes for real.

Not everyone had been able to make it. The president, while offering a strong message of support for the mosque, had declined an
invitation to the rally, promising instead to attend the actual ground-
breaking, assuming there was one. He'd sent a group of Unity Party
functionaries in his place, and the POG, not to be outdone, had
dispatched a delegation of Sauds.

Saddam Hussein had also respectfully declined to attend—and
unlike the president, he hadn't bothered to wait for an invitation
before doing so. Given the identity of the woman in charge of the
guest list, this was a tactically wise move.

One other notable no-show was the Arabian senator, Osama bin
Laden. He had planned to attend the rally and had come down from
Riyadh with the Sauds, only to fall ill at the very last moment. He
was presently recuperating at his hotel.

For Amal's brother Haidar, chief security coordinator for the
event, the news of Bin Laden's absence was a welcome relief. He only

wished it could have come sooner. While all of the rally attendees were concerned about safety, Bin Laden's advance team had been uniquely paranoid, questioning him repeatedly about every detail of the security arrangements. Haidar had no objection to thoroughness, but he did have a problem with people who obviously didn't trust a Shia to do the job correctly.

Now he had a bit more energy to devote to other problems, of which there was no shortage. The security setup consisted of three layers. The outer layer of barricades and checkpoints was being manned by the Baghdad PD. All the necessary bribes had been paid, so Haidar expected little trouble here—unless Saddam, miffed about his nonexistent invite, decided to arrange some sort of payback. The innermost security layer, directly around the stage, was composed mainly of bodyguards of the various attendees. Here the potential for mayhem was greater, since despite the ongoing show of solidarity, many of these people couldn't stand one another. Haidar was particularly troubled by reports of new hostilities between the Mahdi Army and the Badr Corps, both well represented here, and he could only hope that the presence of news cameras would convince them to honor their good-conduct pledges.

But his biggest concern was with the middle layer of security—armed men, some in uniform and some in plainclothes, whose job was to circulate through the crowd, looking for any threats that might have made it past the police checkpoints. Haidar had wanted to use only his own people for this, but several of the more high-profile guests had insisted on detailing additional personnel to the effort. Unable to refuse the help without precipitating a political crisis, Haidar had instead broken the park into separate patrol zones and assigned each group its own territory. The Mahdi Army got a strip on the far west end of the park, next to the Arab Telecom building, while the Badr Corps got the east end, alongside the post office. The Saudi security team was placed in the center, surrounded by members of other, more local Sunni groups, arranged according to Haidar's understanding of their current relations with the Badrists and the Sadrists. Haidar's own men were scattered throughout the park and instructed to watch the watchers.

Haidar himself roamed freely, using radio, eye, and instinct to try to keep tabs on the whole show at once. As his mother stood onstage talking about The Moment, he stopped at one of the police checkpoints to get a head count on the crowd. Turnout was low, around two thousand people in a space that could hold five times that number. Not that it mattered for PR purposes: The estimate released to the press would be inflated to suggest a capacity crowd, and the cameras were all down front near the VIP seating, which was full.

Senator Al Maysani finished her remarks and turned the podium over to the governor, Nouri al Maliki. Haidar walked the northern perimeter, scanning the park. Mist-spraying machines had been set up at various points to keep the crowd cool and to add a none-too-subtle rainbow effect to the proceedings, but they also interfered with the sight lines. As Haidar maneuvered to get clearer views, his suit went from dry to damp and back again.

Al Maliki was followed at the podium by the man who also hoped to succeed him as governor: Muqtada al Sadr. Haidar, now standing among the Guardian Angels, made a quick radio call to the men he had monitoring the Badrs. "It's OK," came the reply. "We've got a few people here who look like they just bit down on lemons, but nobody's acting up."

"No problems by the stage, either," added a second voice.

"The Anbaris are starting to grumble," said a third voice. "I hope we've got some Sunnis on the speakers' list."

"Don't worry," said Haidar. "The mayor of Ramadi is up next." He kept moving.

The rally was approaching the fifty-minute mark, and a few bored spectators were beginning to drift towards the exits, when the only Christian scheduled to speak got up to use the microphone. The Patriarch of Babylon was an old man from Kurdistan. Like a number of the speakers before him, he seemed a bit off-balance at first, unsettled perhaps by the still-shocking emptiness above the plaza to the north. But he gripped the sides of the podium and steadied himself, and looked down at the crowd, and smiled.

"Good afternoon," he began. "I would like to say a few words about peace."

Haidar was over in Badr territory, hunting the source of a strange noise—a metallic bang, possibly a door slam—that he'd heard just a moment before. The murmur that went through the crowd at the Patriarch's first words caused him to look up at the stage. As he was turning away again, he caught a flash of movement out of the corner of his eye: a figure, stepping out from the side of the post office. By the time Haidar turned all the way around the figure had vanished behind a spray of mist, leaving a jumble of impressions: White shirt. Dark vest. Pale skin. Straw-colored hair.

"'Christianity is a religion of peace,'" said the Patriarch. "We've all heard that sentiment many times over the past few years, voiced by well-meaning apologists. I'm sure to many Muslims it must seem an absurd, even an offensive, statement. And nowhere more so than here, in Baghdad, at Ground Zero of the War on Terror." He raised an arm, waved a hand at the empty space where towers should be standing. "Christians, peaceful. How ridiculous!"

Haidar had found what he was looking for. Set into the ground, in a recess along the post office wall, was a hinged metal grate. It should have been padlocked, but the lock was missing, and the front edge of the grate stuck up from its sill, having failed to close properly. "Code yellow, code yellow," Haidar said into his radio. "We have a security breach along the east perimeter."

"How ridiculous," the Patriarch repeated. "And you know, it *is* ridiculous, if by 'religion' we refer to the practitioners of faith. Congregations are not made up of abstractions like peace. They are made up of human beings. Go into any church in the land, any synagogue, yes, any mosque, and that is what you will find: human beings. A few saints, perhaps"—the Patriarch shrugged a shoulder—"and perhaps also one or two demons, hiding their wickedness behind a mask of piety. But the great majority, the body of the faithful, neither angels nor devils, but ordinary sinners: men and women trying to make their way in the world with God's help and forgiveness . . ."

"Suleiman, kill the waterworks," Haidar said, and after a brief hesitation the misters shut off. As the rainbows dissipated, Haidar breasted forward through the crowd, searching for a white man in a dark vest. He stopped to do a three-sixty and spotted something else, something extraordinary: Another man, an Arab in a white desert tunic, who appeared to be floating in midair. The black-and-white keffiyeh around the man's neck fluttered madly in a breeze Haidar couldn't feel, and his eyes were filled with blue fire.

Then Haidar blinked and saw more clearly. The man wasn't levitating; he was perched atop a concrete planter box, bright marigolds clustered around his sandaled feet. His eyes, reflecting the afternoon sunlight, were focused on something in the crowd. Haidar followed the direction of the man's gaze and saw Joe Simeon, headed towards the stage.

"When we speak of a religion of peace, we refer not to Christendom as it is, but as we would like it to be, as we aspire and strive, daily, to make it—a struggle that is not different from the daily struggle of the Muslims. And if we often fail in that struggle, it's not because we worship a different or a lesser God; it's because we are, like you, only human."

Haidar spoke urgently into his radio. He glanced at the man in the white tunic again and saw he was no longer staring; he'd closed his eyes and bowed his head, and his lips were moving as if in prayer.

Feeling a sudden chill, Haidar turned back to Joe Simeon, who had almost reached the edge of the VIP area. As Simeon twisted sideways to slip between two other men, Haidar glimpsed his torso in profile and in a flash of intuition realized what was concealed beneath his vest and shirt.

"Oh God," Haidar said. "Code black! Code black!"

"And so in the name of the Merciful Creator of the Jews and the Christians and the Muslims, I offer you this hope, this wish: Peace be un—"

The Patriarch's blessing was interrupted by a sudden scramble of security personnel on the stage. At the same moment one of Haidar's men tried to grab Joe Simeon. Simeon turned, almost casually, and stabbed the man in the chest with a knife taken from his hotel room. Someone else screamed and the crowd began surging backwards in a panic, trapping the other security guards who were trying to rush forward. Joe Simeon took a few more steps towards the stage, uttering his own benediction. Then he set off the bomb.

The flash that followed dazzled every eye that looked at it and blinded all the cameras, too. No one could say, afterwards, exactly what had happened. But there was no thunderous blast, no shock wave—and, once the light had faded, no scene of carnage. The stage, and the crowd, remained intact, and what should have been a locus of death and destruction had instead become, through some conjuror's trick, a whirring mass of life.

Birds. A flock of birds, arranged around the would-be suicide bomber like points on a globe, and each one holding, in its claws, a single shining nail.

As one they dropped their burdens. The ring of the nails falling harmlessly to the pavement could be heard throughout the park in that moment's hush. Then the birds flew up screaming. They weren't doves. They were ravens, carrion-eaters of the desert, and they were angry, for here today in Baghdad, against all expectations, there was nothing for them—even the man Joe Simeon had stabbed was struggling to his feet, hand pressed to a bleeding gash above his breastbone that was painful but not fatal.

Joe Simeon, his vest and shirt hanging in tatters, stared into the sky, his expression of rapture changing to puzzlement as he realized he too was still among the living. "Jesus?" he said. The ravens ignored him and flew higher. "Wait!" he cried, raising both hands as if to claw his way to heaven. But gravity buckled his knees, and then men with earpieces were tackling him from all sides.

Across the park, away from the commotion, the nomad in the white tunic raised his head and opened his eyes. Nodding minutely in satisfaction, he prepared to step back into the unseen realm from which he'd come, only to find himself frozen in place by the cold steel ring of a gun muzzle pressed against his neck.

"Don't you move," Haidar told him, pulling out handcuffs. "Don't you move a muscle."

"You're right," Amal said, when Mustafa had finished. "That does sound crazy . . . Do you believe it?"

"I don't know," said Mustafa. He looked at the photo, at the brass bottle at his other self's feet. "I do think Saddam believes it. I think he is seeking this jinni to do some wishing of his own, to remake the world closer to his heart's desire."

"And Bin Laden?" Samir said. "What's his game plan? Are Wahhabists even allowed to make wishes?"

"Probably not. But then they're not allowed to commit acts of terror, either, and yet that doesn't seem to have discouraged him."

"So what's our game plan?" asked Amal.

"About the jinn I still can't say," Mustafa replied. "But as long as we're still cops, I was thinking—don't laugh—that we might try enforcing the law."

THE LIBRARY OF ALEXANDRIA
A USER-EDITED REFERENCE SOURCE

Apocalypse

An **apocalypse** is a <u>cataclysmic event</u> that marks the end of an <u>era of history</u> and/or a dramatic change in the world. It can refer to the <u>collapse of a civilization</u>, a natural or man-made <u>ecological disaster</u>, a <u>nuclear war</u>, or, in a religious context, the coming of the <u>End of Days</u> and <u>God's final judgment</u> of humankind.

The <u>Greek</u> word *Apokálypsis* means "unveiling," and oritinally applied to any work of prophetic or revelatory literature. The eschatological navure of th mpst famoxs of these wor s, such as tfe <u>Book of Daniel</u> a the <u>Revelation of John</u>, led to   dy connotz-tion ,mu   idz   k[.d.   dol,gioy   ijykm bd

f   nl;aw

shell-shocked Joe Simeon was sitting in interrogation room A. He had been given a blanket to cover his nakedness but he'd allowed it to slip, exposing a pale torso gone pink with what looked like mild sunburn.

Farouk stood on the other side of the glass, in the observation room. An evidence bag held Joe Simeon's bomb trigger, a simple plunger device trailing half a meter of coated wire that ended in a blob of melted plastic and copper. No trace of actual explosive had been found, nor did the tattered remains of his clothing appear to have any special pockets for holding wildlife. It was a puzzle, but one that, given his near-catatonic state, they were going to have to solve without Simeon's help.

At least they knew his name. Farouk walked around Mustafa's Bible cart to the window of interrogation room B, where the second suspect was being held. The man in the white tunic was alert, and as Farouk approached the glass the fellow appeared to stare at him as if he could see through the mirror.

The observation room door opened and Abdullah came in, his arm in a sling. "Hey boss," he said. "I was just looking for you."

"Do we have an ID on this one yet?"

"No. His fingerprints aren't in the system. We're trying a facial-recognition match now."

"Has he said anything?"

"Not about who he is. He did say he'd talk to you, though."

"He asked for me by name?"

"It wasn't a request," Abdullah said. "More like a prediction. He said he'd like to talk to Mustafa, but he didn't think he'd get here in time."

"Where is Mustafa?"

"Out somewhere. He's not answering his cell phone."

Farouk turned back towards the glass. The man in the white tunic was still staring at him. Smiling. "All right," Farouk said. "Keep trying Mustafa's cell. And see if you can find the other prisoner some clothes."

The apartment was on an upper floor of a high-rise in Mansour. Its balcony faced northwest and offered an excellent view of the approaching sandstorm. The storm's leading edge, a wall of sand and dust several hundred meters high, was advancing in seeming slow motion across Baghdad's outlying suburbs. Behind this, the horizon was covered by a dark smudge that stretched up into the clouds and made it look as though the heavens and the earth were dissolving into a void. Even to a veteran of holy war who prided himself on his fearlessness, the sight was unnerving, and eventually Idris had to turn away in order to concentrate on his phone conversation.

"Yes, Senator," he said. "Yes, zero fatalities . . . No. It wasn't a problem with the device . . . I am sure. I had men in the crowd, they confirm what the news is reporting . . . No, not the hand of God, but not a *human* hand, either . . . Yes, that's what I'm saying . . . I have also received a report from Adhamiyah that that Tikriti thug has his people scouring the city for someone . . . Yes . . . Yes, I think so . . . Homeland Security has two individuals in custody. One of them— . . . I've already dispatched a team. They understand the seriousness . . . Yes, as soon as I hear anything . . . My men have been instructed to bring the creature to the northern safe house. I suggest you head there now, before the storm hits . . . God willing . . . What? . . . Yes, it is a pity. So many targets on one stage. But there will be other opportunities. In the chaos after the mirage collapses, we can hunt many of them down, the ones who aren't dead already . . . Yes . . . Peace be unto you as well, Senator."

He hung up and went back inside. In the living room the TV was on, tuned to Al Jazeera with the sound muted. They were showing the video from the rally: shaky footage of Joe Simeon stabbing the security guard, stepping towards the stage, then several seconds of blackness, and then the ravens, spiraling upwards. The caption read: MIRACLE AT GROUND ZERO?

Idris picked up the remote and switched off the TV. "Khalid!" he shouted. "Get your weapon! We are going out!"

But the person who responded to his call was Mustafa al Baghdadi. Mustafa came out of the kitchen carrying a teapot and two cups and saucers on a silver tray. "You are almost out of sugar," he said.

"What are you doing here?" Idris said. "Khalid!"

"Your servant won't be disturbing us," Mustafa told him, setting the tray on the table in the center of the room. "I asked him to step out so that you and I could have a conversation."

"About what?"

"About Al Qaeda and the 11/9 hijackings," Mustafa said. He began pouring the tea. "About your role in the murder of thousands of innocent people. My wife among them."

There was a leather case on top of a cabinet to Idris's right. He reached for it, flipped open the lid . . . and found the case empty.

Mustafa cleared his throat. Idris turned and saw the gun he'd been seeking lying on the table next to the tea tray.

"You disappoint me," Mustafa said. He settled within arm's length of the gun and picked up one of the teacups. "The crusaders of America, if they kill even a single Muslim, are only too happy to brag about it. But you and Osama bin Laden slaughter multitudes, and you don't want to claim credit? And after all your talk of righteousness. Shouldn't a righteous man be proud of his deeds?"

Idris was still looking at the gun. "I'm not afraid to die," he said.

"Yes, I get that," said Mustafa. "But you aren't in a hurry to die, either, are you? You'd rather let others do the dying for you, while you remain to savor the suffering of their victims. Very well, I get that,

too: You were always a sadist. What I don't see is the connection between this and anything worthy of the name Islam. I don't see how
even you fool yourself that such a connection exists."

"You are right, you don't see," Idris said, growing heated. "But I
am no fool."

"I say you are. I say you are as deluded as the so-called Christians
who spread terror in the name of Jesus."

"Do not compare me to those people!"

"Why not?" Mustafa said. "You chase the same mirage, and worship at the same false altar."

"No!" Idris wagged a finger. "God is on *our* side."

"'Our side.' And whose side was Fadwa on?"

"I cannot say. I did not know her. But I know that she was either
righteous, or unrighteous. If she was righteous, then she died a
martyr and will live on in paradise. If not—why should I care that
she is dead?"

"Because her life was not yours to take!" Mustafa shouted. "I hope
there is a paradise. I hope Fadwa finds her way there, finds the joy
I could not give her. But even if that is so, it was not for you, in your
supreme arrogance, to send her on her way. And not just her. Thousands dead in the towers alone. Thousands! What were you thinking? What was Osama bin Laden thinking? Who do you people think
you are?"

"I am a warrior of God," Idris Abd al Qahhar said proudly. "I, and
Osama bin Laden, and all the men of Al Qaeda. You cannot make us
regret what we have done. When this world passes away and God's
final truth is revealed, even to unbelievers who would deny it, everyone will see we were in the right. But it will be too late for you then,
Mustafa al Baghdadi." Nodding, he continued: "Go ahead. Take your
revenge. It will change nothing."

"My revenge." Mustafa set down his cup and placed a hand on
the gun. Took a breath. "I told Gabriel Costello that if the men re-

sponsible for 11/9 were brought before me, I would show them no mercy . . ."

"To hell with your mercy," Idris said. "I care nothing for it."

"I know," said Mustafa. "And it would be a great pleasure to kill you—like having a wish come true. But God still does care about mercy. I must believe that, if I'm to go on living in this or any other world . . . Yes, I must believe it." With an effort he withdrew his hand from the gun. "Anyway," he went on, "I've used up all my wishes already. Time to give someone else a turn." Sitting back, he called out: "Samir!"

Footsteps in the hall. Samir came in, and Amal, and behind them Abu Naji and Sayyid. Sayyid was holding a tape recorder with a wireless antenna.

Idris shook his head, forcing a smile. "Now you disappoint me," he said to Mustafa. "I tell you I am willing to die. You think you can punish me with prison?"

"We'll see how you feel after the first forty years," Mustafa replied.

Idris laughed. "No," he said. "No, I don't think so."

He lunged for the gun on the table, but Amal had been waiting for this and hit him with a taser before he'd taken two steps.

"Samir," Mustafa said. "Do the honors, please."

Idris had collapsed onto his back. He lay breathing shallowly, red-faced, too stunned to move but still able to summon a look of such hatred that Samir, standing over him, hesitated. Then Samir remembered his sons and his fear dissipated. He crouched down, pulling out handcuffs.

"Idris Abd al Qahhar," he said. "I arrest you for conspiracy to commit murder. By the grace of God the All-Merciful and Compassionate, you have the right to remain silent . . ."

"Hello," Farouk said, closing the interrogation room door behind him. "I understand you wish to speak with me."

"Oh, I try never to make wishes," the man in the white tunic said. "They so rarely turn out the way you expect. I am happy to speak with you, however."

"Good, then. Let's start with a name."

"Of course." The man's smile turned mischievous. "What would you like to call me?"

"How about your real name?"

"It would mean nothing to you, I'm afraid. I'm not in any of your databases."

"What about a home address then?" Farouk pulled out a chair and sat opposite the man. "You don't sound like a Baghdadi to me."

"My family home is in Arabia, in the Rub al Khali."

"I didn't know there were homes in the Empty Quarter. Do you work in the oil industry?"

"We mind our own business." That mischievous smile again. "Most of us."

"And what brings you to Baghdad?"

"I fly all over the country."

"On your family's business?"

"A personal research project of sorts. I've been going from place to place, studying how things have changed."

"Changed since when? Have you been away somewhere?"

"That too," the man in the white tunic said. "I was in prison for many years, and the world changed quite a bit during that time. Since my release, it's changed again. It's the second set of changes I'm most interested in. One should recognize one's own handiwork, but I keep encountering things that surprise me, things that suggest the intervention of another, greater power. So I've been trying to work out what it all means. What the larger plan might be."

"Prison," Farouk said. "I thought you said you weren't in our databases."

"It wasn't one of your prisons."

"You know we have access to Interpol files here too, right?"

"My jailer was not a member of Interpol."

"Where were you locked up, North Korea?" Receiving no answer but that same smile, Farouk continued: "Let's talk about this afternoon. What were you doing at the rally? More research?"

"I was following that man, the one you are holding in the other room."

"Why? Do you know him?"

"I know his type. A maker of burnt offerings. Such men were common in my youth, and time doesn't seem to have lessened their numbers much. I've encountered quite a few in my travels."

"When you encounter them, what do you do?"

"Usually nothing. Interfering in others' affairs, even with the best of intentions, well it's like making wishes—there are always unforeseen consequences. I really should have learned that lesson by now. But today, crossing paths with that man, sensing what he was about to do, I felt a powerful urge to intervene. An impulse not entirely my own."

"What does that mean, not entirely your own?"

"You know how it is," the man in the white tunic said. "God allows evil to exist in the world. Sometimes He permits it to operate unchecked. But sometimes, He puts a stone in the path of the wicked."

"And today you were the stone?"

"I thought so." The smile a bit sheepish now, as he looked down at the steel cuffs on his wrists. "Now I'm thinking I may have been mistaken about the source of the impulse . . ." He shrugged. "Ah well. Ultimately all things proceed from God's will."

"Let's leave God's will aside for the moment," said Farouk, "and get back to what happened at the rally. You say you decided to intervene. How?"

The prisoner sighed. "Forgive me. I don't wish to be uncooperative—"

"Then don't be. Tell me what you did."

"You wouldn't believe it. I could convince you, but it would require yet another intervention. Anyway, we are almost out of time."

"No, we're not," Farouk said, allowing his annoyance to show. "You are a suspect in a terrorism case, and you're not going anywhere until I get answers."

From over his shoulder came the muffled sound of shouting. Farouk turned in his chair and saw the mirror shudder as something slammed the other side of the glass.

"They are here for me," the man in the white tunic said, as Farouk stood up. "Do not resist them. They will only hurt you."

The interrogation room door burst open. A big man stepped through, holding a pistol.

"What's the meaning of this interruption?" Farouk said. "Get the hell out of here!"

Siraj al Din didn't bother to reply. Instead, stepping forward, he brought the butt of the gun crashing down on Farouk's forehead.

The sandstorm arrived as they were loading Idris into the arrest wagon.

Abu Naji and Sayyid had parked on the east side of the block. Idris offered no further resistance as he was led out of the apartment building and manacled to a bench in the back of the wagon. Samir watched from the curb with a mixture of unease and disappointment, the satisfaction he'd felt reading Idris his Mirandas already ebbing away. He turned to Mustafa and said: "You know this isn't the end of it."

"I know," Mustafa said. He held up the tape recorder. "But it's a good start. Now—"

A shadow fell over the street, and at the north end of the block someone cried out in alarm. Mustafa and Samir turned towards the sound. There were people running from the corner, while others stood staring and pointing to the west.

They knew what was coming, of course—they'd seen it from the apartment—but timing was always tricky with sandstorms, and no amount of advance warning could lessen the shock of fear at the appearance of the dust cloud, boiling through the streets of the city like debris from some mighty tower's fall. It surged across the intersection, swallowing up everything—people, cars, streetlights—and came sweeping towards them.

"Fu-u-u-uck!" Abu Naji said, a long exhalation. He jumped down from the back of the wagon and slammed the door. Mustafa looked up. A billow of dust and sand overtopped the apartment building and wrapped around its sides, making it seem for a moment as though the upper floors were pancaking.

"Come on!" Samir shouted, tugging on Mustafa's arm. Leaving Idris in the wagon, they ran back to the building, making it inside with just seconds to spare. As the lobby door swung shut, a woman darted past on the sidewalk, clutching the ends of her headscarf with both hands. Then the dust cloud swept down in a thick curtain, obscuring everything.

The bulbs in the apartment building lobby seemed to flicker, but it was just their eyes adjusting to the sudden loss of daylight. Fine dust puffed through the cracks around the door, bringing a smell like fresh chalk. Abu Naji stifled a sneeze.

As the leading edge of the sandstorm continued sweeping eastward, the air outside cleared enough that they could see again. The Homeland Security agents looked out into the haze at a city transformed, and compared this vision to their memories of another day nearly a decade in the past. They noticed the arrest wagon rocking back and forth, and though it was surely only the wind, none of them were above wishing that it might actually be Idris, driven mad by the storm and tasting just a fraction of the terror he had chosen to inflict on others.

"All right," Mustafa said finally, breaking the silence. "Now we go pick up Osama bin Laden."

"What?" said Sayyid. "You want to drive all the way down to Riyadh? In this?"

"He's not in Riyadh," Amal said. "Bin Laden is here in Baghdad today, for the rally. That will be over now, but he's supposed to be staying at the Rasheed Hotel. We should be able to catch him there."

"The rally?" Abu Naji said. "The Ground Zero rally?" He looked at them. "You mean you guys haven't heard?"

A figure in a black burqa, head bowed against the wind, was pulling a wheeled shopping basket along the sidewalk behind AHS headquarters. All the other pedestrians in the area had been driven indoors by the storm, but Siraj al Din, hands cupped to shield his eyes from blowing sand, made a careful scan of the doorways and rooftops across the street before stepping out into the open.

He made his way to an SUV that was idling at the curb. Three other Qaeda men with drawn pistols were close behind him, and bringing up the rear were two more men with the prisoner between them. The prisoner's handcuffs had been supplemented with a pair of leg irons, so he had to be carried down the steps from the building's rear exit.

The SUV's front passenger door was locked. Siraj al Din yanked impatiently at the door handle and bent his face to the window. He had just enough time to identify the shotgun muzzle on the other side of the glass before the Baath killer in the driver's seat pulled the trigger. Two more Republican Guardsmen in the rear of the SUV opened fire through the tinted side windows, killing the Qaeda men with the pistols. The duo holding the prisoner separated and tried to find cover, but the figure in the burqa had pulled a rifle from the shopping basket and was already taking aim; within seconds, these last two Qaeda agents were dead as well.

The Republican Guardsmen jumped out of the SUV and rushed to secure the prisoner, who'd stood unflinching through the gunfire.

Qusay Hussein stripped off the burqa and dropped it and the rifle back in the basket. Then he went over to take a closer look at their prize. He'd never seen a jinn before and wasn't sure he believed in them. And indeed, the prisoner looked just like a man—defiant and unafraid, perhaps, but human.

"Murder is a sin," the prisoner informed him.

Qusay glanced unconcerned at one of the nearby corpses. "These men were murderers too, you may be sure."

"What does that logic suggest about your own future?" the prisoner said.

Qusay didn't bother to answer. A trio of police cars had just rounded the corner, responding to the gunfire. Qusay stepped to the curb and gestured for them to hurry.

By the time Mustafa and the others arrived, sand had begun to coat the corpses and collect in drifts on their windward sides. Siraj al Din, decapitated by the shotgun blast, resembled a beach sculpture eroded by the tide. The street had been closed off and a mixed group of AHS, ABI, and local police were wandering about the scene.

After a quick look at the bodies, Mustafa, Samir, and Amal took shelter inside the building. While Amal got on her cell phone, Mustafa and Samir spoke to Abdullah, who was battered but conscious. Farouk had been taken to the hospital; Joe Simeon was bound for the morgue.

"They said they were from Riyadh," Abdullah explained. His face was streaked with blood, and he kept an ice pack pressed to his scalp as he spoke. "They said they had orders to collect both prisoners. And they had proper ID, but something about the way they just barged into the interview suite without any advance warning . . . I don't know, it just didn't feel right. So I told them they were going to have to wait outside while I made a call, and that's when the big bastard bounced my head off the glass."

"The prisoner they took with them," Mustafa said. "Can you show us the recording of Farouk's interview with him?"

"No. I checked. They erased it and took the backup disk."

"What did he look like?"

Abdullah described him. "He talked like he knew you . . ."

Amal had finished her phone call. "Abu Naji says we missed Bin Laden at the hotel," she told them. "According to the staff, the senator and his bodyguards checked out right around the time we arrested Idris. They were supposed to fly back to the capital this evening, but they haven't checked in for their flight yet, and now it looks like the planes are all grounded anyway."

"I doubt Bin Laden would leave Baghdad now even if he could get a flight," Mustafa said. "What he wants is here . . . OK, let's assume the dead men outside are Al Qaeda, sent to grab this . . . person of interest. Would anyone care to guess who their killers are?"

"Umm Dabir told me she looked out the window after she heard the shooting," Abdullah offered. "She said she saw police cars pulling up and driving away again . . ."

"Baghdad PD," Amal said. "Saddam."

Samir looked at Mustafa. "You think they'd take him to the Ad-hamiyah estate?"

"They might, especially if Saddam were in a hurry to start making wishes."

"That's simple, then," Amal said. "Let's get some more people together and head across the river."

"We could do that," said Mustafa. "But if the cops outside see us assembling a raid team, they might call ahead and warn Saddam." He considered. "The three of us ought to be able to sneak away unnoticed, however."

"And what are the three of us going to do against the whole Republican Guard?" asked Samir.

"Scout the territory," Mustafa said. "Amal, call Abu Naji back.

Tell him to get over to the Baghdad ABI office and round up as many agents as he can for a raid on Saddam's Adhamiyah estate. Tell him to be careful not to let the police know, and tell him to hurry. Oh, and he needn't bother with a warrant."

"Exigent circumstances?" Amal smiled. "Whose life shall I say is in danger? The missing prisoner's, or ours?"

"That all depends," Mustafa said, "on what the prisoner is really made of."

Saddam Hussein waited at the turnaround in front of his mansion, dressed in an authentic Iraqi military uniform purchased off eBazaar. Oversized mirror shades allowed him to gaze unblinking into the storm. He was grinning broadly in anticipation and every few moments had to turn and spit sand from between his teeth.

Presidential Secretary Abid Hamid Mahmud stood to Saddam's right, looking significantly less jubilant. To Abid's right was the sorcerer Mr. Rammal, his expression hidden beneath the cowl of his robe. Forty Republican Guardsmen were arrayed on the mansion's front steps, weapons at the ready. Their faces were impassive: They might have been awaiting the arrival of a head of state, a shipment of gold bullion, or a battle.

Behind the Guard, sheltering beneath an overhang by the front door, were Tariq Aziz, Uday Hussein, and a small group of male servants. Aziz and the servants looked nervous; Uday, sullen. Uday was furious at having been kept home from the mission to retrieve the jinn. He was also bored: All the women of the house, from his mother down to the lowliest maid, had been sent away.

The police cars arrived and were waved through the front gate. They came up the drive and pulled to a stop at the turnaround. Qusay got out of the lead car. He nodded to his father, then opened up the car's back door and reached inside.

As the prisoner's feet touched the ground the wind whipped up violently. Abid and Mr. Rammal were staggered by it, and the Guard had to struggle to maintain their ranks. Aziz threw up an arm to shield himself and the servants covered their faces in fear. Uday, remembering how he'd shamed himself earlier, balled his hands into fists and leaned into the wind.

Saddam stood his ground. He waited for Qusay to pull the prisoner upright, then removed his sunglasses and peered squinting into the prisoner's eyes. "Welcome to my home!" he said, shouting to be heard above the wind's howl. He tugged playfully at the chain between the prisoner's wrists. "Welcome to my service!"

Halal Enforcement had a boat dock on the river one block east from the Homeland Security building.

The three of them had donned goggles before setting out, and Mustafa and Samir had tied rags over their mouths and noses, while Amal used her headscarf. They looked like bandits, and as they approached the guard shack at the dock entrance Mustafa expected to be challenged. But the shack was deserted, and though the gate was locked the keypad entry code had not been changed in a decade.

They boarded a motor launch with an enclosed cabin and set off upriver. The sandstorm was getting worse. The sky had turned a dull orange from the amount of dust floating above the city, and visibility dropped until it was down to less than fifty meters. Mustafa used the onboard GPS to navigate, while Samir and Amal kept a sharp lookout for approaching vessels. Fortunately most of the other river traffic seemed to have pulled off to wait out the storm.

After about fifteen minutes they rounded a bend in the river and spotted a string of lights that, according to the GPS, marked Saddam's private dock. The dock spanned nearly a hundred meters of waterfront and terminated at its east end in a riverside party and guest house that was larger than most people's primary homes. The house also contained a guard station, so Mustafa steered well clear of it, continuing upriver past the dock's west end before killing the launch's running lights and doubling back. He brought them in on the lowest throttle setting, finally cutting the engine entirely and coasting into an open berth beside a yacht named *Bint Zabibah*.

"Now what?" Samir said, after they'd tied off the launch.

"You remember back in '97, when Halal was planning to raid this place?" Mustafa asked.

"I remember the judge denying us a warrant after our informant turned up in a cement mixer."

"Yes, but before that, when the mission was still a go, I had a good look at the blueprints and reconnaissance photos. The main way up to the estate is through there"—he gestured towards the party/guard house—"but there's also a separate gate above a slipway at this end, for putting boats into and out of the water—and loading liquor onto trucks. That gate's not so well guarded, and at the time it was secured only with a padlock and chain."

Amal was already rummaging in the launch's toolbox. "Will this do?" she said, holding up a pair of long-handled bolt cutters.

They put their goggles and face masks back on and stepped out onto the dock. The gate was where Mustafa said it would be, but unlike Halal, Saddam had upgraded his security since the 1990s. A video camera had been mounted above the gateway, and the gate itself was now a solid sheet of metal, barred and bolted from the inside.

"What about going over the wall?" Amal suggested, as they huddled out of the camera's view. "We can use the bolt cutters on the barbed wire."

"It's got to be at least four meters high," Samir said. "You have a grappling hook, too?"

"If we can pile up some boxes or something for you to stand on, you can give me a boost." Reading their silence as discomfort rather than skepticism, she added: "Pretend you're my brothers."

No one had a better idea, so they crept along the dock looking for some boxes or crates strong enough to bear their weight. Just past the *Bint Zabibah* they found a small, wheeled dumpster chained to a post. They cut the chain and trundled the dumpster back to the slipway.

Mustafa was the tallest of them, so he stood on the dumpster lid and let Amal climb up on his shoulders. Samir stayed on the ground trying to hold the dumpster steady. This circus act would have been difficult even in perfectly calm weather and under these conditions should have been impossible, but the wind was oddly cooperative. More than once, as she stretched to cut the strands of barbed wire, Amal felt herself starting to overbalance, only to have a sudden gust like a firm hand push her back against the wall. She worked as quickly as she could. When the last strand parted, she tossed the bolt cutter to the ground and said, "OK!" Mustafa placed his hands under the soles of Amal's shoes and pushed up, hard. This maneuver proved too much for the dumpster lid, which buckled beneath him and sent him tumbling back to be caught by Samir—but when they looked up, Amal had vanished over the wall.

Five long minutes later, the light on the security camera went out and the gate opened. Amal, now armed with an assault rifle, waved them inside. They passed through a short tunnel. At the other end was a guard shack, inside which a Republican Guardsman lay, bound hand and foot with plastic zip-ties and blindfolded with his own jacket. Mustafa turned to ask Amal a question but she was already forging ahead.

They made for the lights of the main house. They'd covered about half the distance when the wind dropped almost to nothing, and they heard, somewhere off to the left, the asthmatic roar of a lion. This was followed by another, softer wheezing sound. A Republican Guard staggered out of the haze, gasping for breath, and fell facedown in front of them.

While Amal kept watch for the lion, Mustafa and Samir bent down over the Guard. The man hadn't been mauled; he'd been stabbed. A handmade plastic blade had been driven into his upper back, piercing a lung. Mustafa pulled it loose and squinted at the legend on the side of the shiv: XBOX 360.

From behind them they heard the sound of a pump shotgun being cocked. "Don't move!" said a voice. The words were Arabic, but the voice was American . . . and familiar.

Mustafa spoke without thinking: "Captain Lawrence?"

"Stand up slowly," the voice said. "Now all of you turn around. Slowly."

The captain's T-shirt was torn and bloody, and a chunk was missing from his left ear where one of his dying jailers had bitten him. Looking at him, Mustafa experienced a curious sense of doubling. He felt like he knew this man, had worked with him for years. He knew that he didn't know this man; they'd never met before. Not in this life.

Without waiting to be told, Mustafa lifted his goggles up to his forehead and tugged down the rag that covered his nose and mouth. The captain lowered the shotgun. "Mustafa?"

"Hello, Captain Lawrence," Mustafa said. "How is Operation Iraqi Freedom coming?"

The window of the prayer room had been shuttered against the storm and the sand pattern on the floor had been redrawn. A chair of hammered black iron held the captive jinn at the center of the circle. Saddam stood facing the jinn, while Mr. Rammal orbited them both. The sorcerer had donned a peaked cap of densely woven silver thread, and as he walked around the circle with the brass bottle held before him, he muttered incantations in the dead language of Babylon.

Bearing witness to the ritual, their faces lit by flickering torchlight, were Qusay, Uday, Abid Hamid Mahmud, Tariq Aziz, and a half-dozen Republican Guard. The Guardsmen remained impassive—all except for one, who grew increasingly uncomfortable with the blasphemy being committed here and finally opened his mouth to protest. But Uday silenced him with a glance.

Mr. Rammal completed his ninth circuit. He removed his cap and gave the bottle to Saddam, who hefted it in both hands, weighing it like a newborn.

Saddam Hussein addressed the jinn: "Are you ready to do my bidding?"

The jinn stared back at him placidly. "Tell me what it is you want."

Saddam passed the brass bottle back to Mr. Rammal and snapped his fingers. Abid Hamid Mahmud came forward and handed him a globe. Saddam showed it to the jinn; black marker had been applied to the globe's surface, changing borders and renaming nations. "I also have some notes," Saddam said, patting the breast pocket of his uniform. "Perhaps you'd like to study them."

The jinn flexed his wrists beneath the iron bands that held him to the chair. "That's all right," he said. "I believe I understand. You wish to be a ruler again. Arabia will be the seat of your power. From there, your armies will march out, victorious, over Persia and India, Europe and America, and all the rest of the world. Your old enemies will be found and brought to you in chains, to be humbled before you. And you will be the king of all kings, now and forever. Does that about cover it?"

Saddam Hussein grinned. "That will do for a start." He tossed the globe back to Abid and spread his arms to embrace his future. "You've heard my wish," he said. "Now give it to me! I command you!"

"Very well," the jinn said. "My answer is no."

The three Guardsmen stood shoulder to shoulder at the window of the front gatehouse, peering out into the storm.

"It's not natural," said the first Guard.

"Fuck you, it's not natural," said the second.

"Look how dark it's getting!"

"It's a fucking sandstorm, asshole!"

"Yes, and that creature they've got up at the house is responsible! Abu Ramzi told me—"

"Abu Ramzi is a fool!"

"Be quiet, both of you!" said the third Guard, who was looking not at the sky but at the road. "Someone's out there."

"Where? I don't see any headlights."

"Not in a vehicle. Men on foot." He grabbed his rifle. "Call the main house and the other guard stations and tell them we may have intruders trying to get over the front wall." On his way out the door, he hit a switch that brought up extra floodlights.

There *was* someone out there: Just beyond the gate, a figure was crouching to place something against the base of the wall. "Hey!" the Guardsman shouted. "Freeze!" But the figure jumped up and ran back into the storm. The Guardsman continued forward, his eye drawn to the object the figure had left behind: a canvas satchel with a blinking red light on its side.

"What do you mean, 'no'?" Saddam Hussein said. He glanced sharply at Mr. Rammal, who threw up his hands in supplication.

"Don't be too hard on your magician," the jinn said. "His Akkadian isn't bad. A few thousand years ago, his incantation might have worked. But I'm afraid you've both failed to appreciate what it is that I am."

"What you are?" Saddam said. "I told you what you are: You're my servant!"

"Once upon a time I was the property of kings," the jinn demurred. "But during my long imprisonment I heard, from afar, the words of the prophets: Ibrahim, and Jesus, and last of all Mohammed, peace be unto him. Now I've said the words of the shahada and become a Muslim, and pagan enchantments no longer have power over me."

"That's not true!" Mr. Rammal said. "My spell drew you in! It forced you to reveal yourself!"

"My pride did most of the work, there." The jinn shrugged apologetically. "But there is no pride in being a slave of Saddam Hussein—and though I really should stop presuming to know the mind of God, I can't imagine the All-Compassionate would want me to serve such a wicked person."

Saddam trembled with rage. He unsnapped the holster on his belt and drew out a huge revolver. Thumbing back the hammer, he pivoted and took aim at the sorcerer.

"No!" Mr. Rammal cried. Then the gun roared and he toppled over backwards onto the sand-strewn floor.

Uday stepped forward, eyes fixed on the jinn. "Let me hurt this one, father," he said. "I'll get him to do what you want."

"Shut up," Saddam said. He pointed the smoking gun muzzle at the jinn's temple. "I could kill you, too."

"You could," the jinn agreed. "And then when I am dead, I must go before God who will judge me for all eternity. Whose wrath should I fear more?"

Saddam began to tremble again. But before he could pull the trigger a second time, there was an explosion somewhere out on the grounds. "What was that?"

The jinn tilted his head, listening to the wind. "A tall man," he said. "More princely than you, but no less wicked. He means to make a sacrifice of your entire household."

More noise: the clatter of assault rifles. It seemed to be coming from multiple locations.

"Qaeda," said Qusay. He was holding a transceiver to his ear. "They've blown the front gate, and they may be coming up from the river as well."

"You, and you!" Saddam said, gesturing with the revolver at two of his men. "Stay here and guard my property! Qusay, Uday, Abid, and the rest of you, follow me!" He went out into the hall, which was noisy with the shouts of the Republican Guard.

After the others had gone out and the door was shut behind them, a pale Tariq Aziz stepped forward from the shadows and stood wringing his hands over the body of the sorcerer. "This was not my doing," he said. He looked at the jinn. "I didn't do anything!"

"I will not have an evildoer for a friend," the jinn replied.

"I don't actually remember you," Mustafa said. "I feel as though I should, but I don't."

"Nobody remembers me," the captain replied. "Nobody but Saddam even knows who I am. It's made the last couple years kind of difficult . . ."

They had entered the mansion through a back door, overpowering two more Guards in the process. Their goal was the converted prayer room, which Captain Lawrence had learned about from Saddam during one of their late-night sessions, and where he'd guessed the jinn would be taken. But they were still on the ground floor, searching for an unguarded flight of stairs, when all hell broke loose. Now they were hiding in a room just off the chamber that held the Nebuchadnezzar statue. It was the same side room where Mustafa had encountered the English boy; he could still see some toy cars and trucks underneath the furniture.

"You do remember, though," Mustafa said, careful to keep his voice low. "Why? Because you're the one who made the wish?"

"I go back and forth on that," Captain Lawrence said. "Days that I'm feeling sorry for myself, I think God's punishing me. Most days, though, I figure I got what I asked for. What fun would it be to change the world if you didn't remember what you changed it from?"

"And Saddam? How did you become his guest?"

"After I realized I couldn't go back home—that there was no home for me to go back to—I decided I might as well make myself useful."

"You tried to kill him?"

The captain nodded. "Seemed only right, seeing as he's supposed to be dead. But Qusay was in charge of the Guard that night and they caught me coming in. When Saddam figured out what I was, he decided to add me to his collection."

A squad of Republican Guards ran through Nebuchadnezzar's chamber and charged down the hall towards the mansion's front door. Most of the gunfire seemed to be coming from the front of the estate. Mustafa kept hoping that the attackers would announce themselves as ABI, but he knew it was too soon for them to have gotten here.

"So what about you?" the captain said. "You're a cop again, obviously. But what kind?"

"Homeland Security."

Another nod. "Federal law enforcement—*above* Saddam. So you got your wish, too."

"No," Mustafa said pointedly, "I didn't." But then after a moment, he added: "It's not a bad life, though. And most of the problems with it are at least of my own making, not someone else's."

All the power in the house suddenly went out. The side room was plunged into darkness, but Nebuchadnezzar's chamber remained dimly illuminated by the apocalyptic orange glow coming through the windows in the dome.

"All right," Amal said, looking out through the archway. "If we're going to move, I'd say this is the time."

"Go straight across, to that other opening over there," Mustafa said pointing. "I remember I passed a stairwell on the way to Saddam's office."

They were halfway across the chamber when Uday Hussein and a squad of Guardsmen emerged from the very archway they were headed towards. Both parties stopped short and for an instant just stared. Then one of the Guards started to raise his assault rifle and Amal opened fire with hers, killing that Guard and the man behind him. Then everyone was firing, and moving—diving towards the chamber's most obvious source of cover. Uday and the two remaining Guardsmen ended up on one side of the Nebuchadnezzar statue; Amal, Mustafa, Samir, and Captain Lawrence ended up on the other.

Amal sat with her back against the statue's base and fitted a fresh clip into her rifle. "Uday Hussein!" she called out. "We are federal agents! Throw down your weapons and put your hands up!"

Uday laughed. "Is that you, Amal bint Shamal? You want us to surrender? Very well, come over here and show us your ass, and maybe we'll think about it!"

Captain Lawrence rose to a crouch and prepared to make an end run around Nebuchadnezzar. But Mustafa, looking up at the statue, suddenly recalled something; he put a hand on the captain's forearm to restrain him and then leaned over to whisper in Amal's ear.

"Bint Shamal!" Uday crowed. "Daughter of a dead fool, who thought he could stand against a king! Yes, come here, and when I'm done playing with you I'll send you to join him!"

"You are wrong, Uday," Amal replied. "My father was a hero, and even in death he is worth ten of your father—and a hundred of you. As for your father's kingship, I am afraid it is hollow." She stood up, pointed the rifle at the front of Nebuchadnezzar's right ankle, and pulled the trigger. The bullet punched straight through the thin tin shell and came out the other side, striking Uday in the back. As he pitched forward, the Guardsmen tried to scramble up and defend themselves, but Amal kept firing, placing her shots at even intervals, and they never even made it all the way to their feet.

Out in the storm, the soldiers of Al Qaeda fought the men of the Republican Guard. The Guard had greater numbers, but Al Qaeda had the element of surprise. Before the main assault commenced, small groups of commandos had snuck over the wall to set up ambush positions on the grounds. The commandos were equipped with thermal imagers that could pick out warm bodies at a distance, even through swirling sand. This gave them a significant tactical advantage over the Guardsmen, many of whom didn't even bother to don goggles before rushing out of the mansion. The first wave of defenders to respond to the explosion at the gate ran blindly into the ambush and were slaughtered to the last man. A second wave tried to advance more cautiously, but this just gave the commandos more time to aim, and soon enough this second group of Guardsmen had all been killed as well.

There was a lull in the firefight while the Qaeda commandos waited to see whether the Guard would try a third sally. But the Guard had belatedly learned their lesson, and after a moment the commandos picked up and began advancing on the mansion.

By this time Qusay Hussein had taken a squad of men to an up-stairs dining room that overlooked the front of the estate. Qusay set up a sniper rifle with a thermal sight at one window and had the Guardsmen with their AK-47s take position at the others. He let the commandos get close to the house, then ordered his men to fire first. Once they had the commandos' attention, he opened up with the sniper rifle, shifting aim quickly between the glowing man-shaped targets his sight revealed to him. Several rooms away, another squad commanded by Qusay's father began firing as well. In the first few seconds a dozen commandos were killed or wounded, but the Qaeda men didn't panic; the survivors quickly found cover and returned fire.

One of Qusay's men stood exposed too long at a window; an in-coming round shattered his collarbone. As he fell back screaming another Guard turned to look at him and took two bullets in the side of the head. Qusay ducked down to avoid a hail of bullets directed at his window. Cupping a hand over his ear so he could hear over the screams of the wounded man and the whine of incoming rounds, he listened to radio reports from elsewhere on the estate. The river house had been hit by a rocket or possibly a suicide bomber and was on fire; most of the Guards there were dead and the rest were trapped by the flames. The squads Qusay had dispatched to the rear of the mansion said that they, too, were taking fire, and one team reported hearing shots inside the house.

"Oh God save me!" cried the wounded Guardsman, and Qusay barked, "Shut him up!" at no one in particular. Then he raised his head above the windowsill, took aim, and shot a Qaeda commando who was crouching behind a palm tree. He tracked right with the sniper rifle and spied another commando, down on one knee with a long tube balanced on his shoulder. There was a bright flash in the thermal sight and a rocket streaked towards the house, blasting away the front doors and killing several Guards in the grand entrance hall; Qusay heard their dying screams over the radio.

He shot the rocketeer, ducked down, counted three, popped up again, and tracked left to where another commando was kneeling. Qusay never saw this second rocketeer; all he saw was the rocket, which appeared in his gun sight as a black circle ringed with fire, that rapidly grew larger.

Several times, as they listened to the sounds of the battle, the two Republican Guardsmen in the old prayer room had exchanged glances, communicating without speaking. Now, as the rocket barrage shook the mansion, they looked at one another again and came to a wordless decision.

"Hey!" Tariq Aziz said. "Where are you going? Saddam told you to stay here!" But the two didn't even glance back as they fled into the hall.

"Shall I quote you another psalm?" asked the jinn. "The twenty-third perhaps?"

Aziz paced the room, coming to his own decision. "Quote it to yourself," he said finally, and headed for the door. But before he could escape, an armed party burst in.

"Hello, Mr. Aziz," Amal said. "Doing a little frontline reporting?"

Mustafa and Captain Lawrence pushed past the terrified news publisher and ran over to the jinn. The iron bands that held him in the chair were secured with modern steel padlocks. Mustafa asked Aziz: "Do you have the keys for these?"

"What?" Tariq Aziz said. "Certainly not! I have nothing to do with this! Nothing at all!"

"We'll have to smash them off," Lawrence said.

"Don't bother," the jinn said. "There isn't time."

Outside, down the hallway, a voice bellowed in terror: "GOD IS GREAT! . . . GOD IS GREAT! . . . GOD IS GREAT!" There was a blood-curdling scream that cut off abruptly.

"Oh God, let me out of here!" Tariq Aziz cried. Ignoring the rifle Amal had pointed at him, he darted through the open doorway.

"Let him go," Mustafa said, before Amal could chase after him. "Samir, shut and lock that door."

The jinn flashed a mischievous smile at Captain Lawrence. "So. How are you enjoying your wish?"

"You already know the answer to that," Lawrence said. "I've learned my lesson. I'm willing to take it back, if that's what you're offering."

Mustafa, watching Samir bolt the door, spun around at this. "Wait just a minute," he said.

"Yes," Amal said. "Hold on."

"Seriously, dude," said Samir. "That's what Osama bin Laden wants."

"Maybe it's what God wants, too," Lawrence suggested. "Put things back the way they were. The way they're naturally supposed to be."

"Supposed to be?" Mustafa said. "And you say you've learned your lesson, have you?"

The jinn was laughing. "Arabia in a state of nature, untouched by the dreams of the West. Now that would be an alternate reality . . . Alas, I can't oblige you. That doorway is shut and cannot be gone back through."

"All right then," Lawrence said. He placed the butt of his shotgun against one of the padlocks. "I'll have you out of this in a minute . . ."

But the jinn shook his head. "I already told you. It's too late."

Sand flew through a gaping hole in the wall of a formal bedroom, dusting the corpses of Guardsmen whose flesh had been torn by rocket fragments. The bedding had been ripped by shrapnel as well, and the mattress ticking was on fire, though the sand had begun to smother the flames.

The lid of a large hardwood chest opposite the bed creaked open and Saddam Hussein peeped out. When he was sure he could hear no more incoming missiles, he shoved the lid up all the way and half crawled, half rolled out of the chest, the slipped disk in his back making him groan. He grabbed a rifle off one of the dead Guardsmen and used it as a crutch to get to his feet.

He limped into the hall, limped to the dining room where Qusay had been stationed. What Saddam saw, looking in through the shattered doorway, made him groan again.

He shook it off. The jinn, he thought. The jinn could fix this. The creature claimed to be a Muslim: Very well, he would throw himself on its mercy, say whatever it took to get it to protect him. Then later, once he was safe, he would find a way to bend it truly to his will, and undo this nightmare.

But first he had to get back to it. He continued along the hall, not just limping but lurching, and alert to every sound. Al Qaeda was definitely inside the house now—he could hear running, shouting, and sporadic gunfire as they encountered remnants of the Republican Guard—but it sounded as if they were still on the ground floor. It wouldn't take them long to find their way upstairs, though, and he knew they would never stop searching until they found him.

He came to the gallery overlooking Nebuchadnezzar's chamber. He heard movement below and tried to slip by unnoticed, but then a voice with a Gulf accent said, "I think it is the older son." Saddam stepped to the balustrade and looked down. Two commandos stood next to a body on the chamber floor. One of them was shining a flashlight on the corpse's face.

"Uday!" Saddam cried. The commandos looked up and he shot them both. The flashlight, now blood-spattered, rolled to a stop beside Uday's head and continued to illuminate his features like some ghastly spotlight. "Uday," Saddam said. "Wait there. Wait there. I will fix this . . ."

He turned to go to the prayer room and a rifle butt swung out of the shadows, catching him squarely in the face. He spun around, fell against the balustrade, and dropped his own gun over the rail. Another blow hit him in the lower back, fracturing vertebrae. Saddam fell to his knees, insensate with pain.

A rough hand gripped the top of his head and another grabbed the back of his collar. His attacker asked a question. "You," Saddam hissed, disdain breaking through his agony as he recognized that voice. "You go to hell! You can't have it—it's mine! I am a king! A king, you understand? You're not even a dog's asshole!"

The grip on his collar tightened. As he was lifted up he tried to fight, but the blow to his spine had robbed him of his strength and he could only flail and curse. He tipped forward over the rail, the tightness at his throat and the drop below triggering an awful sense of déjà vu, and he began to cry out, affirming God's greatness—a last desperate plea for salvation to which the answer was no.

Then the world turned upside down and he was falling. He landed with a great thud and a crack, and for a moment the whole house fell silent. Osama bin Laden leaned on the balustrade, looking down, the orange light gathered in his eyes making him appear like a demon.

A voice echoed from the hall beyond the gallery: "Oh God, let me out of here!" Bin Laden moved towards the voice, reaching the hall in time to see the narrowing wedge of torchlight as Samir swung the prayer room door closed. Bin Laden stood listening—to the door bolt sliding home, to Tariq Aziz's receding footsteps, and to the soft whisper of his own intuition.

He slung his rifle and reached into his robe, pulling out a canvas satchel. He set the fuse as he was walking down the hall.

The jinn said to Samir: "You should come away from there."

"Why?" Samir said. But he backed away from the door and stood with the others by the magic circle.

Captain Lawrence was hammering at the padlock, which stubbornly refused to break. Mustafa had gone behind the chair to examine the window shutters. "I wonder if we can climb down from here."

"Don't worry about it," the jinn said.

An explosion blew the door apart. Hunks of splintered wood and metal came flying across the chamber and were met by a whirl of air that also extinguished most of the torches. When Mustafa regained his senses, he was slumped against the wall beside the window. Except for the ringing in his ears he wasn't in any discomfort and didn't seem to be wounded, but he couldn't move.

Osama bin Laden came through the doorway cradling his AK-47. He spotted Amal lying facedown in the shadows, but the jinn said, "Leave her be, brother. I am the one you want."

Bin Laden came forward and stood in the same spot Saddam Hussein had occupied not long before. He didn't make a wish or say anything at all, just stared at the jinn with a mixture of curiosity and malice.

The jinn gazed back calmly into the face of death. "There are among us some that are righteous," he said. "And some the contrary . . . Peace be unto you, brother."

Bin Laden pulled the trigger. The jinn bled like a man, and he suffered like one, too—as the first bullets entered his body, he opened his mouth in a gasp and his arms and legs jerked helplessly against the bands that held them. Bin Laden continued firing until the gun's clip was empty. By then the jinn's limbs were still and his head lolled forward on his neck.

Mustafa found he could move again. He tried to stand, but vertigo hit him and he fell back with a groan. Bin Laden turned towards the sound and the two of them locked eyes a moment, the senator trying to decide whether Mustafa was worth reloading for. "God willing," Mustafa said, and Bin Laden with an imperious tilt of the head turned and walked out of the room.

Mustafa slid sideways until he came to rest on the floor with his cheek on a fine layer of sand. From this position he saw the brass jinni bottle, discarded and forgotten beside the body of Saddam's sorcerer. He watched the play of the flickering light on its curved surface, felt the world turn beneath him. Then the wind of the storm, rising to a hurricane fury, tore the shutters from the window and blasted into the chamber, snuffing out the last of the torches.

At that same moment, three thousand kilometers to the west in Tripoli, Wajid Jamil was demoing a software update for his Uncle Muammar. The virtual globe Al Ard—Earth—was one of the Libyan governor's favorite computer programs, and since its introduction he'd made numerous suggestions for improvements. The number-one item on Gaddafi's wish list—real-time updating of Al Ard's satellite imagery—remained technically infeasible in a nonmilitary application, but Wajid had done what he could to make the program feel "live" in other ways.

The new feature presently being demonstrated pulled in data from weather stations around the world and projected it onto the globe, refreshing every fifteen seconds. Wajid had zoomed in on the northeastern UAS so that his Uncle could watch the sandstorm as it spread across Iraq towards the Kuwait and Arabia state lines. Gaddafi was fascinated, almost hypnotized—when Wajid tried to move on to the next phase of the demo, which involved highway traffic data, the governor asked if they could please stick with the weather a bit longer.

"Of course," Wajid said, eager to please as always.

But as luck would have it, at the very next refresh the program hit a glitch: The yellow-crosshatch graphic that represented the sandstorm increased dramatically in size, expanding hundreds of kilometers in all directions. Al Gaddafi jerked his head back, blinking as though the computer monitor had poked him in the eyes. Wajid looked over at his main tech support guy, who winced in embarrassment and bent closer to another screen displaying raw code.

At the next refresh, the sandstorm expanded again. It covered the entire Gulf Peninsula now, as well as Persia, Turkey, and the Caucasus all the way north to Chechnya. Gaddafi chuckled, having regained his composure. "Global warming," he quipped.

"Yeah, this is still a beta," said Wajid.

Refresh. The storm spread through Afghanistan and Pakistan to India, surged into Russia and Eastern Europe, and crossed the Red Sea and the Gulf of Aden to engulf Somalia, Djibouti, Eritrea, Ethiopia, Sudan, Egypt, and Libya as far west as Benghazi.

"We are next," said Gaddafi.

"Uh-huh," said Wajid, shooting his tech guy another look. Then the computer monitors flickered as a heavy gust of wind struck the building and millions of tiny grains began pelting the windows.

Refresh . . .

In Texas it was early morning. In an undistinguished house in the Austin suburbs, a man stood in his kitchen, talking to his dog. Though no one would guess it from his current surroundings, the man was a son of privilege, his father one of the most powerful and respected elders in the Evangelical Republic; in his youth it had naturally been assumed that he too would achieve great things. But he had squandered the advantages of his birth, used up all his second chances, and so come to nothing. Now that his own children were grown, the little black terrier at his feet represented the pinnacle of his responsibilities.

"I know you want the canned food," he said to it. "But you don't get to decide what you eat. *I'm* the decider." He flashed a goofy grin, impressed by his own wit, which the terrier couldn't or wouldn't appreciate. But the dog did seem to understand that it wasn't going to get its wish, and bent its head reluctantly to the bowl of dry kibble. "Good boy," the man said, and went to see about his own breakfast.

The man had slept poorly, plagued as usual by anxiety dreams in which he searched endlessly for something he had promised to find—though whether the something was a person or an object he could never quite remember. The sense of frustration continued to haunt him even now that he was awake. As he stood by the open refrigerator looking blankly within, he wondered, Where are they? and then, Where is what?

He was still staring into the fridge when he heard the patter of what he assumed was rain against the side of the house. The dog, facing the sliding glass patio doors and able to see what was really going on outside, let out a terrified bark and ran to hide in the pantry.

"You whine all you want," the man said. "You're still not getting the canned food." As the storm intensified he shut the refrigerator door and went into the hall and called upstairs to his wife: "Hey Laur? You awake? You better go shut the windows in the spare room!"

Refresh . . .

Ninety miles away in Crawford, the man David Koresh called

the Quail Hunter was in the CIA's interrogation wing, extracting a confession from a recalcitrant Quaker. The basement torture room was windowless and soundproof, but even so he sensed the arrival of the storm as a sudden tremor in his heart.

"Sir?" asked a centurion who was holding a bucket of water above the prisoner's head. "Should I go again?"

The Quail Hunter started to gesture Yes, yes, and something trickled onto the back of his hand. He looked up. A hole had appeared in the ceiling and sand was streaming down through it like the grains in an hourglass. He felt his heart give another kick.

"Sir?" the centurion said. "Sir?"

Refresh . . .

In Virginia, David Koresh sat at his desk with his Bible open to the Book of Revelation. He thought he understood what was happening and ought to have welcomed it, but now that he was getting what he'd prayed for he found himself in doubt, the rasp of the sand on the window behind him sounding more and more like the crackle of a fire.

Across the Potomac, Colonel Yunus stood in the dinosaur gallery of the Smithsonian, marveling at the sand sifting down through the growing cracks in the skylight. He felt no fear, even as the roof began to give way; in the dust cloud that came boiling towards him, he saw the outline of a house, and faces of a family that he knew. He said: "God willing."

Refresh . . .

All around the globe—in Berlin and the occupied territories; in London and Tehran, Kabul and Denver, Chicago and Jakarta, Islamabad and Corpus Christi, Los Angeles and Mumbai; in Alexandria and Alexandria—the storm scoured the landscape, roaring through the homes and hiding places of the powerful and the meek like some mighty voice: Refresh. Refresh. This is the day the world changes . . .

And in Baghdad, a tall man stalking the halls of a mansion found himself suddenly outside, exposed to the storm's full fury. The wind tore the rifle from his hands and the pelting sand drove him to his knees. Blind, he clawed his way forward, seeking shelter, a cave to crawl into. There was nothing. He quickly became exhausted. Sinking down, he felt sand piling up around him and prepared to be buried alive.

The storm abruptly ceased. The tall man raised his head and saw only darkness. He stood up in the black stillness, listening to his own labored breathing, and felt rather than heard the heavy footsteps coming up behind him. The back of his neck prickled. Hot breath whispered in his ear as someone taller even than he was leaned in over his shoulder.

"Who goes there?" Osama bin Laden said, and then he turned around.

Epilogue

The City of

the Future

When Mustafa comes back to himself he's on top of a big pile of sand, one dune among many, a sea of sand extending to the horizon. He doesn't know which desert this is. The Sahara is the obvious guess, but it could just as well be the Rub al Khali, or the Nafud, or something completely new.

He is kneeling as if to pray, and indeed it is about that time: When he looks up, the sun is directly overhead. But instead of prostrating himself, he stands, brushing sand from the robe he has somehow come to be wearing. The hem of the robe hikes up and he sees that his feet are clad in leather sandals, a good pair, nicely broken in.

Straightening, he continues to take inventory. Things he has: A robe. Comfortable shoes. The first hint of a beard. Things he does not have: Pockets. A wallet. A watch. A map. Food. Water. That last could be a problem, though he's not thirsty yet. Supposing that he will be soon enough, he turns around, to see whether perhaps there's an oasis behind him. There isn't; just more dunes. He has all the sand he could wish for.

Continuing to turn, he spots something else, sticking up out of the dune a few meters away from him: a boot. He goes over and pulls it up, pours out the sand, and turns it over in his hands. It's a tall boot, tan leather and nylon with a thick rubber sole. There are no markings on it, inside or out, but it looks military.

Well, Mustafa thinks, now I have a boot. But it's the wrong size for him—he can see this, even before he measures it against the bottom of his sandals—and its mate is nowhere to be found, so after a few moments he tosses it, and watches it roll and bounce down the dune face.

As the boot comes to rest, he detects more motion in his periph-eral vision: Amal and Samir, climbing up opposite sides of the dune.

Amal is wearing a blue abaya that shimmers brightly in the sunlight. Samir is dressed in city clothes: socks and loafers, khakis, a cotton shirt that is already stained with sweat.

Mustafa nods hello to them and they nod back, everybody affecting a casual attitude, as if meeting in the middle of nowhere like this were a natural occurrence. As maybe, in this world, it is. They stand side by side at the top of the dune and look out over the high and rolling sands stretching far away.

Samir is the first to speak. "Well," he says, "here we all are in the desert." Looking down at his empty hands: "With nothing."

"We are alive at least," Amal offers.

"That is one theory," says Mustafa. But he says it good-naturedly, feeling not so much optimistic as philosophical: If this is the same world he woke up in yesterday, then he hasn't lost anything he hadn't already lost. If it is a new world, it is as apt to contain good surprises as bad ones. He supposes he should consider the possibility that they are in hell, but the fact that he can still smile, however faintly, makes that seem unlikely. And in any case, whining will change nothing. "I guess we should start walking."

"OK," Samir says. "Which way?"

Three Muslims adrift in the desert could do worse than follow the Qibla direction. Of course Mustafa has no idea which direction that is, but he remembers the direction he was kneeling in, so they strike out that way. At first they try to travel in a straight line, but after trekking up and down a few dune faces in the noonday sun, they decide to zigzag instead, following the troughs between dunes.

They've only gone two or three kilometers when they come upon the jeep. It is buried nose-down in the sand, its front hood and most of its windshield covered, its tailgate and right rear wheel sticking up at an angle. Like Mustafa's boot, it is unmarked but looks military. Its green paint job has been scoured by the sand.

Under a green canvas tarp in the tail bed they find several plastic jugs full of water. Mustafa cracks one open and drinks. The water is very warm but tastes fine. He passes the jug around.

After they've all drunk their fill, they investigate the front of the jeep. Amal, the smallest of them, crawls in through the open passenger window. She finds the ignition and tries it, but there's not even the click of a solenoid in response. She has better luck with the glove box: Inside is a small pistol, .25-caliber with a nine-round clip. The clip is fully loaded and the barrel is clean; the slide moves easily. Mustafa is mildly troubled by this discovery but Amal takes it as a good omen. "It never hurts to be prepared," she says, slipping the gun into her abaya.

Samir takes another look in the tail bed and finds a leather pouch with tobacco and some rolling papers. "Are there matches, too?" Amal inquires, and Samir produces a lighter from his back pocket.

Mustafa would love a smoke, but there's something else he needs to take care of first. He grabs one of the water jugs and goes to find a private spot around the nearest dune. He washes his face, his hands, and his feet. He still doesn't know the Qibla direction, but there's a workaround for that: He says the required prayers, not once, but four times, each time turning himself by ninety degrees.

He's finishing up the last set when a light breeze comes over the dune, carrying the sound of Amal's voice saying her own prayers. Careful not to disturb her, Mustafa makes his way back to the jeep.

Samir has torn a long strip from the tarp and fashioned a turban for himself. It looks comical but will protect his scalp. Mustafa rolls a cigarette and they pass it back and forth until Amal returns.

They should probably use what's left of the tarp to make some shade and sit out the hottest part of the day, but they are all impatient now to get somewhere, to find out where *somewhere* is, and so without even discussing it they each take a water jug and start walking again.

They walk for several hours, zigzagging between the dunes, using the position of the sun to maintain a more or less steady course. In the middle of the afternoon they find another military vehicle, a canvas-top troop truck, lying on its side. Samir crawls in the back, looking for more goodies. This time there's no water or tobacco, but when he digs in the sand that's drifted up inside, he finds a big tin can filled with something heavy.

Mustafa studies the length of the shadow cast by the truck, does a mental calculation, and goes off to pray again. When he gets back, Samir and Amal have found a can opener. "Figs," Amal says. They sit in the back of the truck and eat fruit, lick syrup from their fingers. Then they get sleepy.

Mustafa naps for about an hour. When he wakes up, Samir is snoring like a buzz saw and Amal is gone. He steps outside and finds her standing up on the truck cab, balanced precariously on the passenger door. She is shading her eyes. "I see a city," she says. Mustafa looks where she is looking but his view is blocked by a dune, so he climbs up beside her.

Now he can see it: out on the horizon, wavering and indistinct, its distance impossible to guess. "I see towers," Amal says. "Do you see towers?"

"I see something," says Mustafa.

They wake up Samir. He sees it too. "I hope it's real," he says. "I hope the people who live there speak Arabic."

"If they speak English," says Mustafa, "I'll translate."

"And if they speak Farsi," says Amal, "I'll tell you what *not* to say."

They set out. The dunes no longer seem so steep, so they begin to travel in a straight line again, and as they climb up and down, they play a game to pass the time. When they are on top of the dunes and the city is visible, they describe what they think they can see. When they are down in the troughs and the city is hidden, they talk about what they would like to see, what they hope they will find when they get there.

"I hope prohibition is over," Samir says. "I'd like to get a cold beer."

"I hope there are more women in Congress," Amal says. "A woman president would be nice."

"I hope there is a Congress," says Mustafa. "A republic—a *real* republic—of some kind."

Hope. They are careful to use that word, and not *wish*. And they are careful not to speak of friends or family. But in the silences, as they labor up or downhill, that is what they think about: who will be waiting for them.

Amal thinks of her father. She pictures him on the steps of the city hall, in uniform, shoulder to shoulder with all the others who gave their lives for justice: These are the ones. She hopes to stand beside him again, but if that's too much to ask, she is prepared to stand for him, and carry on his legacy.

Samir thinks of his sons. In his heart he is certain that they are out there somewhere. What he is less sure of is whether he will be permitted to see them. The majority of his thoughts are focused on this, and on how he will begin to search. But beyond Malik and Jibril, there is room in his hopes for one other—not so much a specific person, a specific man, as an idea of one. It is still not an idea he would dare to voice aloud, but he can at least conceive of it now, and wonder whether, on this side of the storm, some things might be possible that were not before.

Mustafa thinks, of course, of Fadwa. He doesn't know if he will see her again. He doesn't know, if he does, whether anything will be different. He would like a chance to tell her he is sorry, and he would certainly be willing to try again: To be kind. To be honest. To be a bit less of a fool. Trying doesn't mean succeeding, though, and he is still the same man, with the same flaws.

But he is willing to try. And to ask for help. And that more than anything is what he hopes for: that waiting in the city will be one whom he can ask for help with his struggle—the struggle of the future he must still face, and the struggle of the past he must learn to let go.

They walk all the rest of that day, a day that seems to go on endlessly. But it does end, finally. As the sun sinks below the horizon, they crest one last dune, and there it is, sprawled on the plain below them: a white-walled city, with lights of evening just coming on.

They stand on the dune looking down.

"I don't recognize it," Amal says. "Do you?"

"No," Samir says.

"No," says Mustafa.

But it's not entirely foreign to them. Here and there, along the unfamiliar streets, they see shapes they do recognize: domes and steeples and towers. And even now, in a minaret near the outer wall, a muezzin begins his cry, words and a language they know.

They stand on the dune and listen to the call. More lights come on. People move in the streets. "God willing," says Mustafa. And then he and Samir and Amal go down, in hope, to the city.

ACKNOWLEDGMENTS

Thanks are due, as always, to my one and only wife, Lisa Gold, who served as my first reader, sounding board, research assistant, and cheerleader. My agent, Melanie Jackson, offered encouragement at a time when I still wasn't sure the novel would work. My publisher, Jonathan Burnham, and my editor, Rakesh Satyal, were also early supporters, and Rakesh helped me across the finish line with a minimum of pain and suffering. Tim Duggan shepherded me through publication. Others who gave assistance or encouragement include Alison Callahan, Nancy Gold, Rita and Harold Gold, Ernest Lehenbauer, Matthew Snyder, Neal Stephenson, Lydia Weaver, and Henry Wessells. Special thanks to the late (and sorely missed) Reverend Jack Ruff, whose insights into human nature continue to serve me well.

In constructing the mirage world, I drew upon many sources, including works by Peter Bergen, Mark Bowden, Anne Garrels, Shahla Haeri, William R. Polk, Thomas E. Ricks, Zainab Salbi, David Thibodeau, Evan Wright, Lawrence Wright, and Amira El-Zein. Quotations from the Quran are taken from Abdullah Yusuf Ali's English-language translation. Bible quotations are taken from various translations, including the New International Version, the New Revised Standard, and the King James.

Finally, I am indebted to Karen Glass and Caitlin Foito, who started me on my way by asking me to tell them a story. It's taken four and a half years, and the end result is surely not what they had in mind, but I am grateful they made the wish.

ABOUT THE AUTHOR

MATT RUFF was born in New York City in 1965. He is the author of the award-winning novels *Bad Monkeys* and *Set This House in Order*, as well as the cult classics *Fool on the Hill* and *Sewer, Gas & Electric*. He is the recipient of a 2006 National Endowment for the Arts Fellowship. Ruff lives in Seattle with his wife, Lisa Gold.

Visit Matt Ruff on the web at www.bymattruff.com.

E